While serving his country, Curt Nover witnessed enough violence to last a lifetime. As a military veteran, he wanted to heal others... and himself. Unfortunately, Nissassa Inc. has different plans. Curt would soon learn he had become an unwilling pawn in a game of life and death. The clock ticks as Curt races to thwart a World Leader's imminent assassination, save his own life and destroy those trying to kill him.

This publication has been approved by the U.S. Department of Defense Office of Pre-Publication and Security Review (DOPSR) in accordance with the author's security clearances. Questions regarding this review can be directed to whs.pentagon.esd.mbx.secrev@mail.mil for publication 21-SB-156 (see next page).

"The views expressed in this publication are those of the author and do not necessarily reflect the official policy or position of the Department of Defense or the U.S. government."

DEPARTMENT OF DEFENSE
DEFENSE OFFICE OF PREPUBLICATION AND SECURITY REVIEW
1155 DEFENSE PENTAGON
WASHINGTON, DC 20301-1155

21-SB-0156
November 16, 2021

Jeffrey Fischer
█████████████████

Dear Mr. Fischer:

    This is in response to your July 20, 2021, correspondence requesting public release clearance of the manuscript titled, "Live Range." The manuscript submitted for security review is CLEARED AS AMENDED for public release. Enclosed is a copy of the cleared as amended manuscript. Amendments are clearly identified with blacked out text and red text boxes in the margins. This clearance does not include any photograph, picture, exhibit, caption, or other supplemental material not specifically approved by this office, nor does this clearance imply Department of Defense (DoD) endorsement or factual accuracy of the material.

    If you are not satisfied with this response, you may request that this office reconsider the initial determination. Within 60 days of this response, provide any and all information or explanation of facts that you believe this office should know. You may include citations or copies of similar references that show this information was previously released and already in the public domain, although a mere listing of published citations may not necessarily be sufficient to reverse the initial determination. Please note the wide availability of certain information in open sources does not in and of itself constitute an official DoD or U.S. government acknowledgment, release, or declassification of the information. Additionally, you may rewrite portions of the redacted information and resubmit the manuscript for reconsideration.

    You also have the right to appeal this response to the appellate authority. The appeal must offer written justification as described above to support the reversal of each required amendment being appealed. Appeals must be submitted within 60 days from the date of this response. Please submit any reconsiderations, rewrites, or appeals to: whs.pentagon.esd.mbx.secrev@mail.mil.

    This office requests that you add the following disclaimer prior to publishing the manuscript: "The views expressed in this publication are those of the author and do not necessarily reflect the official policy or position of the Department of Defense or the U.S. government." I enclose a cleared copy of the first page of the manuscript. Please direct any questions regarding this case to Daniel Klein █████████████.

Sincerely,

for ████████████████
Chief

Enclosure(s):
As stated

DEDICATIONS

This book is dedicated to my military and U.S. Government colleagues who worked countless hours in the trenches, keeping America safe.

It is also dedicated to my fellow veterans and those still serving who struggle daily to cope with the horrors of warfare and conflict.

Lastly, and most importantly, this book is dedicated to my amazing wife, Barbara, our son, Tobias Josef, the rest of my family and closest friends. For their unwavering love and support, even when I am perhaps less than deserving.

Special thanks to Jack McPeek (jmaviationart2020@gmail.com) for the book cover artistry. If you are a fan of military artwork, he welcomes commissioned opportunities. Below was the first one he did for me and it's still my favorite.

"Prowler on Connie's CAT 3"

And I'd be remiss to not thank my amazing editor who helped me through my first publishing. Pia, you are truly a very patient woman!

Now, to the story.....

Copyright © 2021 Jeffrey H. Fischer
All rights reserved.

Chapters

Chapter One – The Confrontation 11

Chapter Two – The Calling 13

Chapter Three – The Journey 19

Chapter Four – The Arrival 25

Chapter Five – New Home 35

Chapter Six – The Tour 38

Chapter Seven – Broken Truce 46

Chapter Eight – The First 'Real' Workday 50

Chapter Nine – Issam's Dinner 60

Chapter Ten – Along Came a Woman 66

Chapter Eleven – The Interference 73

Chapter Twelve – Dinner with Allison 80

Chapter Thirteen – Catch and Release 86

Chapter Fourteen – Mission Failure 88

Chapter Fifteen – Shadow Money 93

Chapter Sixteen – Daybreak 95

Chapter Seventeen – Lunch with Buck 99

Chapter Eighteen – Medivac 104

Chapter Nineteen – Issam's Interview 106

Chapter Twenty – Longbow 23 110

Chapter Twenty-One – Why Rudy? 114

Chapter Twenty-Two – Strike One 118

Chapter Twenty-Three – Ease of Movement 120

Chapter Twenty-Four – The Second Date 123

Chapter Twenty-Five – Freedom 129
Chapter Twenty-Six – Rewind and Replay 133
Chapter Twenty-Seven – The Article.. 135
Chapter Twenty-Eight – The Fib 137
Chapter Twenty-Nine – The Next Mission 139
Chapter Thirty – The Romance & The Story 142
Chapter Thirty-One – Mission Planning 145
Chapter Thirty-Two – The Training Scenario 148
Chapter Thirty-Three – The Announcement 151
Chapter Thirty-Four – Trouble in Paradise 153
Chapter Thirty-Five – The Celebration 156
Chapter Thirty-Six – Decisions Must Be Made 164
Chapter Thirty-Seven – The Best Laid Plans............................. 166
Chapter Thirty-Eight – The Recruitment 169
Chapter Thirty-Nine – The Search 174
Chapter Forty – The Escape 179
Chapter Forty-One – The Chase 186
Chapter Forty-Two – Tightening the Noose.............................. 194
Chapter Forty-Three – A Friend in Need, Indeed 202
Chapter Forty-Four – One Final Night in Akjoujt 205
Chapter Forty-Five – A Funeral for One 209
Chapter Forty-Six – Time to Cash In.. 213
Chapter Forty-Seven – Raising the Dead 218
Chapter Forty-Eight – Strategic Decisions 221
Chapter Forty-Nine – The Bonds of Battle................................ 224
Chapter Fifty – The Tortoise and the Hare 228
Chapter Fifty-One – Snakes in the Grass 232

Chapter Fifty-Two – Hunting a Jackal 236

Chapter Fifty-Three – Identification Friend or Foe 245

Chapter Fifty-Four – Guernica 253

Chapter Fifty-Five – Queen Sofia's Museum 259

Chapter Fifty-Six – Hopping the Pond 268

Chapter Fifty-Seven – Acquisitions 275

Chapter Fifty-Eight – No Turning Back 282

Chapter Fifty-Nine –The Confrontation - Relived 289

Chapter Sixty – Walking Dead 293

Chapter Sixty-One – Trapping Scurrying Rats 299

Chapter Sixty-Two – Saving Evil 304

Chapter Sixty-Three – Tying Loose Ends 308

Chapter Sixty-Four – We'll Always Have Paris 313

Chapter One

The Confrontation

It was an unseasonably cold autumn evening in Washington, D.C. Steam rose off the Potomac River and the city street manhole covers. The cold welcomed in a clear night sky; however, the lights of the Capitol drown out the viewing of most stars. Rush hour traffic had calmed, and the city pace eased. Evening meals were being served across the city's numerous restaurants. One of them, D.C.'s most famous watering hole, Old Ebbitt Grill on 14th St NE was packed. As the crowded masses stood shoulder to shoulder in the bar, a U.S. Navy Lieutenant dressed in a winter trench coat and white cover walked briskly up the street, passing the restaurant without notice. Ironically, Old Ebbitt had always been one of his favorites, but tonight a greater importance called. He continued north up 14th St. Old Ebbitt behind him and the White House ahead of him to the left; his intended destination.

As he approached the north side of the White House, he quickly scanned the surroundings. There were a few dozen tourists braving the cold. A few protesters were huddled in their makeshift shanties confronting the crisp night air for their worthy cause. As expected, security forces were visible for all to see. The environment was just as the lieutenant had expected minus one critical piece. He kept scanning...

Then, he saw her. The woman he was looking for. A blonde with soft blue eyes. Their eyes caught each other, and it was clear, she was not only familiar, but someone he cared for. A tear ran down her cheek and there was pain in her eyes. She was waiting for him, along the fence line. She stood dead center in front of the White House North Fence line and as close as one could get given the security. He said nothing to her. He didn't have to; his face said it all. It said, 'I love you. I'm sorry, but I have to do this. Someday, you will understand.'

He stopped 10 yards from her. He opened his briefcase. Hundreds of photos flew up into the air and scattered across the ground.

****

Next to the White House front door, a U.S. Marine Sergeant stood, staring out at the North lawn - the Navy Lieutenant's flying papers and commotion catching his attention. Next, the Marine witnessed the Lieutenant pull a handgun and place it against his right temple. Immediately, he notified others and put emergency security protocols into action. Soon, people were screaming and running.

The Sergeant continued to watch. Security guards drew upon the lieutenant. He could hear shouting amongst the screams of tourists. Then, a single shot rang out and the Lieutenant fell lifelessly to the ground. Now even more tourists screamed and ran. Secret Service and Police radios cracked to life, "SHOTS FIRED! WHITE HOUSE NORTH LAWN! SHOTS FIRED!"

Chapter Two

The Calling

(Five Months Earlier)

  The John H. Stroger Jr. Hospital Emergency Room (E.R.) churned at its normally fast pace. Prior to its renaming, this was Chicago's well known 'Cook County Hospital,' with an ER famed for treating the nation's most stabbings, bullet holes, and other unfortunate outcomes of Chicago's gang activity. It was just past noon on a beautiful Spring Day and the emergency room was relatively empty, but the hospital staff packed into the ER staff lounge. Even those who had the day off arrived for this special function. Today would be Curt's last day as he completed his medical residency at the end of his shift and then the farewell party would start.
 Doctor Curt Nover was a striking fellow. He was in his mid-30s, slightly older than most new doctors, but in exceptional physical condition. His facial features were hardened – brownish blonde hair, greyish blue eyes. His skin was worn and there was no hiding some of his wrinkles. But when he smiled, he could melt any heart. To top it all, his personality was infectious. It was obvious why so many coworkers would spend time on their day off back in the Cook County ER.
  Towards the crowd, Curt was escorted by the ER Chief, Dr. Shindel. Hushes fell over the group, and Dr. Shindel spoke, "Curt, what can I say? This hospital is truly going to miss you. You are an exceptional doctor. Your ability to blend humor, wit and seriousness in the most critical of situations is something which cannot be taught – and frankly, you do it better than any I have ever seen. On behalf of the staff here, I want to

congratulate you for completing your residency and a job exceptionally well done." Raising two framed objects, he continued, "As a small farewell gift, our office took the liberty of framing your medical license from the State of Illinois and your residency completion certificate. Congratulations and please take this as a small token of our appreciation for your efforts here. Hopefully it will serve as a reminder of us as you leave our hospital to do great things in this world. You are an inspiration to many of us and we hate to see you leave. And need I not remind you... There will always be an offer for you to come here and work full time, should you change your mind."

Curt was stunned and relieved. The residency was over. Additionally, he'd planned on getting his medical license framed, but just never seemed to have time. It sat around the hospital and clearly, others had taken the liberty to get it done along with his residency certificate. Frankly, that was just how those around Curt felt. He was the guy you just wanted to help. Curt smiled. The crowded office spaces erupted in applause. "Speech! Speech! Speech!" They chanted. Curt had no choice.

"Dr. Shindel, thank you so much for this. I had no idea I would be receiving such wonderful gifts. I cannot begin to tell you how relieved I am to be holding my residency certificate and my framed medical license." He paused and stared at them. Looking up, he continued, "I also had no clue so many of you would come into work on your day off and try to sneak overtime on the books just to see me out the door!" He paused as the crowd laughed. He then continued. "I truly am blessed to have met each and every one of you. Many of you don't know much of my past, but I can tell you this. I needed to become a doctor to heal others just as much as I needed to become one to heal me. Someday, I hope that makes sense."

Curt again paused, "I wouldn't have succeeded here without the support of this hospital and the staff. The credit belongs to all of you." He meant it. Nurses who worked with Curt were fighting back tears. "Dr. Shindel, again, I thank you for the offer to stay, but as you know, I have a bigger calling and it must take me away from here. I assure you, I'd love to stay and harass your nursing staff just a while longer and continue my practical jokes, but the time has come, and I must say farewell. Oh, and if any of you make it to the African Desert in the next few years, look me up!" Again, the crowd laughed. Curt had no more words and the applause soon followed. He cut the farewell cake and they began to eat.

As folks gathered around, said their good-byes, Curt noticed off in the corner of the room, Nurse Wanda stood leaning against the wall, all alone and staring at him. She was a large, no nonsense black woman; the kind that would serve you up food at the local diner, and by the end of the meal, you couldn't help but fall in love with her. He knew, he owed her a private goodbye. She was one of his favorites. Curt politely excused himself from the group and started walking her way. Nurse Wanda's face began to smile. "Hey, Nurse Wanda, ma'am."

"Yeah. You really leaving us? Eh, sugar?" Although Wanda was a nurse, she was one of those who somehow strangely was able to flip seniority protocols and titles. Curt wasn't 'Doctor Nover' but rather any number of pet names Wanda felt appropriate. No one said a word about it.

"Yes ma'am. You know, I meant what I said... The part about being a better person now. A great deal of that credit belongs to you."

"Naw, baby, you was just a piece of clay when you arrived. Thank the Lord above you was wet clay though, so we could mold ya. Lord have mercy, some of you residents are hard as rocks!"

Curt chuckled. He knew Nurse Wanda well enough to realize that humor was her defense mechanism for pain and sorrow. She didn't want to see him go. Curt's real mom was over 1000 miles away. Nurse Wanda was filling that role in Chicago, and she didn't want to see one of her prize birdies leave the nest.

"I just don't understand..... Curt, why can't you stay? Dr. Shindel done offered you the best job in the hospital for a new doctor, and you are somehow all high and mighty on saving the world. Didn't you see enough of the world's shit holes already when you was in the Navy?"

"But Nurse Wanda, if I don't try to save the world, who will?" And another smile cracked from his face. She knew he was joking, but there was just enough sarcasm for her to realize there was a hint of truth in how he perceived his own statement. Curt wanted to make a difference to someone, somewhere... and the more people and places he could make that happen, the better.

Wanda's voice began to rise. She was agitated. "OK, save the world here! Lord knows this hospital needs a Superman. We have more ER visitors who need good doctors on an average night than any other hospital in the nation! Seems to me if ya wanted to be Doctor Superman, this is as good of place as any to do it! We got people walking through our doors with more holes in em than a dang spaghetti strainer."

"Ms. Wanda, that's true, but there are also plenty of doctors here in Chicago who will take this job. There are very few who will volunteer to go to the ends of the earth for two years and treat people who have no other access to medical care. Nurse Wanda, ma'am, I have done more than my fair share of hurting people in this world. I need to make that right. It is payback time for me, and this is what I need to do. I'm sorry. I hope someday you will understand."

Wanda's eyes watered. "Aww, come here, you fool. I'm gonna miss you something fierce. If you need to do this, OK, but I still say it ain't right." With that, she placed something in his hand. He looked down and his eyes lit up and his cheeks locked into a smile.

"Is that the world-famous Nurse Wanda Jalapeño corn bread? You know how much I love that stuff!"

"Yeah, well it's a long flight to Africa and I didn't want you starving to death on the plane. Now come here and give me a hug." As they embraced, the affection between them was obvious. A part of each didn't want to let the other go. The hug lasted longer than most, and then Curt said, "Nurse Wanda, you didn't poison the corn bread in hopes I'd miss my flight, did you?" And with that, the tears in Wanda's eyes transition from sadness to laughter. She didn't know if she should hit him or love him. Curt was just that way.

The party ended and Curt left the hospital. It was straight to the hotel room he had booked for the past few nights. Africa would be his next home. Curt had checked out of his apartment days earlier, put most of his personal belongings in storage, and packed everything he needed for the two-year trip nearly a week ago. The hotel was nice. The Palmer House, a Chicago icon, was the location where he would lay his head one last time breathing American air. No reason not to splurge a bit on his last few days in the USA.

As he looked around his room, Curt chuckled thinking that the personal effects in the room must be puzzling to hotel staff. Juxtaposed antique furniture, a classic look, an amazing view of the Chicago skyline, were five Navy Sea Bags stacked horizontally like bowling pins. He stared out at the lights of Chicago. To Curt, the city was intoxicating, and he knew he'd miss it. Spring flowers were in bloom, the city was awakening out of its slumber and ready for Summer. The two local baseball clubs, the Cubs and the Sox, would soon have their openers and the beaches on LSD (Lake Shore Drive) would soon come to life. Curt leaned to the window and looked down Monroe Street out towards Michigan Avenue and beyond to Lake Michigan. The lake and the horizon met somewhere in the distance. Curt reflected on that distance, and then chuckled – realizing it was a pittance compared to his travels over the next few days. Curt went to the bathroom, brushed his teeth and cleaned up for dinner. His reservations were in a few hours at Gino's East; one last attack on a Chicago Deep Dish pizza classic.

Post dinner and making his way back to the hotel, his stomach ached from the heavy meal. It was exactly how he wanted it. Curt lay in the bed reflecting on a great day. Unfortunately, while alone, his mind drifted to his past. Just like many other nights, he worked hard to stop it. The memories, the flash backs, the nightmares. This was his secret, and subconsciously, it was also the reason he needed to make right with the world. The time had come, and he was more than ready to begin to make good on all the damage he had inflicted to others and himself.

Chapter Three

The Journey

Curt stared at the ceiling. He checked his watch; it was 0650Hrs. His alarm would go off in 10 minutes, but he didn't need it. He was wide awake. Trying to sleep any longer was pointless as he rarely slept well anyway. He climbed out of bed, made coffee in his hotel room and prepared for the long journey. He looked out the window one last time. The city lights were now dormant, and the sun would soon appear where Lake Michigan and the horizon met. As he drank his coffee, he opened his briefcase and pulled out a folder. The outside had a symbol and said, "MÉDECINS SANS FRONTIÈRES," or more commonly known in English, Doctors without Borders. He looked at his flight itinerary. Chicago, IL, O'Hare to Charles De Gaulle in Paris, France. He would change flights in Paris and continue to Rabat, Morocco. From Rabat, he would hop a flight to Nouakchott, Mauritania and then meet a chaperone who would facilitate his continued travel to Akjoujt, Mauritania. His stomach churned just thinking about his next two and a half days. He showered and dressed, then packed away the last few personal items into his duffle bags. One last look around the hotel room and he headed to the lobby. The checkout line took five minutes and his obligations to the Palmer House were met. A bell hop assisted him with his bags and a cab took him to the international terminal at O'Hare airport. Curt arrived and proceeded to the check-in clerk.

"Good morning, Curt Nover flying to Rabat, Morocco."

"Good morning Mr. Nover. Is that your final destination?" He wondered if she really wanted to hear about the follow-on diatribe of his travels to get to his final destination.

Quickly, he realized his humor might be lost on the Air France check-in attendant and just said, "Yes ma'am." Check-in went well and within 30 minutes he was through security and waiting at the gate. There were plenty of people mulling around and he soon realized the flight was going to be fairly packed. He would have little luck at empty seats in his row.

As he boarded the flight, it was just as he predicted, the seat next to him was not vacant. An elderly gentleman sat next to Curt's assigned seat. The man was frail, clearly over 80, and had a nervous appearance about him.

"Hello, sir," said Curt.

"Hello, young man. My name is Arnie. Arnie Johnson from North Eagle Butte, South Dakota. What's your name?"

A bit strange to offer so much information so quickly, he thought. "Curt. Curt Nover. Nice to meet you, Arnie. And thanks. I can't remember the last time I was called a young man." Curt chuckled under his breath. Everything is relative he thought.

"Curt, are you going to Paris too?"

"Well, on this airplane, I hope so. After that, I will head to Africa. Do you fly often, Arnie?"

"Nope. First time flying in 15 years. I'm a little nervous," said Arnie, admitting what Curt had already perceived.

"Well, the good news is, I have flown many times and you couldn't have picked a better seat. I'm a doctor and I promise, I will take good care of you. Arnie, what takes you to Paris if you don't mind me asking?" Curt tried to shift Arnie's mind to something else.

"Son, it's a long story, but suffice it to say, I need closure." Curt thought, *'Wow, don't we all.'* Arnie continued. "When I was young, I lied about my age and enlisted into the Army. I fought on the battlefields in France during World War II. Not a day goes by that I don't think about a battle, a friend or an event tied to that war. I promised my wife that someday I would return there and get closure. I figure I'd put if off long enough. Nancy, my wife, died two years ago and I miss her so.

So, now I got two things nagging me every day and that's just too much. I figure I owe this to her, and I need to keep my promise. Plus, maybe I can get one of these confounded things outta my head which pester me. It won't be easy but it's the right thing to do."

"Are you going alone?"

"Yep. I don't need anybody watching over me or seeing me cry. That ain't right."

"Well, Arnie, I am impressed. You know, I too fought for our country in Iraq and Afghanistan. Maybe someday those countries will find peace and I can return and get closure just like you."

"Well, son, if those countries ever do find peace, I recommend you attempt to find closure sooner than later. You never understand the grief and pain you carry sometimes. It can be overwhelming, and you don't even realize it's there."

"Thanks, Arnie. I appreciate the advice."

The flight attendant announcements for departure came on and both settled in for the flight. The aircraft taxied out and waited for clearance from the tower.

The takeoff was uneventful for Curt. He had flown more times than he could count, and the dull static engine and cabin noise had become soothing. Arnie sat wide awake, reading a book and ordering a beer. After passing 10,000ft in the climb out, Curt pulled out his iPad and began to tinker. The iPad was a recent purchase as a gift to himself for completing his residency. A new toy. Arnie's comments from earlier touched Curt and he opened his photos application and began to view pictures from his combat time. He reminisced about old friends. The pictures were treasured. Backdrops of mountains, Humvees, sand dunes – all the pictures of buddies in faraway lands appearing invincible with weapons and body armor. He closed his iPad and looked over at Arnie. After half his beer,

Arnie was deep in sleep. Curt realized he'd likely never see Arnie again but was grateful he had the chance to make his acquaintance. Curt leaned back, closed his eyes and fell asleep.

****

"Last Checks!" Curt heard his team lead scream. He stared through the green hues of his night vision goggles at his chute, pack, weapon, O2 bottle and comm gear. He was ready. It was the eighth time he had checked his gear in the last 30 minutes. His blood pressure was up; more alert than one could imagine. He was ready. The MC-130 Talon depressurized, and the aft ramp slowly opened. Curt activated his O2 bottle. At the altitude they were flying, a man breathing normal air would be unconscious in 45 seconds. His heart rate increased. The cargo bay of the MC-130 cooled rapidly. It was cold outside at that altitude – minus 40 degrees Celsius. A green light illuminated on the aircraft wall. Soon thereafter, the command. "GO, GO, GO!" Curt and his team ran off the back ramp into the night darkness.

The mission was a HALO (High Altitude Low Opening) parachute jump into Helmand Province Afghanistan. They would depart the aircraft from a high altitude and free fall in the night sky until the team was close to the earth. While dangerous, the intent is to minimize vulnerable time to enemy fire or being spotted in their parachutes. It is also one of the greatest rushes a para jumper can experience. It was, however, no ordinary mission. Normal infiltration / exfiltration (infill / exfill) missions in Afghanistan were conducted via helicopter but the loud thumping of the helicopter rotors gave away the element of surprise. A high-flying MC-130 Talon was the perfect delivery system for capturing or killing high value targets (HVTs).

Faster and faster, they screamed towards the earth until they reached terminal velocity. Back arched, legs spread, hands and arms out to control the decent. Curt lived for this stuff. He was a true adrenalin junkie. 10 seconds more. He could see the earth rapidly approaching. 'NOW!' he said to himself and yanked the rip cord. The drag chute deployed and yanked the main chute out a fraction of a second later. WHAM! The harness shock grabbed Curt as if he was kicked by a mule. His decent towards earth decreased from roughly 120 MPH to a few feet per second. From violent and loud to eerily peaceful and serene…. So very odd he always thought.

"Bravo Team, Check." The team lead came up on the secure radio.
"Two's good chute."
"Three's good chute."
Curt's turn. "Four's good chute."
"Five's good chute."
"Six's good chute."

The entire team had managed to survive the HALO jump and would soon face the enemy. Out of the fire and into the frying pan so to speak. Slowly drifting to the earth now, silent as could be. Night vision goggles scanning for movement. The descent was quiet. The ground was approaching…. Bent knees, feet together…. Thud. Curt was one with the earth again. Rolling up his chute and preparing to make contact with his team, the adrenaline increased even further……

****

Curt awoke. He had slept through the entire flight. The aircraft was in a descent and the flight crew was preparing for landing. Curt looked at his shirt. It was full of sweat. He then looked at Arnie. Arnie was staring back at Curt. Arnie spoke, "Son, I don't know what you were dreaming about, but you might want to get to Afghanistan or Iraq sooner than I got back to France."

Curt smiled and said, "You know, Arnie, I think you might be right."

The plane landed. Arnie and Curt said their farewells. Curt thought to himself, *"What caused me to have a dream that intense? I haven't had one that strong for years."* It was puzzling... And frightening. Curt didn't want the dreams to escalate. While his dreams over the past year weren't pleasant, they were also mild or as he might say 'controlled.' He realized this dream was a bit beyond mild, and there was the potential for them to get out of hand. He thought and thought about it and finally gave up. He dismissed the dream to his conversation with Arnie and the background aircraft noise which sparked the dream. No need to dwell.

A quick change of planes in Paris and Curt was on his way to Rabat, Morocco. A much shorter and uneventful flight, it was over before he knew it. Curt cleared customs and wandered out into the baggage claim area. *'Halfway through the adventure'* he thought. After retrieving his bags, Curt headed back to departures. It would be four hours before his flight to Nouakchott. He grabbed some coffee and a sandwich.

While sitting at the airport coffee shop, Curt remembered he met a Moroccan army soldier years ago during an international training exercise. They became somewhat friendly, but as with most military contacts, you part ways. Curt remembered his name, Faycal. How was he doing? How was his family? Was he dead? Unfortunately, an all-too-common thought in a military mind when reminiscing about old battle buddies. Four hours came and went; Curt was on a Cessna 208 Caravan to Nouakchott and his first steps in the country he would call home for the next two years – Mauritania. After seeing the quality of the aircraft, Curt also wondered if he'd make it.

Chapter Four

The Arrival

The airport in Nouakchott was nothing to write home about. Curt stepped off the plane and although it was early spring and evening time, the temperature was sweltering. The passengers, all eight of them, walked from the aircraft to the airport terminal to collect their personal belongings. Once again, just like in Rabat, Curt gathered his duffle bags and proceeded to the waiting area.

A young African man held a sign which read, "Doctor Nover." Under his breath, Curt joked, *'I wonder how many Dr. Novers were on this flight?'* Curt approached the man and said, "Alsalam Alaikum."

"Dr. Nover? Hello! Glad you make it. Let me help with your bags." The young man grabbed a cart and threw on all the bags. While his English was choppy, the man continued, "Sir, you speak Arabic?"

Curt answered, "I know a few words. Enough to get by but I can't have a conversation." He had learned a little Arabic in Iraq as well as some Pashtu in Afghanistan. Many of the words and phrases he had learned however were not ones you might throw out in normal conversation. Curt immediately thought of the Arabic phrase, *'Oof Slahek bil-ga'a!'* As an example, this might be a touch inappropriate. The translation, *'Drop your weapon!'* Curt smiled.

"Excuse me, what is your name?" Curt asked.

"Ahmed." The man answered. "I work here in Nouakchott and help foreigners transfer from the airport to where they go. The job pay good. You are easy. I just take you from here to that plane over there." Ahmed pointed to a small cargo plane on the other side of the ramp. It was white with a blue stripe down the side. It had a high wing line and an engine on each wing. The aircraft was anything but aerodynamic. The Cessna Caravan he just left was a peach compared to this one. They both approached the aircraft, and an individual came out to meet them – it was the pilot. He was stocky, in his late 40s with token aviator shades. The gentleman's shirt was somewhat buttoned in effort to convey a mere hint of professionalism, but the cargo shorts, white socks and gym shoes combination killed any resemblance. As Curt got closer, he began to make out the pilot's facial features. It was strange, Curt had a feeling he knew this man. Closer now, the man stopped and stared back.

"You're new here," the pilot said. "Kinda strange, but have I seen you before?"

"Hi, I'm Curt Nover. I must confess, I think I know you too. You're American, right?"

"Yup. Born and raised. Philly. My name is Thiessen, Doug Thiessen, but folks around here call me Buck."

"Ok, Buck. Is that a nickname?"

"Nope, my callsign from days back in the U.S. Air Force. I flew 130s. Left the Air Force a few years ago when they tried to make me fly a Pentagon desk. That wasn't for me. I retired from that gig and have been flying down here ever since."

And with that, Curt knew exactly where he had met Buck before, but the conversation would end there for now. "OK, Buck. What do you say we get the aircraft loaded and fire up the engines? I am dying in this heat!"

"Absolutely. Not sure why you are wearing pants down here, though. Don't you know you are only 18 degrees north of the equator? And they tell me you are a doctor? I hope you know how to treat yourself for heat stroke!" Buck laughed out loud at his own joke. He didn't care.

Curt said goodbye to Ahmed and thanked him for his services. He reached in his wallet to pull out a tip. Ahmed absolutely refused. He was paid handsomely to ensure Dr. Nover's safe travels. Odd, Curt thought. Doctors Without Borders is a nonprofit. Why would they throw such money around? Then it occurred to him. Yes, he remembered now. He was a doctor! Maybe they have to do this as some doctors let their profession go to their head. Curt wasn't like that, but after nearly a day and a half of travel to this point, he was mighty grateful for the care and feeding others were bestowing upon him.

Ahmed walked away from the aircraft, pulled out his cellphone and placed a call. "Your package arrived safely. He departs here in the next hour as planned."

The voice on the other end replied, "Perfect. Good news, Ahmed. Thanks for the update. Bye."

"Al Salam," Ahmed replied and hung up the phone.

Curt entered the aircraft cargo compartment area hoping to escape the heat. He didn't think it could get hotter. He was wrong. Inside the aircraft was even more miserable than outside. He tried not to think about it. The name on the aircraft safety pamphlet said, 'Casa 212.' The cargo compartment had a large pallet of goods loaded in the middle, all of Curt's seabags, and a few seats along the outside. Curt grabbed a seat along the fuselage wall and strapped in.   Within minutes, the left prop engine began to spin. A puff of smoke and she had started. Soon thereafter, the right engine wound and started. As the engines idled, a meager amount of cool air began to fill the cargo area.

Buck taxied the plane out to the runway. He wound up the engines with his feet on the brakes. Ahhh…. Cool air littered the cabin. The brakes released and the plane rumbled down the surface and into the air. Just like any small aircraft in a hot environment, it bounced around like a county fair ride for the first few minutes. Eventually, the bumpiness calmed. Buck and Curt were the only two on the airplane.

Curt unstrapped as they headed to his final destination. He walked up toward the cockpit. It was a two-seat cockpit – pilot and copilot. The right seat was empty. Buck noticed Curt standing behind him and handed back a headset and mic.

"Curt, you up?" Buck spoke over the crackly aircraft intercom system. "When you want to talk to me, push this button on the cord. Speak, and then let go of...."

"Buck, I'm familiar. It's similar to the comm system in a C-130."

Buck's head spun around. "How do you know that?"

"I figured out where I know you from. You flew 130s out of Hurlburt Airfield for a while; back in let's say 2002-2004. I think I might have been in some operational briefings with you and also on missions with you down range. At a minimum, I know we've eaten in the same chow hall in the middle of only God knows where."

"Holy Shit! Yes! But let's be clear. I flew Special 130s. I didn't haul trash. I hauled special trash and also shot special guns. Which branch of service were you?"

"Navy," Curt answered.

"Ahh... You were perhaps my cargo on occasion. Special cargo, no doubt, but cargo just the same. Now it kinda makes sense. Every now and then I take your types to Akjoujt."

"My types? You mean Special Ops guys?"

"Yeah, not sure why or what they are doing. You know the code – 'Don't ask and don't speak about it.' I probably already said too much."

Curt agreed. "You're probably right. Anyway, I must confess, it is good to see a familiar face on this side of the globe. Do you spend time up in Akjoujt? You might have figured; I don't think I am going to have many American friends in this part of the world, and it would be nice to grab a drink with you. If nothing else, I know where you can get some great medical care at a phenomenally cheap rate."

"Cheap?! HA! You mean free! Every now and then I spend nights up in Akjoujt, but it is rare. I do make a run up there about two to three times a week. Maybe during my layover, we could grab lunch. The good news is Nissassa, the mining company, is paying to move my bed down location from Nouakchott to Rabat. Next week will be the last I see of Nouakchott. Rabat is a far bigger and better city. All that said, I agree with you, it would be nice. Akjoujt has a few decent restaurants."

"Decent restaurants?!! Are you serious? I am being sent to Akjoujt for Doctors Without Borders on a humanitarian mission – and this place has nice restaurants! Well, I must confess, part of me is relieved to know I will have some level of comfort, but I am a bit confused!"

"Curt, don't get me wrong. Akjoujt has its problems. The town does decent, and the mining operation is creating jobs and money. The problem with Akjoujt is the Injus and the Satris. They are rival groups or gangs and fight nonstop. Best not to get in their crossfire. The local politicians are indifferent. It has gone on so long, there is a sense of normalcy and complacency about the whole thing. Also, the local authorities are helpless. The Injus and Satris, much like Taliban or ISIS, fight in head gear wraps and civilian clothes so you never know who's who in all the commotion." Buck's mic went silent.

"Great. Just like Cook County Hospital. Gunshot wounds and stabbings will be..."

Buck waived his hand in the air attempting to get Curt to stop. Curt noticed Buck was talking into his mic but couldn't hear him. Then he figured it out. Buck was talking on the radio, likely getting clearance and instructions for the descent. They must be getting close. Curt went back to his normal seat where he had begun the flight and sat down. As he was strapping into his seat in the cargo area, he looked up. There was Buck, standing in front of him.

"BUCK!! WHAT IN THE HELL?? WHO'S FLYING THE DAMN PLANE!!??" Curt screamed over the engine roar echoing through the cargo bay. Neither were on headset.

Buck replied loudly, "ALICE!"

Confused, Curt belted out, "ALICE? WHO THE FUCK IS ALICE?"

"SHE'S THE AUTO PILOT. SHE'S AWESOME AT STRAIGHT AND LEVEL, BUT SHE SUCKS HUGE DONKEY BALLS AT LANDINGS! LOOK, I GOTTA LAND THIS THING IN ABOUT 15 MINUTES. IF YOU WANT, YOU CAN SIT IN THE COPILOT SEAT

RATHER THAN BACK HERE. THE VIEW IS MUCH NICER, I ASSURE YOU!"

"THANKS!" Curt screamed. They both turned and went up to the cockpit. Buck sat down on the left seat and Curt in the right and they put on their headsets. Curt reflected, *'Huge Donkey Balls... Hmmm.... I'm gonna guess Buck isn't married; or at least his wife isn't anywhere near Mauritania.'*

Buck set up Curt's headset to monitor controlling frequencies as well as the aircraft interphone. Buck started the descent and ran the landing checklist. Curt observed. Buck was a character, and it was apparent he loved flying. A desk job in the Pentagon would have killed this guy. The left wing banked up and Buck drew back the yoke. He was bleeding altitude and airspeed in preparation for landing. Buck was in the zone and there was something almost artistic in his movement. Curt was practically mesmerized.

The wings leveled and Curt looked out the cockpit window. Roughly five miles ahead was a dirt strip and a small town in the vicinity about a mile away. Curt remembered his conversation with Buck and realized he need not ever refer to Akjoujt as a city again. The place was tiny. Contrasting the skyline to Chicago was almost an offense to Chicago. Closer they approached the field. Curt just stared straight out of the aircraft. Buck set the flaps to the correct location and the landing checklist was done.

Curt's headset cracked to life. "Your aircraft," Buck said. Curt swung his eyes to Buck and instantly saw Buck staring back at him with no hands on the yoke.

"What? You're Crazy!" Curt screamed... and he forgot to push his mic button for the interphone. Calmly, Buck pointed to the button. Again. "Dude! You're Crazy!"

Buck replied. "Maybe, but it's either you or Alice which is gonna land this plane, and my money is on you. As I said before, Alice sucks big donkey balls at landing."

Curt grabbed the yoke. Instantly, adrenaline burst through his veins. His blood pressure spiked and heart raced.

While he was taken aback by the surprise, there was no denying he loved every second of the experience.

Buck began to calmly speak via the intercom, "That's it. You're doing great. Ease the nose down. OK, I am going to control the throttles. You just handle the yoke." Buck also had a hand shadow the yolk too. He may be a bit crazy, but today wasn't the day he wanted to die. The engines dulled as Buck reduced power. Curt kept turning the yoke to the right, then straight, then right, then straight. He was clearly fighting winds and didn't understand it. Buck spoke. "Put your right foot on the rudder and push it about a quarter of the way down. You have a slight cross wind which is pushing you off runway heading." Curt obeyed. It fixed the problem. The plane continued to descend now maintaining lineup on the runway. Curt was nervous, but also in heaven. What a great experience he thought. He'd NEVER get to do this at Cook County Hospital.

"You're dropping the nose." Buck mentioned a bit forcefully.

"Shit!" Curt replied... then realized reminiscing about Chicago was perhaps better saved for a later time.

Ten feet over the runway... now five feet. Touch down. Curt slightly pulled back on the yoke, and they were up in the air again. A second landing soon followed. And another. It was a triple bouncer. The landing wasn't pretty. Curt's hands were sweating and were wrapped tighter than a clinched fist around the yoke handles.

As the plane slowed, Buck said, "My aircraft," and Curt reluctantly let go. The aircraft lumbered to a stop and then taxied off the runway. "Not bad for a squid!" Buck said.

"Buck, that was amazing. Any chance you want to change jobs? I'll fly and you practice medicine?"

"Curt, I appreciate the offer, but my efforts in the medical profession would not even resemble the notion of *'practicing.'*" They both chuckled. Buck flipped some switches, ran the post-landing checklist and then taxied into parking. The aircraft was met by just a few people and there were no visible airport facilities. It was a dirt strip in the middle of nowhere next to a small village. Buck shut the engines down. The plane began to heat up quickly. "Now is a good time to get out if you wish to beat the heat." Buck jumped up, popped open the doors and they both exited the aircraft.

Some locals helped empty the aircraft cargo. One gentleman approached Curt and extended his hand. "Good evening, Doctor. I am Jawad, your assistant. I am a certified physician's assistant and am a native Mauritanian. Welcome to Akjoujt."

"Thanks, Jawad. It is a pleasure to meet you." Two things were instantly obvious. Jawad was proud of his medical training and was also proud to be native to his land. Both of them were admirable traits in Curt's book.

Buck interrupted the conversation, handing out a piece of paper towards Curt. "Hey, Doc. I am gonna head out now. Here is my cell phone number and email. Cell coverage and Internet here are spotty unless you're near the mine or in town but it's the best we got. Give me a shout and we can meet back up. It's good to see a friendly American face in these parts. Most other Americans I fly are quiet and unengaging. I appreciate our time today. You take care and don't forget to mind yourself around the Injus and Satris!" Buck smiled. Jawad did not. It was apparent the comment did not resonate well with Jawad. Buck turned back towards his aircraft, leaving the other two alone.

"That pilot knows what he speaks of. Akjoujt has so much potential. This fighting is literally killing our people and is our black eye to the world." Jawad paused. The fighting clearly frustrated him. Eventually, he changed the subject and again spoke, "Come sir, let's get your things and get you settled. You have had a long day of travel."

Day? Curt thought... Umm, try two. Curt said nothing and just smiled. Jawad started walking towards a dusty Toyota Forerunner. Curt could see his bags already packed in the cargo area.

"Your quarters are ready, and I have prepared a meal for you. Tonight, you will just eat and sleep." Jawad reached in his pocket and pulled out an iPhone. "Sir, this is your work phone. My number along with many others are already programmed in. It previously belonged to your predecessor. The PIN is on a piece of paper taped to the back." Curt took the phone and they continued walking. "Tomorrow, I will pick you up from your apartment at 8AM and then show you around the hospital. Is that acceptable, sir?"

"Jawad, that sounds perfect. Thanks. At some point, I need to let Doctors Without Borders know I am here."

"Sir, I will take care of that this evening after I drop you off. Come this way." Jawad and Curt jumped into the SUV, and they drove towards Akjoujt.

****

A phone rang in an office high-rise somewhere in Rosslyn, Virginia. A large high-back leather swivel chair faced a window with the back towards an oversized dark walnut desk. Over the top of the chair, a man's head was partially visible and cigar smoke slowly rose. The phone from the desk was blinking and the cord wrapped around to the other side of the chair.

Just outside that room, a receptionist's phone rang. She answered, "Nissassa Incorporated, how may I help you?"

"Hello, this is Jerry from the Akjoujt mining operation."

"Hold one moment, I will transfer you." She placed the call on hold for a minute and pushed it into the plush office next door.

"Jerry, hey, do you have good news?"

"Don, yes, in fact I do. Dr. Nover arrived today. He will be working soon, and we will be fully operational within two days."

"Perfect. I will notify our friends that we will soon resume efforts. This is great news. Our customers have been waiting and I think their patience is wearing thin. Take care, Jerry, and keep us informed."

"Will do. Goodbye." An arm reached out from behind the chair and placed the receiver into the phone cradle. A critical piece of the operation was now in place, and it appeared from headquarters' perspective, it was not a moment too soon. Unbeknownst to Curt, he would become a pawn in a game he never wished to play.

Chapter Five

New Home

  Curt said goodbye and thanked Jawad one more time, and the front door closed. Alone, Curt stood inside his new apartment, his home for the foreseeable future. It wasn't much. Cement wall construction, the single-story structure was extremely nice for Akjoujt standards, but would not pass for more than an adobe hut in the United States. In Chicago, it would take more money to bribe the city inspectors to deem it habitable than it would cost to build the place.

  It was, however, cozy. Curt had a small kitchen and table, a sofa with a coffee table, a TV on a makeshift stand of cinder blocks and plywood, a bathroom and bedroom. He took a deep breath. The sofa was completely hidden by five duffle bags which local staff threw into the apartment while Curt and Jawad said their goodbyes. There was a somewhat odd aroma emanating from the kitchen table. Curt investigated and opened the Styrofoam container sitting on the table. The rice and perhaps some pieces of chicken were identifiable. The sauce and other entities in the container were all unknown. It was obviously the meal Jawad had referenced earlier. The food looked interesting, but Curt passed. His stomach was already queasy from the travel; there was no need to press his luck. It was only 1830Hrs, but Curt was exhausted.

  Curt's new iPhone vibrated. He entered the PIN and learned he'd received an email. Opening it, Jawad had in fact sent notification to Doctors without Borders and courtesy copied Curt. There was a small comfort in this somewhat insignificant event. Curt realized many of the small details were already complete. Curt had an email account that was linked to his phone and his staff was already communicating via electronic medium. Capitalizing on that comfort, Curt set down his phone and went straight to the bedroom. He was asleep in 10 minutes – fully clothed.

Curt awoke. His first realization was this was one of the first nights in many that he could recall no negative dreams. He also couldn't recall any positive ones either, but clearly a win in his book. His next thought, *'What time is it? Did I oversleep? Where am I and why am I in all my clothes?'* A deep breath. Then he remembered he was in Akjoujt. He looked at his watch. 0417Hrs. *'Perfect,'* he thought. *'Only four hours until Jawad picks me up.'* He was never a big fan of circadian rhythms and time zone travel. Curt could sleep no longer and got out of bed.

Choosing to waste no time, Curt turned on the lights and began unpacking his belongings. He started with the duffle bags full of clothes and toiletries. This took all of twenty minutes. Next, he grabbed another duffle bag, opened the top and looked in. Curt smiled. *'God Bless you, Ms. Wanda,'* he thought. There, on the top, was a Ziploc bag full of jalapeño corn bread muffins. He opened the bag and began devouring them as he continued to unpack. His queasy stomach was cured by some good old fashioned southern cooking. In another duffle, Curt found his medical supplies and tossed that duffle towards the door. There was no need to unpack that until arriving at the hospital.

The laptop was next to come out of the packing. He pushed the 'on' button and let it begin to fire up. Unable to connect to the internet, Curt abandoned his laptop and began pulling out framed photos and albums. Some were family and friends. Others were battle buddies, and then a last one - the staff at Cook County Hospital. Noticeably, the unpacking slowed as Curt found the pictures. His heart sunk a bit and he became overwhelmed. Thousands of miles from home and loved ones, alone and facing an unknown future, sadness touched Curt. With a sigh, then a deep breath, he found places for all of his pictures; a meager effort to make his new residence a 'home.'

Curt grabbed his briefcase, remembering Doctors Without Borders had provided him a 3G Wireless USB stick. Curt inserted the USB stick into his computer. He had tested the system in the U.S., and it worked perfect. That said, Curt had plenty of experience in foreign lands where things didn't work exactly as advertised. He went to the kitchen table and sat down in front of his laptop. Albeit slow, the system worked, and Curt was downloading emails and surfing the Internet.

Once done rummaging through his email inbox, Curt created a new email. Adding his mom first onto the 'To' line, then other relatives and friends to the CC line. Once complete, he began writing:

15 May 2019

Dear Friends and Family,
My world travels are complete, and I have arrived in Akjoujt safe and sound.. Well, other than worn out from jetlag. I don't have much to report at this time but will keep you updated. I am sure my next few days are going to be filled with adventure!
All for now,
Curt

Curt hit the send button and the email shot into the abyss of the cyber world. A piece of him felt relieved knowing he had contact with those far away. Finishing the corn bread muffins, he navigated his small quarters towards the shower. Soon, he would be cleaned, refreshed and begin to feel human again.

Unpacking complete, breakfast complete, internet connection established, and showered – the time was now 0630Hrs. Jawad would arrive in 1.5 hours. Curt attempted to lay back down on his sofa and sleep. He knew he was in for a long day. The clock stared back at him. 0645Hrs, 0705Hrs, 0721Hrs, and many other times. There would be no more golden moments of shut eye.

Chapter Six

<u>The Tour</u>

Knock! Knock! Knock!

Curt's eyes sprang open. He looked at his watch. 0800Hrs. It was Jawad. On the positive side, Curt had acquired some much-needed sleep. On the negative side, he'd overslept. Luckily, he was lying in bed fully clothed. "Wait a minute! I'll be right there." He jumped out of bed, ran to the bathroom and splashed some water on his face. He stared in the mirror over the sink. His first day was about to begin.

He opened the door and there stood Jawad. "Good morning, Sir! Are you ready for your first day?"

"Jawad, I'm so excited, I've been up since 4:30AM waiting for you."

"Really!? It looks like you just woke up?" Jawad was puzzled.

"Well, never mind. Let's go. I am excited to see what you have in store for me." And with that, they left, Curt's work duffle bag forgotten next to the door in all the haste. The first stop was the hospital. It was approximately 400 yards down the street from Curt's residence. Although Jawad drove him to the hospital, Curt was quite pleased to learn he'd be able to walk or bike to work every day.

It was impossible not to notice the two well-armed police officers which stood guard at the hospital entrance. Clear signs of the Injus and Satris conflict, Curt thought. Surprisingly, the Akjoujt hospital was more than Curt could have hoped for. The facilities were clean, the staff was youthful, energetic and happy. Jawad was proud of his hospital. Jawad was one of only a few males in the staff as most others were female. The hospital was small. There was an Operating Room, an

Emergency Room and two exam rooms. Further down the hall, Curt noticed a well-supplied medical cabinet as well as a decently stocked pharmacy. Both good signs, he thought to himself. Walking through the hospital, Jawad introduced Dr. Nover to all the staff. Curt learned more names than he could imagine and was trying to remember them all. Additionally, Jawad introduced him to local villagers who shuffled in and out picking up prescriptions, performing physical therapy or other reasons for visiting the hospital that day. All of this was somewhat overwhelming – just as Curt had expected.

As they continued through the hospital, Jawad showed Curt the Recovery Unit which attempted to separate out critical and non-critical recovery patients in a large open room. The Recovery Unit also had armed guards. Interestingly, the beds were nearly all vacant.

"Jawad, why are there so few patients?"

"Sir, local clan fighting generates 90% of our patients. Recently, the leaders of both the Satris and Injus established a cease fire for peace talks. The government and local people are hopeful this will end fighting. Lately, there has been no conflict which means less patients."

A little farther down the hall was Curt's new office. On the door, a cheaply made small placard hung at eye level. Nonetheless, it said:

Dr. Curt Nover
Chief of Medicine – Akjoujt Hospital
Doctors Without Borders

"Sir, this is your office. I know it is not like the one you had in the United States, but it is the best we have. I hope you like it."

"Jawad, it's perfect." Curt wasn't just saying this. The place was spotless and obviously had new furniture. There was an air-conditioning unit in the window and beautiful pictures on the walls. The bookcase was filled with medical books and the flooring was new – much nicer than that in the other parts of the hospital. Thus far, everything Curt saw far surpassed his expectations. Evidently Doctors Without Borders has some serious funding to facilitate, supply and staff such a hospital.

"I'm glad you like it, Sir. We spent a great deal of time and effort getting it redone."

"Redone? Why did it need to be redone? You did not have to do this just for me."

Jawad paused. He was hesitant in his reply but realized he had already said too much. "Sir, it wasn't all for you. Unfortunately, the office was a disaster from your predecessor. It is a sad story. Dr. Wilson became too overwhelmed with the work here in Akjoujt and killed himself. We have been without a permanent doctor for eight weeks. I am sorry to have to tell you this, but I don't believe in secrets, and I think you have the right to know."

Curt's interest was piqued, but he was not shocked. Given his past, it was perhaps easier for Curt to process this than for others. Suicide had become an all too common in the U.S. military and he had lost friends to the disease.

Jawad looked at his watch. "Sir, It's nearly 11AM. We should get to lunch." Realizing this was a half-hearted effort by Jawad to change the subject, Curt let it go. And with that, they left the hospital in Jawad's vehicle, the same mid-1990s Toyota Forerunner from the airport. Curt would soon learn the vehicle was provided by Doctors Without Borders for him, but it was clearly a prize possession of Jawad.

The SUV came to a dusty stop in front of The Café. By Akjoujt standards, the place was extremely nice. Jawad and Curt entered. They were greeted by a very friendly man who appeared to be in his 50s, hastily running towards them. "Hello! Hello! Welcome!"

Jawad smiled and said, "Sir, this is Anbar. He owns this place. He insisted you have your first meal here. Actually, he made the food you had in your room last night. Did you like it?"

Curt was cornered and put his diplomatic skills to the test. "Actually, I fell asleep, Jawad, and by the time I awoke, I was afraid it might not be any good, so I didn't eat it. I must confess, it looked very good and now that I know Mr. Anbar made it, I am looking forward to lunch even more!"

Jawad stared at him. He knew Curt could have lied and he also realized Curt did not. Jawad's respect for Curt increased at that moment.

"Dr. Nover, it is such an honor to meet you. I have never been to the United States, but I decorate my entire restaurant with U.S. things. You see?"

"Yes, Mr. Anbar. It looks great."

"I have a table here for you. Please sit. I will bring your food soon." And with that, Jawad and Curt took their seats.

Curt broke the silence and asked. "Jawad, I'm confused. Which warring faction do we treat at our hospital? The Injus or Satris?"

"What do you mean? We are the only hospital in the area. We treat both. The Injus and Satris have deemed a few locations in the town as either neutral or 'no fight' areas. Lucky for us, the hospital is one such location. Normally in the recovery room, Satri patients are on one side and Injus on the other. Outside the hospital, they want to kill each other, inside, they don't look at each other or talk. Years ago, a fight broke out in the hospital between the Injus and Satris. The guards shot them dead. Ever since then, the rule has been if a fighter comes to the hospital for care, he is dropped off out front by his fellow fighters, he is disarmed, and remains so until he leaves the hospital. It is strange, but it works."

Curt was intrigued but not surprised. During his fighting in Afghanistan, things were similar. Local hospitals funded by the coalition partners commonly treated Taliban and Al Qaeda wounded. Many times, in warfare, things don't make sense. As more and more of the Akjoujt story unfolded, Curt began to have a sense of why he was selected to come to this town.

Anbar brought drinks and something which resembled bread. It was flat like a pita but clearly not as thick. Almost as if it were floppy Indian bread. They both thanked him, and Jawad ripped off a piece, beginning to eat. Curt continued, "Does either side ever try to break the rules and fight in the safe zones?"

"No. That would never happen. While the weak local government can't stop the warring factions, it is strong enough to enforce law. Fighting in safe zones would anger the locals that don't condone the fighting and neither of the warring faction's leaders wants this. Sadly, the local people have become numb to the fighting as there are rarely civilian casualties. Fighting in safe zones could potentially bring with it civilian casualties. This would most likely cause the locals to rise up. Again, neither leader desires this. So, the conflict is managed. It never seems to escalate which means it never gets international exposure. It also means it never ends."

Curt knew of such wars all too well. There were many conflicts ongoing throughout the globe. Not just Iraq and Afghanistan, but places few have heard of. Nagorno Karabagh, Transnistria, South Ossetia, Abkhazia, Crimea, Luhansk, Islands in South Asia, and just like Akjoujt, many places across Africa. Most have continued for years but few in the world knew they existed – or ever worse – few even knew of the countries in which the conflicts were fought.

Anbar approached rapidly. "Gentlemen, here is your food! I made one of my specials, lamb curry and rice, just for you. I hope you like it." Curt looked down at his plate. Ironically, it appeared identical to the food in Curt's kitchen last night. He scanned around at the restaurant one more time. Pictures of Sinatra, Elvis, the Rat Pack, James Dean hung from the walls. The Cafe had a retro U.S. diner feel. Curt chuckled and thought, *'If Anbar wanted to resemble a U.S. Diner, lamb curry and rice perhaps isn't in keeping with the motif.'* "Anbar, it looks great! Thanks." They both began to eat. Curt took his first bite. He soon realized; his earlier concerns of the Cafe were unwarranted. The food was delicious.

"Ok," Curt continued with their previous conversation, "Well then, Jawad, what do they fight over?"

"That, sir, is one of the best questions of Akjoujt. Here in our town, there is good revenue from the company which mines gold, copper and other minerals. Some say the warring factions would love to capture the mine, but given it is run by an American company with well-equipped security, I don't believe this. Also, they barely have enough weapons to fight each other. Introducing another faction into the mix for either side would prove challenging."

Jawad continued, "The mine is actually our town's bright spot. We receive a decent amount from them via taxes for their effort. This is good, but our government is weak. Lastly, our society is almost 95% Muslim. Given all this, it doesn't appear the factions fight over money, power, or religion. The best answer I can give you is honor. Long ago, the two largest local families were the subject of honor killings. No one really knows the details, but from that, the conflict has grown. Sadly, young boys with little opportunity pick sides much like picking a favorite sports team. They get recruited, paid and begin to fight. It's tragic. There are not many prospects here for our youth. This fighting is what they see as a rite to manhood. I wish there was a way to make it stop. Many have tried and none have succeeded."

Curt finally cut into Jawad's speech, "So, it's the Hatfields and McCoys?"

"Excuse me, sir?"

"Ha. Never mind, Jawad. I was just commenting to myself. I think I have asked you enough questions. Let's eat before our food gets cold."

Jawad agreed. "Yes. Thank you. Sir, I know there is much for you to digest today. We are very happy you are here." They began to eat, and the table was quiet.

The two finished lunch and Anbar's staff cleared the table. It was time to leave, and Anbar presented the bill. It was 850 in Ouguiya, the currency in Mauritania. Curt had come prepared. He opened his wallet and pulled out a 1000 Ouguiya bill. The tab was settled and the two of them left. The total cost was roughly four U.S. dollars.

The remainder of the afternoon, Jawad took Curt around the village. Vendors in a local bazaar exchanged goods and cash. A small makeshift school for the children was nestled into a corner lot. Curt absorbed it in. As they drove, Curt noticed most signs were in Arabic, the official language of Mauritania, but nearly every sign referencing the gold and copper mine was in English. "Jawad, why are the signs for the mine in English?"

"Sir, they are in both. The English ones are for the Americans. Many of the mine workers / managers come from the U.S. Every now and then, they visit the city for food, goods or services. It is great for our economy."

"There are U.S. citizens at the mine? Why don't we go? I would like to say hello."

"Sir, that is not possible. The mine has very tight security and unless you are invited, it is impossible to go. Many have tried to go, but the company refuses. The mine officials can't tell Injus from Satris from local Akjoujt civilians, and thus, they let no one near. The mining company is tremendously protective of their operation. I am told that the minerals they harvest are extremely valuable. The mine company, Nisassa Inc, takes no changes. They are well liked here by our people and our government and given a very long leash. I would suspect you will eventually meet some Americans in town. Make friends with them there, it is better."

The hour of 4PM was approaching and Curt was exhausted. The road they were on appeared familiar. It was the road where Curt's quarters resided. As they approached his residence, he was delighted to see his home.

Jawad parked the car and turned to Curt. "Sir, that was a lot for your first day. There is a grocery store up the street and some restaurants as well. If you need anything, please call me anytime of the day or night."

"Thanks, Jawad. For everything. I greatly appreciate all the effort you put into today. I can tell you are very proud of your town. I respect that and I look forward to working with you." Curt's words touched Jawad. He was pleased and proud of his new boss's comments. They departed ways.

Curt walked into his residence. The aroma of two-day old lamb curry and rice filled the place. He had forgotten to get rid of the food from last night. Curt grabbed the Styrofoam container, threw it in the trash and set it outside the door. He opened the windows and let out the smell – and the cold. The house heated up quickly. About 10 minutes later, he closed the windows. Curt was beat. He lay down on the couch with his laptop and lasted an hour before he fell asleep.

A loud car passing outside woke Curt. He had only been asleep for a few hours. While the sofa was comfortable, Curt knew he needed to go to bed for quality slumber. Curt got up, took a shower and prepared for bed. Today was a big day and tomorrow would be bigger. It would be his first day practicing medicine in Akjoujt.

Chapter Seven

Broken Truce

  Akim was 12 years old. He had grown up his entire life in Akjoujt. Although he didn't know it, today was the day he might lose his life. Akim was a low level Inju fighter. The son of a deceased father who also fought for the Injus, Akim made money to provide for his mother and siblings. At such a young age, he was still the man of the house. Dressed head to toe in robes and a cloth around his face, he was ready to fight to the death for Abdul-Salam, his Inju leader. It was before dawn in the early morning and Akim stood guard, armed with an AK-47, the world's most widely disseminated assault rifle, and a large handheld military style Ultra High Frequency (UHF) radio. His post was known to all as Inju territory. The Inju area was a few kilometers towards the East out of town. Only one road came near the location which made defense of checkpoint unchallenging. The land was relatively flat near the post. A few random rock outcroppings in the desert existed.   Akim was bored. A car approached and Akim stood, slightly brandishing his weapon. As the car approached, the headlights blinked in a preset sequence. Akim lowered his weapon and raised the makeshift gate arm crossing over the road. A senior Inju clansman rolled down his window as the vehicle approached and stopped. Akim began speaking to his superior in Arabic.
  //Translated to English//
  "Peace be with you, my fellow warrior."
  "And also with you, sir."
  "How is your post, Akim?"
  "Sir, it is perfect. No traffic, no movement and nothing to report. We are safe from any Satri attack. The Satris seem to

be abiding by the cease fire, but I don't trust them. They are liars, cheats and thieves."

"You are wise, Akim. Very wise. I will leave you now as I see our safety here is in good hands. I will pass to Abdul-Salam of your bravery and courage."

And in an Arabic tongue, Akim replied, "Shookrahn," (Thank you). Soon, Akim again stood alone at the post, awaiting the sunrise in the east.

****

In a rock cropping, 1000 meters away from Akim, the motionless desert came to life and the silence was broken. A tiny speaker inside a well camouflaged human's ear crackled, "Longbow 23, Base. Longbow 23, base." The transmission piped via high-tech military radios, through a thin wire and into a customized earpiece. Only one person would hear this communication. A voice in the desert, as if from nowhere, spoke. "Go," is all he said; softly.

"Are you in position?" The other end questioned.

"Affirmative. I am visual on the target. Awaiting orders," the man said, again in a hushed voice and a well concealed location.

"Roger, be advised, bird is overhead, and you are cleared on target, shoot to wound." The 'bird' was an unmanned aerial vehicle which was broadcasting live full motion video back to some location. While the electro optic camera could only pick out Akim, the thermal imaging camera clearly identified Longbow 23 laying hundreds of meters away in a rock outcropping. The transmission continued, "Not authorized shoot to kill, how copy?"

"Understand, shoot to wound." Orders were received. Longbow 23 became machine-like. As if from nowhere, he slowly emerged from a grouping of rocks. He had been there for well over a day awaiting his orders. Covered in dirt, dressed in local traditional attire, his face covered by a cloth, Longbow 23 would be a perfect match for a local from Akjoujt; minus his perfect English. He was just under 6 feet tall and built like a tank. To see someone that muscular move so quietly and gracefully was impressive.

Camouflaged and embedded in the rocks, Longbow 23 slowly and methodically opened a camouflaged weapon case. Inside was a Barrett M82A1 sniper rifle with an AN/PVS-10 Sniper Night Sight scope and an extremely modern silencer on the end. The weapon had obviously been used before, but it was clean and in excellent condition. The .50 caliber rifle had an 'unofficial' maximum range of roughly 3 kilometers. Today's shot would only be one kilometer. Still, this was no easy shot. Slowly and methodically, the man extracted the weapon. He affixed the tripod, removed the scope lens covers, and positioned himself for the shot – all as if it were a scripted robotic effort.   It took him mere minutes to get into position and he was so quiet, anyone or anything greater than 50 meters away would have been oblivious to his actions.

The man began to control his breathing. His eyes slowly closed and opened with each breath. Laid out in a prone position, Longbow 23 and his M82A1, blending into the desert floor. He slowly shifted the weapon scope onto Akim, dialing in range and attempting to adjust for wind. A handheld laser range finder displayed his target was 1005 meters away as Akim, a 15-year-old warrior with his rifle and radio, stood alone in the desert next to his makeshift guard hut and a tree branch which served as a road gate. The sniper inserted the magazine and quietly bolted a round. Desert animals were oblivious to him. Longbow 23 would only need one shot. The other magazine rounds were irrelevant.

Making final adjustments to his scope, Longbow 23 calmed his breathing and cleared his head. The crosshairs climbed up out of the earth and squared themselves upon Akim's left knee. Slowly, Longbow 23 wrapped his finger around the trigger. He breathed in deeply. A long exhale, combine with increasing pressure on the trigger. Crack! The gun jumped to life and a puff of fine desert dust swirled near the end of the barrel. He quickly re-centered the scope onto the target and watched. A mere two seconds later, Akim fell to the earth.

In a professional and calm voice, Longbow 23 spoke into his microphone, "Target down." The transmission was pointless. Those receiving it had just watched the entire events unfold on the full motion video. The only difference was Longbow 23 could hear Akim screaming in pain.

"Copy, Longbow 23. Expediate exfil."

Longbow 23 quickly put away his weapon, closed the case and began to egress approximately a kilometer and a half over the next few hours. The sunrise was roughly 30 minutes away and he would be forced to 'hole up' until nightfall. Then, he would rendezvous with arranged transportation. An exceptional training event.

Chapter Eight

The First 'Real' Workday

Curt woke early and crawled out of bed. From his former military lifestyle, early rising was an unbreakable habit. After making coffee, he put on some running attire and set out for an early morning jog. The desert air was cool and the Akjoujt streets were empty. Curt headed down the 'safe' road out of town. The 'safe' road, according to Jawad, was the one that led to the mine. As the road rose over the horizon, Curt could see the mine in the distance. It was unlike any other mine he'd seen. Yes, there were large scars on the earth exposing stone and some heavy machinery, but there was also double layered perimeter concertina wire fencing, a helicopter pad, and a large building. In other places, such security measures would be deemed excessive. In Akjoujt, it made sense. Owned by a foreign (non-Mauritanian) company, there were warring factions in the area, the local roads were atrocious, etc. Curt could only see a few personnel moving about. Maybe it was just too early. Behind Curt, the silent morning air was disrupted by noise emanating from Akjoujt. The mosques began to transmit the morning prayer, and Curt knew he must return. As he turned and began jogging, comparisons of the modern mine and old Akjoujt were just as contrasting as the geographical distance that separated them. Curt reflected on this as he ran home but dismissed much of the contrast. He'd fought in many places and learned that around the world, several things just don't make sense to a western mindset.

After returning, Curt took a shower, made breakfast, cleaned up and put on his hospital attire. It was still too early for work, so he sat down at his computer and read some news from back home. The headlines included a massive car pileup in

Arizona, some state and federal political / government scandals, a weather report for Chicago. None of the headlines captured his interest. Curt believed it was always the same news articles, only the names and places changed. Surfing the net, he left the normal headlines and went to the sports page. The Chicago Cubs would be playing Milwaukee at Wrigley Field and Curt was already missing baseball, Chicago, and home. He wondered how he would watch the games in Akjoujt. The internet was a wonderful invention, he thought, but the time zone difference was seven hours from Chicago. Hence, watching day games at Wrigley Field was doable – they'd start at 2000Hrs his time. Watching night games would not be an option due to the time zone differences. Now linked to his apartment Wi-Fi, Curt streamed some clips from yesterday's game. The internet speed and quality were impressive and far better than the 3G system provided by Doctors Without Borders. Akjoujt wasn't so bad.

    It was approaching 0700Hrs and it was time to go to work. Curt made a point to grab his duffle bag full of work gear and headed out the door. The streets were now alive with donkeys, carts and just a handful of old cars that most would consider death traps. He passed street vendors, strolling through the makeshift market. Although early, it was already warm, but nowhere near the heat of the afternoon. Curt arrived at the hospital; the walk took him a total of ten minutes. Later when he would return in the sweltering sun, Curt was sure he could cut that time to seven minutes.

    The hospital security guards recognized Dr. Nover as he entered. He was grateful to see they began remembering his face. As he walked between them into the door, Curt looked down at their weapons – a standard practice of every ex-military veteran. They were armed quite interestingly. Normally, he would have expected the standard third world rifle – the AK-47, but these guards both held U.S. made Colt M-4s outfitted with Close Combat Optic scopes. The weapons were clean, new, and that scope was expensive as its technology eliminated parallax associated with traditional front sight / rear sight weapons. With this scope, just place the red dot on your target and shoot. It was no wonder the fighting clans respected safe zones. The security that enforced them were well armed. Curt was a bit more comfortable knowing these weapons protected his work. As he entered, a few staff members were cleaning the facility. The place was spotless. Along one wall, a line of villagers had formed and patiently waited. Such was the daily occurrence. Curt had seen such lines in war torn regions and knew these people would be the days patients. A nurse walked through the line with a clipboard, writing down names.

"Good morning, Dr. Nover!" said Kamil in an exceptionally energetic way. Kamil was Curt's interpreter, raised in Akjoujt and roughly in his late teens, early 20s. One of the few his age to gain employment outside the warring clans. "I have prepared your office and made you some tea. Or do you prefer coffee today?" Kamil would do this every day but still felt obliged to tell Curt. His English was blanketed in a thick Arabic accent. But he truly was a good kid. Curt was a bit taken aback by Kamil's youthful energy. Curt saw Kamil as Akjoujt's Energizer Bunny, albeit, a bit overwhelming that early in the morning. "Good morning, Kamil, and Thank you. Today I'd love some Coffee if that's not a problem."

"No problem, Dr. Nover! Come with me!" Kamil grabbed Dr. Nover's duffle bag and quickly led Curt down the hall to his office. The light was on, the computer on the desk was operating, and a cup of hot tea sat on the desk with steam rising from the top. Kamil set down the bag and quickly took the tea from the desk. "I'll take this now and be back with Coffee immediately."

"Kamil, you are too kind. Thanks. OK. I am going to unpack some of my things in my office. What time do we start seeing patients today?"

Another voice echoed into the office from the hall, "Dr, Nover, sir, at 8AM." It was Jawad. He turned and looked at Kamil. "Assalamualaikum, Kamil." (A common Arabic greeting).

Kamil looked at Jawad and said, "Aleikum-salam, Mr. Jawad." (A common Arabic greeting reply). His energetic antics had vanished. Kamil had respect for Jawad and was subordinate in the hierarchy.

Jawad replied, "Kamil, please go help the nurses interview and prepare the patients for today. Learn of their illnesses or requests and be ready to explain them to Dr. Nover."

"Yes, sir." And with that, Kamil departed.

"Good morning, Dr. Nover. Did you sleep well?"

Curt was unpacking his personal belongings and professional gear in his office. "Assalamualaikum, Jawad. Yes, I slept fine, and the jet lag is all but gone. It is however starting to remain hot at night. Does that increase even more into the summer?" Jawad smiled and laughed lightly. "Dr. Nover, for the people of Akjoujt, this is still cold."

"Jawad, I noticed the patient line seemed long." There were approximately 30 people.

"Yes, sir. The news of your arrival has spread, and many have been waiting on a doctor. I did the best I could as a Physician's Assistant (PA), but my knowledge is limited and many here decided to wait until your arrival to seek medical care. Sir, your presence is special for the people of Akjoujt."

The weight of what Jawad explained was not lost and Curt felt a slight burden placed on his shoulders. *'They came to see me, so I could take their pain away,'* he thought. This was EXACTLY why he left the Navy, for Med School. It was years in the making and he could not be more honored. "Well, Jawad, I hope I don't let them down."

"I believe you won't, sir. We are lucky you are here." If Kamil was the Energizer Bunny, Jawad was Spock from Star Trek. Intellectual, but emotionless. No matter. Curt appreciated Jawad's help.

"Thanks. OK, I will finish settling into my office and will open my door for patients around five till eight."

"Great, sir. Kamil will be outside your door and escort in your first patient." With that, Jawad left.

Curt had roughly 20 minutes to himself and logged into his computer. The hospital file system still was on physical paper. The computer was for email and research. Curt sat down. He realized he wasn't the Chief of a big American Hospital, but he was the Chief of Medicine in Akjoujt. There was no one above him. He was in charge. Yes, he had to answer to Doctors Without Borders from time to time, but he was on his own. The leadership skills he had learned from the U.S. Navy would pay off as he was not just a manager. He would lead this hospital. There was no hiding Curt's excitement. He pulled up his email account and jotted off a quick email:

20 May 2019

>Ms. Wanda –
>A quick note to let you know I'm fine. It's been a few days and I am finally settled in.
>Guess what? I am the chief doctor here. I have a small staff and am seeking a good candidate for a Head Nurse position. Are you interested? ☺ It doesn't pay well, but I hear the boss is a dream to work for.
>I can't begin to tell you how happy I am.
> Miss you,
Curt

A shuffling and commotion were obvious outside his office door. Dr. Nover looked at his watch. It was 0750Hrs. The noise was no doubt Kamil. He was five minutes early, and if Jawad would have allowed, Kamil would have been five days early. He was so eager it wasn't funny. Luckily, Curt was just as eager.

Curt opened the door, greeted Kamil, who led him to Exam Room One. Inside, a small girl sat patiently on the bed as her mother dressed in black robing sat in a chair next to the door. Kamil relayed that the child was brought in for an ear infection. It had been festering for a while and it was fairly well developed. Through Kamil, Curt instructed the mother how to keep the ear clean. Curt prescribed some medicine, taught the mother how to administer it and wished the little girl a good day. The entire event took nearly 20 minutes. The line of patients was now nearly 40 people. Curt did some quick math in his head. "Kamil, how am I going to see all these people today?"

"Sir, you probably won't. If you don't see them today, they will come back tomorrow. Most of them are nomads or wives with no work responsibilities. To them, you are the big event for their week. If they don't see you today, they will be back. I assure you." Again, Curt felt a burden placed on his shoulders.

The next three patients were taken care of over the next hour. As Curt was finishing his last of the three, the exam room door burst open, and a nurse was screaming in Arabic. Kamil responded to her quickly then turned to Curt. "Dr. Nover, we must go. They are bringing a severely wounded boy. He will be here soon." Curt acknowledged and quickly said his farewells to his current patient.

An Isuzu truck rapidly approached the hospital with its horn blowing. It stopped in front and two Inju clansmen with weapons jumped from the vehicle. The hospital guards gripped their M-4s and raised them so that the barrel was pointed at the ground in front of where the Injus stood. Any sudden move and the guards would continue to raise their guns and place them squarely on the Injus. Oddly, this was standard procedure. In the back of the truck, another Inju was screaming and laying in a pool of blood that covered the truck bed. They took the injured warrior from the vehicle and left their weapons. The hospital guards lowered their M-4s. All, according to informally agreed upon procedures between the warring factions. Soon the boy would be on the Emergency Room table.

Curt looked at the patient. His leg had either suffered a large caliber strike or some sort of small explosion below the knee. Further up the leg, Curt noticed a makeshift tourniquet. It was working, but below the tourniquet the leg was blue and had been for quite some time. Akim was violently screaming and struggling as one would expect a scared young boy to react. Over and over, Akim screamed, "ALLAH AKBAR! ALLAH

AKBAR!!!" (God have mercy!). To a scared boy, that phrase was a plea for God's help. To Curt, every time he heard it, he was certain an explosion, gun fire, or horrific war related event was certain to unfold. Curt tried to calm his nerves. *'Focus, Nover!'* He thought to himself. *'Now is NOT the time to have a break down.'*

Kamil was able to begin to calm Akim and started extracting information.

"Dr. Nover, the boy's name is Akim. He is Inju. He says he was guarding a post and then a bullet from nowhere struck him. He was alone and didn't see anything or anyone leave. He says it happened about 3 hours ago." Akim and Kamil continued to scream at each other in Arabic.

After a quick look, Curt realized there was no saving the leg. The tourniquet had probably saved the boy's life, but the lower extremity of the leg was mangled beyond repair and had seen no fresh blood for hours. The leg required a below the knee amputation. The nurses had already dropped an intravenous drip as well as extra blood and began medication.

"Kamil, tell the nurses to prepare the Operating Room. I need to amputate this leg. Jawad, I need you. I am unfamiliar with the Operating Room here and your assistance is critical."

Both agreed and went about their business. As they were preparing the O.R., a woman entered the hospital screaming. It was Akim's mother. She was in tears and beside herself. It took two guards to contain her from barging into the emergency room. Via Kamil, Curt had one of the nurses give the mother valium to calm her down. There was no way Curt would be able to perform a surgery listening to any more screaming, his nerves were already on the edge of breaking down.

Curt entered the O.R. and was amazed. While none of the equipment was new, nearly all of it was far more modern than he had expected. His predecessor had obviously made significant efforts in hospital acquisitions. Over the next few hours, Curt did not perform the most elegant surgery of his career. Unfamiliarity with the O.R. proved difficult but the end result was a success. Akim would live. He was moved into the open recovery room (the corner with the ICU) and was joined by his mother. Curt looked into the waiting room. Along with the mother, another visitor was present. He was a tall man. He appeared stoic and dressed far better than anyone Curt had seen in town.

"Jawad, who is that man with the little boy's mom? Is it his father?"

"No sir, that is our village elder. He is like what you may call a mayor. His name is Issam." Curt kept looking. Issam turned and noticed Curt. Their eyes locked. Issam turned around, said something to the little boy's mom, turned back and then moved towards Curt.

"You must be the new doctor and the one I should thank for saving Akim's life."

"Assalamualaikum. My name is Curt. Doctor Curt Nover. Akim is lucky. Whoever applied the original tourniquet is the real hero. Without it, he would have died."

"You speak Arabic, Dr. Nover? Interesting."

"No, sir. I don't. I know a little... enough to be respectful of your culture."

"Very well. I am Issam. I am the leader of the Akjoujt people; at least those who don't align with our warring factions. My people and I are very grateful you are here. If you do not have plans for tonight, I would like to dine with you at my house. Is this acceptable?"

Curt looked at Jawad. While they had only known each other for days, he could tell by Jawad's eyes this was not an offer he should reject. "Sir, it would be my honor."

"Good to hear, Dr. Nover. I shall have a car at your residence at 7:30PM."

"Mr. Issam, Sir.... about the boy. I understand he is an Inju clansman. The wound he suffered was no accident. Has the cease fire between the Injus and Satris ended?" Curt wanted an answer.

"Dr. Nover, some things are not as simple as yes and no. Let us discuss this over dinner tonight. You and I are busy men, and the business hours are upon us. Inshallah, we will have this discussion over our meal." They shook hands and Issam left before Curt could respond. *'Inshallah?'* Curt knew what this meant – God willing. *'What did Issam mean by 'God Willing' in the context of this conversation?'*

Curt looked around. He had nearly forgotten there were numerous patients left to see. He quickly cleaned up and began cycling patients in and out of exam rooms. Working with Kamil was getting easier and the nursing staff quickly began to adapt to his style. Jawad observed Dr. Nover's actions and was pleased. Doctors Without Borders had sent them a good one. Jawad began to withdraw himself from practicing medicine and spent more emphasis on the administration and upkeep of the hospital – a job that had been sorely ignored for the past two months.

The end of the workday approached. There were eight patients that would come back tomorrow. They did not complain, this was how they lived. Jawad finished writing up orders for supplies and managing the staff schedule for the next few weeks. He walked down the hall and saw Dr. Nover and Kamil chatting.

"Dr. Nover, before you leave today, may I speak with you?" Jawad requested.

"Absolutely, Jawad. How about now? Kamil, will you excuse us?" And with that, Kamil was gone.

"Sir, I overheard your conversation with our village elder. Tonight, you will eat dinner with him. I heard you ask about the fighting between the Injus and Satris. I caution you. It is not normal in our culture to confront such an issue so abruptly in public. I know you say you are respectful of our culture, but realize, Issam was politely dismissing you."

Curt thought about what he remembered of Arabic culture, and realized, Jawad was correct. "Jawad, you are right. I forgot how direct our culture is compared to yours."

"It is OK, sir. That is one of the reasons I am here." Jawad smiled and continued. "Sir, I do not know if tonight's discussion with Issam will warrant this, but I have created a list of things our hospital needs. If he asks how he can help, here is that list. I have prioritized our needs as you can see." While Curt looked down, he didn't really even look at the list. He seriously doubted a 'town mayor' of this poverty-stricken village would be able to afford expensive and delicate medical equipment. More importantly, he had no idea how to indirectly approach such an issue with Issam. Curt took the list and put it in his pocket.

"OK, Jawad. Thanks. If it comes up, I will discuss it with Issam." Curt perceived this as a fruitless effort, but he was pleased with Jawad and the last thing he wished to do was upset the one person whom he relied on most.

"Doctor, it is getting late and there is little left to do here. Please go home and prepare for dinner. It should be an enjoyable evening."

"Thanks, Jawad. I think you are right. I will head home now and get ready. Have a good night yourself and I will see you tomorrow." They began to separate and then Curt stopped and said, "By the way, I meant to tell you. Today with Akim you were extremely good. I have seen a fair amount of physician assistants in the O.R. and I must confess, you were one of the best I have ever seen."

Jawad replied in a somber tone. "Thank you, sir, but when you have done nearly thirty amputations, you tend to get very proficient at the procedure." Jawad turned and walked away. Curt had no idea of Jawad's amputation experiences and felt a bit awkward. He said nothing more.

Chapter Nine

Issam's Dinner

It was 1730Hrs when Curt finally headed home. The later afternoon heat was intense during the walk. As he grabbed his front door, he looked at his watch and thought, *'Seven minutes and forty seconds…. I can do better.'* With time to kill, Curt lifted his coffee table and placed it on the sofa to create some room and began to workout. The apartment was warm, but he needed this. Sit-ups, push-ups, crunches, and dips – nearly every exercise under the sun one could imagine in a cramped place. This was his first two-a-day workouts since arriving in Akjoujt and he wanted to make it part of his daily routine. Sweat dripped from his face. His legs and arms burned. The endorphins soon began to circulate in his blood stream – it felt good. An hour later, he was exhausted, and he had built up an appetite – unfortunately, he had no idea what would be served and given the culture, there was a 50/50 chance he wouldn't recognize any of it.

Cleaned up and ready, Curt waited for his ride. At precisely 1930Hrs, a clean high gloss black Chevy Tahoe with tinted windows pulled up in front of his residence. The car looked completely out of place for Akjoujt. Curt walked out and the rear passenger door opened.

"Dr. Nover?" A deep voice said from inside the vehicle.

"Yes," Curt replied.

"Sir, Welcome. Please get in." Curt entered the Tahoe. A driver sat alone in front and a very large man in a uniform sat in the back seat armed with an M-4 assault rifle – the same weapon hospital guards carried. Curt closed the door and the car sped away – ignoring nearly every Akjoujt traffic law. This was not really all that disconcerting, from Curt's short time in the town, he noticed few, if any, followed the traffic laws, they were more or less traffic suggestions, but this driver seemed to ignore more than the average person.

The SUV approached a small compound. A drop gate was raised by local guards which appeared to be security and the vehicle continued into the compound. It was surrounded by 10ft walls. Again, the vehicle stopped and a small man in nice local attire opened the rear passenger door. The entire trip took less than 10 minutes.

"Dr. Nover. Good evening, sir. His excellency awaits you inside."

'Excellency?' Curt thought, 'And I was on a first name basis with this guy just a few hours ago???' "Thanks," Curt replied to the gentleman.

"Please, come this way." The servant escorted Curt into the house. It was more than Curt could have imagined for a small African village. While the exterior presented an appearance similar to other village buildings, the inside was clean, well maintained and well adorned. Artwork hung on the walls and the light fixtures had covers – a luxury not afforded to many lights in Akjoujt. Jawad's list was beginning to make more sense.

Issam walked towards Curt and broke the silence. "Ah. It is good to see you." Curt was too busy scanning the environment to realize Issam was approaching.

Quickly he looked up and said, "Sir, it is good to see you as well. You have a beautiful house."

"Ah, one cannot judge a man on his house alone. Come with me. My staff has prepared tea for us in the sitting room while the final touches are prepared for the dinner." Issam led him into a room filled with carpets and overstuffed sofas. They sat as tea was poured.

"Sir," Curt said. "What should I call you? At the hospital you introduced yourself as Issam, but when I exited your car, you were referred to as 'Your Excellency' by a staff member. I am not sure how to address you."

Issam laughed. "Dr. Nover, please, call me Issam. Titles and formal names serve me little purpose here. I know who I am, and my people do as well. I know little of you, but I imagine you know your place in society as well."

"Issam, Ok. Thanks for the clarification. But I do please ask you call me Curt." If Issam was to accept a first name basis, Curt was going to do the same.

The two drank tea and exchanged formalities. Curt was very cognizant to remember Arabic culture and to refrain from letting the discussion topic become too confrontational or too forward. Curt errored in the hospital earlier and was attempting to heal a wound before it became serious. "Issam, do you have family?"

"Of course!" And with that, Issam magically pulled a wallet from under his robing as if it appeared from nowhere. Inside was a picture of Issam's family. "This is my wife, and five children."

"What a beautiful family. Will they be joining us for dinner?"

"No. I am afraid they cannot. They do not live in Akjoujt. It is too dangerous. They live in Nouakchott, the capital, and I see them upon occasion. And you? Do you have a family?"

"Issam, I wish I had a family but as of yet, I have not been blessed with one." A perfect answer in Arabic culture. Families were one way in which a man was judged. Not having a family was somewhat frowned upon, however, the religious reference and placing the issue in 'God's Hands' would mitigate the ill perceptions.

"I see," said Issam. "Well, I have good news, there are a great deal more women in Akjoujt than men. You can have your pick of a wife." They both laughed. Curt knew the reason for the disproportionate ratio of women to men – The Satris and Injus. He bit his tongue, literally, to keep from asking. An awkward silence fell upon them.

A servant entered the room and rattled off something in Arabic. Issam responded with another phrase and the only word Curt recognized was "Shookrahn," (Thank You). "Curt, dinner is served. Please, come with me."

They entered the dining room. The table was set for two but could easily seat twelve. He looked down at the food. He recognized it! Lamb and rice. He thanked God tonight would not involve a rendezvous with 'mystery meat,' a common Western reference to unknown flesh served throughout the globe. They sat and began to eat.

The food was excellent which was apparent by the lack of communication between the two. Slowly, they began to fill up and the conversation returned. Issam spoke. "Very sad about Akim. I am pleased that he will live."

"Yes. It is. He seems to be a good young boy. "

"Curt, I must confess, it appears you were correct today. The Injus and Satris have again begun to fight. The truce is now broken, and I fear more bloodshed in the near future. We have Allah to thank that you are here to save our youth."

"I am humbled you believe in me so, Issam, but you are the elder. Isn't there any way you can stop the fighting?"

"I truly wish I could. Abdul-Salam and Qudamah are the rulers of the two armies. Sadly, I grew up with both since the time we were little boys. I really thought this current truce could make peace. Their hatred for each other is indescribable."

'Armies?' Curt thought to himself. 'Somehow, the strength of these entities had grown from clans to armies in a matter of hours.' "Do you talk to either? Do they understand what their fight is doing to your town?"

"Yes, I do speak to them regularly and yes, they understand, but do you?" Curt was a bit taken back and he quickly realized his directness had surfaced. Issam was not about to give him another free pass. "In our culture, hatred this deep is rarely understood by your kind. It is rooted in generations and family honor is one of the few pieces of pride my people can hold. Resolving fights like this does not just happen when a magic man waves his hand. From my experience, they never stop."

"Issam, I am sorry. My comment was ignorant, and I should have known better. I have spent time on battlefields in Iraq and Afghanistan and I understand they each have unique cultural differences from your people. One thing however you all have in common is a displeasure with American directness. I shall work on this."

Issam paused and stared at Curt. "It is OK, my friend. I accept your apology. You are not the first American I have met." Issam flashed a quick smile. "The subject of the Injus and Satris will not be solved tonight. Let us stop talking of it. I ask you. How do you like our hospital?"

And with that, the subject was changed, and all was forgotten. "It is nice. Very nice. Actually, more than I had hoped for."

"Yes, we are proud of it. The mining operation here does very well and they pay good money to keep the hospital well sourced in the event of a mine emergency. It is a bonus we can use it for the people of Akjoujt as well. Our town receives more support from the mine than from our capital, Nouakchott."

"I see," Curt said. "Let me ask, does the mine provide a doctor as well?"

"No, there is no need. A doctor would cost them additional funds. The mining company believes the money they save on paying for a doctor could be better used in providing funds to our hospital and allowing a volunteer doctor come into Akjoujt."

With this, Curt wondered how long it would be until he was providing medical care to a U.S. citizen in the middle of Africa. "Yes, I guess that makes sense."

"You don't seem pleased with the arrangement, Curt. Why is this? Is there something wrong with the hospital? Is there something you need to make the hospital better?"

Curt couldn't believe his ears. *'How did Jawad know!?'* "Issam, I have only been in the hospital a day. I really have not taken inventory."

"Come. There must be something you need. Let me talk to the mining company – I have a meeting with them tomorrow."

"Well, I do have a list, but I really have not reviewed it. Jawad created it and handed it to me today." And with that, the list exited Curt's pocket and was being handed across the table.

"Perfect. I shall see what I can do. I make no promises." Issam looked at the list and began to chuckle. "Jawad. He is a character. Always asking for an MRI machine. As if the hospital had room for an MRI machine. I tell you; he is a good assistant. You should listen to him. He dreams big, but he means well."

Curt was shocked and thought, *"An MRI Machine?! Issam openly asks for a list? Does Jawad have ESP (Extra Sensory Perception)? What just happened?"* Curt was utterly confused. "Ha. Yes…. An MRI. I think he was attempting a joke. And, I agree, Jawad is very good, and I appreciate his efforts. I would be lost without him."

"I am glad he is working out. Curt, the time is late, and I must complete some work. I thank you for being my guest tonight and I am deeply touched with your efforts to save Akim. Our town owes you and we pray to Allah you can save many more." Issam stood and so did Curt.

"Thank you Issam, for everything. Again, I shall work on my directness."

"It will come with time, my friend. I don't doubt it." Issam walked him to the door. The Black Tahoe was waiting. The two said their goodbyes and 10 minutes later, Curt was back home.

After Curt left, Issam picked up the phone and placed a call. The number rang and Issam spoke. "Hello….. Yes, he saved the boy's life. It is God's Will. I believe in him. He can do good things. Yes, Jerry, I have a list for you. My people will deliver it tomorrow. Please, try to get all you can…… We will talk tomorrow….. Goodbye."

Chapter Ten

Along Came a Woman

The next few weeks were filled with exactly what Curt and his staff had come to expect. Other than Akim, there were four more warriors wounded in Inju and Satri fighting. Morbidly, this was considered a positive as none had died in the renewed fighting. Three suffered gunshot wounds and one was the victim of rocket propelled grenade shrapnel which blew a hole in a wall and the frag pattern caused surface injuries to a Satri clansman.

It was a slow day, other than the elderly, the mothers and the daughters lined up to donate blood... a common scene with increased fighting. The morning line of patients other than blood donors was manageable; four or five who required more intensive medical attention. The rest were there to receive their weekly fill of prescription medications. Curt was finishing with an elderly lady who had a serious infection on her leg. From outward appearance, the wound was old and untreated. Curt grabbed an empty bag and filled it with medicine and fresh gauze. While Curt was gathering these items, Kamil attempted to inform the woman that she needed to change the dressing daily and put new medicine on the wound each time, but the woman didn't care to listen. Curt opened the door. Jawad, standing out in the hall, noticed the troubles Kamil faced and walked into the room as Curt walked out. In two minutes, Jawad had calmed the situation. The woman understood the instructions and would follow them to a tee. Jawad had a way with the people of Akjoujt.

"Jawad. It appears we are out of patients for now. I think I am going to go to The Café and see what Anbar has on his menu today. Do you wish to join me?"

Jawad was still trying to catch up on administrative issues in the hospital. While a normal hospital could have been caught up by now, the Akjoujt hospital was not normal. The only computer in the hospital sat on Dr. Nover's desk. All records and bookkeeping were done by hand. "Sir, I cannot. I need to get some work done here."

"OK. I understand." Curt would eat alone. "Well, I have my cell phone. Call me if something happens." And with that, Curt took off his hospital coat and walked out of the hospital into the noon day sun.

Curt strolled by the bazaar. This was going to be the perfect place to pick out holiday gifts for family and friends. Rugs, hookah pipes, hand carved wooden objects…. Gift options were endless. Daily, he would look at the seller's wares and he mentally began matching items against his gift list. It was a welcome mental exercise and helped him decompress from his hospital work.

The walk to The Café took about 5 minutes. The lunch crowd today was large but as soon as Anbar saw Dr. Nover, he was certain there was a place for him to sit.

"Good day, Dr. Nover! Welcome. Welcome!!"

"Thank you, Anbar. How are you today?"

"Sir, I am perfect. Business is good, inshallah, and the summer heat doesn't appear to be too bad this year. Autumn will eventually be here. What more could I ask for!?" Curt quickly thought *'the heat isn't bad this year??'* He was amazed it could get worse. Regarding *'what more could one ask for,'* Curt bit his tongue give the desire to make an off-color comment regarding Satri/Inju peace, but held it in. *'I must keep working on this directness problem'* he thought in his head.

"What is the special today, Anbar?"

"Oh, it is a family specialty." In any foreign land, this phrase was cause for alarm in a westerner's mind. "Today we have marinated goat with vegetables."

Curt had eaten more goat than he ever wished to while in Afghanistan. He didn't care how special Anbar's family recipe was, there was no chance he was eating goat today. "Anbar, that sounds great, but I think I would like to see the regular menu."

"No problem, sir. I'll get it for you right away." Anbar left the table in a haste.

Curt began to look around. The crowd contained a significant number of locals, but at one table, three well-dressed western men sat along with an attractive western dressed blonde. One of the gentlemen looked familiar but given how many folks Curt had met over the past few weeks, there was no placing a name with a face. The entire table looked extremely out of place at Anbar's restaurant. Curt had not seen an attractive female for a while. Not because the women of Akjoujt weren't beautiful. Frankly, Curt wouldn't know as they were often covered head to toe in clothing. An attractive woman in western attire? He couldn't help but stare. He knew it was awkward, but it was as if his muscles were frozen.

She had blonde hair, blue eyes and a well-constructed face. Her jaw line was strong, and her neck and shoulder proportions were as if they were taken from a model. It was either that, or Curt had completely forgotten what a woman looked like. The three men spoke to her in English, and she took notes as fast as any court stenographer. She didn't stop writing, she rarely looked up, and never noticed Curt's Medusa stare.

"Sir…. Sir….. Sir! Here is the menu you requested." It was Anbar. Attempting to get Curt's attention. Finally, Curt's eyes broke lock and took the menu.

"Sorry, Anbar. I was thinking about something."

"Yes, sir. You are not the only one thinking about something in this restaurant. Many people are 'thinking something' about her." Anbar smiled. "She is new in town. Some reporter invited by the mining company to write about Akjoujt. We are all excited she is here. Soon, Akjoujt will be famous!" Comically, Anbar truly believed this. "Sir, you seem to be more 'thinking about something' than our people though." Anbar smiled and walked away. His sentence was a grammatical train wreck, but he was pleased with his little joke.

Curt ordered his food and received it. He ate, all the while wondering what news story was so pressing for the mine to get out. *'Did they bring her here to shed light on the clan fighting? Did they hope international exposure might bring diplomatic negotiators and eventual peace? Did the mine desire to bring in UN peacekeepers in an effort to make Akjoujt a safer place for its workers?'* He also wondered what her name was. Where was she from? He didn't know why he was so taken aback by this female, but whatever the reason, Curt was.

As he contemplated numerous questions, his phone rang. He pulled out the phone and the number was visible, but he did not recognize it.

Curt answered, "Hello. Dr. Nover."

"Dr. Nover? I heard you are a closet pilot!"

"Buck? Is this you?!"

"Yup. Just landed in Akjoujt and was wondering if you wanted to get a bite to eat. I'll be here until about 5 tonight."

"Buck, I would love to, but I am eating right now. I need a little more lead time! When do you come back? I really could use a pointless conversation with a crazy man." Curt knew full well he could throw smack with Buck. It was obvious in his nature.

"Yes, and I need a refill on my Viagra too, so we need to get together sooner rather than later. OK. Next time I will try to give the important doctor some lead time. Sound good?"

"Yes, Buck, that sounds perfect. And thanks for calling. Is this your number?"

"Yup. Load me into your contacts!"

"Hey, Buck, by the way, how did you get my number?"

"I called the hospital and told them I had an ever-increasing blister on my nut sack, and it was getting close to exploding. I said I had a knife and was going to lance it and asked if they would talk me through the procedure step by step. I had your number in 3 minutes."

Curt began to laugh out loud; so loud in fact the other patrons noticed him – to include the blonde. "Great job, Buck. Next time you are in town, the meal is on me. Take care and goodbye." Curt hung up the phone and continued eating.

The three men seated with the female all stood up. They shook the reporter's hand and left The Café. She was alone. No matter, she was clueless to the scene around her. She feverishly wrote in her journal as if she was fearful she might forget something one of the three had said. Curt kept eating and watched her.

She eventually stopped writing. Curt was still staring. After nearly a full five minutes, she finally caught him. It wasn't awkward at all as Curt had been planning to catch her eye for a while. He didn't look away, he just kept staring and slowly began to smile. After a short pause, she smiled back. Curt's foot casually pushed out one of the three empty seats at his table and simultaneously motioned with his hand for her to come join him. She grabbed her purse, gathered her things and stood. She walked towards him. His plan worked. She stopped right behind the chair. And... She did not sit down.

"Dr. Nover, I presume."

"Umm... Yes. How do you..."

"How do I know who you are? I have only been here a day, but I assure you, the town's people have told me all about the 'magic one.'"

"Ironic. I have been here for a week now and not one has mentioned anything to me about the 'furious writing one.'" Curt smiled. So did she.

She smiled. "Give them time. They'll know me soon enough. Look. I have already eaten lunch with the three men from the mine. I have other things to do right now but I would like to interview you for my article. Is there a chance you are available tomorrow for lunch?"

"Nope. I'm sorry. Not available."

"OK. How about the next day?"

"Nope. Busy then too."

"Fine. When are you available?"

Curt didn't waste a second in his response. "Tonight. For dinner."

"Dinner!? Wow. A bit direct, aren't you?"

"Yes, but I've assured the town elder I am working on that."

"Dinner, huh? Alright... but just dinner. Where would you like to meet?"

"My place."

She looked at him quizzically. "I thought you said you are working on not being so direct."

"I am working on it. I didn't say I was doing well. Maybe you could help me. Tonight? Seriously, just dinner. I have not had a chance to cook here, and this seems like a good reason to test out my kitchen. I assure you I am a perfect gentleman. I even have references." Curt again flashed a shit-eating grin of a smile.

She couldn't help but be attracted by his humor. Nonetheless, her guard was up. She was a western woman in an unknown culture. This story was a big break, and she didn't want to let anything interfere. To that end, she also knew she really wanted to interview the village doctor. "OK. Dinner at your place but we need to make it early. And you answer all my questions. Deal?"

Curt was smitten with his effort. "It's a deal. I do need one more favor though."

She was nearly shocked by his audacity. "What is it now?"

"Your name?" Curt asked.

A bit of relief fell over her. "Allison. Allison Donley. Where do you live and what time do I meet you?"

"How about 6:30PM, in front of the hospital. I'll meet you there." He extended his hand as if to seal the deal.

She reached out and shook his hand. "OK. Dr. Nover, I'll be there."

Their hands released and with one last comment, Curt said, "It's a date."

"No." She replied. "It's an interview in the vicinity of food." She smiled back and let him know Curt was not the only one with quick wit. He was impressed. She turned and walked away.

Anbar stood behind Curt and witnessed the entire exchange. "Dr. Nover. Would you like something else?"

"Anbar, yes… I do want something else. But I don't believe I'll find it on your menu. Can I get my check? I need to get back to the hospital. There is much to be done." Curt settled his bill. As he did, Anbar came back to the table with a bag.

"Dr. Nover. You will have dinner with this woman tonight. Yes?"

"Yes, Anbar. That is the plan. Why do you ask?"

"I have a present for you." Anbar handed the bag to Curt in a secretive manner. Curt looked in. The bag contained a nice bottle of wine. In Akjoujt, like other predominately Muslim nations, alcohol was available but difficult to come by publicly. Additionally, it was frowned upon in public spaces. In private, however, and in the right circles, villagers drank often. Interestingly though, no one confessed openly about their private libations. To acquire alcohol, there were black markets and such, but Curt did not have time to scope these out as of yet. The gift was very appreciated.

"Anbar, you are a saint. How much do I owe you?"

"Nothing, sir. It is on the house. Have a good time tonight." Anbar smiled directly at Curt as he walked away. Curt chuckled, took the bag and returned to the hospital. His new plan was to leave early and hit the market. Tonight's meal would be something special.

Chapter Eleven

The Interference

Later at his office, Curt began shutting down his computer and gathering his effects. "Dr. Nover, are you done for the day?" Jawad asked. The time was only 1500Hrs, but it was clear there were no new patients and those in the care wards had already been seen.

"Yes, Jawad, I need to get some personal things done today. Is there something pressing you wish for me to attend to before I leave?" Curt didn't really wish to stay any longer, but Jawad was very good to him and the last thing he wished to do was upset one of his closest allies.

"No, sir. Everything is good. I was just checking. I am sorry. I didn't mean to meddle."

Curt was puzzled. Again, he failed to recognize the culture. "Jawad, there is no need to apologize. It is just some shopping and such. Nothing earth shattering. I will see you tomorrow."

"OK, sir. Have a good evening."

"You too, Jawad. Don't stay too late."

Curt left the hospital and headed to the market. As of yet, he had no idea what he was going to cook tonight, but it was going to be good. More importantly, Curt knew this was good for his mental health as well. He had not done anything other than work and exercise since his time in Akjoujt. Curt thought, *'This relaxing cooking effort and dinner was exactly what the doctor ordered.'* His own corny joke made him smile.

Curt checked the market produce and food. The vegetables were decent as it was the late summer harvest. He grabbed some onions, potatoes and tomatoes along with some fresh bread. 'Now for some meat,' he thought. Curt continued to walk around the market and then noticed something. He stopped in his tracks. In front of him was a tall man of about six feet in traditional attire. But that face??? It couldn't be... But it was. Smitty!!!! Mark Smith, a military man who Curt served with in more far off places than Curt cared to ever count. When stationed together, they were best of friends. Unfortunately, much like many other military relationships, once they separated, they lost contact.

"Smitty?" Curt questioned. The man turned and saw Curt. A quick smile on the man's face confirmed it.

"Curt? What are you doing here?"

"What am I doing here!? I am the town doctor assigned here on a humanitarian mission. What they hell are YOU doing here!?"

Smitty stuttered for a minute, "I, um, work for the mining company."

Curt couldn't help but notice the nearly invisible wire running up to Smitty's neck and into his ear. It was relatively discrete, but Curt was trained to notice these things. "I see you're mic'ed up. What are you doing, working security for the mine?"

"Uhh... Yes. There's a great deal of money in the mining operation, and they pay to protect their assets you know.... Curt, I can't really talk now. I am sorry. Do you have a card or a phone number or something so we can catch up later?" Curt was well aware that in security and military work, there are times to talk and times to focus. He completely understood Smitty's plight.

Curt scribbled down his number on a piece of paper and handed it to Mark. "Smitty, it's great to see you. Give me a call when you are off the clock, and we can catch up."

"Yeah, great. Sure." They hugged and Curt immediately realized Smitty was carrying a concealed weapon, which of course made sense given his current employment.

Smitty put the number in his pocket buried in his local garb. It was obvious he was trying to listen to the conversation in his ear bud while trying to say his goodbyes to Curt. Smitty turned and began to walk away as he raised his right cuff to his mouth and spoke. Curt assumed the mine company must be pulling in some good money. Smitty was trained as one of the elites in the U.S. military; so was Curt. Additionally, Curt could tell Smitty's communication system was quite pricey. It didn't matter, Curt smiled. He knew someone... a REAL someone finally in Akjoujt, five thousand miles from the U.S. Maybe the world wasn't as big as he had thought.

Curt continued to move through the market, with a little more stride in his step. He continued toward a meat vendor selling his goods. As he walked in that direction, Curt noticed there was a well-dressed Akjoujt man walking among the crowd. His attire was similar to that of Issam, suggesting the man was of wealth and status. In the market however, he clearly looked out of place. Akjoujt locals were in garb, which was worn, torn, full of dirt or all the above. This man's clothing was in immaculate, and he was well groomed. *'He must be important'* thought Curt as the man was completely out of place. While Curt didn't know the man, the locals all knew him as Kameel, a high level Satri officer. In his near vicinity, his small protective detail walked and watched the crowd. To Curt, however, such scenarios in third world places was commonplace. Curt looked back down and continued shopping for his evening meal.

Just then, an engine roared and a yellow Toyota truck screamed into the bazaar. In the truck were three men: two in back and one in front. They were dressed head to toe in local garb and their faces were wrapped. As the vehicle approached, villagers screamed and fled the streets like mice chased by cats. Chaos was about to ensue. As the truck approached, Kameel's security detail raised their weapons. Curt began to realize the truck was tracking on Kameel, the man in the grey clothing.

Kameel's security detail was so focused on the Toyota truck, they failed to realize each had someone shadowing them, also dressed in local attire. As the security detail raised their weapons to fire on the vehicle, the shadows lunged at them from their backs. One was knocked unconscious from behind.

The second was knifed below the ribcage. The last was quickly disarmed of his AK-47, running away. Kameel watched his security detail neutralized in five seconds. He didn't move. Two men in the truck jumped out and captured Kameel without a fight. The driver kept the car running and was continually on the lookout. Curt knew exactly what was happening. It was a textbook grab and go.

Curt's adrenaline started to pump. His blood pressure and pulse both rose. He couldn't help himself. Eyes widened; pupils shrunk to pinheads. 'Where was Smitty?' No matter…. He was 'in.' Curt dropped his bags and moved towards the truck; quickly but controlled. As he got closer, the henchmen were lifting Kameel into the truck bed. The assailants said nothing, remaining eerily silent. As their victim fell into the Toyota, the other attackers in local garb closed in on the truck, planning to jump in for a coordinated get away. Curt arrived at the side of the truck, unbeknownst to the attackers. He reached up and grabbed one of the men standing in the truck bed. Curt realized the man's legs were unprotected. He quickly coiled his body to the left. Quickly, he uncoiled, using every muscle in his body. His right arm flew through the air gaining speed and momentum. In a sideways karate chop motion, his fist made contact with the man's shin with significant force against the edge of the truck bed rail. Curt distinctly felt leg bones crack as the man fell to the bed clutching his leg. Another attacker noticed Curt and jumped from the truck bed onto the ground. The two began wrestling and through the man's garb, Curt realized his opponent was in excellent shape. Curt wondered if he had somehow picked a fight with literally the fittest man in Akjoujt. The driver looked back with concern in his eyes. This was clearly not part of the plan. Curt's wrestling partner freed an arm and reached into his chest area. Curt looked down and saw the attacker pulling a semiautomatic handgun poorly concealed in his robes. Curt was in trouble.

Well-concealed under the attacker's facial wrappings was an ear bud attached to a communication device. It had been relatively silent until now. As the man reached for his

weapon, the communication device transmitted in English, "Do not shoot! He's American! I repeat you are not cleared to fire on that individual!" Somewhere, someone was witnessing these events unfold. Curt was unaware of the communication device and the command. All he realized was the attacker was armed, and he was not. Quickly, he scanned the truck bed. Mounted to the inside rail of the bed was an M-4 semi-automatic assault rifle, a weapon familiar to Curt. It was his only chance. He reached in to grab it. As he reached for the rifle, he and the attacker locked eyes. The man's face was wrapped in cloth, but his eyes were steel blue and cold – extremely rare for a north African. The little facial skin which was exposed was milky white. Curt's hand was close to the M-4, but without taking his eyes off his opponent, he couldn't find it. Breaking eye contact, he looked down to establish contact with the weapon. As soon as he did, a crushing blow slammed down onto the back of Curt's head. Another assailant, standing next to the truck bed, smashed the butt of his rifle onto Curt. Curt's head bounded downward, violently striking the side of the truck rail then bouncing back up. Instinctively, he rapidly looked up to see where the blow had originated.
Unfortunately, gazing up at his attacker exposed Curt's face and a second blow connected with Curt's left cheek, directly under his eye. Curt went limp and he fell to the ground, releasing the side of the truck bed. The assailants, now all in the truck, sped off. The henchmen had acquired their target without firing a shot. 30 seconds later, the truck had vanished in the dust it kicked up blanketing the market. Curt lay motionless in the dusty streets of Akjoujt.

From a distance, Smitty witnessed the whole thing. As he saw Curt lie there, he was torn. Instinct tugged at him to help a fallen brother in arms. Reality said he needed to turn and leave. Reality won. He entered the passenger seat of a waiting vehicle and sped off.

Eventually, the Akjoujt market began to crawl with villagers again. It was as if they were trained to clear out during fighting and then return on cue once it ended. Many attempted to help the beaten Satri protection detail. Those knocked unconscious were lucky. The stabbing victim unfortunately was sliced in a way that caused significant bleeding. A local man ran to help up Curt. "Doctor! Are you ok?" Curt recognized him. He was one of the shop keeps from the Bazaar.

"Yes. Shookran. (Thank you) You speak English?"

"Yes. A little. It helps to sell my goods to the mine workers."

"I see." Curt was standing now and moving to render first aid to the stabbing victim. It was pointless. He was dead. Curt thought to himself... *'Where was Smitty? Surely, he heard and saw this? Is he OK?'* Curt looked around. Smitty was nowhere to be seen. "Excuse me. Do you know who the man that the men in the truck took?"

"Yes. We all know him. He is Kameel. A Satri Officer. The Injus wanted him in retaliation for breaking the truce. If he is lucky, he will be bartered and traded for Inju prisoners. If he is not lucky, he will be killed."

"Sir, what you did was very brave. But also, very stupid. Both sides that fight have very good weapons. You had nothing. Better to be a living coward than a dead hero."

"Yes, I suppose you are right." Curt went back to where his bags were dropped with the man. He picked up his bags. "Thanks again for helping me. You are very kind. Shookran."

"'Afwan" (You are welcome). Doctor, if I can say. We need you here alive. You save our children and our families." The man moved closer to Curt and began to whisper. "If you need, I know a friend who can get you weapons for a good price."

Curt acted the obligatory surprised and then said, "Oh! Really?! No, thanks, but I think I am OK." Curt was well aware of the third world black markets. They were always the unspoken soft underbelly that societies all knew existed, but few spoke of. He thought to himself, 'I don't need anyone else's weapons. I'm all good.'

"OK, doctor. If you change your mind, I am Hamal."

"Hamal?"

"Yes," Hamal replied.

"Doesn't Hamal in Arabic mean 'Lamb?" Curt asked.

"Yes! Yes it does!" Hamal was excited.

"Funny," Curt replied. "You wouldn't know where I could find some lamb to cook for dinner do you?" While Curt's head was still in pain, his mind slowly began to refocus on the evening dinner.

"Of course! Come with me." In an instant, Hamal was guiding Curt through the market to a friend who sold Lamb.

Chapter Twelve

Dinner with Allison

Curt arrived home around 1700Hrs. Plenty of time remained to prepare the meal and get cleaned up. He went to the bathroom and looked in the mirror. His face was a mess. *'So much for impressing a woman tonight,'* he thought. Curt reached into the medicine cabinet, grabbed some 'Ranger Candy' or 'Vitamin M' as it was known to military types. Civilians would know it as 800mg of Motrin. Back to the kitchen, he placed some ice on his cheek and began to unpack the groceries.

The lamb and vegetables were placed in a pot with some herbs which Curt acquired from the market. He preheated the oven and then inserted the lamb. The bottle of wine chilled in the fridge and the kitchen was clean. It was now 1745Hrs. He needed to be in front of the Hospital by 1830Hrs. Time was getting tight.

He jumped in the shower and began to clean up. As he toweled off, a loud knock at the door startled him. It was not a casual knock, but rather an aggressive BANG! BANG! BANG! After his market event, Curt took no chances. Curt quietly moved out of the bathroom and towards the kitchen. His adrenaline again began to race, his pulse and blood pressure swelled. With only a towel around his waist he quickly grabbed a large kitchen knife. BANG! BANG! BANG! The pounding continued. There was no peep hole. Curt got into a position he had practiced many times in the military. He was ready.

"Who is it!?" Curt said from behind the locked door. The knife raised. His back against an adjoining wall and ready to leap should the door fly open.

"It's Allison! For Christ's Sake! Are you OK!? News is spreading through town that you were in a fight and were knocked out?"

Curt relaxed. The door opened. She was alone, but clearly worried. "Yes, I'm fine."

"Did you really jump into a fight with armed men!!?? What were you thinking? People are saying you acted like some idiot superhero trying to stop the kidnapping without even a weapon. Oh My God! Look at your eye!?" She was genuinely concerned.

"How did you find out where I live?" Curt was calming himself down from what he thought was an unwelcome visit from the Injus.

"Look, I'm a journalist. It's my job. Seriously. You need to go to the hospital!"

"And see who? Myself, the doctor? I think I can do that here just fine. By the way…..," "You're early." Curt's humor was back. She soon began to realize he was fine…. Still just as cocky, but fine.

"Hmmm… Humor… at a time like this? You must not be in too much pain. And you're right. I'm early. I'll come back when you can at least answer the door like a gentleman and not some Neanderthal in a towel." Allison may have said that, but she was far from unimpressed with seeing Curt in merely a towel. He was fit. Curt's shoulders, chest and abdomen muscles were well defined given his continued workout routine.

Curt smiled. "Well, since you're here, you are welcome to come in and I will put on some more appropriate attire." Curt moved back out of the doorway, clutching his towel in one hand and waving his other hand as if to invite her in. Unfortunately, though, he forgot he was clutching a knife with that hand.

Allison was surprised…. "Do you often shower with a large knife?"

"Funny," Curt responded and then fired a question back of his own. "Do you often pound on doors of individuals who within the past few hours have had a run in with a heavily armed clan?"

"Touché," she said. She entered and he closed the door. He also locked it. No need to tempt fate.

"Sit here. I will change and be out in a few minutes. Make yourself comfortable. There is a bottle of wine in the fridge." Curt headed for the bedroom and changed into some more appropriate clothing. Before he walked out the door, he looked in the mirror. His eye was nearly swollen shut, his cheek was redder than a fire truck, his head was pounding, and the bulge had fully established itself on the crown of his skull. If something else could go wrong, Curt didn't know what it was. He opened the door and walked out.

Allison had poured two glasses of wine and set them on the coffee table. Curt plugged his iPad into some cheap speakers and began playing some music. He walked over and sat down. Allison raised her glass to toast him, he responded. She said, "Here's to that big old shiner on your face." Curt smiled, their glasses clinked, and they drank. The wine was acceptable quality at best. Obviously, Anbar was not an African sommelier.

"So, what's for dinner? The food smells great."

"Lamb stew. Or at least the closest I could come with broken Arabic and English at the local market and with the limited ingredients." Curt was proud and confident of the meal he was cooking but laying out every excuse just in case the meal was going to mirror his day and be a disaster too.

The two sat and made small talk for a while. They discussed hometowns, favorite cities, where they had been in the US. The conversation flowed and Curt was smitten to be sitting with her. There was something about Allison. He just couldn't get enough of her. Curt checked the dinner, and it was ready. He cleared off the coffee table and they ate on the sofa, continuing the conversation from where they left off.

Dinner ended and Allison soon remembered why she had agreed to come over in the first place; to interview Dr.

Nover. "So, dinner was great, but I think you forgot why I came here."

"Actually, for a while, I thought you forgot why you came here. I never forgot; I was just hoping you did." Curt paused and smiled at her. Then he continued, "OK. A deal is a deal. Fire away with your questions there, Ms. Journalist."

"OK, first. What brought you to Akjoujt?"

"Well, technically, a bunch of airplanes, but I don't think that is the answer you were looking for. In all honesty, my humanitarian agency picked it for me. Really, it is a matter of fate. Originally, I was slated to go to a village in Southeast Asia. Everything was going well and about a month before I intended to depart, I was redirected here. As I understand, my predecessor departed unexpectedly so there was clearly a need."

Allison got out her notebook and pen. She began to settle into work mode. "OK, but why a humanitarian mission?"

"Well, I served multiple years in the U.S. Navy. I did some things I am very proud of and performed my nations bidding and made the United States a safer place. After I exited the military, I used my GI Bill for Med School. I was accepted and at some point, felt it was more important to do a humanitarian mission and save people rather than make my first million in three years. So, I am here."

Her hands wrote feverishly and there was a pause. Finally, she spoke again. "What did you do in the Navy?" She questioned.

Curt grinned. "I was with some units. Nothing special."

Allison smiled. "You do know, every time someone in the Navy doesn't divulge about their career and then says it was 'nothing special' it kinda means it was 'Special.' kinda like Special Operations. Care to elaborate?"

"No elaboration desired or required." Curt smiled.

"And what connection do you have with the mine and Nissassa Inc?"

Given the day's events, this question stung a bit. "Actually, I have no ties to the mine. I work for my NGO and take care of the local people but have been told if the mine has an accident and needs medical help, I'd provide it. That said, I have yet to treat any foreign national who works out at the mine. By the way, have you been to the mine?"

"Me? No? Why do you ask?........... Hey! Wait. I'm asking the questions here! Nice try, Dr. Nover."

"Ah, it was worth an effort."

Allison continued with her questions. It became apparent her story was to focus on the issues of Akjoujt and she really was looking for a 'good news' story. She stayed clear of the Inju and Satri clan fighting in her questions. Additionally, she wondered what philanthropic efforts the mine had performed in support of the city. At the end of the interview, Curt was willing to bet a large amount that she was there on Nissassa Inc's dime, and they had 'shaped' her story before she ever got to Akjoujt. As beautiful as Curt thought she was, this by far was the ugliest part of her to Curt. That said, her other attributes far outweighed this ugliness.

They drank the last bit of wine and began to reengage in small talk. Allison smiled and laughed at Curt. He responded in kind. It was getting late.

"Curt, I really have to get going. I had a great night, though. Maybe we could do it again?" Exactly what Curt wanted to hear.

She stood up and so did he. As he stood, his legs began to give out and his head spun. He could barely stand. Curt tried to catch himself on the sofa, but it was of little use. Allison saw him fall and thrust her small frame at him hopelessly trying to catch him. They both crashed to the floor. "Curt! Curt! Are you OK?" He lay flat on his back and she on top of him.

Curt opened his eyes, let out a small smirk. "I am now." His arms wrapped around Allison's back and held her to him. She didn't push away.

"You Jerk! I thought something was wrong! Using your injury to seduce me? How utterly inappropriate." Her hands gave a halfhearted attempt at punching him in the chest.

"Yes. Yes, I am. May I ask... Is it working?" He stared into her blue eyes. She couldn't look away. Their faces slowly moved towards each other.

Softly, she answered in a whisper, "Yes." Their lips touched and their eyes closed. The intensity began to increase, and their hands began exploring. Curt had no recollection he had a headache. He was completely focused and entranced by Allison. The feeling was mutual. Clothing began to be removed. Shirts and then a bra. Soon, they were completely naked. The passion was intense. For the next three hours, they made love. Exhausted, they fell into his bed. They didn't awake until the morning.

Chapter Thirteen

Catch and Release

The Isuzu truck sped out of Akjoujt. In the truck bed, Kameel lay bound with a sack over his head. One henchman winced in pain with every bump, and another helped try to stabilize his leg. Overhead, an unmanned aerial vehicle captured the entire events on video, feeding them to a control center. In the middle of the African desert, the Isuzu truck approached a large black SUV and stopped. Everyone but Kameel exited the vehicles. Kameel remained motionless, lying in the truck bed.

"How did it go?" A gentleman from the SUV dressed in military camo asked one of the assailants.

"How did it go?!! Rudy has a freaking broken leg! You mind telling me what the fuck Nover is doing in Akjoujt!?" It was clear the assailants knew Curt.

"Excuse me?" There was a long pause and a menacing stare. "You're out of line, son. That's not why we are here. Get the target out of the truck. We will address this later back at headquarters." The gentleman from the SUV made it clear who was in charge and what the discussion topics would be.

Under orders, Kameel was removed from the truck bed. His hands were freed and the bag over his head removed.

In a warm greeting, the same man from the SUV spoke. "Kameel!" he said, "Well done. How are you? Did they rough you up too much?"

"I'm great. All in a day's work. I thank you for the opportunity."

"You are very welcome. Here is your payment. Please pass along our appreciation to your leader Qudamah." Another person from the SUV approached Kameel and handed over a small bag of money. It was more than an Akjoujt citizen could make in a year. "When you return, your story is the Inju clan captured you and beat you. A ransom was offered by the Satri and the Inju accepted. Do you have any questions?"

"I have no questions. I am happy to help the USA. I am getting older though, and these are becoming more painful. I am hopeful the payments may increase, Inshallah. God bless you and God be good. I shall pass along your kind words to Qudamah." Kameel began walking away, back towards Satri territory. It would take him hours to get home. It didn't matter, he had nothing but time.

With Kameel out of range, Rudy began to speak, clearly in pain from his injury. "Hey, I'm fine. I can still go on the upcoming mission."

"Rudy, we can talk about it later."

"Look, I need this money. I need to go on this mission," Rudy was unwilling to wait until later. "Cast it up and I can go. I'm certain." His pleas were compelling but ignored.

"Get everyone in the vehicles. We're going back to HQ to un-fuck your mission failure." The team did as they were directed.

Chapter Fourteen

Mission Failure

"We have a problem," a familiar voice said with concern. It was Smitty. He was sitting with a group of men at a table in a large room. Some were the assailants; one was the gentleman from the SUV. The room was dark, but the table was well lit. There were flat panel screens stretched around the room, each with different bits of information or video flashing across displays. It was obviously a Command Post or an Operations Center of some sort.

"I agree, we observed the mission today from the aerial video feed." Another familiar voice. It was Jerry, the man who had phoned in Curt's arrival to headquarters back in the United States. "What is the status of the grab and go team?"

Smitty replied, "Not great. Rudy has a broken Fibula. He is in medical now. The doctor on staff recommends not sending him with the rest of the team. Rudy, however, still wishes to participate." In fairness, Rudy's position was understandable. Each team member for this mission would receive $200k tax free.

"Smitty, I need to know your assessment? Can he perform? The last thing we need is to continue this training problem into the actual mission."

"Jerry, I believe he's out. We will have to get a replacement. Would you like to set up another 'snatch' training event?"

"I would, but unfortunately, there is no time. Find a replacement and have the team perform rehearsal drills here on the base. They depart in 48 hours for downrange. Our customer needs this event to happen soon. Arranging another live training event is just not possible." Jerry was right. Given who the customer was and how much they were paying, providing his services on time was of utmost importance. "And what is the status of the Satri commander, Kameel I believe is his name?"

The man from the Black SUV spoke up, "He has been returned to the Satris for the standard ransom payment. He keeps asking for more money. It's getting tiresome. Sir, I realize the concern on meeting our customer's expectations, but we just had some bad luck on this."

Jerry paused and stared at Smitty. He said nothing for nearly a minute. The silence broke. "Yes, bad luck. I presume you mean Dr. Nover. Let me ask you something. Wasn't it just months ago, you and your colleagues told me he was going to be, a 'solution?' What I see is an expensive solution that has now cost me an even more expensive problem. So... I ask you," Jerry's voice and pace began to rise as each word was spoken, "Why is that son of a bitch a problem?"

The group was silent. Jerry rarely raised his voice. It was apparent he was pissed. "This training operation we have created is unique. No, let me rephrase that, it is One of a Kind. And expensive. You told me Nover had operational experience in hostile areas and would be a 'good fit' to be the local doctor. I confess I welcomed the notion of him helping regenerate our target set, but his meddling in our training events is unacceptable. I can't even begin to tell you how much corporate paid Doctors Without Borders in the form of a 'charitable contribution' to move Nover to here. And now, less than one month after his arrival and resuming training events, he has effectively neutralized one of our key personnel for months and jeopardized a critical mission."

"Yes sir," Smitty responded softly. It was all he said. His years of military culture began to kick in. It was the only thing to say.

"Smitty, I pay you to instruct, monitor and critique our training events. You are paid handsomely. Since this operation began, you have done exceptionally well, and I value your perspective." Jerry began to calm down. "I ask you, how do you suggest we fix this? I know Nover is a brother in your community, but we have a mission here which cannot be threatened. The last doctor in Akjoujt had an unfortunate ending. I would hate to see the same happen to Dr. Nover."

A lump rose in Smitty's throat. Curt was a friend and a brother in arms. Smitty was aware how the previous doctor had been disposed of. To imagine the same fate for Curt was disheartening. "Sir, I will work on a solution. Until then, we can continue with sniper training and other events."

"OK. But Nover makes no further impact to our training. Is that clear?" Jerry turned his thoughts to other issues. "Smitty, by the way, speaking of sniper training, how is our target from last week? Correct me if I am wrong, but wasn't that one of the first events where Nover was in place?"

"Yes sir." Now was not the time for first name informalities. "The boy was struck in the leg on a perfect shot. Nover saved the boy's life but had to amputate the leg. Given the target was struck with a round from a .50 cal, this was the best we could have hoped for. To date, Nover has worked on over a dozen targets. All but one has been regenerated. I think we lost another today due to a deep knife wound."

"So, Nover has done some good. Encouraging. I know headquarters had concerns we would be unable to sustain a viable target base. Hopefully, Nover can continue this trend." This news increased Curt's value even further to Jerry.

"Well sir, he did his residency in Cook County Hospital. If anyone has the experience to patch up conflict related wounds, it's Curt." Smitty was trying to inflate Curt's stock.

"Noted." Jerry's response was short. "OK, onto another issue. I ate lunch with that reporter today, Donley, I believe is her name. I paid for her to come here and craft a good news story about our mining efforts in Akjoujt. She is to ensure the positive effects of Nissassa's mining influence in the area overshadows tribal infighting. Her time is important and if she asked to interview you, stick to the mining operation talking points but she doesn't come onto the compound. We have too many training events ongoing, and she is a liability."

Smitty couldn't agree more. If there was one thing military personnel dreaded, it was having reporters snooping around ongoing operations. While military brass back in the Pentagon embraced the idea of 'embedded reporters' ever since Operation IRAQI FREEDOM, the troops executing the mission at the tactical level were still wary. Some of those same military operators were now the ones working for Nissassa. "Yes, sir. When is she to go back?"

"A week or so, but I am certain we can manage the risk." Jerry turned to another member at the table. He was a moderately overweight man, who obviously had not been in the service for quite some time. "Tiny, I want your folks to monitor her telephone and other communications. Notify me if her story begins to center on the tribal infighting as opposed to the positive effects our 'mining' operation has on the town. Also, Smitty, let's keep her geographically separated from training events while she is here."

The rotund man, Tiny, and Smitty both responded, "Yes sir." Apparently, Tiny was the senior intelligence piece of the operation.

"Also, Tiny, I need you to monitor and predict Nover's whereabouts. Make sure you work with Smitty and deconflict future training events from Nover's anticipated location." Both Tiny and Smitty acknowledged and wrote in their notebooks. Jerry's tasks were flying fast now. It was apparent he mentally was managing his way forward from this point.

Again, Jerry spoke, "Pete, I would like to have dinner with Issam. I want to discuss this Nover issue with him. Have him come here to the mine within the next couple of days. Also, have we received any funds from headquarters to pass along to Issam?" Pete was the Chief of Staff for the mining operation. He was tall and lanky. Pete did have a military background as a naval surface warfare officer. He arose to the rank of Commander, holding the position of "XO" (Executive Officer / Second in Command) as his last leadership role and was well known for his ability to manage operations and personnel. A perfect fit for Jerry's right-hand man.

Pete answered, "Sir, I will call Issam this evening and make arrangements for dinner. As for funds, yes, we received authorization to pass along $30k in humanitarian aid for this month."

"OK. That's not enough. We are going to need more. I will call back to Headquarters and report today's events. Let's meet back together this evening at 1900 Hours. I would like a pre-brief of tomorrow's training event."

The men left the room. Jerry slowly proceeded to his office. He would soon make a phone call he would rather not make. His unpleasant task was to inform headquarters of the following: today's mission was a failure, a critical team member, Rudy, was injured and unable to proceed with his team, a future mission for a very special high paying customer was now at risk and it was all because of Dr. Curt Nover, an individual he had personally recommended corporate get into Akjoujt. The phone call would not go well.

Chapter Fifteen

Shadow Money

A phone rang in a high-rise Rosslyn, Virginia office. Rosslyn was perhaps the greatest example of real estate's most famous three words…. Location, location, location. A stone's throw from the Pentagon and only two metro stops away, the city quickly grew to be the mecca for the defense industry. From contractors to industry headquarters to lobbyist, the town was packed. Their presence was important in many ways, from an availability to quickly answer the Department of Defense's (DoD) questions on future weapon system development to also rubbing elbows and grease palms of key decision makers. The Ying and Yang of D.C.

From appearances, the office was pricey – much like nearly every other Executive Rosslyn office. The walls were filled with military awards, citations, farewell gifts. The heavy walnut desk gently covered in family photos. And a thick black leather chair. A hand reached for the phone and answered, "Hello, Don here." It was the same man Jerry spoke to when Curt arrived at the operation.

"Don, it's Jerry. Good morning."

"Good afternoon, Jerry." There was a six-hour time difference. "How are things going?"

"OK, but not as well as we hoped. We had a small issue with our live range snatch and grab today. One member was injured and will be unable to participate in the actual operation in a few days."

"Excuse me? Jerry, I have stressed to you this mission will be our largest revenue generator yet. We are still under proof of concept. If we can pull this off, the sky is the limit."

Jerry tried to calm the discussion, "I realize that. I have some options to fill the gap."

"No, you have one option. Smitty is going." Don's response was clear.

"Don, he's our lead instructor. You're jeopardizing the continued operation for this mission. That's not what we agreed to."

"You're correct. We also agreed to no fuck ups. And yet, here we are. Smitty is taking the place." Don was not budging. "Onto another topic. I received initial payment for the mission from Ft Bragg. We have $2M in hand to facilitate the mission and upon completion, we will have the remaining $2M. I am wiring you $500k to facilitate the team's movement into place."

"Thanks for the funding update. I've secured air travel for the team as well as all required support / equipment. Is there any chance you'll consider another replacement team member? I can't lose Smitty."

"Jerry, I appreciate your position, but your heart is driving your position and not your brain. Goodbye."

Don hung up and paged his secretary. "Helen, please get the White House Chief of Staff on the line. Tell him the subject is Operation HEPVACS. In five minutes, Helen buzzed in, "Sir, your party is on the line."

"Steve, Don here. Operation HEPVACS is on track. No issues." Obviously not true but worrying the White House could potentially scrub the mission.

"Don, stop calling me here. Our deal is no discussion via text, email or phone. At no point no more than 5 are to know outside the teams. Do we need to meet?

"No sir, I apologize." The line went dead.

Chapter Sixteen

<u>Daybreak</u>

The sun crept into the doctor's bedroom and began to splash light onto Curt and Allison's bodies. They both awoke. She looked into his eyes and felt vulnerable. This was not the kind of girl she was – or wanted to be, but she had feelings for Curt. "Good morning, handsome," she said. Trying to hide her weakness.

"Who are you and what's your name again?" Curt responded. He smiled into her eyes. She knew he was kidding, and with that, the two began playfully wrestling. She didn't stand a chance. Curt had pinned her in under 10 seconds. It only took another 5 seconds to identify her ticklish locations. She laughed and screamed. There was something about the chemistry between these two. They were comfortable around each other. Truth be told, neither wanted to leave his bed. Departing for work today would be a chore.

"I give! I give! Stop!" Allison screamed. Curt stopped tickling her. They embraced in another hug.

"Allison, I had a great time with you last night. I want you to know that."

"I did as well. I can't believe I spent the night. This is not who I am." Again, Allison felt uncomfortable.

"Eh.... don't feel that way," Curt responded. "Honestly, it's not your fault. When I turn on my charms, women are helpless. You were powerless."

"Really? How often do these powers come out?" In Curt's effort to be funny and calm the situation, the message was crossed. Allison began to feel like a statistic and her uneasiness began to grow.

Curt back tracked quickly. "OK. Not what I meant. Allison, I'm sorry. I was trying to put you at ease. Look. I really like you. I have not felt this way for a very long time, and it feels great. I dread walking out the door today as I know we are both going to go different ways. If I were king for a day, I would spend the next 24 hours with you. Sadly, that is not possible." As he stared into her eyes and spoke, it was obvious he meant every word.

Allison finally could relax. She felt the exact same way about Curt but was a bit coyer. "Really, I don't think I could spend the whole day with you. Frankly, you bore me." Her wit and sarcasm stung… and Curt loved it. She shared his sarcastic humor. As her last word fell from her lips, she smiled and began to defend herself.

Curt was happy. A feeling void to him for quite some time. He knew if Allison could resort to sarcasm, her fears and concerns were fading. Surprisingly to Allison, he didn't strike back – no saucy comeback, no tickling. He just smiled and said, "God, I really like you." That was it. She was hooked, and Curt knew it.

The two begrudgingly crawled out of bed and prepared for the day. As Allison showered, Curt attempted to slap together some sort of breakfast. While he had hoped the evening would go well, he had not envisioned it would lead to breakfast for two. Allison emerged from the shower and had a troubled look on her face as she entered the kitchen.

"What wrong?" Curt asked?

"Nothing really. It's just. I am going to have to wear the same clothes today and I'm muddling through the associated stigma in my mind. It's no big deal. You made breakfast? Impressive."

"Well, you can try to call it breakfast. Not sure the local bread is really 'toasting' worthy, but I tried. Here, have a seat. I made coffee; would you like some?"

"Yes, please. You are awesome." Allison too, was happy. She felt Curt was different than the others. And even as cliché all this may have appeared, every action through the morning made her feel more and more comfortable around him. She sat down into the chair and began to eat. She was still wearing only a towel from her shower. As comfortable as she was becoming, she could have worn nothing and been OK.

Curt left the kitchen and headed for his bedroom. "Hold on a second." She could hear him rummaging through his drawers. Minutes later, he emerged with a T-shirt in his hand. "Here. See if this fits." He tossed the shirt at her. She dropped her towel and put on the shirt.

"Awww... thanks. It's a bit big but it is better than wearing what I had on yesterday." She was very appreciative. She looked at the shirt. It was green with the word 'Mc Ps' on the front. "What is Mc Ps?"

"A blast from my past," Curt said. "It's from a bar in.... California. One of my old stomping grounds. I've had that shirt for years. It's about the smallest thing I have."

"It's perfect. Thanks." The two kept eating and soon breakfast was over. They would both have to depart for work soon – the dreaded goodbye.

Allison reached out for a piece of paper. "Curt, here is my local phone number. I know I joke around a bit, but I am being serious now. Call me. Please. I like you, and I don't want to get hurt. Well, I don't want to get hurt any more than you could already hurt me. And that amount right now is significant, even though we have only spent a short time together. I really want to see you again. Soon. Do you understand?"

The words could not have been more welcome to Curt. He took the paper and pulled her close. She felt safe, and so did he. They kissed softly again for an extended period. Just enjoying each other's presence.

Curt broke the silence and spoke. "I promise. I will call. But I can't call you for 3 days. It's the rule." He smiled as he made reference to the common 'man rule' which states a man should never contact a girl within the first 72 hours of a first date. In his heart, he knew there was no way he could perform such an act but wanted to at least demonstrate some manhood resolve.

"Uggg! You drive me crazy. Well, I guess this is short lived then, because I am likely leaving in five days. Waiting 72 hours could be a problem." While the sarcasm smacked a bit, there was no denying she loved his sense of humor.

Curt looked her in the eye and without pause said, "Dinner, tomorrow night."

Her comfort soon returned. "Yes. And I promise not to tell the man club you violated the 3-day rule."

"Deal." Curt was also relieved. He knew when they would meet again. They kissed again and walked out into Akjoujt. They would miss each other a bit. This was a good thing.

Chapter Seventeen

Lunch with Buck

Given Curt's late night, his arrival at work was... 'delayed.' There was little harm, however, given the short patient line. As he walked in, Jawad and Kamil were waiting. "Good morning gentlemen." Curt was trying to conceal his tardiness; he hated to be late. What Curt didn't realize was tardiness was a well-established and common occurrence in such cultures.

"Good morning, Dr. Nover," both Jawad and Kamil replied. Jawad continued, "Sir, are you OK?"

"Yes, Jawad. I just overslept. It won't happen again."

Jawad looked puzzled... "Sir, time is not a big issue in Akjoujt. I was talking about yesterday's attack. The entire village says you jumped into a fight to save Kameel. Are you crazy? No one who isn't in the Satri or Inju clans does anything to help them. Why did you do this? You could have been killed."

"I'm fine. It was nothing." Given Jawad's question, Curt was reminded of his head and his shiner. "I don't wish to discuss it. Let's try to get to work."

"Dr. Nover, I appreciate your desire to help people, but I will say one last thing. You are more important to the people of this village than you are to the Satri's or Injus. They could all die and this would be a better place. Do not forget that." Jawad did not wait for a reply. He turned and walked away. Curt and Kamil stood there quietly. Finally, Kamil spoke.

"Doctor, don't take Jawad's anger too seriously. Jawad lost some of his family members to the clans and for him, this is personal."

"Thanks, Kamil. I did not know."

Curt and Kamil began their rounds. The morning patients began to process through. A few infections. A few colds. Nothing extraordinary. The morning soon began to draw to mid-day.

Curt's phone rang. He looked at the number. It was Buck. He answered, "Dr. Nover."

"Doctor? That's how you greet me? OK. Hello Dr. Nover, this is Pilot Buck!"

"Buck. Great to hear from you. What's going on?"

"I know it's short notice again, but I'm on a layover here and was wondering if you want to do lunch."

Curt didn't have to think long. "Buck, I'd love to. Meet you at Anbar's in about 30 minutes?"

"Sounds great. See you then, 'Dr. Nover.' Pilot Buck, out."

Curt looked at Kamil. "Kamil, change of plans, I'm going to head to lunch in about 15 minutes. I'll be back after lunch."

"Yes sir! No issues at all! Have a good lunch."

As Curt walked into Anbar's, he could see Buck sitting alone. Dressed as a common African bush pilot, he didn't fit in well, but better than some other westerners he'd seen. As Curt approached, he was cut off... "Dr. Nover! Welcome to Anbar's!" It was Anbar and an expected standard greeting.

"Thanks, Anbar. Good afternoon. I am going to sit with Buck over there if that's OK."

"The pilot? You know him?"

"Not well, Anbar, but I agreed to lunch with him. Is he OK?"

"Well, Dr. Nover, I don't know if he is OK or not. No one does. He flies in and out but no one from Akjoujt travels with him."

"Interesting." And with that Buck noticed Curt and stood up.

"Doctor Nover! Good to see ya!"

"Hey, Buck. You too." They shook hands and took their seats. Anbar handed them both menus.

"Anbar, what is the special today?" Asked Curt.

"Dr. Nover. Why do you ask? Every time I tell you the daily special, you order something else. Other than the first day, you have never eaten the special"

"Anbar, you're right. For me, no menu. Bring me the special."

"PERFECT, SIR!" It was clear, Anbar was beaming that Curt would try some good cultural food.

"For me, I'll just have a burger and fries," said Buck.

Anbar's excitement dissipated just as fast as it arrived. Every American almost always ordered the burger and fries. "Yes, sir."

"So Buck, what brings you to Akjoujt today?"

"Actually, I'm not sure. I wasn't scheduled to come in for a few days and then last night I was told to come in today to fly out two passengers. They also asked for me to arrange an ambulance in Rabat. Frankly, I'd rather die than have medical treatment in Rabat, but hey, their dime, their time. The good news is this allows me more opportunity to transition my main operating base to Rabat."

Obviously, Curt was initially puzzled. He is the local doctor. What other entity would be sending out a medical passenger? "Do you know the age of the injured? Is it a 15-year-old boy?" Curt had treated numerous Satri and Inju injuries to date, but the one that stuck out was the little boy. Frankly, it could have been any of them, but Curt could not get past Akim's future prosthetic needs.

"I don't know the name, age or sex. Frankly, I rarely ask. And for that, I get paid well. That said, it's boring as all get out on this end of the missions into Akjoujt. Hence why I bother you."

"Thanks, Buck. It's great to be needed." Curt's sarcasm was perfect. "Just seems weird. I'm the local doctor and have no clue who'd be ordering a medivac."

"I don't know. I just get a phone call. Anyway, how are things with you. Are you sampling any of the local talent?"

"Ah, Buck. I missed you. No, none of the local talent, but I did meet an American reporter." Curt was still smitten with his former evening and was none too shy to share.

"American? That's about all I fly in and out. Was she a hot blonde chick from about a week ago? Yeah. I remember her. Tried to strike up conversation with her for the whole flight and she'd have nothing to do with me. Seemed a bit bitchy if you ask me."

"Maybe she doesn't like flying. I'm sure it wasn't you," Curt said… thinking to himself he was CERTAIN it was exactly Buck. The food arrived. Buck's burger was set down first. It was poorly plated, and aesthetically unpleasing. Curt thought to himself, 'Ha! Buck made a huge mistake with that order.'

"And for you sir, khubz dimagh almaeiz!" Anbar said with pride. The plate was large. In the middle was a goat's skull crafted into a serving dish and surrounded by rice. Neither Curt's nor Buck's Arabic was good enough to translate the dish. Other than the skull staring Curt in the face, the presentation was amazing.

"Looks…. Interesting!" the closest Curt could come to a compliment. "I apologize, my Arabic is not that good, can you translate the dish?"

Anbar didn't hesitate. "Baked Goats Brain!" Again, he beamed with pride.

Curt was stuck. Anbar stood next to the table with pride. Awaiting Curt's first bite. Curt pulled out his fork and began to eat. Buck could barely contain his laughter. Frankly, both of them in the past likely ate worse in many villages they don't discuss, but to eat it on your own invite and pay for it? Buck found this just hilarious. Curt gave Anbar a convincing nod up and down as he said "Mmmmmm." Anbar could not have been happier. In fairness, the food didn't taste bad, it was just quite different.

"When is the next time you come into town, Buck?"

"Right now, I'm still scheduled to pick up a group of folks in a few days. That said, if you continue to eat that meal, I may be back tonight."

Curt didn't laugh. "Funny.... Hey, question for you, do you possibly do private charter flights?"

"If the money is right and my schedule is clear, I'll fly anybody. What did you have in mind?"

"Well, I haven't been on vacation yet and I was hoping to get to Casablanca for a weekend or so to unwind. Can your aircraft make it to Casablanca?"

"Easily. Casablanca is my divert field when planning for Rabat and potential weather."

"Great, if you're available, maybe we could work something out."

"Sounds good. Let me know when. If the money is right, I'll take you anywhere."

"Good. Thanks." Curt kept slowly eating his meal. He also noticed he was the only person eating with a goat head on his plate. After watching the restaurant for a while, it dawned on him the plate he was eating wasn't the restaurant's daily special, but rather Anbar's daily special for him. It was an exceptionally kind gesture, and he ate every bite. Curt realized he was becoming accepted in Akjoujt and that made him happy.

The plates were empty, Anbar took them away, and Buck offered to pay. "My invite. You got the next one." Curt didn't challenge him and took solace in the fact he didn't have to pay for what he just consumed.

"Well, if you're in town in a few days, next one's on me."

"Deal," Buck replied. They both got up from the table and headed their separate ways after standard farewells.

Chapter Eighteen

<u>Medivac</u>

Buck arrived at the airport and walked to his plane. Next to it a large black SUV sat parked… idling. This was the standard for Buck's passengers. As he began opening the aircraft, the SUV door opened, and two gentlemen got out. The first approached.

"Hey, Buck, good to see you." Said Jerry.

"You too, Mr. Faulk. How are things here?"

"Great, Buck. We just had a small accident at the mine. Nothing major but just wanted to get our guy some better medical care."

"Understandable." Buck considered mentioning Curt, the 'Akjoujt Doc,' but thought better of it. Not his business.

"How soon before you're ready to go?"

"Five to ten minutes. I refueled the aircraft before lunch. Do you have the money?"

"It's right here." As usual, a briefcase was handed over full of cash. Buck opened it, quickly scanned it and was satisfied.

"Dead Presidents on paper. Gorgeous. Always a pleasure doing business with you. Cash….. my favorite payment."

"Likewise," Jerry responded. As Buck opened up the aircraft and began the preflight sequence, he noticed a gentleman exit the SUV with a cast on his lower leg. It was Rudy, someone Buck didn't know. Rudy was being helped out of the vehicle by two other guys, one large and one small. Rudy settled into the aircraft's cargo area along with the short guy who was clearly tending to Rudy's medical issue. They both strapped in and made no contact with Buck. That was standard for Jerry's cargo. No questions and no discussion.

Buck fired up the aircraft, taxied out, and took off. At altitude, he engaged the autopilot and sat there. Boredom overtook him. He pulled out his phone and texted Curt,

> 'Doc, FYI. My PAX (passenger) isn't the 15-year-old boy. Some big dude with a broken lower leg. See ya soon. Buck'

Chapter Nineteen

Issam's Interview

In other parts of Akjoujt, Allison was attempting to line up interviews. Per her contract with Nissassa, she wasn't to interview any of the warring factions. Being a journalist, this frustrated Allison as she believed the tribal conflict was the far better story. Money is money however, so she followed instructions. After a brief discussion on the phone with Issam's people, she was afforded an interview later that day. She welcomed the opportunity. The interview would be at 1400Hrs in Issam's office. Unlike Curt, Allison was well versed in the local culture and reviewed her questions closely to ensure they gained information but simultaneously did not insult. She looked forward to the interview.

At 1350Hrs, Allison arrived at the Village Elder's office. She wore long sleeves and a scarf which modestly masked her hair. The greeting Allison received was a bit cold. To be fair, her greeting would have been offensive to a male, but she was not male and thus received a welcoming fit for a female in the local culture. She sat in Issam's waiting area for 15 minutes.

At 1405Hrs, Issam walked out and greeted her. "Ms. Donley, I presume. Welcome."

"Thank you, your excellency. I appreciate you making the time." Allison learned of his title from others in town. She was not a novice reporter.

"You're very welcome, and please call me Issam. Shall we go into my office? Would you like some tea?"

"I'd love some, thank you." Before Issam could say a word, his staff was already scurrying to make tea. They also were scurrying because this was one of the few females they had ever seen Issam allow them to use his informal name. This female was important…. But still female.

They sat in his office on couches far nicer than Akjoujt warranted. His office was well decorated. It wasn't a Mauritanian Palace, but far better than what anyone in the village could afford.

"So, Ms. Donley, how do you like Akjoujt?"

Allison quickly realized she had not reciprocated the offer of her informal name. Rookie mistake, she thought. "Please, call me Allison. Akjoujt is quite interesting. I've had a chance to meet some local residents and they all seem rather nice. There is a sense of pride here, among the people. They are welcoming and inquisitive. I'm not sure who's more intrigued." Just then, the office door opened, and tea was placed in front them. Piping hot with a bowl full of sugar cubes.

"You are wise, and correct. Many in the town rarely get to see an American, especially a female. While the mine is American, it is rare they venture into the town. I have learned that you are quite of interest to our people. Are you married and do you have any children?" In Arabic cultures, this was the common first discussion. For the next 10 minutes, small talk about family ensued. It was a safe subject and one that allowed each time to measure up the other.

"No, I am not married, nor do I have children. How about you, Issam?"

"Yes, I have a wife and five children. Here is a photo." He reached onto his desk and shared a framed picture with her. He was proud of his tribe. "Perhaps someday you as well will have five children." Allison tried to hide her wince. One or two kids had always been her dream. Five, however…. A bit much.

Eventually the small talk faded and Issam directed the discussion towards the interview. "I am happy the mine has sent you to do a story. Frankly, it was I who asked for it." This was untrue, as it was Jerry who initially surfaced the idea. That said, Issam saw no harm in taking partial credit for a good idea. Another common practice among African Arabic cultures.

"I did not know that. Fascinating. Can you tell me why?"

"Sure. For years, the mine has been working here. Less than one year ago, Nissassa bought the mine. They fired most of the people from Akjoujt and brought in westerners. They built compounds to house the workers and didn't frequent our city. The local people in and around Akjoujt were furious as those jobs were our livelihood and the minerals were our natural resources. Many protested, but within weeks, the mine donated a new school to our village. After that, they paid to refurbish all our village elder offices. Then they donated to upgrade our hospital. Slowly, many began to change their opinions and be supportive of Nissassa. The mine was again providing for Akjoujt. Our hospital is better than many others in all of Mauritania. And our village's security is facilitated by the mining company. We are very grateful. Because of this, I wanted to tell the world of how a company can do good things in Africa. In Africa, many mines have been purchased by the Chinese. In those mines, the Chinese try to assimilate villages to their culture, or worse simply destroy the villages in which they operate. They are like a cancer. The relationship between our villagers and Nissassa could not be better. It is one to serve as a model and for others to learn from."

"That's a really good story, Issam. You sound very proud of your relationship with the mine. May I ask, if Nissassa has done so much for Akjoujt, why hasn't it tried to help to address the local challenges?" It was the closest Allison could get to asking about the Satri and Inju conflict without being overt and inappropriate.

"I think I understand your question. The mine does many things, but it cannot do everything. Much in the way the warring factions avoid confrontation with the mine, the reciprocal is perhaps also true. The mine's goal is profit. I am guessing here, but any expense or effort outside of mining would harm that goal. That is my guess, but I confess, I do not know why they don't do more, nor is it my place to ask them. The mine company has been very good to us. Within Akjoujt, the clan fighting is extremely limited and that is because of the mine. To ask for more I believe would be an insult."

"I understand," Allison replied. Unsatisfied with the answer, she tried to dig deeper. "Issam, does Nissassa hire any locals? If so, what do they do? Don't they want jobs?"

"They hire very few. Some interpreters. Some are the people they use to engage with the village. Yes, our people want jobs, but they can find them in other fields. The mine provides many with food, clothing, shelter, education, medical and more. We have very little to complain about. The mine gets our resources, and they provide our welfare. It is working quite well."

"Perhaps, and I truly understand your desire to share your good news story. But I confess, anyone who reads my story and does any further digging will learn of the warring factions. It may be better if you help me find the right words to say about them to help shape the story before others seek out their own answers." Allison's question was perfect. While it touched on a taboo subject, it offered Issam the chance to shape the narrative and be in control, something far more important in this culture than verbal miscues.

"That is an interesting proposition, Allison. Would you allow me to think about it?"

"Sure, take your time though, I am only here for a short time."

"I shall. Thank you for meeting me. I believe we have shared enough for now." It was Allison's cue to depart.

"Yes, Issam. I agree. And I thank you as well. Have a good day."

Chapter Twenty

Longbow 23

Somewhere in the United Arabic Emirates desert, an old beat-up SUV trundled down a dirt road. 20 Kilometers ahead, a radio transmission into a small earpiece broke the desert silence. "Longbow 23, Darkstar….. Longbow 23, Darkstar." The callsign 'Darkstar' was clearly some sort of controlling agency.

"Darkstar, this is Longbow 23. Go."

"Longbow 23. Imagery verifies your target approaching from the north, approx. 20 kilometers. Confirm the device in place."

"Darkstar, Affirmative." The 'device' was a remote-controlled electromagnetic pulse weapon (EMP) buried below the road. Once activated by Longbow 23, the device would draw energy from the massive battery into its capacitors. When the next car engaged the pressure plate, the energy would be rapidly discharged through an amplifier into a flat, subterranean antennal, destroying any circuitry devices within 10 meters, ironically, to include its own controlling circuit board. Every electronic device within 10 meters would be destroyed, to include the electrical components in an SUV. Devices out to 50 meters could be damaged. Beyond that, the weapon had no effect.

"Longbow 23. Hostile target approaching in black, older SUV, traveling as a single vehicle. Your target is in the passenger seat. Activate the device. You're cleared hostile."

"Copy. Cleared Hostile." Darkstar's message was military terminology for *'kill the guy in the passenger seat.'* Longbow 23 slowly emerged from the desert floor, blending as if he didn't exist. Methodically, he prepared his weapon. Hours earlier, Longbow 23 had carefully measured the distances. It was 1.5 kilometers to the EMP weapon. The car would likely roll to a stop 100-200 meters past the device, where he'd placed some inconspicuous stones along the road as distance markers. He was prepared for a shot between 1.0 and 1.5 kilometers. As Longbow 23 was executing his final steps, the SUV emerged over a hill, traveling towards the EMP device. The plan was clockwork. He pushed the remote button to activate the weapon and the EMP capacitors loaded with energy. Five seconds later, he received a green light on his remote. The device was ready.

As the front tires drove over a pressure sensor, the EMP weapon transmitted a massive energy pulse up into the vehicle. While the passengers were unaware of the event, the electromagnetic spectrum erupted as if there were a nuclear detonation. The engine immediately stopped, and the car coasted to a halt 125 meters from the device, still buried and camouflaged under the road.

As Longbow 23 watched through his rifle scope, three passengers emerged from the vehicle. Two had AK-47s and were apparently close protection for the high value target (HVT), Mohammed Al Ibari. According to Western intelligence, Mohammed was the key interlocutor for transitioning 'clean' money and weapons to terrorist organizations such as Hamas and ISIS. He was wanted for years but proved to be an extremely difficult target, traveling only through nations that the U.S. and other western forces were prohibited from operating in. High overhead the Gulf States, Wester reconnaissance sensors would often monitor and track Al Ibari's movements. A strike opportunity never materialized, until the creation of Nissassa. Given the company was, in theory, a non-nationally sanctioned private company, Nissassa could operate where nations could not. Now, the best option, according to the decision makers was crafting a plausibly deniable unconventional sniper strike opportunity.

The three men exited the car and opened the hood. Visibly, the engine appeared fine. They tried to start it a few times with no luck. Next, they attempted a few calls for help on their cell phones, but those too, were destroyed by the EMP detonation. Slowly, the three began to stop moving around the vehicle. They looked around, began to stand still in one location and discuss what they should do.

Longbow 23 set his sights on Mohammed's chest. He began controlling his breathing. One of the stones approximately 2 meters from Mohammed's foot told Longbow 23 the shot would be 1.4 kilometers; this was also verified on his laser range finder. Methodically, he dialed in the distance to the weapon's scope. As he dialed, the crosshairs lowered. Set at 1.4 kilometers, he raised the crosshairs again to Mohammed's chest. Slowing his breathing.....

Back at the car, Mohammed began yelling at his security detail, blaming them for his dilemma. Unbeknownst to him, an inoperable vehicle was about to be the least of his concerns.

Longbow 23 squeezed the trigger. The .50 cal jumped to life, quietly due to the silencer. A small cloud of dust swirled near the end of the barrel. Longbow 23 re-caged his scope on Mohammed and watched. Roughly two seconds later, Mohammed's chest exploded, and he fell to the ground. His two comrades immediately raised their AK-47s, looking aimlessly into the surroundings. They drug Mohammed's lifeless body to the other side of the vehicle, attempting to revive him. It was hopeless. Mohammed was dead. One of the men opened the trunk and pulled out a large radio, frantically screaming into the microphone. Again, useless. The radio circuitry was destroyed. Longbow 23 lay motionless, watching the entire spectacle.

After 15 minutes, the two men began walking briskly down the road, backtracking towards the direction they came. Longbow 23 watched them crest the hill until they were out of sight. *"Have a nice stroll, gentlemen,"* he thought to himself.

"Darkstar, Longbow 23."

"Longbow 23, Darkstar. Go."

"Darkstar, target neutralized. Area secure."

"Longbow 23. Copy. Imagery confirms. Target neutralized. Execute Exfil as fragged."

"Darkstar, Copy. Longbow 23, Out."

Days later, a group of Nissassa men disguised as a local road work crew would dig up and recover the EMP device. They'd exit the country and return it to its rightful owner. After a quick swap of the circuitry card within the EMP weapon, it would again be operational and ready for its next mission.

Chapter Twenty-One

<u>Why Rudy?</u>

Curt looked down at his phone.

'Doc, FYI. My PAX (passenger) isn't the 15-year-old boy. Some big dude with a broken lower leg. See ya soon. -- Buck'

He replied, *'Thanks, Buck. Have a safe flight and will see you soon.'*

Curt was fairly sure he knew who was on the flight. It was the Inju clansman he fought in the market. But how did the Injus afford to pay for such medical treatment? Why didn't this man come to his hospital for treatment? Who cared for him? As he thought about it, more questions arose than answers.

After lunch, Curt returned to the hospital where Jawad and Kamil greeted him.

"Welcome back, Dr. Nover," Kamil said.

"Thanks, Kamil. Do we have any patients?"

Jawad spoke up. "Yes, sir. We have one. It is a woman who complains of pain in her breast with a lump. I am afraid it isn't good."

Curt met the patient. As Jawad said, the woman, in her 30s had an obvious lump in her breast. The hospital had no Mammogram equipment nor an MRI. Curt took a biopsy of the tumor but was fairly certain it was cancer. This woman needed medical support beyond his capacity. He and Jawad stepped out of the exam room.

"Kamil, can you ask her when she noticed the lump?"

Kamil asked and she responded. Kamil looked at Curt, "Sir, it was six months ago."

'Six months!?' Curt thought... "Kamil, is this the first visit to the hospital and if so, why did she wait so long?"

Kamil did not communicate in Arabic with the patient, he looked at Curt and said, "Doctor. Many women here are very private and would rather not expose themselves. She waited until the pain became unbearable, is my guess. It is perhaps better if we just do not ask this question."

"Jawad, what options do we have to get this woman a mastectomy?"

"Sir, we do not know if it is cancer but if we had the equipment that we asked Issam for, we would know." Jawad was clearly upset. His awareness of modern medicine marvels in first world countries was both a blessing and a curse. Curt knew Jawad was right. However, that did little to solve the current issue at hand.

"Yes, Jawad, and I am working on that. For now, what are the options for our patient?"

"Sir, in such cases we usually help the patient find transportation to Nouakchott or Morocco where she can receive the required care. This can take weeks."

"OK, start working that, I will also work to get her biopsy reviewed somewhere."

"Sir, that too must be done in Nouakchott or Morocco."

Curt's heart sank. He'd done well solving the medical challenges of Akjoujt, and now, he felt helpless.... Worse yet, he knew that had the timing been better, Buck could have flown either the biopsy or the patient out for care. Luck was not on his side today.

The patient line was empty. Jawad worked to help solve the problems for the patient with the breast lump. Curt felt helpless and hopeless. Unfortunately, this was a feeling that had often set in on Curt. It was far from welcome. This feeling had a way of consuming him and, in the past, he struggled with it significantly. Curt needed space. He left the hospital and went to his apartment.

The afternoon sun was setting in Akjoujt. Curt exited his apartment in running attire, his headphones, and his phone.

A long run, some endorphins and a chance to think were just what the doctor ordered. He headed out on the road towards the mine.

His pace was slow. At first, he lamented the hospital facilities. They were far better than he'd imagined. It was unrealistic to even consider some of the items on Jawad's list. A low-end MRI machine would cost $150k and some are over $3 million. But how did the hospital already have other good equipment? Did Issam truly have access to decent funding? And what was Issam's relationship with Abdul Salam, the leader of the Injus, and Qudamah, the Satri's leader? He must know them?? Right?? Did Issam fund the medical evacuation for the injured Inju fighter with a broken leg or do the Injus have their own financing? Who trains these fighters? Why didn't the two leaders attempt to leverage control over Issam? Why have neither made an effort to gain favor with Curt himself? Nothing made sense. Curt wanted answers, and few presented themselves.

Curt's eyes were entranced on the road in front of him as he ran. Eventually he looked up. He was about 500 yards from the mine. He was far closer this time. The security fences were even more prevalent with a large "NISSASSA, Inc" sign out front. A makeshift billboard stood in front of him. It was adorned with a cleanly dressed western mine worker in a construction hat handing food to a child dressed in local attire. Curt may not know much about Nissassa, but he was smart enough to realize the company was dedicated to developing and maintaining a positive relationship with the village.

Curt stopped running and checked the timer on his watch. He sat there and observed the mine. A few cars passed through the dual gate security structures. The heavy equipment he'd seen on previous runs also was visible, but again, most of it was idle. Curt couldn't be certain, but they even appeared to be in the same location he'd seen them before. Perhaps these are their parking locations? Maybe they are down for maintenance? Both logical.

His heartrate slowed from the short break… It was time to turn around and head back. He restarted his watch and ran towards Akjoujt, watching the sunset. The endorphins were working. The numerous questions he pondered all helped drown out the very reason he had started the run. It worked. Curt had suppressed his helpless and hopeless feelings. He was proud of this, and rightly so. Many of his colleagues struggled far worse than he did. Curt arrived back at his apartment, covered in sweat and dust, but with a far clearer mind than which he'd departed.

Chapter Twenty-Two

Strike One

The Nissassa Ops room was dark and quiet. A group sat around the table, clearly mulling over an issue. That issue was Curt.

"I am not sure why I let you talk me into this," Jerry said to Smitty. "Nover is becoming a far greater liability than an asset." They were both looking up at a big screen on the wall, which had a video feed of Nover, looking at the mine, likely being piped in by an UAV overhead.

"Sir, I disagree. He's already repaired numerous Inju and Satri clansmen keeping the target pool at or near capacity," Smitty responded. "Our mission is to provide top off training in a live range setting. He is delivering as I predicted."

"Yes, but he's also stumbled upon you, he's interfered in one of our training scenarios and is clearly intrigued with our mining operation," Jerry responded. "I believe he is giving us little choice."

"What do you mean by 'little choice?' I am hopeful it does not lead down the same path as Curt's predecessor," Smitty responded. It was clear Smitty cared for Curt.

The others in the room, Tiny and Pete as well as some other unknown faces all remained silent. Jerry was a bottom-line kind of guy with no Special Forces background. Curt was nothing and no one to him. For Tiny and Pete however, it was different. Each, like Smitty, held a Special Forces background and thus, there was a bond to Curt. The conversation was becoming uneasy. "Smitty, you recommended Curt. Your rationale at the time appeared to make sense. I agreed to his arrival, as well as paying a hefty sum to revector him here. I don't like loose ends, nor do I care for unpredictability in our operation."

"Sir, there is no issue. Curt is performing well."

"You're right, there currently is no issue. And it will remain that way. This is Strike One, and he doesn't get three." The room remained quiet. Jerry spoke again. "Gentlemen, we have few options, and we need to deliver our services in a few days. Rudy is temporarily off our team, and I have but one choice for a replacement. Smitty, you will take Rudy's spot. You're the only one who knows the mission and team. Your integration will be the least disruptive."

Smitty's heart sank. He was hired to train and had little appetite to be on an operational team again. While part of him enjoyed the rush, that was overshadowed by the demons that already haunted him. However upset he was though, Smitty knew Jerry was right. "Yes, sir. I'll prepare my things."

"Good. The team departs tomorrow."

Chapter Twenty-Three

Ease of Movement

Nissassa's seven-man team moved north across the African desert late in the evening via a closed cargo truck. Seven members with full gear in any open-air truck would be too conspicuous. The plan had been formulated and in place for months. They drove north, crossing the border into Morocco and then approached the port town of Nador where all but one commercial fishing trawlers slept. A single fisherman prepared his boat. Diesels running, mooring lines loose. The cargo truck approached the dock and in a casual, quiet and nearly stealth manner, the team exited the truck, boarded the vessel and she slowly departed the harbor.

As the Moroccan coastal lights faded into the horizon, Smitty opened up his cargo bags, checking his gear for the third time. Another member of the team spoke up, "Smitty, it's all still there…. Just like it was when you checked it in the truck."

"Funny. Thanks for the reassurance." Smitty stopped his inventory and sealed the bag. He was never supposed to be a part of another operational mission. That was his deal with Jerry. Unfortunately, Don in Rosslyn was not privy to that agreement, and even if he was, it would matter little. Smitty was a near legend while assigned to U.S. Special Forces. Unfortunately, during his last mission, things did not go as planned and to this day, the scars and the nightmares still haunted him. Working for Nissassa was a great opportunity to leverage his expertise in a training environment without the exposure to a real operation….. and the pay was exceptional. Smitty calculated that in three years, he'd be able to retire with over seven figures in the bank on top of his military retirement pay. All that changed when Rudy broke his leg. Now, Smitty was again on a team. His apprehension was palpable although he hid it well from the other team members. Smitty closed his eyes and tried to rest as the ship steamed through the night towards Spain.

The captain began waking up the team as the morning dawn splashed onto the fishing trawler. As the makeshift fleet of Spanish fishing boats departed Gibraltar, this vessel was entering the harbor. It attracted little attention. The harbor was quiet given the numerous vacant docks. A white van waited in the harbor and would be the next leg of the mission. Smitty and the team piled into the van. They didn't say anything, nor did the driver who wore a U.S. Navy uniform and drove a vehicle with U.S. military license plates. The drive would take the team from Gibraltar to Rota, Spain, a U.S. Military installation. As the driver approached the gate, he flashed his headlights twice, then once, then twice again. He was cleared onto the base without stopping. The plan was progressing.

The van drove straight to the flight line. A U.S. Air Force C-130 awaited, its engines running. Again, the transition onto the next form of travel was just as uneventful as the others. The C-130 ramp and door opened and closed. The crew acquired flight clearance and departed Rota, Spain, climbing east. The team was getting closer to the mission.

As the flight continued, the C-130 refueled over Saudi Arabia. This mission would be longer than most C-130 missions but risking a stop in a foreign land was not possible. Per the manifest, the only cargo on the C-130 was medical supplies for the U.S. Embassy in Kabul. The flight path would continue from Saudi, over the Indian Ocean, north into Pakistan, continuing into Afghanistan and landing in Kabul.

About thirty minutes after entering Pakistani airspace, the C-130 Crew chief approached Smitty. "Sir, we've reached the point you asked to be notified." The crew chief had no knowledge of the mission but knew these seven gentlemen were never officially on the manifest. Smitty rallied to the rest of the team. They began suiting up for a High-Altitude / Low-

Opening (HALO) jump. The jump required supplemental oxygen as well as cold weather gear. Much of this gear would be discarded upon landing, but the cost was far outweighed should this mission succeed.

The aircrew went onto oxygen. The team of seven stood by the aft ramp. The aircraft depressurized and the ramp slowly opened. A red light along the side of the door illuminated the cargo area. The night sky was black with only 45% moon illumination. The red light switched to green. One by one, the team jumped into the darkness. The adrenaline flowed. As they hurled towards the earth, team members scanned the ground with their night vision devices (NVDs). Closely watching their specialized wristwatches, the team monitored their altitude. Screaming towards the ground, the team pulled their rip chords with 2000 feet remaining and opened their parachutes. What was once a loud rush of thundering air past their faces, transitioned to a soft breeze. NVDs afforded the opportunity to see night as if it were day. The terrain, villages, and other team members. All had good chutes, and all were advancing to the rendezvous point. The insertion was complete, and the C-130 continued on its mission as if nothing had happened, because according to the flight records, nothing did.

Chapter Twenty-Four

<u>The Second Date</u>

Back in Akjoujt, Curt was preparing for his second date with Allison. That was the easy part. Frankly, Akjoujt's night life offered little in the way of dinner dates beyond Anbar's Café. Dr. Nover was going to have to be creative. Departing his apartment, he headed to meet Allison at her hotel. The town was bustling, the shop keepers and street vendors were wrapping up for the day. Along the walk, he grabbed a small bouquet of flowers. The sun setting and the sweltering heat beginning to dissipate.

Curt walked into Allison's hotel. It was nice for Akjoujt standards, but on par with a jazzed-up Motel 6 in the U.S. The clerk was scurrying around keeping busy, although he and Curt were the only two in the lobby. Curt interrupted his work, "Excuse me. Can I please have a courtesy call to Ms. Allison Donley's room?"

"Dr. Nover! Good evening. Yes sir, I will ring it for you, but I regret to inform you, she is not in her room."

Puzzled, Curt replied, "She's not? Do you know where she might be?"

"Yes, sir. She is in the back room behind our kitchen. She is waiting for you. Come. I show you the way."

Curt followed the clerk. Through the front of the restaurant, into the kitchen where line cooks were busy preparing the evening meal. He led Curt to a back door. When it opened, Curt saw a neatly prepared dinner table, candles, wine, and two chairs. And behind it all stood Allison.

She smiled and said, "Good evening, Dr. Nover. Hungry?"

Curt was stunned. "Uhh... What is all this? I am speechless."

The clerk looked at Allison with a smile which she returned with the words, "Thanks, Mr. Mohammed, for everything." They both winked.

"My pleasure, Ms. Donley. Enjoy your meal." He darted off, with the smile permanently affixed to his face.

"I figured you made dinner for me on our previous date, it was only fair I returned the favor."

"How on earth did you cook this in a hotel!?" He walked over to her, hugged and kissed her. "By the way, these are for you.... But I've clearly been outdone." He handed her the bouquet.

"Aww, thanks for the flowers." She kissed him again. "Mr. Mohammed is a wonderful man. I had dinner with his family last night. I told him that we would meet tonight for dinner, and he insisted to cook for us. I eventually convinced him that I would prepare our meal in his kitchen and teach him how to make some American cuisine. It was a deal."

"OK then. Let's eat. I'm starving. What's on the menu?"

"For starters, a garden salad and carpaccio. The main meal was to be buttermilk fried chicken but is now goat milk fried chicken and local veggies. Dessert in the desert is a chocolate mud pie that's as close as I could get to my mom's recipe given the local markets."

The food was all on the table. It looked magnificent. He pulled out her chair. They both sat. Curt opened the wine, poured two glasses, raised his and said, "A toast, to a wonderful night."

Allison raised her glass and replied, "Toast, but the night has just begun?"

Curt responded...... "I just got a hunch."

They ate and spoke of their past few days. Allison discussed her interviews, Curt talked about medical procedures and lunch with Buck. It was like they had been on thousands of dates before. At a break in the conversation, Allison reached below the table and pulled out a folded T-shirt and said, "By the way, I washed your McP's shirt and wanted to give it back. Wouldn't want your SEAL buddies to see you without it."

Curt stopped moving and looked at her. "OK, thanks....." he considered saying more but chose not to.

"Curt, do you honestly think that as a journalist, I wasn't going to do some digging? What info shall I share? Your BUDS graduation class? Where you were stationed? Which Teams you were on? Or perhaps none of it, because it's something you're not ready to share. I'm good either way. But to be fair, I'd think most folks who were Navy SEALS would boast. I'm curious why you keep it hidden?"

"I'd like to select, *'it's not something I'm ready to share,'* Mr. Trabek, for five hundred," it was Curt's poor attempt at a humorous Jeopardy reference.

"I get it. But I'll say thank you for your service. You are an impressive man, Mr. Nover. Former SEAL, now a doctor and yet again, serving in the middle of nowhere to an under privileged community. Are you working on a Nobel or something?"

Curt chuckled. "Good one. No. It is just something I felt I needed to do."

"Fair enough," Allison responded, "But why Akjoujt?"

"Why not?" Curt shot back. "Actually, Doctors Without Borders selected my location. I was a worldwide volunteer. I cared little where I went, as long as I went somewhere that needed me. Oddly, up until a few weeks before I departed Chicago, I was to go to a small island in the Pacific. Somewhat comical in that I began prepping and learning about Island diseases in the Asian theater, most due to high humidity and water borne illnesses. Then, all of the sudden, Doctors Without Borders called and said I was being moved to a higher priority mission in the middle of an African desert. I gave up trying to do specialized preparation. The good news is, Akjoujt needed me, so that's where I am."

"Interesting story. I have a college friend who went to work for Doctors Without Borders. She's an amazing organizer and was brought into their administration to help. The stories she shares about the accomplishments of that organization are awe inspiring. So, after this, are you going to cure cancer? Solve the global climate crisis?"

"Again, funny. I don't know. I really haven't thought that far ahead. I know this. I love my country. I love what it stands for and that's why I joined the military. The power we wield internationally is 90% good in my book; however, some things I don't agree with. As a SEAL, I had to follow orders, whether I liked them or not. Now, I can make my own choices, and, in a way, I am remedying part of that 10% I disagreed with. To many, that sounds crazy – especially to my mother who wanted me to practice medicine in the U.S., make good money, find a lovely wife and raise a family. I don't think she'll be visiting Akjoujt anytime soon."

"Curt, that is extremely commendable. And yes, your nation needed you, the people of Akjoujt need you, but don't forget, at some point, you also need you."

"Allison, I get that. Someday. I promise. Enough about me…. Please. Tell me the Allison Donley story."

"Are you crazy?! I'm sitting across from a Navy SEAL, who's now a humanitarian doctor. My story sucks."

"Come on… It can't be that bad. Please. Go."

"OK. I grew up in Tucson, AZ. The entire time in school, I couldn't wait to get out. It was hot, dry, and it just wasn't me. I got a scholarship to Duke and packed my bags. About three months into college, I missed Tucson and couldn't for the life of me imagine why. I went home for Christmas break, saw friends and family. From that moment on, I fell in love with Tucson. I graduated Duke with a journalism degree and like every budding scribe, I was going to expose the next Watergate. Unfortunately, I quickly learned that while trying to uncover Watergate Part II, journalists are not exempt from rent, electric, water, phone, cable and all the other bills that piled up. So, I volunteered to do an imbedded journalist job with a Provincial Reconstruction Team in Iraq. I spent three months with a Marine unit which also had a State Department Foreign Service

Officer and a U.S. Aid Rep. Frankly, it was fascinating to see them work together. At the tactical level, facing common challenges, these three entities could work together better than any would imagine. Far better than at the strategic level, back in parochial D.C. where they constantly fought over policy and budgets. I wrote about that and how sometimes D.C., Politics and Senior Service Officials serve more as a hindrance to accomplishing U.S. goals than help. My stories were well received by the public, but not so much by those in the National Capital Region. I was offered a job with the Boston Herald and took it. That lasted about three months. As much as I hated the Tucson heat growing up, Boston winters are not survivable by true human beings. I began freelancing and I love it. I now live in Mesa, AZ. It's close enough to my family in Tucson but far enough to ensure my distance."

"That's extremely disappointing."

"Excuse me?" She was taken back by his comment. "My story disappoints you?"

"Of course. I'm a Chicago boy. I love a cold brisk wind off of Lake Michigan in the wintertime. There's nothing better. It's clear this wasn't meant to be." Curt's sarcasm was thick and was not missed by Allison.

"Out of that entire diatribe, you narrow in on climate temperatures? When Jawad said you were a nitpicker, I had no idea how right he was."

"What? Jawad said I nitpick?!" Curt could not imagine Jawad speaking ill of him to a stranger.

"No. I just made that up. Two can play your game." They both laughed. And it was clear, their chemistry was perfect. Curt was pleased to have someone in Akjoujt he could relax with. Little did he know it would be someone he'd fall in love with. He leaned over the table, took her hand and gently kissed her. She'd been waiting for two days for another kiss like that. It was long overdue. The passion increased and they retired to her hotel room, making only a few awkward situations as they stumbled through the kitchen and through the lobby. The line cooks tried hard not to look up out of embarrassment. Public affection was not common in Muslim culture, but to be fair, many have seen enough American movies to realize it was a part of U.S. culture.

They barely made it to her room before their public exploits would begin to offend not only Muslims but Americans as well. The door closed and this night would prove to be just as passionate as their first.

Chapter Twenty-Five

Freedom

One week before the Nissassa team's insertion, a few key Pakistani medical personnel deemed Shakeel's health to be terminal. His long-standing food strike had taken its toll on his internal organs and as a prisoner serving a life term in Pakistan, few if any in the Pakistani government cared about it. Shakeel however, was not an average prisoner. He was famous. Doctor Shakeel Afridi was the key reason Osama Bin Laden was dead. Dr. Afridi, with the help of the CIA, had been able to identify Bin Laden's location via DNA collected for Hepatitis Vaccinations. While the U.S. Government was successful at killing Bin Laden, it failed to extract Shakeel and his family before he could be arrested. The Pakistani government captured him first, found him guilty of criminal charges and sentenced him to death.

A doctor within the hospital medical staff demanded that Shakeel be transported to the hospital in Multan, Pakistan, where he could be force fed via an intravenous drip and feeding tube. Multan was the nearest medical facility capable of treating Shakeel who was sitting in a jail in Sahiwal. The Pakistani government originally protested but realizing the political value of Dr. Afridi remaining alive (a key reason they never continued through with the execution), finally relented. Dr. Afridi was loaded up into a two-vehicle convoy and began the movement to Multan. Given his fame, numerous locals chanted, screamed, and captured the event on their phone cameras. One local who took his phone video pushed it out on Twitter. Yet another piece of the plan continuing like clockwork. The video identified the time of departure, number of security guards, the types of vehicles and the license plates.

Smitty and the team had already changed into Kuchi tribesmen attire. They slowly moved to the edge of town. Once there, they lingered and sat. The Kuchi were nomads from Afghanistan and Northern Pakistan. While not locals, they could easily blend into a town as they often did to acquire goods and services.

An undisclosed command post was tracking Dr. Afridi's convoy via overhead video. When it was approximately one hour out of Multan, a radio transmission broke the silence in the team's earpieces... "HEPVACS, Merlin, target one hour out."

Smitty replied, "HEPVACS copies. Moving now."

Five of the team descended into Multan via foot. The other two had 'acquired' a pickup truck. Just like they rehearsed.

It was time.... Smitty's hands shook. He was never supposed to be in this position again.

The Pakistani prison guards drove slowly into Multan. While the locals in Sahiwal knew of Dr. Afridi's movements, locals in Multan were clueless. Life continued just like any other day. This was just how the prison guards wanted it.

The two-car convoy stopped outside the Multani Hospital. Three guards emerged from the first vehicle with their weapons drawn. Curious locals moved in, amongst that crowd were the team of five, each visually selecting their unsuspecting targets. Two more emerged from the second vehicle along with two medical staff and Shakeel Afridi.

From the other end of the street, a small pickup, with two passengers roared towards the hospital, honking the horn wildly. The Prison guards took notice, clutching their weapons. Just like they'd practiced, other team members methodically moved closer behind their targets. As the truck approached, the first guard raised his weapon. That was the catalyst. Just as they had rehearsed, the team neutralized each guard. The two medical staff tending to Shakeel, fled, leaving him lying in the street dirt, too weak to get up. Like clockwork, the team wrapped up Shakeel, loaded him in the truck and all piled in. A local Pakistani police officer noticed the commotion and charged to the scene screaming with his weapon raised. The team member responsible for that sector of fire raised his weapon and fired twice. The police officer fell instantly. With precision, the entire team was now in the vehicle and ready to go. One banged on the side of the truck bed… The signal to start driving. Smitty reached into his clothes, pulled out a piece of paper and threw it on the ground as the truck sped away. As they departed, a sense of success began to set in. The driver speeding faster down the narrow streets of Multan.

In a small Pakistani hut, a small girl jumped with joy at the news her mother would take her out for ice cream. Her exuberance was unbound, and she rushed from her front door out into the street.

Without notice, 15 meters ahead of the truck, that same small Pakistani girl stood, facing the truck. There was no time to react. The truck slammed into her, carrying her body approximately 40 meters until she slid over the cab, landing in the truck bed. She gurgled, unconscious with her eyes wide open. Smitty froze. Another team member grabbed her body and flung it from the bed onto the side of the road. Her dress in tatters and covered in dirt, she slowly rolled to a motionless stop as the truck continued.

The team members looked at each other. Without saying a word, they knew it was the right thing to do… Except Smitty. His stomach churned. The sense of success muted.

Back at the hospital, the guards called their posts for support. A local Multan villager picked up the paper tossed by Smitty. The paper was a handwritten letter in Pashto. It was from the Taliban, who claimed responsibility for the event, taking Dr. Afridi hostage with plans to execute him, completing his court sentencing that Pakistan failed to do. The note continued that the Taliban would wait no longer for justice to be served. Within minutes, the news of the events as well as the letter blanketed social media.

No one spoke in the truck. One member dropped an IV drip into Shakeel. The truck continued to the northwest towards the Ravi River. Eventually, the team abandoned the vehicle, crossing the river on foot. They took turns carrying Shakeel. They climbed a ridgeline to gain a vantage and scan for any enemy response force. None came.

        Slowly, Shakeel began to gain strength and night set in. Under the dark of night, two heavily modified and blacked out HH-60 helicopters descended out of nowhere and picked up the team. They flew north, continuing towards an undisclosed U.S. base in Afghanistan. An hour later, they were physically safe from harm. Smitty however, could not erase the image of the little girl's last breath.

****

        Back in Rosslyn, Don learned that Operation HEPVACS (Hepatitis Vaccination) was successful. He sent a quick text to Steve. *"Success."* The remaining funds would be wired into Nissassa's accounts from a black U.S. Government account.

        Within days, Dr. Afridi would reunite with his family in a small Oklahoma town under the witness protection program. Surrogates of the U.S. would generate social media postings which claimed the Taliban killed Shakeel while the actual Taliban would staunchly deny these false reports. The effort, along with the Taliban's long standing credibility challenges, fiction would trump fact and globally, few would believe the Taliban. Nissassa had proven itself invaluable.

Chapter Twenty-Six

Rewind and Replay

Jerry greeted the team back at Nissassa with top end food and drink. This successful mission was the boost Nissassa needed, and the team deserved reward. They wasted no time and dove in. Steaks, lobster, wine, whiskey and beer. Later, there would be Cuban cigars. The atmosphere was festive. Jerry began to speak.

"Gentlemen. On behalf of the Nissassa leadership, I want to congratulate you and thank you for your service." Another employee began handing envelopes to each team member. "Additionally, I've been instructed to tell you that your $200,000 pay has been increased to $250,000 tax free. Each of these envelopes contain a Cayman bank account in your name with the funds in place. Great job."

The team began hugging and high fiving. They'd each spent approximately one month training and executing this event. $250k a month was far more than they'd received in the past performing similar missions while on active duty.

As the celebration continued, Jerry had Tiny pull up a video on the Ops Center main screens. It was overhead video of the event. The lights went dim and the large screens around the room came to life. The entire scenario played out; just as it had happened. This time however, the participants were the audience, talking about each micro-event, critiquing and complimenting each as if it was a full military debrief. Gun muzzle flashes filled the screen for a few moments and then the truck sped away. It was the moment the Pakistani police officer was shot. Next, the truck sped away. The film cut out; the lights turned on. The team clinked glasses to a successful mission.

Every member of the team knew what happened next. But it would not be part of the Nissassa video, nor part of the debrief. War is hell. Shit happens. Best to ignore that which the mind can't process. Jerry too, saw no sense in replaying that scene. The mission was a success.

Chapter Twenty-Seven

The Article

Allison had finished her article. She knew it was a fluff piece, but the money was good, and she met Curt. Her next article will be stronger she told herself. As she sat in Anbar's Café, she drank her coffee with her article in paper form laying on the table. Jerry walked in and approached.

"Good morning, Allison."

"Good morning, Jerry. How are you?"

"I'm great. Thanks for asking. How is the article?"

"It's complete. I think you're going to like it. By all accounts, Nissassa is truly helping the people of Akjoujt. They are lucky to have you."

"Great! I look forward to reading it and even more importantly getting it out into the media. We are very proud of our operation and want to ensure the world knows what it is we do here. We will wire transfer the remaining payments to your account and coordinate your flight back to the U.S."

She welcomed the news on her pay. The notion of a flight back sat in her stomach like a rock. She really liked Curt and did not want to leave. "Thanks, Jerry. But I may stick around Akjoujt a while."

"Ha ha! Ok. I heard you had a good sense of humor. That must be a joke!"

"Actually no. I am thinking about another story here in Akjoujt." This was far from the truth. There was no other story, but she needed a reason to stay. Her near term plans back in the U.S. were non-existent. There truly was nothing forcing her to return.

This was unwelcome news to Jerry. "I hope it has nothing to do with the Inju and Satri conflict. That's dangerous stuff." This was clearly not Jerry's main concern, but he needed something to dissuade her stay.

"No, nothing like that, Jerry." Actually, that was exactly the type of story she would like to do but clearly did not have the resources to make it possible. "I met Dr. Nover and learned of his story. When I was embedded as a journalist in an Iraqi Provincial Reconstruction Team (PRT), I wrote about how medical professionals make a difference in war impoverished regions. Hence, I think I see a story here." She was making the entire narrative up on the fly, but in truth, she also was convincing herself of the story. Unfortunately, convincing Curt of the story? That would be a bit more of a challenge.

Jerry was a bit surprised but relieved her story was only tangential to the Nissassa operation. "OK then. Just let us know when you wish to leave, and we will make the arrangements. And enjoy your stay in Akjoujt." She handed Jerry the article, and he left. A vehicle was waiting outside the café. Once inside, Jerry placed a call. "I think we have another problem, and again, it involves Nover." He hung up.

As the car drove away, he looked at the article. It was perfect. Allison had captured exactly what Nissassa wanted her to describe. A U.S. company, ethically committed to the local community in which it was entrenched. Doing good for Akjoujt, the U.S., and the world. In Jerry's mind, that's exactly what Nissassa was doing, albeit far from a mining operation.

Back in the café, Allison sat conflicted and alone at the table. 'What a bunch of horse shit' she thought regarding her idea she sprang onto Jerry. Curt was never going to go for it. Given how he hid his Navy career from her, she was certain he'd cut her suggestion off at the knees. The only thing she knew was she wanted to stay close to Curt for a while longer. She just needed a reason. As she looked up from her table, her heart melted, and her pulse raced. She'd better come up with a reason soon. Curt was walking towards her table.

Chapter Twenty-Eight

The Fib

"Hey, Beautiful!" Curt said as he approached. He leaned down and kissed her. Pleasantly surprised to see her at the café.

"Hey, handsome," she replied. He pulled out a chair and joined her.

"What are you doing here alone?"

"Well, I wasn't alone. I just handed over my article to Nissassa. It's complete." Her tone was far less energetic than his and she hoped he'd pick up on the notion that she'd be leaving given her work was complete.

"Oh," Curt replied. "Did they like the piece?" He wasn't obtuse to the fact she'd be leaving, but he too didn't want to discuss the topic.

"I am sure they will. It's what they paid for. They are reading it now. I doubt they will have any changes, but should they, I'll consider them." Allison too, was avoiding the elephant in the room. Finally, Curt addressed it.

"So, what now? What do you do?" It was as close as he could muster to asking if she was going to leave. Neither wanted to appear as the clingy, crazy lover, but they also didn't want this to end.

"I don't know. I kinda like Akjoujt. The temperature and sand remind me of Tucson."

"Frankly, I think Akjoujt likes you too." It was Curt's subtle, but not so subtle hint he'd like her to stay.

"Remember when I told you about my college friend at Doctors Without Borders? Well, I am thinking of reaching out to her and doing a story about their mission and using the one in Akjoujt as a backdrop. If you wish, I won't mention you directly." Again, Allison's mind had hastily crafted yet another narrative. This one just might work. She anxiously awaited Curt's response.

She had nothing to fear. Curt was elated. "That sounds great! I'm happy to give you access to the hospital." In reality, Curt had not really thought through the idea of her article and to what degree it would include him. He was just happy this weeklong romance was given a stay of execution. "Will you stay in the hotel?"

"Probably. I need to talk to Mr. Mohammed and ensure there is space and negotiate a price. This article will be a freelance effort so until I sell it, the costs come out of my pocket." Given the money Allison received from Nissassa, she could have afforded to stay in Akjoujt for life. Money was not the issue.

"Well, if Mr. Mohammed doesn't have anything, I may have something for you." He smiled. "Just let me know...... Look, baby, I gotta run back to the Hospital. I actually just came to get breakfast to go. Can I see you tonight?"

"I'd love that." Allison's heart rate slowed, and calmness swept over her. The thought of sharing Curt's apartment was a bit fast, but she couldn't have been happier. She kissed Curt goodbye and watched him walk away. She chuckled under her breath. Allison was relieved by the notion of voluntarily staying in a third world African village vs going home to the U.S. That said, another part of her contemplated having her head examined.

Chapter Twenty-Nine

The Next Mission

Back in Rosslyn, Don was partly working in his office. He was also partly staring out of the window over the Potomac River. Autumn had set in and the leaves blanketing the banks of the Potomac were gorgeous. *'There is just something about D.C. in the fall,'* he thought to himself. Slightly startled, his phone rang. "Don," he said.

"Don, hello. It's Steve." He knew who it was and recognized the voice. "Can we meet today. The normal spot. Let's say noon?"

Don would of course take a meeting with the White House Chief of Staff. It was his company's main customer. "Of course. See you there." Don hung up the phone. No more time for daydreaming over the Potomac. He quickly began collecting papers, reviewing recent emails from Jerry, and gathering as many datapoints as he felt he needed for the meeting.

Don picked up the phone again and called his secretary. "Helen, please clear my calendar for today."

"Yes, sir." She was used to such tasks as well as such directness. Don Harrison could be as polite as they come, but also just as militant and direct. He was conditioned from his former career in Special Forces. Don was a former Special Forces operator and later served as a staff officer in the Pentagon. His family was politically active and while in D.C., Don befriended a decent number of power players. Through discussions and some help, he founded Nissassa and was making exceptional money. While Don's title was CEO, he was clueless how much of a pawn he was to the U.S. Government.

Don exited his cab at the Lincoln Memorial. Tourists packed the area. The monument's strength and positioning at the end of the reflecting pond never gets old. He stood at the steps of the memorial, staring towards the Washington Monument. The trees that lined either side of the reflecting pond had all changed from lush summer green to a brilliant yellow, almost in unison. It was beautiful and a sight Don would never grow tired of. In fact, through the rest of the year, he'd yearn for just this very view.

Don walked along the left-hand side of the reflecting pond in the canopy of the yellow leaves. After five minutes, he reached the end of the pond and stood at the edge of the World War II memorial. It too had some tourists, but far less than the big named memorials. In the distance, Don saw Steve approaching. "Hey, Steve. Thanks for the call. What can I do for you?"

"Don, let's walk." They both reached in their pockets and turned off their phones. This was the protocol. They walked away from the World War II Memorial towards the Constitutional Gardens Pond, a memorial that had even fewer unwelcome tourist ears. "Don, leadership was pleased with your last efforts, and we'd like to get a team trained for another mission. This one will be a bit more difficult, but we believe you can do it. Basically, the job involves a covert deep infill into Iran. In Tehran, the mission calls for one sniper hit and one pax exfil. You will infill in the vicinity of Baku, Azerbaijan and exfil through Ashgabat, Turkmenistan."

"Those involve some tough border crossings. Is that as close as you can get us? Also, what about logistic support to Baku and from Ashgabat?"

"The same people who facilitated logistics for your previous mission will perform the same function again. But from Baku to Ashgabat, you are on your own. U.S. assets cannot get you into Iranian territory. If you can't do it, just let us know." Steve knew this line was like a worm on a hook. Don never backed away from a challenge. It was one of his key weaknesses.

"Understood. I'll take a look at it and get you a cost in a day. When does the mission need to go?"

"End of October. You have some time. The hit is planned to coincide with a significant public speech in Teheran. The mission won't be easy, but then again, that's why we hire you."

"I got it. I'll call you later today with an estimate."

"Great. I appreciate it, Don. And the standard rules apply. This talk didn't happen. The White House has plausible deniability. Nissassa assumes all the risk."

"I wouldn't have it any other way. Take care, Steve. We will talk soon." They shook hands, parted and went their separate ways.

As Don walked back to the Lincoln Memorial to catch a cab, he texted Jerry. *"Jerry, we have an offer for two missions, one lollipop and one baggage. Location is one door west of our previous party. Halloween. Can you make it happen?"* Don jumped in a cab. Before returning to the office, a text alert came in. *"Affirm. Send me the details when able."*

Don sat back in the cab. The last mission netted him six figures. This one would be seven. His eyes were lost in dollar signs and autumn leaves as the cab drove up George Washington Parkway towards Rosslyn.

Once back in Rosslyn, Don ran the numbers and calculated the risk. He sent a text to Steve. *'$35M. $20M up front'*

Immediately, a reply, *'Done.'* A funds transfer that day would fill the Nissassa bank account with twenty million dollars. Easy day.

Chapter Thirty

The Romance & The Story

Allison spoke to Mr. Mohammed about extending her room. He was more than happy to do so. Akjoujt saw few visitors. The cost for the room would be the same. She appreciated his offer, but her heart hoped the room was unavailable. Later that day she met Curt at the hospital.

"Hey, you!" She saw him standing in the middle of the hallway reviewing a chart.

"Allison. Great to see you! What did Mr. Mohammed say?"

"He says my room is still available for the same price."

"Well, I can offer you something that is far cheaper. In fact, it's free." This was music to Allison's ears. Sharing Curt's apartment was exactly what she was hoping for.

"Interesting. What's the offer?" She was trying to be coy.

He said, "Come with me." He led her down the hall and opened one of the hospital doors. It was a musty, dusty old exam room that was turned into a single bedroom for medical staff to get sleep. "Voila! Your new home!" Her heart sank. She mustered the best *'I'm so grateful'* appearance she could.

"Thanks........" It was all she could say.

Curt stared at her for a second and didn't say anything. He finally spoke up and said, "I know it's not much, but with a little cleaning, it could really be nice. Far better than staying at my place. Don't you agree?" With that, Curt's face lit up with a 'practical joke' smile.

Her disappointment quickly shifted to anger. She'd been played. "You Asshole!" She repeatedly slapped him in the shoulder. He defended her blows as he laughed out loud.

"Do you really think I'd let you sleep where I work?! Come on. I'll help you get your things from Mr. Mohammed's hotel. You can move in today."

She hugged him... but wanted to kill him. They left the hospital hand in hand.

****

The romance between Curt and Allison flourished. They talked about Chicago, about Tucson, about the Chicago Cubs, although she was not a baseball fan. When he wasn't working, they were together. When he was working, she was halfheartedly working on her story sitting in Anbar's Café. She was smitten. One day as she sat in Anbar's Café, she checked her email. It was a response from Karen, her college friend who worked for Doctors Without Borders. Given her halfhearted story effort, Allison had reached out to learn more about the Akjoujt mission... and a bit more about Curt.

29 Jun 2019

Alli!

Great to hear from you! It's been FAR too long! So... given me more details about this hunk, please!!!?? Any guy who can keep you in third world Africa must be a huge keeper. Not only that, but he also clearly has rich friends. Evidently an anonymous donation for $2.5M was made to Doctors Without Borders with only the request to re-station Curt into Akjoujt and to not inform him. With friends like that, you better find a way to lock that guy down!

Take care!! I miss you! I hope we can visit soon!

Love ya!
Kar

Allison was confused. $2.5 Million dollars for Curt? Why wouldn't Curt have told her about this? He had to know? Didn't he? Was it another one of his secrets? If he truly didn't know? Who could have paid that kind of cash… and more importantly, why?

Chapter Thirty-One

Mission Planning

One of the more special Nissassa ops center computers sprung to life and began downloading encrypted files. Those files contained all the tasking and supporting material for the new mission. Where they originated from would be masked and the data would jump across over 50 Virtual Private Networks (VPN) to hide their point of origin. Trying to trace it would be pointless. Once at Nissassa, the files were unencrypted, and the planning team began their work. The target would be the Ayatollah of Iran. Given the state of global affairs, this was not surprising. The Ayatollah's rhetoric had grown untenable to the West, and something needed to be done. In fact, it had grown so obnoxious, other prominent Muslim nations had begun to align with the west against Iran.

More details of the plan emerged and provided greater context for the infill location. The team would take on the cover of Azerbaijani sympathizers who were on a pilgrimage to see the Ayatollah speak. Enough crumbs of this narrative would be left to completely cover the team's identity. In late October, the Ayatollah would speak at Mawlid, the celebrated birthday of the Prophet Mohammed. While this presented a great opportunity, it also presented great risk. The crowds and security would be massive. The second part of the mission was far less difficult. They were to grab Iran's chief nuclear scientist.

Jerry and Smitty began discussing the task with the planners.

"Jerry, the second part of the task is the easiest. We can take the last team, add Rudy back in after his leg heals. We will need some rehearsals which involve a larger security posture around the target, but this should be doable."

"Smitty, I concur. But we are going to need a completely separate team for the hit. Longbow 23 can be the trigger, but getting him in and out of Tehran will require an effort far greater than what we've provided him in the past. Let's see if the planners can come up with a scenario where we infill Longbow 23 into Akjoujt with a significant crowd. Get the shot off and get him out. I'll meet with Abdul-Salam and Qudamah and come up with a target." This was far from ideal. Akjoujt was far smaller than Tehran. It was not enough to present a sniper with a long enough shot for valid training. The mission planners would have their work cut out for them.

The planners departed to their individual workstations. Jerry and Smitty, alone now, were comfortable with the guidance they provided. Jerry spoke, "Smitty, I need to discuss something with you."

"Sure, what is it, Jerry?"

"Can you tell me how the family of the little Pakistani girl ended up with $10,000 U.S. Dollars?"

Smitty's face showed a hint of surprise. Secretly, he had leveraged some old contacts in the area and pushed the money to the family. He had to. He couldn't sleep. The nightmares were so vivid, so real. Her eyes... they just stared at him. Lifeless. "Yeah... sir, I just thought she was an innocent victim and I wanted to help."

"I understand that, but your meddling has caused issues. That family arrived in Islamabad at the U.S. Embassy with the money asking for it to be converted to Rupees. A poor family with that much money draws attention. Such attention helps give life to the Taliban's narrative. Your good deed puts Shakeel and his family in danger. I expect better from you."

Smitty's eyes were pinpointed. His heart raced. He knew in his heart he did the right thing. The Taliban would never find Shakeel, even if the world knew the truth..... The truth he thought. The entire Nissassa mission was eating at him. "Copy, boss. I understand you expect better." Smitty paused.... Then he continued, "I think we all have expectations."

Jerry paused and stared at Smitty. He was taken aback..... "Excuse me? And what pray tell are your expectations?"

Smitty had over spoke and knew it. "Nothing, boss. Never mind. I'm good."

"Smitty, do we have a problem?"

"No sir. We're good." Smitty left the room. A few minutes later, Jerry also left and stepped outside. He raised his phone and began texting Don. *"Looks like we need a second catering company. The party needs to be twice as big as the last one."*

Don wrote back, *"Agree and working on it. Feelers out at all the known hangouts. Perhaps some of the original catering company has some recommendations?"*

"Will check."

Jerry returned into the ops center, leaving his phone outside. He went to the team that was planning the mission and asked for any former Special Forces friends who were looking for work. A few names surfaced and were passed.

Within two weeks, they had enough men in Akjoujt to perform the mission and train. Rudy was also back on the team... a relief to Smitty. The mission planning for the event was completed and agreed to by Jerry and Smitty. Now the rehearsals and training would begin. Within the mine, the sand box (a small map on the ground used to rehearse the plan) was used, and some makeshift buildings were erected to also facilitate training. Eventually the training within the mine was complete. It would soon be time to practice in Akjoujt.

Chapter Thirty-Two

<u>The Training Scenario</u>

A small fire along the edge of a dusty road lit up the desert night. For miles, there was nothing but sand. Next to the fire, a large black SUV and a makeshift table with four chairs. Jerry was seated with Issam, the Akjoujt village elder. The time was nearing 2100Hrs. Like clockwork, two vehicles appeared. One approaching from the north, the other the south. As they arrived, only one member exited each vehicle. One was Abdul-Salam, the Satri leader and the other Qudamah, the Inju leader. They walked towards Jerry and Issam and greeted each other. Unexpectedly, they shook hands and hugged as if they were long lost friends. A far cry from what one would have ever imagined.

Jerry spoke, "Greetings, Qudamah and Abdul-Salam and welcome." Tea was prepared and sitting on the table.

"Greetings to you as well and to you, Issam. Abdul, you look healthy!"

"Ha! I feel healthy! Assalamu Alaikum my friends." They all sat down. It was as if three long lost friends had met again for the first time. They discussed family and other issues. Jerry knew it was inappropriate to immediately discuss work.

After a while, Qudamah asked, "Jerry, my friend, why have you called this meeting? What is it we can do for you?"

Jerry didn't miss the chance. In his mind, he'd wasted enough time on small talk. "Gentlemen, I need another training event. I need a sniper target outside the city approximately 800 meters."

"This is simple!" Abdul stated. "We need not a meeting for such things. This is a standard request with a standard price." It was clear Abdul was just as focused on the payment as he was on the process.

Jerry continued. "Yes, but there is one other part. We need a large festival in Akjoujt."

Now the issue involved the town which was Issam's territory, and he didn't miss the chance to inject, "You may have any festival you like as long as you pay."

"Yes, we will pay everything." Jerry wanted to assuage concerns. To him, money wasn't the issue, but he also knew it was the drug that kept them coming back. "I believe we need a large celebration. As big as we can get. We must come up with an occasion. It would be helpful if it was a holiday, people were free from work to be in the city. In fact, it would be great if people from other villages were enticed to come. The streets must be packed."

"OK, my friend, I understand. Perhaps we celebrate the mine?"

Jerry didn't like the idea. "I appreciate that, but let's not make the party about the mine." Jerry knew how this party would end and didn't want such a stigma tied to the mine.

"I have an idea," Abdul-Salam spoke up. "One of my small warriors, Akim, lost his lower leg in an unfortunate training incident. His family has taken it quite hard and shuns him. He is a good boy and I understand his new prosthetic leg will be here soon. Perhaps we can celebrate the arrival of this new leg along with some significant medical donations to the hospital."

The idea had merit. The prosthetic would be just a small piece but tie the hospital to the people where they could see its value. It would also bring in many other villagers to see and learn of the new equipment. The cost to generate the party would be larger than the anticipated budget, but Jerry was confident he could get the money.

"OK. Let's go with that. I will work on the prosthetic leg and donations. We will funnel them through you, Issam. As for the target, I believe this time the target should be Inju to keep balance." They all nodded in agreement.

"I shall have you a target soon. He will be at your prescribed location during the festivities." Abdul's tone was coldly matter of fact. It was what must be done.

"Great, and if you plan to use Kameel, please let him know the prices for our work are not negotiable. This is the third time he's hinted at more money. Speaking of money……" The doors of the large black SUV opened. Three large bags weighted down with money, gold and gems emerged and were placed on the table.

"Gentlemen, I believe you will find this to your liking."

"Shookran, my friend." They all said it in unison.

"Offwan. Let's plan a party."

Chapter Thirty-Three

The Announcement

Jawad came running into the hospital exam room, "Dr. Nover, Dr. Nover! Great news!"

Curt was stunned a bit as Jawad never seemed this excited before. "What is it, Jawad?"

"Our hospital will receive an MRI machine. A REAL MRI machine. We will be the only hospital within hundreds of kilometers with this capability! Issam says it is already on its way. He is also overjoyed and stated that Akjoujt will celebrate its arrival with a festival and a mandated day off for everyone. This is the greatest news!"

Curt was speechless. How on earth did Issam get an MRI? Who paid for this? Was it Doctors Without Borders? Was it the mine? As much as he wanted to celebrate, something just didn't add up. "This is great news, Jawad. Let me finish up with this patient and I will come out to talk to you."

"Yes, sir! In Shala! Allah Akbar!"

That last phrase caught Curt off guard. During military training, he was instructed that should he hear that phrase, he should seek cover immediately as the next few seconds were likely going to be unpleasant. This would be the second time he heard it in a far different light.

Curt finished up with his patient. It was a simple check up from a gunshot wound. The fighting between the factions had increased over the summer. Casually, the entire town and others blamed it on the heat. Curt was anxious for the heat and the fighting to subside as fall was in the air. Curt stepped into the hallway. Kamil, who was translating, accompanied him. Jawad was holding a clipboard which contained a list of items that were inbound to the hospital. Along with the MRI, numerous supplies were coming and additionally a high-tech prosthetic for Akim, just as Jerry had promised.

"Dr. Nover. This is like your Christmas! It's everything we wanted. And finally, we have a supplier of real prosthetics. You MUST call Issam immediately and thank him."

"Yes, Jawad. I shall." Curt pulled out his phone and dialed Issam.

"Issam," he answered.

"Assalamu Alaikum, Issam. This is Curt."

"Curt! Greetings! I presume you have heard the good news. God is good and has provided! Your items will be here in two days, and I would like to host a celebration. Everyone from near and far should see our new MRI. And they should see Akim with his new leg."

"Yes. It is impressive, but Akim's new leg will take time to fit properly and then he must undergo significant physical therapy on how to control and use the device. Putting this on and having him walk in front of a crowd immediately could embarrass him. As his doctor, I must say this is not acceptable." Curt was right, but Issam was in no mood to hear of it.

"Fine. But he will at least be presented with his leg. This is a very important event for our village. Do you understand?"

"Yes, Issam. I understand. And thank you. What you have provided will be of great value to your people. Shookran."

"Offwan, my friend! I must plan the party. It is in two days!"

Chapter Thirty-Four

Trouble in Paradise

Later that day, Curt returned home. Allison was in the kitchen, making dinner. "Hey, baby." Curt said as if he'd had a tough day.

"Hey," she replied. He halfhearted kissed her and her return effort was just as poor.

"You're not going to believe this," Curt said, "But Issam has secured hundreds of thousands of dollars in new medical equipment for Akjoujt, to include an MRI."

"That's interesting," Allison responded. "Who or where do you think that money came from?" Her question seemed innocent enough to him, but it was far guiltier than he realized.

"I have no idea, but I would imagine Nissassa and the mine. They are the ones that have funded most of the things. I'd like to know just as much as you, but it is not something I can ask."

"Why not? Asking questions is my job. I can teach you." Allison's journalist side was overshadowing her personal side. She wanted answers and felt Curt had them. She stopped cooking and approached him face to face.

"It's not me. It just all doesn't make much sense. This place doesn't warrant a humanitarian doctor. It can afford far more."

"Well, I don't know about Akjoujt, but I do know someone can afford much more."

"What are you getting at?" Curt was confused.

"Curt, I need you to be honest with me. Why are you here?"

"Uhhh... I told you why I was here."

"Yes, you said you were originally going to some place in Asia and then 'magically' were rerouted here."

"Yes, that's true." Curt was still confused.

"I spoke to my college friend at Doctors Without Borders. It appears a large donation was made with a singular request to have you shifted to Akjoujt. Do you know anything about that?"

"Huh? I've never heard that, nor do I believe it."

Allison paused and stared at Curt. She was trying to confirm if he was telling the truth. By all indications, he was, and she wanted to believe him. But something didn't make sense. "So, you don't have any idea why or how someone donated $2.5 million to Doctors Without Borders… but here you are. Excuse me if that seems hard to believe."

Curt was confused and didn't appreciate the insinuations. "What? $2.5 million dollars? What are you talking about?

"My friend who works for the organization confirmed it. To someone, you are worth $2.5 mil."

"I have no idea about that. You got to believe me!" He was getting upset.

"Look, I want to believe you. But this wouldn't be the first thing you hid from me. My concerns are not without merit."

That was it. Curt no longer wanted any part of this conversation. "Allison, I don't know about the donation, and at this point nor do I care. Yes, some things initially were not discussed openly but we are in a far different place now, compared to when we first met. You clearly don't believe me. A lack of belief is a lack of trust. If you can't trust me, why are you even here?"

His tone had finally set off Allison as well. "Actually, Curt, I don't know why I am here." With that, she got up and left.

Curt sat down in the kitchen, frustrated. He dropped his head into his hands…. Just then a small grease fire ignited in the kitchen. Curt quickly extinguished it, but the neglected dinner was destroyed. Curt found this a fitting way to end this day. He opened his laptop and checked his email. One of numerous responses popped up from Ms. Wanda. He read it and then replied.

1 Jul 2019

Ms. Wanda,
>Things here are OK. A few minor women problems, but hey, isn't that life? I wish there was a book on you types. Understanding women is an eternal mystery. By the way, this hospital seems to have more money than I originally presumed. Any chance you want to come work in North Africa!?"
>
>Take Care
>Curt

Chapter Thirty-Five

The Celebration

The morning sun splashed onto a festive vibe stretching across Akjoujt. Shop keepers and street vendors all had their best wares displayed. Locals dressed in their best attire. Makeshift banners hung across the streets and a few small platforms were erected so that entertainers could perform. In the middle of the town, a very nice platform was set up as well. The outside of the hospital was also well decorated. Issam was in rare form, running around, smiling, shaking hands with locals as well as those visiting from afar. "Good morning! Good morning! What a beautiful day!" To anyone around him for longer than three minutes, he sounded like a broken record.

Curt rolled out of bed, alone. He had no idea where Allison was, but he was sure he'd be able to patch things up. He opened his computer and saw Wanda had replied.

2 Jul 2019

Doc,
Just to be clear, she's right and you're wrong. You don't need no book. I'm sure of it. Go fix it. And I ain't ever working in Africa. You crazy!???
Keep doing good
Wanda

Damn….. Ms. Wanda was never wrong, he thought. Curt's priority today would be to get to the medical clinic and prepare for the day's events. He showered, put on fresh clothes and departed his apartment. On his way to the clinic, many in the village shook his hand. "Shookran! Shookran! (Thank you! Thank You!)," they screamed; assuming it was Curt who deserved the credit for the new medical equipment. He knew their thanks was misguided, but he didn't have the time or the heart to tell them differently.

Curt arrived at the clinic. Jawad, Kamil and the entire staff were scurrying around getting everything ready. The MRI machine nearly filled one of the old, empty rooms in the clinic. It was massive. "Good morning, Dr. Nover," Jawad said. "Look at this. It is beautiful! Should we start seeking out patients and schedule them in the coming days for screenings?"

Again, Curt didn't have the heart to burst Jawad's bubble. The truth is that it would take days to calibrate the machine – working with the vender. Additionally, once the imaging was calibrated, the clinic would need to find a radiologist who could read and interpret the images. This problem was one Curt had seen over and over again in many deployed locations. An 'item' was purchased to address a problem, but the asset was only one part of a capability system. The MRI hardware was a step forward but would be of little value without the associated maintenance, training, and professionals.

"Yes, Jawad. Let's start looking out to see what patients may need this service. Additionally, can you please contact the vendor and work to get the machine calibrated as well as some assemblance of basic training for our staff?"

Jawad realized from Curt's comments there was far more to do before patients could be examined and was grateful to have such a 'strategic thinker' in his midst. "Yes, sir!" Jawad grabbed the MRI paperwork and immediately went to call the manufacturer.

"Dr. Nover, you don't seem happy about today?" Kamil said with a puzzled look.

"Good morning, Kamil. I am happy. I just had a tough night. How are the plans for today?"

"Sir, they are all set. We will have our open house from 9AM to 11:30AM. At noon, Issam will speak in the middle of Akjoujt. He has asked if you will be there. Akim's new prosthetic device arrived, and he would like to have you present it. After this, there will be food, drinks and entertainment for all. It will be a great day."

"Thanks, Kamil. I will go to my office and create a speech for the event. Please keep welcoming locals into the clinic and show them around. If nothing else, perhaps we can generate more interest in the clinic and convince some more females to come forward and seek needed medical help."

"Yes, Doctor. Good luck with writing your speech. I am sure you will do great." Kamil turned around and walked towards the crowd of folks in the clinic. Curt went to his office.

At 1130Hrs, the hospital closed up and Curt went to Issam's office. As he passed the center stage, a group of school kids dressed in very old traditional garb attempted to sing and dance in unison. The crowd of parents, aunts, uncles and grandparents clapped as if it was a Broadway performance. It was far from perfect, but Curt smiled. Wellness, he thought to himself, is such an important aspect to overall health. He was happy for the people of Akjoujt. A gift-wrapped box laid on Issam's sofa. If Curt didn't know what it was, the box could have easily passed for flowers. "Good morning, Issam. How are you?"

"Curt! I am great! How are you?! Are you ready for our event?"

"Yes. As ready as I'll ever be." In truth, Curt didn't want to be in the limelight. He was partly an introvert, and crowds and public festivities were something his SEAL time taught him to avoid. Nothing about this event was appealing.

"Great. Let's discuss our speeches and how the flow of the event will go." The door to Issam's office closed shut.

****

Around half hour prior to Curt visiting Issam, a group of nomads had wondered into Akjoujt. They were strangers just like many of the other strangers who'd come to visit Akjoujt for the big festival. They traveled with a donkey and a cart. In the cart were some burlap bags and blankets. Nothing out of the ordinary. As the men got closer to town, they turned down an alley, behind Mohammed's hotel. It was one of the taller buildings in Akjoujt at three stories. While some of the nomads stood guard, one grabbed a blanket that was clearly concealing something. He darted up the side of the building and within seconds was on the roof. A small speaker in the ear of the nomad holding the donkey still cracked to life, "Longbow 23 in place." The nomads said nothing to each other and began to slowly walk back out into the public. The donkey and cart would remain, tied up in the ally. Infill was complete.

As the hour of noon approached, Issam and Curt waited for Akim. He, nor his family were anywhere to be found. "Where is Akim?!" Issam shouted at his staff. They were all on different phones and talking to messengers trying to find him.

"I am sure he will be here," Curt reassured Issam. "Stressing yourself out will do no good."

On the roof of Mohammed's hotel, Longbow held up binoculars out towards the mine. Just as planned, a small truck was moving slowly towards Akjoujt. The driver of that vehicle would be his target.

Finally, Akim arrived with his family. He was on crutches and was quite good at maneuvering with them. Issam stated there was no time for an informal meeting and the speeches MUST begin immediately. A member of Issam's staff ran out onto the stage. The school children on their third rendition of a local tribal song were scurried off the stage and the music stopped. Another staff member grabbed the mic in front of the crowd and began to introduce the stage party. And with that, Issam, Akim, Curt and an interpreter took the stage. The streets of Akjoujt were packed and the applause was impressive. Curt nor Issam had ever seen so many people in the town.

Issam spoke fast in Arabic and the interpreter whispered into Curt's ear, trying his best to translate. Curt was not really paying attention. His eyes scanned the crowd slowly. He saw Anbar and smiled. Standing next to each other, Kamil and Jawad were also among the crowd. Kamil made eye contact. Kamil waived with a sense of beaming pride. Curt smiled and nodded back. Also in the crowd, he finally saw Allison. At this point, he had lost all interest in the translation. He stared at her. She too stared at him. Ms. Wanda was right. He mouthed the words, "I'm sorry," to her. She raised her arms and held her fingers in the shape of a heart over her chest.

Curt smiled. She then started clapping, along with the rest of the crowd. The interpreter nudged him. "Doctor! It's your turn! They introduced you." Curt had missed his cue. The clapping turned to a bit of chuckling as Curt jumped out of his chair. He waved and slowly walked to the podium.

"A Salam Alekum. Welcome all the people of Akjoujt and visitors. Today is a great day for this region." Curt paused and allowed the interpreter to speak. His eyes again scanning the crowd. "As many of you know, we have received wonderful new medical equipment to include a new leg for Akim." The translator spoke and the crowd applauded. Akim's eyes lit up as he smiled. While not part of the plan, Issam couldn't help himself. He opened the box and held up the leg as if it were a victory trophy. The crowd applauded loudly. Issam handed the leg to Akim. He took it and held it as if he was given a new soccer ball. The applause died down and Curt continued. "Yes, congratulations, Akim. I hope to see you in the clinic tomorrow so we can fit your new leg properly and provide you the appropriate physical therapy to ensure you use it correctly." Akim shook his head up and down during the translation.

"As a medical professional, my hope is to serve the community and make a difference. While I am happy for Akim, I truly hope that in the future, the needs of all people in and around Akjoujt can be addressed. It's my hope that both men and women of all ages receive the care they deserve." The translator relayed his message. The crowd grew a bit more silent. They accepted his comment given he was western, but Curt had touched on the sensitive topic of women. It was clear, their appetite for further discussion on this topic was limited. Curt shifted his speech. "It is also my hope that the need for prosthetics related to the Inju and Satri conflict can become a part of Akjoujt's history." Curt's speech was political, and he watched closely to observe the crowd's reaction. On this narrative, the locals all could cheer. They'd lost too many brothers, uncles, fathers and grandfathers. The applause wasn't overpowering, but strong enough to let Curt know his shift from the topic of women was welcomed. Curt watched the crowd clap. All but one. The individual was not paying attention and given much of Curt's former training, this was a sign. Something wasn't right.

****

On an Akjoujt roof, Longbow 23 had set up his rifle. This time he would be shooting an SSG 69 from the Austrian company 'Steyr Arms.' Not Longbow 23's favorite weapon, but part of this overall mission included ditching the sniper weapon given the difficulty of getting it out of Tehran. Using a non-U.S. weapon would add just one more layer between the truth and the fabricated story. Through a high-powered binocular set, Longbow 23 watched a distance vehicle approach. Holding a remote in his hand, he pressed the button as the car passed a road sign – another distance marker for Longbow. The button activated the in ground EMP device, disabling the truck as it drove over the pressure plate. The driver side door swung open and out stepped Kameel. Kameel circled the vehicle, looking for obvious signs of malfunction. Finding none, he opened the hood. The problem was a mystery to him. On the street below the applause and the speeches didn't faze Longbow 23. He watched the target coolly through his scope. His earpiece cracked to live, "Longbow 23, Darkstar. Confirm your target."

"Darkstar, yellow Isuzu. One lone pax (military abbreviation for passenger). Wearing a white man dress and currently attempting a cell phone call."

"Longbow 23. Affirm. Cleared, headshot. Darkstar."

"Longbow 23." It was all he needed to say.

Curt continued to speak. His eyes moved around the crowd but kept circling back to Allison and the disinterested man. A loud crack ripped through the air. There was no mistake. It was a gun shot. Longbow 23 recenter the scope's reticle and watched. Kameel's head burst open, and he fell to the ground. Longbow 23 stood up and quickly moved to get off the roof.

Curt ducked, then locked eyes on Allison. She was scared and the crowd began to scatter and panic. He looked around for the victim; however, in this crowd, there was no finding the victim until the streets were cleared. Oddly, no one was screaming in pain as if he'd been hit. *'Were they killed immediately? Where did the shot come from?'* Curt had no answers. Akim next to Curt had dug his hands into Curt's leg and froze. Akim was in shock. Curt lunged from the stage taking Akim under his arm like a football. He raced through the crowd towards Allison.

One of the visiting nomads reached under his robe. He popped a smoke canister and then set off a string of fireworks mimicking the sound of further gunfire. Approximately 30 meters away, another member of the nomad clan rolled out three 'flash bangs' creating loud explosions. Just as predicted, the crowds fled these noises. Their efforts were corralling the crowd much in the way a shepherd herds sheep. Curt, however, gave little attention to the commotion, he must get to Allison. As Curt looked for her and scanned the crowd, he saw three other men advancing into the crowd versus running with them and appeared to be screaming. Curt was right. Each was calling out a feminine name acting as if they were also looking for someone. Curt finally found Allison, who was now OK. She kissed him and took Akim's hand. "Baby! Are you OK?"

"Yeah. I'm fine. I'll take Akim. Go get that fucker." Allison was angry.

Curt looked up. Before he could get the shooter, he wanted to ensure everyone was safe. He too 'swam upstream' into the crowd. He heard a Nomad say the name 'Ayda' and now he too screamed the name "Ayda." The nomad, hearing another call out Ayda, looked puzzled at Curt. Unbeknownst to Curt, the nomad was not really a nomad and there was no Ayda. Again, Curt was going to screw up the live fire training event.

Three of the men had moved through the crowd and converged on where the smoke and fireworks were set off. That location had a small alley and a clear way out of town. A small SUV waited for Longbow 23 and the others. Curt was 30 meters from the nomads who were converging on each other. The nomads huddled.

"Fucking Nover again!" Curt approached and he knew something wasn't right with this group. They had stopped calling out for people.

One of the nomads transmitted into the radio, "We need to eliminate him."

Smitty cut in onto the radio, "Negative! You can incapacitate him. That's it! Do you copy?" Clearly Smitty was observing the events from somewhere.

One of the men turned quickly at Curt with a flowerpot in hand. He threw it at Curt. Curt's apprehensions about these men were validated. His ability to dodge the flowerpot however was not. It hit him square in the chest and he fell back. The men ran to the truck and began piling in. Curt recovered and ran to the truck; arriving before it could depart. One of the men lifted a semi-automatic gun from under his robe, flashed it at Curt and screamed, "Back the fuck off, Nover!" It was Rudy.

Curt froze. Perfect English. Their eyes remained locked as the truck drove away.

What had just happened, he thought?

Chapter Thirty-Six

Decisions Must Be Made

The truck sped towards the mine via a service road on the back side of the mine's embankment, hidden from Akjoujt. A gate opened and closed with an efficiency that ensured the truck did not have to slow. Once inside, the truck quickly came to a halt, throwing dust into the air. The occupants jumped out. From one of the office buildings, Smitty emerged to meet them.

"Smitty... I swear, I'm gonna kill that fucker."

"Rudy. Shut up. You're still pissed he broke your leg. Everything is fine. The training mission was a success. Congrats. We will be beaming the training video to our customer in about an hour to demonstrate capability."

Unbeknownst to Smitty, Jerry had also emerged from the building. "Rudy is right. Nover was a problem. I'm sorry to say, this experiment with him has run its course. It's not working out. Rudy, take the team inside to debrief. Smitty, stay here with me."

Rudy led the team inside. The entire time he stared at Smitty. Eventually, only Jerry and Smitty remained.

"Smitty, I'm sorry. Nover has to go. Because of your friendship with him, I am going to let you come up with how that happens."

"Jerry, I won't do that. You and I both know, he's not like his predecessor. He's one of us. He's eaten the same dirt. Suffered the same pains. Experienced the same losses."

"He's one of 'you.' I am not Special Ops."

"Jerry, please. There is another way. What if we fully expose him to the operation and bring him in?"

Jerry's jaw just hung open... "Have you lost your mind?"

"No. Hear me out. I signed up for this as did my bros because we bought your concept. As distasteful as some may find our operation, it is the most realistic way to conduct live training. The experience our operators get before heading out on missions is second to none, and it has saved many of their lives. Nover's existence here brings a level of ethical balance to our mission. I know I can make Nover see that."

"You honestly believe that?"

"Yes, with your help." It was Smitty's only other option.

"OK. Let's see if we can make Dr. Nover see wrong from right."

They both walked into the Nissassa complex. Smitty was right. Aside from Nover's interference, the mission was a success and the team had proved they could infill and exfill a shooter in a dense crowd. The customer would be pleased.

Chapter Thirty-Seven

The Best Laid Plans

Curt was finishing the last few stitches on a villager injured during the chaos. There were some other sprains and twists but luckily Curt treated no gunshot wounds. Between patients, Curt called Allison. She and Akim were fine. Allison walked Akim to his house and would be back at their apartment later. Curt offered to meet her at Anbar in two hours as a bit of a makeup date. She welcomed the idea.

The clinic door opened, and another patient was slowly rolled in on a gurney. There was no rush and the sheet over the entire body explained the nonchalant nature. Curt stopped the gurney and lifted the sheet. It was Kameel. Both his eyes were frozen wide open. A single gunshot wound had entered through the right cheekbone. It was a fairly large caliber entry wound. However, the exit wound was a mess, and a large section of his rear skull was missing. There was nothing to be done.

Some of the staff continued tending to those with minor injuries. Curt stood there. He missed Allison and wanted time to prepare for their date. There were no more patients that required a doctor's skill set. Fidgety, Curt could not wait to get to Anbar, see her, and decompress from the day. He raced home, changed into workout clothes. He knocked out his pushups and sit ups, then looked at his watch. There was just enough time to get in a run. He opened the door and flew out into the street. His pace was fast, and his mood was good.

Curt ran out of the town, down the road with the mine far off in the distance. His headsets playing some music but his mind pondering the coming evening. He was unaware of the traffic on the road, he was unaware that he just passed

Kameel's disabled vehicle. On all his previous runs, there was very little traffic, and many broken down vehicles. Why would today be different?

Curt looked at his watch. Time to turn around. He began running back to town. A pickup truck in the distance observed him turn around. As he ran back towards town, the truck began to roll and approach him from behind. Three men were in the truck bed. Curt never saw them coming.

Once the truck was abeam Curt, two men jumped from the bed, tackling him. The truck continued forward approximately 15 meters and stopped. The driver scanned the road ahead for any other traffic. The third man in the truck started walking towards Curt who was slowly being subdued.

"Curt, stop fighting." The voice was Smitty.

Curt looked up and saw him. "Smitty, what the fuck!? I was looking forward to seeing you, but this is a bit over the top. Call off your goons, please."

"I'm sorry. I can't. I promise you all this will make sense, but you need to come with us. You also need to put this over your head." Smitty was holding a small sack. Clearly Curt was not to see where they were going.

"Sorry, buddy, no can do. I have plans tonight. How about tomorrow?" And with that Curt broke free of those restraining him. He fought relentlessly, kicking one of the goons so hard it nearly knocked him unconscious. As Curt's foot struck his chest, the assailant tried to grab Curt's foot and mitigate the blow. He did little other than to catch Curt's shoe as it struck him in the chest. As Curt's foot retracted, the shoe remained in the goon's chest. Curt turned to face the second attacker, who began wrestling Curt in close combat. With one shoe, Curt kept fighting and although outnumbered, was gaining an upper hand. Then, Smitty closed in on the fighting. In an extremely graceful move, Smitty withdrew a syringe, stabbed Curt, injected the serum, and withdrew the needle. Curt knew he'd been stuck but was unsure what the needle contained. Within seconds, he knew it was a sedative. "Smitty!" He screamed as his legs grew week. "No! Allison!!" Curt fell to the ground. Smitty and one of the assailants lifted Curt's limp body into the truck. They then, helped their groggy comrade up from the ground. Once all were in the truck, they drove towards the mine.

****

Allison sat at Anbar. She dialed Curt's phone numerous times. There was no answer. She also kept looking at her phone. There were no missed calls or messages. She walked back to the apartment. Curt wasn't coming. There must be an explanation, she thought. Allison fixed dinner and tried to call Curt's phone one more time. She heard his ringer! It was coming from the sofa. His phone was in the apartment, but Curt was nowhere to be found. Strange......

Chapter Thirty-Eight

The Recruitment

Curt slowly began to awake. He was seated with his hands and feet restrained in front of the Nissassa Ops Center conference table. Jerry and Smitty were the only other two in the room. At first, everything was blurry, but soon, everything was clear.

"Smitty. What on earth are you doing? Fucking untie me!"

"Curt. I am really sorry about all this, but it's for your own good, our own good and frankly for the nation's own good."

"What are you talking about?"

Jerry interrupted, "Nissassa is what he's talking about, Dr. Nover, it was at the recommendation of Mr. Smith here that we bring you in to be the local humanitarian doctor in Akjoujt. You see, to us, Akjoujt and her residents are very important to Nissassa."

Curt replied. "Let me guess... did that cost you $2.5 million?

Jerry ignored Curt and continued. "As you perhaps have come to suspect, our operation here has little to do with mining. I will make this short. That business is a front for our actual operation which is top off special forces live range training."

To Curt, the pieces were falling into place.

"After an extensive search for a realistic training environment, our company bought the mine. We then began negotiating with the leaders of the Satri and Inju warring factions. We gave them what they wanted – a bit of money and power. They, along with Issam, agreed to help Nissassa perform live fire training operations as proof of concept and top off training in preparation for near time real world operations that are extremely unique."

Curt could take being quiet no longer. "So, you train Elite Special Forces here?"

Jerry chuckled. "Absolutely not. The U.S. Defense Department would never be able to acquire funding for such a training mission. Nor would the U.S. Military be able to execute the types of missions our company provides. We recruit prior service Special Forces who are looking to make some substantial money from employing some of their extremely unique skillsets."

"So, you train mercenaries." Curt said bluntly.

"No, Curt. You're not listening. We train exceptionally skilled mercenaries, grab and go teams and assassins. All who perform missions the U.S. Government could never even consider due to political or other sensitivities. Many of them are former Elite Special Forces, mostly from the U.S. or Western Nations. Should any of our teams ever be captured or killed, there are layers of insulation between our employees and the U.S. That said, we make the world a safer place. Especially for every American that walks the face of the earth."

"Safer for Americans? Really?"

"Yes, Curt. When you hear of high-level terrorist leaders or financiers killed in places like the Saudi Peninsula, or you hear of an American citizen being rescued in inaccessible lands, who do you think does that work? In a good number of cases, when Western nations are unwilling to commit Special Forces, there are few options left other than Nissassa. So, not only does Nissassa rid the world of bad actors and save our citizens, but it also sets conditions to inhibit other bad actors out of fear."

"Yes, but what you do is illegal." Curt was not impressed.

"Illegal.... That word is not as black and white as it may appear in a realistic world. Perhaps what we do is illegal by your definition, but I would suggest the meaning of that word from an international security perspective has lost much of its gravitas. Can you show me the U.S. Congressional Declaration of War for the Afghanistan conflict? Or Iraq? According to 'the law' such a Declaration should have existed for the past decade. Sure, Congress created a makeshift bill that bypassed this requirement, only to diminish and blur the actual law. On the other side of the coin, I can show you the Budapest Memorandum of 1994, a legally binding treaty between the US, Ukraine and Russia that clearly states all would recognize Ukrainian borders forever. As of 2014, Russia has taken over Crimea, Ukraine and facilitated an ongoing war in a region of Ukraine called the Donbas. So, how's that working out for Ukraine? Frankly, in today's world, those that scream 'Illegal' often use it as a last resort from a position of weakness with no intent to hold the perceived violator accountable."

"OK. Great. So, you have your little operation. I get it, but I don't have to like it. That said. Why me? Why am I here?"

Jerry calmly continued. "Curt. You are of more help than you know. First, you provide exceptional medical care to the community which helps advance the Nissassa's local image. Second, and most importantly, you keep our target set viable."

"Excuse me?"

"Yes. It's maybe a bit distasteful to some, but if Nissassa is to perform training on a live range, we use live ammunition. That means we must, on occasion, strike targets. In a place like Akjoujt with a small population, we needed a way to facilitate target regeneration."

"So, you were the ones who shot Akim?"

"Yes."

"And the Satri commander Kameel?"

"Yes."

"Well, I don't know what kind of miracles you think I can work, but Kameel's entire aft skull was detached from his head. A bit challenging even for the best doctors to 'regenerate' that target."

"Kameel unfortunately was becoming a problem that had to be eliminated. He began asking for too much money and was threatening to expose our mission. The good news is that his death will increase the friction between the Satri and Inju factions which our company desperately needs. More missions and more customers are seeking out our services every week. In fact, I'll let you in on a secret. Kameel's death was not in vain. That mission was a final rehearsal for an assassination of the Iranian Ayatollah. Again, making the world a safer place. We do good work here, Curt. I hope you see that."

"So, If I understand correctly. Your entire effort to bring me here and share this is to convince me to play along. Right?"

Jerry turned serious. "I need not convince you of anything. You have a choice. You can support our mission or not. Should you choose the later, I am hopeful we can craft another beautiful suicide note like the one we generated for your predecessor." And with that, Jerry got up. "Again, the choice is yours." Jerry walked away, leaving Smitty and Curt.

"Never ever, Smitty. Never would I have imagined you involved in something like this."

"Not true, buddy. You and I both know my biggest frustration was training for a mission only to have it turned off due to political sensitives, excessive risk, or some other bullshit. Here, if the training is successful, the mission is a go. And frankly the money has two more zeros at the end of what we made during active duty."

"So, it's money?"

"No, Nover. I explained it. The money is a bonus. Did you read the headline a few months ago? About Shakeel Afridi?"

Curt knew the name. Nearly every Special Forces member did. Curt also wondered how on earth the U.S. would risk a Special Forces Operation into Pakistan again. Getting Bin Laden was one thing, going after Dr. Afridi was another.

Smitty continued, "Yes. That was us. And you know as well as I do that man should have been living a hero's life for the past decade."

Curt paused. What Smitty said made sense... but... "Smitty. You're intentionally injuring and maiming innocent people here in Akjoujt. How is that right?"

"Innocent people? Are we? The way I see it, if Nissassa never came to Akjoujt, Satri and Inju warriors would be fighting and killing each other in far greater numbers. And the town would have nowhere near the medical staff available to them as the one that exists today."

"Fair, but what would have happened if the Inju and Satris had stopped fighting and found peace. Then all your exploits are in excess of the maiming and death they would have experienced."

Smitty realized Curt had a point. No one could predict the future. "You mean like the Sunni and Shia?" Smitty's reference to the two conflicting factions of Islam that to this day feud over interpretation of the religion.

"Smitty, look me in the eye and tell me you are truly OK with all this."

He couldn't. The demons of his Pakistan mission still haunted him. He also knew he couldn't remain silent. "Nover, I am good with this training, and that is my part." This too was not completely true. Smitty became unnerved. "This discussion is over." Smitty called for the guards. "Take Dr. Nover to his room."

"My room? You're not letting me go?"

"Curt, if you don't agree to help us. You won't be walking out of here alive. Jerry is not fucking around. In his mind, you've disrupted two of our training events. There won't be a third." Smitty turned and walked away. The guards untied Curt, picked him up, led him down some extremely sterile hallways then into a black 4x6ft room. It had a small light over the door frame and an extremely thick door. A pillow and blanket lay on the cold cement floor. In the corner was an old Folgers coffee can for his 'relief.' This would be his home for the night, far from the loving arms of Allison. Allison, he thought. Curious if she was angry that he stood her up.

Chapter Thirty-Nine

The Search

The next morning, Allison went straight to the hospital, hoping she'd find Curt. As she waited, Jawad and Kamil both arrived and approached her.

"Jawad, Kamil, have you seen or heard from Curt in the past 12 hours?"

"No, ma'am. But that is not special. We never hear from Curt at night. Is he missing?"

"I don't know. He didn't come home last night but left his cell phone there." Allison's voice did not hide her concern.

Kamil tried to offer reassurance. "You are welcome to wait for him to come into work today. I am sure he will be here. He has never missed a day."

"Thanks, Kamil. I think I'd like to go see Issam. Can either of you call me if he shows up?"

Both Kamil and Jawad responded, "Yes, ma'am."

Allison departed and went straight to Issam's office. She did not have an appointment, but to be clear, Issam was never really that busy. "Allison! Good morning! Are you OK after yesterday's incident? Tragic someone had to destroy our big day and even more upsetting about Kameel. He was a good man."

"Hello, Issam. Yes, I am fine. Thanks for asking. And I agree about yesterday. Look, the reason I am here is I can't find Curt. He did not return to his apartment last night and he has not reported to work today."

"This is strange. I have not seen him. Do you think he was somehow involved in the incident yesterday?"

"What do you mean 'involved' in the incident?"

"I don't know, but we have not caught the cowards yet who did this horrible act. We are looking very hard. Justice will be done! Perhaps Curt was the target? Perhaps Curt was a participant? Perhaps Curt went after them? There are many possibilities to describe how Dr. Nover may have been involved."

"Issam, I think we both know Curt would never be a supporter of open violence in a heavily packed town center. And I don't believe he was the target because after the shots, he was fine. The last thing I said to him was to go after them, which he did. But later, he was at the hospital, caring for people, so I know he was safe."

"Allison, I see you are worried. I will have my security look into this immediately and if I learn of anything, I will contact you."

"Thank you, Issam. I appreciate it."

"You are welcome. Now, I must tend to other business. If you will excuse me." Issam motioned to the door. Allison obliged and departed. Once out of the area, Issam picked up his phone and dialed Jerry.

"Jerry, good morning. It is Issam."

"Issam! Great to hear from you and thank you for yesterday's event. It worked out exceptionally well."

"You are very welcome, and I am happy it was a success. I am disappointed about Kameel. We agreed that killing would be limited."

"Yes, Issam. We did agree to this. But as you know, Kameel was pushing to get more money and threatening to expose our operation. Neither of these are good for us…. And by that, I mean 'All of us.' Would you like to have given him more of your pay?"

"No. Of course not." Issam's tone changed quickly when he recalled that Kameel sought more pay. "Kameel never knew when to keep quiet. This is unfortunate, but I agree it must have been done. Jerry, I am calling to ask you if you know what happened to Dr. Nover. He is not at work and hasn't been home for a day."

Jerry remained silent for a bit. He didn't think he would be fielding this call so quickly. "Issam, I do not know about Dr. Nover, but I will ask around." Issam was street smart and suspected Jerry wasn't being completely open.

"OK, Jerry. I thank you for this." While Jerry was neck deep into this operation, he also knew he was slithering with snakes that he could only trust so far. Jerry wasn't being honest. "I too will keep looking and let you know."

"OK, thanks, Issam. I appreciate that. I must go. We have work to do." Jerry said his goodbyes and hung up the phone.

Issam was conflicted. Should he investigate or not? While uneasy, he wanted to know what was going on, and as the village elder of Akjoujt, he felt it his right. Issam was involved with Nissassa, but he also felt a responsibility to his people. Issam summoned his driver, and they began to drive around town.

As they drove, nothing seemed out of place. The makeshift stages were being taken down along with the celebratory banners. Locals were talking in the streets blaming both the Inju and the Satri for yesterday's violence. Issam had already started the narrative that he did not know which faction it was, but he would immediately meet with both leaders separately to learn the truth – which, of course, he had no intent of actually doing. Nothing was out of place. Issam decided to leave the town and drive towards the mine. He passed Kameel's disabled and abandoned vehicle. A bit further up the road, his driver pointed to a single shoe sitting on the embankment. They stopped. Around the shoe, the sand has been recently disrupted. Issam realized a struggle had occurred here. Identifying the owner of the shoe would not be difficult. Few Akjoujtis wore anything but sandals. If they did wear gym shoes, they were cheap and only from a few local brands. If this wasn't Curt's shoe, it was another westerner… and Issam could count all the Westerners outside the mining operation he knew on one hand. Issam kept the shoe and returned to the vehicle; informing his driver to return to Akjoujt.

Issam picked up the phone and placed another call. "Abdul. A Salam Alekim." He spoke in Arabic. Translated, he said, "I am calling to inquire if you know anything about the disappearance of Dr. Nover."

Abdul Salam, the leader of the Injus, responded in Arabic, "I know of nothing." It was clear to Issam Abdul was telling the truth. He quickly said, "Thank you," and ended the call. He then placed another call. "Qudamah, I am calling to inquire if you know anything about the disappearance of Dr. Nover."

"No, I know nothing of your doctor, but can you tell me why I have a dead commander in my unit?" Qudamah was angry about Kameel's death as it was clearly not the arrangement. Issam explained the situation to Qudamah just as it was explained to him. It ended with a question if Qudamah wished to share any of his profits with Kameel. Qudamah responded to Issam just the way Issam had to Jerry. The life of every Satri warrior was important. The money in his pocket was more important. The issue of Kameel was closed. Curt, however, was another story.

Upon return to Akjoujt, Issam saw Allison walking through the bazar. He ordered his driver to stop. "Allison!" He shouted. "Please come here."

She approached his vehicle. "Issam. Did you find him!?"

"No, Allison, I did not. By the sounds of it, you as well have not found him. May I ask you; do you know what kind of shoes Curt wore?"

"Yes. In the hospital, all he wore were Crocs - a kind of rubber sandal. When out from the hospital he wore some kind of 'Ghost' tennis shoe. I only know this because he swears they are the best for his feet. Why would you ask this?"

"My security team asked as they would like to know the tread of shoes he would likely wear. Did he wear any other work shoe?"

"Those are the only two sets of shoes I've seen him in here, but I will look in the closet when I get home."

"Thank you. I shall pass this info to my security team."

They said their goodbyes and Issam's driver slowly pulled away. Issam pulled out the shoe. The brand was Brooks, and the make was "Ghost." The shoe was Curt's. Issam was on the trail to finding the answers. He placed one last call. "Jerry, this is Issam. You asked me to call you if I learned of anything."

Jerry responded, "Yes. Please share with me what you know."

Issam measured his delivery and was keen to how Jerry would respond. "Well, it seems he may have been kidnapped. Someone found his shoe on the road to the mine, and they said there were signs of a struggle."

Jerry showed little concern and tried to flip the script. "Damn it, Issam. Why would the Injus or Satris kidnap him!? We pay you good money to keep order in this area."

"Yes, Jerry. I agree. I will get to the bottom of it." Issam knew neither the Satri nor Injus had Curt. And as this mystery unraveled, he was fairly certain he knew who did.

Chapter Forty

The Great Escape

Curt sat on the cell floor attempting to process what he'd learned. In an effort to balance out the violence he committed in combat; he pursued a medical degree to heal. Was it all for nothing? For months, he was 'patching up' targets. The thought made his stomach churn. Instinctively, Curt's training and former life began to kick in.... There was time to process all of this later. Now, he needed to focus on escape. He looked at his watch. It read 0125Hrs. Earlier when he entered the cell, Curt made a mental note as to the door thickness. It was clearly built to contain. He did not have the time or energy to get through that door. Curt ran his hands against the side walls and realized immediately, they were either cinder block or cement. Again, this was not going to be easy to escape. He looked up to consider the ceiling. It was too far. Disappointed, he gently knocked his head against the back wall. It made a hollow 'thump,' as in the sound of drywall. *'It couldn't be? Drywall for a prison wall?'* He did it again. 'Thump.' Curt turned and knocked gently with his hand along the wall. It was in fact drywall and clearly the studs were roughly a foot and a half apart.

Curt began to scrap where the wall adjoined the floor. He progressed relatively quick. Soon, the hole was the size of his head and drywall dust covered the floor. Curt looked into the hole he'd just created. His excitement quickly vanished. The drywall appeared to be a false wall just four inches in front of another cement wall. This would not likely be his escape. Again... dejected. He thought to himself, *'There must be a way.... THINK Nover! Figure it out. Why build a false wall in front of a cinderblock wall? To run conduit? Through a holding cell?'* Puzzled, and with few other options, Curt continued to expand the hole, hoping it would offer a way out.

The lock on the door rattled. Someone was soon to enter. Curt put his back over the hole, covered himself and the white gypsum dust with the blanket. He was certain he'd get caught; it was a pathetic concealment effort. The door swung open. It was Smitty.

"Hey," Smitty said.

Curt replied with the same…. "Hey."

"You doing OK?" Smitty inquired. He really didn't know what to say.

"Smitty, cut the shit. Tell me what you want? I'm stuck in a one-man makeshift cell, haven't eaten since lunch, can't get sleep and now you want to have a small talk chat?"

"You're right. Sorry. Curt, I need you to understand. You don't have a choice in this. Nissassa is bigger than you realize. It may not be the mob, but it's perhaps as close as one can come. I know you didn't ask to be involved, but now you are. There is really only one way out of this relationship, and I don't want to see that happen to you."

"Well, I appreciate your concern, but come on! This isn't you! Why are you involved in this? I know you! Or at least I thought I knew you."

"Curt, we have been apart a long time. You don't know what's gone on in my life and now is not the time for me to explain my actions. It is what it is. I can't change that. I just ask that you do not make me, or my team members do something I know I won't be able to stomach."

Curt had learned all he needed to know. He also knew the longer Smitty remained in the cell, the more likely his efforts would be exposed. This was not the time or the place to continue the discussion. "Smitty, fair enough. It's late and I haven't eaten. Is there any chance I could get some food and perhaps water?"

Those words were welcome news to Smitty. Knowing that Curt was no longer argumentative and was requesting assistance from his captors….. these were very positive signs.

"Yes, of course. I'll have the guard bring something to you. Can we continue discussing this in the morning?"

"Sure. I'd like that." Curt replied, with no intention of being there.

Smitty left, the door made a loud thud and the lock rattled shut. Curt could hear Smitty give instructions to the guard to fetch food and water. The door would open again soon, and Curt needed to hatch a plan. He began feverishly digging harder into the drywall, making the hole roughly 1.5ft wide by 2ft tall, with larger pieces loosely placed back to cover the hole. He may not be Houdini, but this hole was going to serve a critical piece in his newly devised escape plan.

The lock again rattled, the guard announced himself and he entered the room. As the door swung open, the guard's eyes immediately fixated on the hole and gypsum dust on the floor. There was no prisoner. The guard ran in, pulling pieces from the hole to follow the detainee on his escape route. As he pulled the first piece away, he puzzled at seeing the second wall only four inches deep. It was the last thing he'd contemplate for a while. Curt had pinned himself against the ceiling given the walls were only 4ft apart. Drawn to the hole, the guard never noticed Curt above him. Curt dropped from the ceiling, jutting his elbow into the back of the guard's skull. He immediately fell unconscious. Curt closed the door, inventoried the guard's belongings, salvaging the ID card, radio, 9mm Glock and holster. He also stripped the guard to his underwear and dressed himself in the uniform. All the while, he downed the food brought by the now sleeping guard. No sense in letting it go to waste.

Curt opened the door, carrying the food tray. He proceeded slowly, keeping his head down as if looking at the tray. Curt in actuality was not looking aimlessly at the tray. He was looking directly into the water glass he'd placed in the forward center of the tray, using it as a rudimentary mirror, attempting to 'see' who or what around him without making eye contact. Curt continued to the end of the hall which opened up to the Ops Center where he'd sat during 'discussions' with Jerry and Smitty. A few workers in the area were looking up at the full motion video screens; fixated on watching Unmanned Aerial Vehicles (UAV)s flying in some other land. One screen showed a vehicle being tracked and another held firmly centered on a building that had individuals entering and exiting. The workers paid little attention to Curt, as they were memorized by watching what the intel community informally refers to as "Predator Porn" given the hypnotic effect the video has. Curt continued through the Ops center and followed a hallway that appeared to lead out of the building. Every fiber of his body wanted to accelerate and run, but he knew he MUST maintain the pace of a security guard on the night shift.... Which meant SLOW. He kept breathing deeply... concentrating on every step.

Curt approached the door. The good news of his slow pace meant he could evaluate how to get through. He scanned the door. There was no buzzer, no button; however, there was a magnetic card swipe with a numeric keypad. Curt prayed it would just be as simple as pushing the door open. No such luck. He pushed and learned the door was locked. As calmly as he could, Curt grabbed the guard's ID card and swiped it in the magnetic scanner, again praying the door would open. As he swiped, a keypad lit up, and the door remained locked. Curt quickly looked at the ID card looking for a pin. There was none. Curt tried four random numbers. It didn't work. After failing to open the door, Curt slowly bent down and placed the tray on the ground. He then moved to tie his shoe, which was already tied, in an effort to buy time. He faked the entire effort, hoping to buy time. What could the guard's pin be? Frankly he had no clue and couldn't stay bent down forever. He picked back up his tray and again prepared to swipe, hoping for a miracle.

Just then, the door swung into him, and he barely managed to balance the tray in his other hand. A single man continued through the door into the building and noticed he'd nearly upended the food tray. "Sorry, buddy! You OK?"

Curt quickly replied. "Yeah, yeah. It was a good glove save. Thanks." Curt walked through the door, hoping it was the end of the discussion. It was. Curt was now outside. The perimeter fence had few visible guards, but closed-circuit TV (CCTV) cameras as well as EO and IR sensors blanket the fence line. The chances of him departing Nissassa undetected was nearly zero.

    Standing still would do Curt no favors, so he continued walking. This time, he moved towards the vehicle yard, filled with trucks, SUVs, and other large 'mining' vehicles. Curt slowly entered one of the smaller trucks, the very ones he'd seen out in town. Once inside, he saw no keys, not that such an issue would stop him. Curt could easily hotwire the vehicle. On the visor was a singular garage door opener. There was only one door such a device would open. Watching the main gate, Curt pressed the button. Slowly, the door lurched to life. Curt quickly pressed the button again and the door stopped. He had an escape plan. Now, to start the truck. Curt opened the door again, looking for a large rock, something the grounds of a mine offered in plenty. Grabbing a hand sized rock, he reentered the vehicle and broke open the steering column cover, exposing the wires. Within seconds the car started. Curt turned on the lights, and slowly pulled away. He pushed the gate button. The gate did not open, but rather closed for approximately 2 seconds. Curt nearly had a heart attack. He stopped the truck, took a deep breath, and pressed the button again. This time, the door opened. As he drove through, Curt held his arm up in the side window and kept his head low to obscure any CCTV, EO, or IR video feeds. He was sure they'd suspect it was him once the escape was uncovered, but there was no need to assist them in the tracing.

    Curt continued out of Nissassa, driving towards town at an unsuspecting pace. Approximately 1 mile away, the lights of Nissassa beamed on. There was no blaring horn one would associate with a prison break, but it was clear a fully illuminated Nissassa mining operation at 4 AM could only mean one thing, his escape was known. There was no time to lose.

    Curt ditched the truck outside his apartment. He knew they'd look for him there first, but he also knew going to his apartment was his only chance to remain on the run. Curt entered the apartment. As he did, he heard rumblings in the bedroom. His first thought was Nissassa had beaten him home…. Then he realized, it was Allison. He was so fixated, he'd forgotten.

"Curt?" Coming out of the bedroom, she saw him. "CURT! Thank God! You're OK!" She ran to hug him. "Where have you been! What happened?"

"Allison. What a sight for sore eyes." He held her, but again, knew time was limited. "Look. I am in danger. And because of our relationship, you may be as well. The mine is a front for something very bad. I don't have time to explain."

"Curt, why are you wearing a Nissassa Guard uniform?"

"OK. I get it. Questions are your job. But please. Not now. I need you to help me. Please get all the cash I have as well as my passport." Curt's eyes showed her the true danger he faced. Allison knew where he kept both and quickly got them.

"OK," she said confused. Curt grabbed his phone, and his wallet. Curt then opened his computer and booked a flight for that afternoon from Rabat to Paris.

"Curt. I'm scared. What are you doing?"

"Baby, this is a part of me I never wanted you to see. When I say I am in danger, there are people on the way here right now to kill me. That's not hyperbole. Keep your phone on. Answer calls that are from unknown numbers only. I won't call you from my phone. Please pack a bag and go to the hospital. Sleep there and if questioned, say you were waiting to see if I came back to work. You did NOT see me now. You trust NO ONE and you tell NO ONE that you saw me. Do you understand?"

Allison just stood there. She was overwhelmed.

"DO YOU UNDERSTAND! BABY PLEASE… WE DON'T HAVE TIME!" Curt ran to the bedroom. He ditched the guard uniform and changed into another set of running attire, this time with Crocs on his feet. Curt turned off his phone's cellular and wireless connections, grabbed Allison's arm and departed the apartment. It would be the last time he saw it. He began running towards the hospital with Allison in tow. Abruptly, he stopped her, held her and kissed her one last time. After that, he let her go, pushed her away and said, "I love you! Now run!" Confused and scared, Allison again started running. Running from the very thing she loved and believed could protect her from anything. She was scared and started to cry.

The early dawn was beginning to cast light onto Akjoujt. Curt ducked down an ally as he saw Allison running to the hospital. A lone vehicle engine pierced the silent morning air. It grew stronger. Curt looked around the corner and saw a Nissassa truck racing towards his apartment. It was time to go.

Chapter Forty-One

The Chase

A ring of Jerry's apartment doorbell at 0400Hrs was never good news. Jerry got out of bed and opened the door. It was Smitty. "Nover escaped." It was all he needed to say.

"How on EARTH did that happen!? Did you fucking let him go!?"

"No, Jerry. I did not. He overpowered a guard and somehow made it off the grounds. We are investigating now and sending a team to his apartment."

"Don't bullshit me. I know your history with him. Senior Chief Smith come clean with me. Where are your loyalties?" 'Senior Chief Smith' was something Smitty had not been called in a long time and it didn't sit well with him. Smitty's blood began to simmer. It was one thing for Curt to question Smitty's involvement with Nissassa, but Jerry's questioning of his loyalty cut deep. That wound would take a long time to heal.

Smitty stared at him, refusing to answer as he deemed the question unworthy of a response. "Again, we are tracking him. I'll let you know when he's found."

"Jesus! Do you have any idea what he could expose? You are the one that recommended him! You are the one who brought him in! If he sings, we are screwed. I want a contract on him, now!"

As much as Smitty hated to hear those words, he knew Curt had made his choice. "I'll pass the word to our teams, and we will come up with a cover story."

"Yes. You will. Get out of my sight." Jerry closed the door in Smitty's face. It was unpleasant, but not surprising.

Jerry turned back towards his bed and reached to his nightstand. He immediately grabbed his phone and hastily looked for a contact, then dialed a number.

A phone rang on a nightstand in the National Capital Region. It was close to midnight. "Hello?" The voice said groggily.

"Don, It's Jerry. Wake up. We have a problem. Nover was read into our operation and is now on the loose."

"You're shitting me."

"I wish I was. Right now, we are tracking him, and I'll keep you posted. Should I need your support and that of your contacts, I presume it will be made available?"

"Of course, without question. Again, you need to tell me how this happened."

"I can't at this point, but suffice it to say, I think Chief Smith's tenure with our organization may be reaching its end."

"That's unfortunate, but you're the guy on the ground there. Your call. I'll coordinate support from this end. Before I hang up, tell me, what does he know?" Don's question was one Jerry did not wish to answer.

Jerry paused, "Everything."

"Fuck. Find him. Got it? Good night."

"Yes, Don. Good morning." Jerry hung up. Don took a deep breath, and sent a text message, *"Can we meet tomorrow in the morning? The usual place."* A phone in the White House west wing buzzed, displaying the same message. It was Steve's work phone.

****

Back in Akjoujt, three Nissassa employees were pulling up to Curt's apartment. They knocked on the door and waited. There was no answer. One went back to the truck and returned with a door breach. After a few loud thuds, the door was open, and locks destroyed. As the sun rose, the mosque's call to prayer blared across the town. It was of little notice to the Nissassa employees. They entered the apartment in well trained military / SWAT team style, weapons at the ready and hands on each other with the point man leading the way. Immediately, they saw the guard uniform laying on the living room floor. Slowly, they cleared the apartment. Once cleared, the effort quickly became an intelligence gathering exercise. Curt's money and passport were gone. The apartment was in disarray. They grabbed the uniform, his laptop, and all the papers he had laying around. Call to prayer had ended. The streets were coming alive. It was time to go.

The three exited the apartment and began walking to the truck. As they did, they heard a man yell "HEY!" while running towards them. Instinctively, they turned hands on their holsters. It was Kamil.

"HEY! What are you doing!?"

One of the Nissassa men spoke, "Have you seen Dr. Nover?"

"No, everyone has been looking for him. Why are you in his apartment and why are you taking his things?" Kamil was puzzled and growing more concerned by the second.

"We too are looking for him. We were asked to gather some of his things and try to use them to help find him." Not actually far from the truth, but also far from conveying their actual intent.

"Oh. Who asked you to do this? Allison? Doctors Without Borders? Issam, our village Elder?"

The man didn't answer. "Look, we must go. If you see Dr. Nover, please let Issam know or anyone associated with the mine. Do you understand?"

Kamil was at a loss. He was alone and the three of them had weapons. Now was not the time or place to challenge. He replied, "OK. I will." He also knew from instinct that something was wrong. Why were security guards from the mine breaking into Curt's apartment?

Where was Issam and his security team?

****

Allison made it to the hospital. She was scared and nervous. She tried to relax but it was pointless. She looked at her phone ten times a minute. Would Curt call now? What could she do? Who could she call? Allison felt helpless. It was agonizing.

As Issam walked to work down the streets of Akjoujt, his phone rang. "Hello?" He spoke.

It was one of his security detail. "Sir, Nissassa guards just ransacked Nover's apartment. They are leaving now."

"Thank you." He hung up the phone. The puzzle pieces were aligning for Issam and the picture they presented was one that concerned him. He raised his phone again and placed a call.

The phone rang and a female voice answered, "Hello?"

"Good morning, Allison. It is Issam. I wanted to ask if you have found Dr. Nover. I have kept trying his phone, but there is no answer."

Allison was alarmed. Could this be coincidence? Should she share with Issam her encounter with Curt? Could he be trusted? In the end, she followed Curt's instructions. "Issam, I have not. Have you heard anything more?"

Her response was unrevealing and Issam could not tell if she was being honest. "Sadly, no. Perhaps we should meet to discuss this. Are you at the apartment you share with Curt?" Issam knew if she was there, she'd know about the Nissassa effort.

"No, I am at the hospital. I slept here hoping Curt would come back here first." The chances that Issam's call and questions were coincidence were beginning to fade. Her journalistic instinct suggested Issam knew something. "Yes, it may be good to meet and compare notes. I miss Curt terribly and I fear something bad has happened."

"It has only been one night. Let's remain hopeful that there is a reasonable explanation, and he is OK." Issam knew such a likelihood was unrealistic.

"Shall I come to your office today?" Allison was determined to meet Issam.

"Yes. Shall we say in one hour?"

"Great, Issam. I will be there. Take care." Allison hung up the phone. In an odd way, Issam's phone call was exactly what she needed. Her anxiety from feeling hopeless and uninformed now shifted to opportunity and purpose. Allison put her phone in her pocket. She walked down the hall to grab a cup of coffee.

"Ms. Allison! Ms. Allison!" She heard from behind her. It was Kamil.

"Ms. Allison! Your apartment! The door is broken and Nissassa guards have taken Curt's things!"

"Kamil. Slow down. Tell me what happened." He explained it all. Her stomach churned. Her hopes that Curt was exaggerating the danger faded as he spoke. "Thanks, Kamil. I will go to the apartment now. Would you join me?" He agreed.

As they approached the apartment, a crowd had gathered around. Kamil tried to clear the way and help her enter. Just hours before, she'd held Curt in this very spot. Her heart hurt. "Well, Kamil... It looks like the door is broken to the point I cannot stay here. I will gather some things and find a place to stay tonight."

"Yes, Ms. Allison. I will try to contact the apartment owner and get the door fixed. Please do not leave anything valuable." As they stood in the apartment, someone knocked on the door frame. It was one of Issam's security team. Kamil spoke to him in Arabic. The man stood at the door and the local villagers slowly dispersed.

"Ms. Allison. This man works for Issam. He says he will stay here until the landlord boards up and secures the apartment."

"Thanks, Kamil. I'm curious. Did he just stumble upon this situation? Who told him to guard the apartment?"

Kamil turned to the guard and again shared another exchange in Arabic. Once finished, he turned back to Allison. "Ms. Allison, he says that Issam directed him to come here and watch the house."

"Thanks, Kamil. It appears I will need to thank Issam for such a kind gesture." This information was timely, as her meeting with Issam would be soon. Given Issam's earlier questions and the answers from this guard, things were far from consistent. Something was wrong with Issam's story. Allison departed the apartment on her way to his office. Curt needed her help, and her best course of action was to leverage every investigative journalistic skill she had. Issam was the perfect place to start. The questions for him grew by the second.

****

Curt had broken into one of the local vendor's shops, hiding in the back of the store. As the shop keeper arrived for the morning opening, he was startled to see Curt inside his shop. "Dr. Nover! What are you doing here!?"

Curt tried his best to cover and deescalate the situation. "Good morning, Mohammed! How are you!?"

"I am fine. But why are you in my shop?"

"Mohammed, I need a favor and I was so excited I couldn't wait. Please forgive me. One of my good friend's birthdays is soon approaching and I wish to send him you nicest traditional clothing from Akjoujt. I need this to remain a secret though as I don't wish to spoil the surprise. Can you help me?"

Mohammed's concern about Curt's break-in were quickly vanished. His first customer of the day and before he even opened. Allah was good. "Yes! Yes! Please! Tell me what you would like and what size is he?"

"Great. He is actually my size, so I can try on the clothes if that is ok?"

"Yes, Dr. Nover!" Within 15 minutes, Curt was provided a set of full traditional garb, from headdress to footwear. His running outfit and Crocs would soon be disposed. Curt paid Mohammed and reminded him to remain silent.

"Yes, Dr. Nover. It is our secret. But if it is a gift, why are you wearing it?"

"Ha! Great question. To be honest, I wanted to see what it felt like to be in traditional attire. It's comfortable. I understand why you wear it." Curt was lying. Many times in his Special Ops career, he had worn what military types refer to as a "Man Dress," the term used to describe traditional Arabic attire. He disliked them but knew if they kept him camouflaged when he was a SEAL, they'd keep him safe now. Far safer than a running outfit with Crocs.

"Yes!" Again, Mohammed was pleased. "They are the most comfortable!" The glow in Mohammed's face was beaming. A westerner embracing his culture was one of his greatest pleasures.

"OK, Mohammed. Take care and have a great day."

"Yes, Dr. Nover. You too. And Happy Birthday to your friend."

Curt proceeded out into the street. Within seconds, he looked like every other Akjoujt man. Curt slowly walked through the market. Soon, he saw what he was looking for. A local man was haggling over the cost of kiwis with a fruit vendor. On the box of kiwis was the man's cell phone. Curt approached and stood next to the man and in front of the phone, casually reviewing the vendor's fruit. Slowly, he reached up and grabbed an apple, examining it. Again, he slowly put it down, but as his hand retreated, he nonchalantly grabbed the phone and put it in his sleeve. With that, he walked away. *'Tactical communications system, secured,'* he thought to himself.

In Nissassa's Ops Center, a worker walked up to Jerry. "Sir, I have an update. Two issues. First, we have information that Issam and Allison spoke. They are again meeting today in about 20 minutes in Issam's office."

"What did they say?" Jerry inquired.

"Sir, our systems monitored the entire call. Here is the text." He handed Jerry the exchange verbatim.

Jerry was pleased. "Activate either one of their phones for the meeting. If either gives any indication they know where Nover is, I want to know immediately."

"Yes sir. Second, Nover booked a flight for later today out of Rabat to Paris."

"Get me the flight information and ticket number."

"It's right here, sir." The worker handed over a piece of paper then departed back to sit at one of the many desks along the Ops Center walls.

Jerry took a photo of the paper and sent it to Don back in D.C. with the words *'Your resources would be helpful. This is Nover's flight out of Rabat.'*

Catching Nover would not be easy. But Jerry knew he had the advantage with special resources from Washington on his side.

Chapter Forty-Two

Tightening the Noose

In Virginia, Don stood near the WWII memorial, explaining the recent events in Akjoujt. The anger in Steve's face was easily visible. "How does something like this happen? Our agreement from the very beginning was 'no loose ends.' Now, not only is there a loose end, but there's also a freaking uncontrolled noose rope flapping in the breeze. I'll be damned sure that thing isn't going to catch my neck!"

"Steve, I understand your frustration, but we see this more as a hiccup. Look, the good news is, we know his next move. He booked a flight out of Rabat. Here is his flight and passport info." Don knew he was underselling the existing danger, but at this point, agreeing with Steve was unhelpful.

"OK. I'll have State Department and Department of Justice flag his passport. We also will have the USG assets work with Mauritania to watch for border crossings and with Morocco to have authorities pull him from the flight. Don, these are extremely limited resources. We don't use them regularly. Do you understand?"

"Yes, I do. And we are very appreciative. I thank you greatly for your offer. Once he is in a Mauritanian or Moroccan police custody, we will have a team ready to execute an operation to clean up this small mess."

"I presume the emphasis in that sentence is on 'execute.' Speaking of, how are we on Iran?"

Iran….. Don had almost forgotten. "Yes, Iran. Everything is a go." The teams are assembled and will begin their infill within the next few days. Did you see the training video?"

"No, but I heard about it. Good to hear that part of your efforts are as well planned. Don, if you pull this off, you'll have a sole source contract from this administration for eternity." Don knew that meant one thing. Money. Lots of money.

"Got it. Just help me get Nover."

"Yeah. OK." The displeasure in Steve's voice was not lost on Don.

"Steve, I'm sorry about this. It won't happen again."

Steve stared at Don thinking *'How could you even fathom this happening again?'* Then he spoke. "You're right. It won't." Without shaking hands, Steve turned and walked away.

****

Back in Akjoujt, Curt meandered amongst the locals, finding an Akjoujt hookah and coffee shop. He sat on pillows ordering a coffee and pipe. His back against the wall with full view of the street and blending like a chameleon, Curt was safe here and it gave him time to think. If Jerry was telling the truth, the Ayatollah assassination would take place soon. Final top off training had a short shelf life and the closer that took place to the actual operation the better. Given global tensions, Curt also knew that the fallout from such an assassination had repercussions that likely could include anything from retaliatory chemical and or biological weapons attack up to World War Three. *'Great,'* Curt thought to himself. *'Not only do I have to save myself, but I also have to save the freaking world.'*

Curt's moves were limited. He pulled out his phone that still had the transmit/receive function disabled. He looked up a number and then dialed it on his newly acquired fruit vendor phone.

"Hello?" The person answered.

"Buck. It's Curt."

"Doc! What's going on! What number are you calling from? Are you ready for that get away weekend you were lamenting!"

"Ha… funny you should ask. I may need that flight sooner than you think. Sorry about the strange number, I lost my phone. Where are you right now."

"Sitting in Rabat. I thought this place would be livelier than Mauritania. I'm not sure I was right. Anyway, no flights today but I have one tomorrow down your way. Bringing some mine workers back up here and arranged their follow on to Baku. Any chance you want to do lunch tomorrow?"

Buck's innocence was endearing, it also reassured Curt that Buck was unaware of the mine's actual operations. "Yes, Buck, maybe. Hey, can you do me a favor. There's a flight from Rabat to Paris today in about three hours. I sent some medical cargo on the flight which is time sensitive. Can you monitor it and ensure it gets off the ground on time?" Curt never intended to be on the flight. It was a decoy. But it was one way to try and expose how deep Nissassa's connections were.

"Sure. I'm not doing anything else. I'll see you tomorrow!"

"Great. I look forward to it." They both hung up. Curt called over the waiter and paid for his pipe and coffee. He then placed one more call.

Somewhere across the ocean, a phone rang in the United States. An angry woman answered the unknown number….. "If this is one of them damn Nigerian Princes needing my money again I'z gonna kill you!"

"Great to hear your voice too, Ms. Wanda." Curt said. Ms. Wanda back in Chicago was about one of the only people Curt could trust. And at this point, trust to Curt was critical.

"Oh Lord Have Mercy! Doctor Nover! Well, I'll be! Good Lord! I thought you were some crazy scam caller!"

"No Ms. Wanda. It's me. Hey, I am sorry to be short with you, but I need help. Can you do me some favors?"

"Suga, you know I'd do anything for you."

With that, Curt rattled off his instructions. Wanda grew more concerned as he listed off the requests. She could tell he was in trouble, but also had great faith in Curt. From his time with her in Cook County's Emergency Room, Curt knew whether it was a young kids broken bone on a playground or a gangbanger's five bullet holes clinging to life, Wanda was unflinching in getting things done. He could sense her concern, but this was not the time to try and calm her.

They both said their goodbyes. Was Nissassa monitoring local phones? He knew his phone was likely being monitored which is why it was in Airplane mode, but how good was Nissassa's technology? Could they monitor all phone lines and cross identification via voice recognition? While such technology exists, Curt thought it was unlikely they could acquire it but at this point, anything was possible. He could take no chances. Curt erased both calls from the phone registry and left the phone under the pillow he sat on. He then got up and walked a few dozen meters down the street, still blending with his surroundings.

****

Across town, Issam was welcoming Allison into his office.

"Good morning, Issam. Thank you for seeing me. I'm concerned about Curt. This is not like him."

"Yes, Good morning, Allison. Come in, sit down. Would you like some tea? I had some made for us."

"Excellent, thank you."

"You are welcome. Yes, this does seem odd. My security has asked many questions across the community. It appears no one has seen him. I am hopeful he is not in the desert without water. The sun is punishing." Issam offered up one of numerous explanations. It was the start of the game with Allison.

"Yes, I hope he is not as well. I am surprised and perhaps a bit relieved to hear you do not accuse the Inju or Satris. Knowing these warring factions exist, I was worried one of them would be to blame."

"No. I do not believe either would be so foolish. They fight among themselves, but they do nothing that would upset the local people. Their conflict remains limited. Bringing harm to someone who brings our local people health and wellness would be unacceptable." Issam had rehearsed this line hundreds of times. Accusations about anything against the Inju and Satris were always met with a similar response.

"Well, if it isn't the warring factions, he isn't in Akjoujt and he isn't lost in the desert, what else or who else could it be?" Allison framed her question in a way to leave the mine as a possible culprit.

"This is a good question. I do not know who it may be." Issam did not take the bait.

"That's weird, Issam. Because when I went to my apartment today that was ransacked by Nissassa security, I am curious if the mine may have something to do with this?"

Issam became uneasy. "No, no…. I called the mine yesterday evening and told them about his disappearance. They are likely just trying to help in finding him. Nothing more."

"Issam, the state of my front door would suggest differently. And you sending a guard to our apartment to 'protect it,' also doesn't fit neatly, especially after you asked me if I was at the apartment when you called earlier?" Allison was done playing nice. "What are you not telling me?"

Issam was angered. How dare a western female in her western attire enter his office and speak to him in such a tone. Issam slowly sat down his teacup. He leaned forward in his chair and fixated his angered eyes on Allison. "Child, you are pushing when you should not push. I quickly sent a guard out of kindness. That guard which remains there as overwatch can be recalled just as quickly. Your tongue is sharp, and if you're not careful, you may cut yourself on it. I know the mine is good for Akjoujt. I know the Inju and Satri are not involved. I know Dr.

Nover is missing. That is a far better situation than what I know about our last doctor."

As Issam lectured Allison, her phone buzzed. The ringer was muted as not to interrupt her meeting with Issam. She casually looked down. It was a U.S. number from area code 312. *'Chicago'* she thought to herself. *'It was Curt. It had to be.'* Allison was prepared to unload on Issam for calling her a 'child' and inferring to the death of the previous doctor. None of that mattered now. She needed to get to her phone immediately.

"Issam, you're right. I am sorry. I am embarrassed. It was just the journalist in me. Again, I thank you for the meeting." Allison tried desperately to exit the office before the call disconnected. She would fail.

"Allison. Your apology is accepted. You should not seek out things that do not exist. You know the mine is good. You wrote your article. We will all keep praying for Curt's safe return." Issam rose to show Allison out. She rose just as fast and exited as politely as she could. Issam was not convinced he'd changed her mind. He was also sure that sharing this meeting with Jerry was not helpful. Best to keep this to himself for a while. Little did he know his phone captured the entire discussion which was currently being transitioned to text format per Jerry's instructions.

Allison scurried into the street. She raised her phone and dialed the number back. Wanda answered, "Hello? Is this Allison?"

"Yes! Yes! This is Allison!! Who is this?"

"Allison, Dear Girl. This is your great aunt from Chicago. You know, the one that loves the Cubs!"

Allison had no great aunt in Chicago. Nor did she know anyone who loved to watch the Cubs (other than Curt), but she also knew now was not the time to challenge the caller. "Yes! Yes! How are you? What can I do for you?"

"Oh, Dear Girl. I am sitting in this small coffee shop where we first met, and it made me think of you and how much I love you so. That's all I really wanted to say. You be safe. K?"

"Yes, Auntie. I will. And thank you for the call." They both hung up, and Allison knew exactly where to go. Curt was waiting at Anbar, the coffee house where they first met.

Allison walked quickly towards Anbar. As she approached through the market people were walking about. She moved quickly, brushing against locals in the crowded streets. As she did, one brushed back and said, "Hey Baby," in perfect English. She froze and looked back. It was those eyes. Curt's eyes. Other than that, she did not notice Curt dressed in his local attire.

Allison looked him up and down. She never would have suspected.... *'Damn... He's good'* she thought. She turned around and followed. Curt swung his head as if to say, *'follow me,'* turned and then walked away. He walked deeper into the local market, eventually slowly turning into an empty ally.

She followed. They were finally alone. "Jesus, Curt! I would have never suspected!"

"Yeah. A good-looking Man Dress can knock off about 10 years and 10 pounds. Not bad, eh?" His humor remained, and frankly, he was happy to be alone again with Allison.

"OK. Curt. Tell me what is going on."

"Allison. The mine is a front for elite 'Top Off' mercenary training, some of the guys with which I used to serve. Unknowingly, I was brought here at one of their recommendations to 'patch up' locals who are used as training targets."

The notion to Allison was implausible. She just shook her head. "No. Seriously, that can't be true."

"It is. Trust me. I am just as shocked. I was taken prisoner. Jerry explained the entire operation and tried to persuade me to support the effort. I escaped and now they are likely trying to kill me. Know this. No matter what happens, I need you to help me expose this."

"OK." Allison's mouth moved, but she still could not process reality.

"I need to get out of the country and back to D.C. I have some friends there that I know can help me. We don't have much time. Nissassa's planning to assassinate the Ayatollah soon."

Allison's shock of Nissassa's true operations was now turning to fear given her deep knowledge on global affairs. Allison knew the Ayatollah and the U.S. were far from friends and that Iran was aggressively pursuing nuclear weapons. "The Ayatollah?"

"Yes."

"Jesus. Do you know what the fallout from that could be?"

"Yes. And I am sure you do as well."

"Curt, how do we get you back to the U.S.?"

"I have a plan." Curt began explaining. Allison's assistance would be integral. They hugged and kissed goodbye. All of which was captured on a camera belonging to one of Issam's men. Allison was followed from his office. The image was sent via phone to Issam with the message, '*Nover is in Akjoujt.*'

Issam looked at his phone and watched the video. He smiled…. It appeared Ms. Donley was just as dishonest has he.

Chapter Forty-Three

A Friend in Need, Indeed

Curt purchased another phone from a street vendor. The transaction was insignificant. After setting up the SIM card, Curt called Buck again.

"Hey, Buck, it's Curt."

"Doc! Dude, this is the third number I have for you now! Ha Ha Ha!!! Are you in trouble?"

"Ha! No, not at all!" Curt tried to dissuade Buck from concern. It was pointless.

Buck shot back at Curt, "Well, for a guy 'not' in trouble, I don't know why your passport has been flagged by national security, your name is on the Rabat to Paris manifest, and there's enough police and military around that flight to stop a major uprising. Other than that, I have no clue why I'd guess you're in trouble."

Curt paused. He realized eventually he'd have to begin to trust Buck. Now was as good of time as any. "OK, yes, I'm in a bit of a jam. I didn't do anything wrong, and I really could use some help. Buck, I know you don't know me well, but you're one of my only hopes. Can I count on you?"

"Count on me? Buddy, I miss doing crazy shit so much, I'd be pissed if you didn't ask for help! What can I do?"

Curt released a big sigh. "You have no idea how relieved I am to hear this. I am working on getting a false passport. That said, tomorrow when you come here, I need you to plan to take some additional cargo out on your flight. Will you have room?"

"Yeah. The current manifest is about 10 guys. I'll have room for about another 500 pounds. Do you need me to get you a fake passport?"

Curt was a bit surprised by the question, but the truth is, Curt had no contacts for such things. "Buck, I love you. How quick can you have it"?

"I'll have it with me when I land. I got a guy who owes me a favor."

"Perfect. When you land, you may not see me, but you'll see a gal named Allison. Please do what she asks."

"Got it. Is that the American chick? If so, she better be nicer to me! Hey, by the way, is there any danger involved in this?"

"Actually tons."

"Perfect! Til tomorrow!"

"Thanks, Buck." Asking Buck for help was a risk but a calculated one. While Curt knew he couldn't be certain of Buck's level of knowledge with Nissassa, Buck was truly his only hope. Buck was Akjoujt's conduit to the outside world for Nissassa and they likely couldn't risk him knowing about their true operation. Buck's personality lent well to their secret as Buck didn't care about much or ask too many questions.

****

Allison went back to their apartment and packed up as much as she could take. It would be her last time in the place where she and Curt first fell in love. She paused, with a sense of controlled anger. She picked up her phone and called Jerry. "Hello, Jerry?"

"Yes, Allison, is that you?"

Allison was crying. "Yes. Jerry, it's me. I am losing my mind. I can't take Curt's disappearance anymore. I'm going crazy. I can't sleep. I can't eat." She was having a nervous breakdown on the phone. "Jerry, I need to get out of here. Now. When can I get that ticket you promised me?"

Allison's request was well received by Jerry. Allison's article was a good PR idea for the mine, a journalist with idle hands remaining in Akjoujt was far from welcome. Extracting her from situation and tying up that small loose end was a great idea. "Allison, could you be ready to fly out tomorrow?"

"Tomorrow is too late. I need to leave today. If you can't fly me out, I'll take a bus to Nouakchott, Rabat or Casablanca."

"Allison, slow down. I'd rather you not travel on a bus. Please relax and take a deep breath. I can assure you, tomorrow you can fly. We already have a flight scheduled to Casablanca tomorrow. Can you wait until then?"

"Ugh.... OK. You're right. I'll try to calm down. Thanks, Jerry." They hung up. A smile filled Allison's face. She turned off her phone and walked to the hospital.

Jerry called Pete, his assistant. "Pete, add one more to the manifest for tomorrow. Our journalist will be leaving the country with our team. Have Buck work her flight from Casablanca back to the US."

"Yes, Sir." Pete would relay the message down to his logistics staff. He could tell; however, Jerry's voice was cold. Something was wrong.

Chapter Forty-Four

One Final Night in Akjoujt

Allison entered the hospital and found Kamil sitting in the break room, drinking coffee. "Kamil, hello."

"Hello, Ms. Allison. Have you found Dr. Nover?" Kamil was far from his lively self.

"Kamil, no. I haven't. Hey, can I take you to Anbar's for real coffee?"

"Yes, Ms. Allison." With that, Kamil got up and they walked out of the hospital together. As they walked, Allison began to speak.

"Kamil, I have some good news for you, but I need you to promise you can never tell anyone. I also need a favor, for Curt."

"For Dr. Nover? Yes, Ms. Allison! Anything! Is he OK?"

"Curt is safe now; I've seen him recently. But he is in danger."

"No! What is wrong?"

"Kamil, I cannot explain everything to you. You can ask no questions. OK?"

"Yes, Ms. Allison. I will do anything for you and Dr. Nover"

"OK. I am glad to hear you say that." They kept walking. "Kamil, I need you to get me a casket and I need paperwork of a death for a man from Casablanca. He will die tomorrow in Akjoujt. Do you understand?"

Oddly, Kamil did not question any of the request. Instead, he looked at Allison and said, "Ms. Allison, what is the name of the dead man?"

"Kamil, you can make his name anything you wish. Ok? You need to have the death certificate and empty casket in a truck parked behind the hospital tomorrow at 10:00AM. Once they are in place, I need you to wait in the truck for further instructions. Can you do this?"

"Yes, Ms. Allison." She hugged Kamil and thanked him. He was one of her favorites. She would miss him greatly.

****

The sun began setting over Akjoujt. Nover was nowhere to be found, but for Nissassa, that would have to wait. Jerry and Smitty were giving their final instructions to the two teams preparing to enter Iran. One last tabletop dry run, a final pack check, a radio check. Everything was set. Tomorrow, the teams would fly to Casablanca where a U.S. Air Force C-130 would be waiting. The C-130 had flown into Morocco yesterday and today was performing a bilateral paratroop jump exercise as part of a building partnership capacity effort. The flight crew was unaware they'd have pax tomorrow, nor that their flight plans would terminate in Baku, that change was being held by higher authorities to share at the last possible moment.

The Nissassa teams turned in for the night. The next few days would be challenging. *'Sleep while you can'* was the motto. As the team turned in, so did the rest of Akjoujt. Issam was preparing to retire in his house, curious as to what opportunities would surface from the knowledge he possessed. In Mohammed's Hotel, Allison was offered a hotel room free of charge. As for Curt, he was bedding down in one of the few places he felt safe.... 'The high ground.' Curt was curled up on the roof of Mohammed's Hotel, one of the highest points in Akjoujt. Little did he know it was the same place Longbow 23 had taken the fatal shot on Kameel. More importantly, it was also the roof over the very room Allison lay in bed. Physically, there were just feet apart, but mentally it felt like worlds away.

****

Issam's phone rang. The caller ID said it was Jerry. "Hello, Jerry. What can I do for you this evening? It is late."

"Issam, have you had any luck at finding Nover? We are concerned about him as well as the health and welfare of the good people in Akjoujt."

"Jerry, this is disappointing. My men have not found anything. But he will eventually turn up. I believe this." Issam clearly sensed a shift in Jerry's voice. In previous calls, Jerry was far calmer than now. He also knew from his video that Curt was on the run.

"Thanks, Issam. You will call me when you know something, yes?"

"Of course, Jerry. We are friends."

"Thanks. Have a good night."

"You too." They both hung up. Issam stared at the photo of Curt and Allison in his phone, smiling. His decision to keep the information to himself was purely based in greed. Issam realized Jerry wanted Nover and when Jerry wants something, there was profit to be made. Before sharing his information, Issam needed to know what price he should place on Curt's head.

****

Back in Nissassa, Jerry called Don. "Don, the teams depart tomorrow. They are prepped and ready."

"Good news. What about Nover?"

"We have nothing. His phone is inactive, and he has not returned back to his apartment. We also know he never got on the flight to Paris."

"Jerry, damn it. My help locked down that flight and both Morocco and Mauritania. I thought you were sure he'd be on the flight."

"We were, but he never showed. Maybe he was tipped off by the security."

Don was frustrated. "Jerry, the dude is a former SEAL. Finding him won't be easy. Try harder. I've mobilized all the forces I can from this side and those resources dwindle fast at great expense. The sooner this goes away, the sooner our 'customer' is happy. Do you understand?"

"Yes, Don. Got it."

Don changed the subject. "Did you make a decision on Smitty?"

Jerry took pause. Then he said, "Yes. Start looking for a replacement, please."

"Got it. Give me a few weeks." Don knew what that meant. "OK, I've gotta run. Take care." They both hung up.

And with that, Akjoujt slept.

Chapter Forty-Five

A Funeral for One

Kamil did as he was instructed. He placed the truck behind the hospital with a casket in the truck bed. Inside the hospital, he snuck into Dr. Nover's office and hastily borrowed his stamp, certifying the death of Kareem Al Salam, a thirty-four-year-old male who tragically died from a motor vehicle accident in the early hours just outside Akjoujt. Kamil held up the death certificate and admired it. He was quite proud of his work.

Allison ate breakfast at Mohammed's hotel. She said her goodbyes and could have won an Oscar given the mourning she spewed. She returned to the room and packed her belongings.

Curt woke far earlier than all, he departed the roof before sunrise. Slowly, he had wandered to the outskirts of town and then a quick work out. Push-ups, sit-ups and a small run, as much as possible in 'Jesus Sandals,' anyway. Curt had not showered for two days and had no possibility to do so. He also had two workouts under his belt. He stunk horribly. Soon enough he'd shower, he thought. More important things awaited…. The time had come, he walked to the hospital much like other villagers who sought care. As he approached, he broke away from the crowd and circled around the back. There was Kamil; sitting in the truck, just as planned.

"Kamil. How are you doing?" Curt smiled at him.

"Dr. Nover!!!! It's you! You're OK! Kamil jumped out of the truck and hugged him, oblivious to his body stench.

"Kamil. It's great to see you. I'm sorry we involved you in this, but I needed help and you were the first-person Allison and I thought of."

"Dr. Nover, I would do anything for you!" Kamil was proud of his loyalty and that was exactly why Curt knew he could count on Kamil.

"Dr. Nover, where is the dead body?"

"Kamil, I am the dead body. The casket is for me."

"Dr. Nover, you can't go in the casket!" Kamil protested.

"I can with an O2 bottle. I need you to go back in the hospital and get one along with a small hose and nasal cannula. OK?"

"Sir, what is a 'cannula?'"

"Ha. It's the nasal dispenser of O2, it looks like prongs."

"Yes sir, but I don't approve!"

"It's OK, Kamil, I'm a doctor." Curt smiled... Kamil went in and did as he was instructed. While gone, Curt removed the casket top with a hammer claw, then gouged out two holes in the bottom. Kamil returned with the items, and with that, the two of them headed to the airport; for now, Curt was in the passenger seat.

"Kamil, there is one last thing I need you to do. When we get to the airport, there will be a small airplane, you will see Allison with some other men. Drive up to that aircraft. You and Allison must get me on that plane. Do you understand?"

"Yes, Sir." They approached the airport and Kamil pulled over. Curt entered the casket with the O2 bottle. Kamil hammered the casket shut.

Kamil began driving again, and just as Curt had said, Allison was on the ramp with a plane and some men. The men included the two Nissassa teams as well as Jerry who'd be paying Buck for his services. Kamil pulled up.

"Mr. Pilot! Mr. Pilot! Are you going to Casablanca?"

Buck was surprised. "Yes, how did you know?"

"Ms. Allison is my friend and said you go! If this is true, you MUST take this casket with you?"

Jerry had no idea who Kamil was, but he was going to have no part of it. "No, sorry buddy. This is a private flight. You'll need to find another."

"Mister! You do not understand. There are NO other flights to Casablanca. The man in this coffin was a devote Muslim and he MUST get to Casablanca before sunset. This is one of our most important customs! If he is not buried before the sun sets in his home, he will not ascend to heaven. This is in accordance with the traditions and customs of Islam."

"I hear you but there is no room on this plane." While Kamil and Jerry were arguing, Allison looked at Buck, whom she'd only met when originally flying into Akjoujt. She gently nodded to him. It was all Buck needed to see.

"Alright, Alright... Hold on." Buck turned to look at Jerry, "Hey boss, I have the space if you want. Also, good PR for the mine. Your call, but I can make it happen."

Jerry looked at Buck. He had a point, and dead men tell no tales. "OK, but let's move. My men have a flight in Casablanca soon." Inside the casket, Curt heard everything. He clenched his hand in a small fist pump. He was getting on the flight. He also realized he was beginning to feel the effects of hypoxia. He turned on the O2 bottle, took one large breath of O2 and then turned it off to ensure no one heard the hiss from the bottle's exhaust.

The Nissassa teams helped load the casket onto the aircraft. Buck and Allison sat there and watched; the irony of the situation not lost on either. The casket was strapped down in the center and the teams boarded, taking seats along the sides of the aircraft. Curt was doing everything possible to control his breath, but he could sense the blur of unconsciousness setting in. *'Start the engines, Buck! Start the engines!'* he thought. Once there was loud background noise in the cabin, he could again start the O2 with its associated hissing. Eventually, he heard the whine of an engine, and with that, he cracked open the bottle. After one large breath, his vision immediately cleared. Curt was leaving Akjoujt in a casket, just like his predecessor. The plane taxied out and took off.

Curt increased the O2 now and was feeling better. As the O2 bottle fed Curt, it also pushed the stagnant ambient air from inside the coffin into the aircraft cabin. Curt's stench proved to be a perfect cover. If the Nissassa teams had any questions about the deceased prior to take off, they had none after takeoff.

Chapter Forty-Six

Time to Cash In

As Jerry drove back to Nissassa, his phone buzzed. A text came across from Issam, "*I have information on Nover. Come to my Office.*" Jerry redirected his driver to Issam's office. They arrived in 20 minutes.

Issam welcomed Jerry into his office. As usual, tea was set out, for which Jerry was in no mood. Additionally, Issam was flanked by two from his security team. "Issam, I don't have time. You have information, I want it. Now."

"Jerry, slowly. All in due time." Issam was in control of this meeting. Something culturally important when establishing negotiations. What Issam failed to realize was Jerry was in no mood to play 'culture time.'

"Issam, don't fuck with me. I want to know now."

"Jerry, you seem to want to know quite desperately. Do you truly care this much for Akjoujt's wellbeing?"

Issam was right. Jerry was overplaying his hand. "Issam, I just want to help."

"Perhaps if you wished to help, you would have shared all your information earlier." And with that, Issam displayed a single running shoe.

"What is that?" Jerry asked confused.

"This is one of Dr. Nover's running shoes; found on the road between Akjoujt and the mine. It was sitting in sand that was heavily disturbed, suggesting a struggle. I know that neither the Inju nor Satri took him, which leaves very few other options."

Jerry fumed. This loose end could unravel the entire operation. "Issam, I don't have time for this. Do you have other information?"

"Jerry, do you want to tell me anything yet?" Issam just stared at Jerry.

"Issam, I am here to hear what you have to tell me, the other way around."

"Of course." With that, Issam pulled a photo of Allison kissing Curt. "This was taken yesterday afternoon."

"Damn it…. That bitch knew where he was."

"No, she knows where he IS. and so do I."

"Issam, God Damn it! Tell me now."

"I will, but you will pay one million dollars. Today. Now."

"Excuse me?"

"This is non-negotiable. The truth is you won't do anything to Allison. How would it look if the journalist who write a good news story ends up dead? Your only source is me. You have no other option and I assure you; time is not on your side. So, what will it be?"

Jerry raised his phone and called Pete. "Send one million now to Issam's office. Fast! Do you understand?"

"Yes, sir." Pete would do as he was told. But the once smooth operation of Nissassa was cracking. It took over 60 minutes to get to the money and get to Issam's office.

Pete handed the money to Jerry and Jerry passed it to Issam. "OK, NOW!"

One of Issam's men counted the money quickly and nodded. Issam reached back to the other security officer who handed him a photo. Issam passed it to Jerry who looked at it. With a deep sign, Jerry said. "That Son of a Bitch!" The photo was of Curt climbing into the Coffin outside the Akjoujt airstrip while Kamil assisted.

Jerry looked at his watch. Buck would be landing in 10 minutes at Casablanca airport, an airfield where Jerry knew no one. Jerry had not made contacts in Morocco yet but still had plenty in Nouakchott. Unfortunately, those would be useless. Jerry tried to call Buck. As Buck was descending onto glideslope, he saw the call come in. He let the call go to voice mail. It rang again… and again… Buck quickly surmised who was after Curt. The calls were followed by a text that said, *'DON'T LET THE CASKET OUT OF YOUR SIGHT!'* Buck knew Jerry was onto Curt, but Buck had given his word to Curt, and that bond would not easily break. Plus, he could easily argue he was flying and didn't hear his phone.

****

    The plane landed in Casablanca and Buck taxied to the terminal. He parked and shut down the engines. As they wound down, Curt turned off his oxygen. The cabin door as well as ramp opened to fresh air. The teams rushed out quickly. A U.S. Air Force Lieutenant was waiting for the teams to lead them to the C-130 for boarding. A Moroccan customs agent approached Buck, shook his hand, and left. Because of the sensitive Nissassa mission, this customs check was pencil whipped. It also made things quite convenient for Allison and Curt. The teams gave a meager goodbye to Buck, took their gear and left. Buck, Allison and Curt remained at the aircraft.
    Buck and Allison went back into the cargo area and quickly cracked open the casket, praying Curt was still breathing. As the casket open, Curt smiled, but the other two retched. "Dear God! You smell horrible!!!" Buck said.
    "Good to see you too, my friend. Are we in Casablanca?"
    "Yes. The other passengers are gone. It's just us."
    Curt jumped out of the coffin, grabbed Allison's arm, and said, "Here's looking at you, kid!" He smiled; Buck laughed. Allison's heart melted just a bit. It was Casablanca after all.....
    Allison was relieved to see Curt safe, but she also was not going anywhere near Curt until he showered. "Very funny, sweetheart. But you smell atrociously."
    Curt's humor shifted again to seriousness. He said, "Eventually they are going to find out what's going on and track us. We need to keep moving."

Buck was about to share info about the calls from Jerry but was interrupted by a morgue truck approaching the aircraft. All three were puzzled. Quickly, Curt jumped into the coffin, and they closed it up as a driver approached the aircraft.

"Mr. Kareem Al Salam?"

"Excuse me?" Said Buck back to the driver, "Is that your name?"

"No sir! It's the name of the deceased man. Kamil Jaffari sent us a copy of the death certificate and we are here to pick up the body."

Realizing there was little chance of them talking the coroner's office into keeping the body, Allison and Buck helped the man load the coffin in his truck. Allison rode with the coroner, claiming to be a relative, as Buck remained with the aircraft and closed it up. The truck drove away.

As Buck was finishing his post flight and closing up the aircraft, a U.S. Air Force Security Police vehicle rapidly approached. The guards jumped out of the vehicle with M4 rifles at the ready, "Sir, step away from the aircraft!"

Buck did as they instructed and instinctively raised his hand. The Security Forces open the aircraft only to find it empty.

"Sir, did you transport a coffin here?"

"Yes, I have the paperwork in my cockpit."

"Can you get it for us?" Buck shook his head and went to the cockpit. The papers were directly on top of his manifest, but he fumbled for a few minutes. He had no idea what kind of trouble Curt was in, but he was certain this was not good.

Buck exited the aircraft and handed the papers to the Security Forces.

"Sir, where is the casket now?"

"I don't know. The local coroner took it." Buck was telling the truth.

One of the Security Forces raised his radio mic and relayed the situation. They both put their M4s assault rifles down, thanked Buck for his cooperation and departed.

Buck picked up his phone. He had to make one call, and he had to make it sound convincing. In a pleasant voice, he said, "Hello, Jerry!"

"BUCK! Where the fuck is the coffin!? Why didn't you call me ASAP?"

Bucks tone turned just as harsh as Jerry's, "Call you ASAP???!!!!. The local coroner has the coffin! Now, can you tell me why fucking U.S. Air Force Security Forces with weapons raised dressed me and my aircraft down? Look, I welcome your business, but this is nuts!"

"Had you NOT taken the coffin on the flight to begin with, this wouldn't have happened! Look, no more deviations. You do what we direct! Do you understand?!!"

"Sure, no sweat off my skin. I don't particularly enjoy being held at gunpoint. Can you tell me what this is about?"

"No. Goodbye." Jerry hung up the phone.

Buck thought to himself, *'Perfect. No chance he suspects a thing.'* Buck pulled a bottle of scotch out from under the co-pilot seat and poured a glass..... *'All in a day's work.'*

Chapter Forty-Seven

Raising the Dead

The coroner truck pulled into the morgue parking lot. It was a small facility close to the Casablanca hospital. The driver looked at Allison, who had a tear in her eye. She asked, "Do you mind if I have a minute alone with him?"

"No problem. Just come in and get me when you're ready for us to process him in."

Allison thanked him. They both opened their doors; the attendee went inside, and Allison went to the back of the truck. "Curt! Curt! It's safe, come out now! We must hurry."

Allison pried open the coffin. Curt was unconscious and blue. He had run out of oxygen. "Shit!" She screamed. Allison frantically searched for a pulse. She immediately began resuscitative breathing. After a minute, Curt reacted and had barely woke.

"Baby, come on, we gotta go! And you GOTTA shower!" Curt crawled out of the casket still groggy. She helped him up.

"Wait!" He screamed. He reached back into the casket and took the O2 bottle and hoses. Curt tucked them under his Man Dress, and they fled on foot. Roughly a block away, Curt ditched the spent O2 bottle.

After a half hour, the morgue attendant grew concerned and went out to the parking lot, to find an empty open casket. *'What on earth!? Allahu Akbar!'* He freaked out and instead of calling the authorities, headed straight to the mosque and began to pray. Dead men coming back to life isn't a crime, but it is scary as hell.

Curt and Allison found a local hotel, paid cash and secured their room. As Curt took a shower, Allison laid out some of his clothes she'd placed in her luggage. After that, she went to a local store and bought another burner phone. For a journalist, Allison was proving to be an extremely good fugitive.

The two laid on the bed, tired but full of adrenaline. They needed a plan. Allison pulled out a small envelope. There was a passport inside with Curt's phone. The name on the passport read "John Holmes." Curt thought to himself, 'Funny, Buck.'

Just then, a knock was on their door. They both froze. How could they make it this far so fast and still be caught? They remained silent as mice.

A second knock followed. Then a voice, "Hey, Dude! It's me, Buck! Open the freaking door!"

Curt let Buck in and quickly shut the door. "Buck, how the hell did you find us?"

"Seriously? A few phone calls to some hotels asking if two Americans checked in and the guy smelled like ass? It took 10 minutes. Dude, you gotta go." Buck relayed what happened at the airport.

"Thanks, Buck. Man do I owe you. Just so you're aware, what's going on in Akjoujt."

Buck stopped him in his tracks. "Eh, Eh, Eh, EH!!! Stop! I do much better when I don't know what I shouldn't know. Doc, I think I know what goes on at that mine ain't mining. And I don't wanna know much more. You get it?"

"Yeah, Buck, I get it. Thanks."

"Look, I gotta go. I need to fly back to Rabat today or folks will get suspicious."

"Any chance we can stow away?" Allison asked.

"Look, I'm not the fugitive, but if you want my advice, stay away from the airport and any international trains or buses. If these guys can get the U.S. Air Force Security Forces to do their bidding, they clearly have the U.S. Government at their disposal. I'd take the bus to Al Hoceima and then take a ferry to Spain. It won't be glamorous, but its perhaps your safest route."

"Buck, great idea. Thanks." They hugged and said their goodbyes.

Allison and Curt packed up again and made their way to a cab stand. They took a cab to Mohammedia, one town closer to Al Hoceima so they could catch a bus away from the Casablanca bus station. Once there, they secured travel to Al Hoceima.

Chapter Forty-Eight

Strategic Decisions

The call came back from the U.S. Air Force Security Forces. The casket was gone. They didn't know why they were asked to secure a casket, nor did they wish to. All they knew was that one of the Nissassa team members told the flight crew the casket was to come with them – that member getting a call from Jerry at the airport courtesy desk. In fairness, the aircrew were far happier the casket would not be on the aircraft. Ferrying a few 'black ops' guys is one thing. Smuggling a dead body across international lines was a far more challenging feat. Jerry was taking more and more dumb risks. He potentially exposed his teams in Casablanca by leveraging U.S. Air Force contacts to try and capture Curt. He could afford no more unwanted exposure to the teams.

Jerry picked up the phone and called Don. He explained the situation, to include a loss of one million in revenue. Don was furious, but there was little value in arguing. In both of their minds, the blame for this fell squarely on Smitty, who would soon be out of the company. As Jerry explained the events of the past day, he intentionally omitted one piece of the puzzle. Jerry did not share with Don that Allison was involved. Allison's story was Jerry's idea, and he was the one who had brought her to Akjoujt, against Don's wishes. Jerry would give no opportunity for Don to accuse and punish himself in the same manner he did Smitty. The trend for those who failed to deliver or screwed up with Nissassa had grave consequences and Jerry chose to set the conditions to avoid adding to that statistic. It was a decision that would prove catastrophic.

Jerry quickly turned the discussion to the team's advancement on the objectives. He relayed they were onboard the C-130 headed for Baku. Once there, additional travel was secured through Nissassa to get them into place. At least that part of the plan was progressing well.

Jerry hung up the phone and sat in the Ops room. The C-130 flight was tracking across one of the screens. That mission was their rain maker. Jerry watched it for a minute or so.

Smitty walked in and found Jerry in a daze. "Jerry, you ok?"

"Yes, sorry. I was just spacing out."

"I heard about Nover. That fucker is smart."

"No shit. Speaking of Nover, both Don and I have decided Nover is your problem. Tomorrow, Buck is flying you to Casablanca to find him and that bitch and rid them from this earth. Do you understand?"

Smitty was stunned. His pause was noticeable. "Sir, I'm not the right gu....."

"You will DO WHAT I FUCKING SAY! DO YOU UNDERSTAND?" Jerry's anger burst forward.

Smitty was stuck. "Yes, sir. I'll pack now." Smitty departed.

Jerry took a deep breath. If he still cared for Smitty, that order should have been painful. In actuality, it felt good. Jerry could feel things had changed.

Jerry got up and went outside the building into the smoking area, finding exactly who he was looking for. A lanky thin man stood alone, smoking a cigarette.

Jerry spoke to him. "Hey. Just the guy I've been looking for. I have a job for you."

"Good. I'm sick of waiting. When does my training start?"

Jerry replied, "There's no training. You're going straight out on an op. It's a sniper shot. Can you handle that?"

The man was excited. "Easy day, boss. Who's the hit?"

"Slow down. Let's walk." Once they were clearly alone out on the Nissassa grounds, Jerry continued to speak. "Only you and I are to know about this. Do you understand?"

"Sure boss." That seemed logical. Assassinations were the type of thing you didn't advertise.

Jerry continued. "You're leaving for Casablanca tonight via car. You'll wait at the airport. Smitty will land there. Once he does, tail him at a distance. He has been ordered to take out the Doc and his girlfriend. Once he does that, you hit Smitty. Do you understand?"

"Got it." A smile filled the menacing face.

Jerry ended the conversation. "Again, you and I are the only to know. Payout is $35k. Is it a deal, Jackal?"

"Deal." 'Jackal,' his callsign, put out his cigarette and shook Jerry's hand. He went to his room, packed his bags, loaded his weapon into one of the Nissassa vehicles and departed under the cover of darkness. Jackal wasn't Jerry's first pick, but Longbow 23 was in the backwoods of Iran. Jackal was a new hire given the expected increase in future missions. He wasn't Special Operations, but rather a former NY Army Guard who was an instructor at the 2nd Squadron, 101st Cavalry Regiment sniper training. Jackal had seen significant action in Afghanistan and had a reputation as being the Army's best shot for over three years. His training in NY however grew boring and he no longer found excitement in shooting paper targets at long distances. His application read like a shark who missed the taste of blood. With 11 kills to his credit in war, Jackal was a proficient combat sniper. Jerry was certain he had little to worry about.

Chapter Forty-Nine

The Bonds of Battle

Buck landed back in Akjoujt early the next morning. On the ramp were Jerry and Smitty. Buck parked, shut down the engines and exited the aircraft. His last call with Jerry was cold and Buck had no intention of warming the situation.

"Good morning, Buck," Jerry said, as if trying to perform some level of damage control.

"Good morning, sir. What's the mission today? My manifest says one passenger to Casablanca?"

"That's correct."

"OK, but if Casablanca is going to become a regular route, we will need to discuss compensation for that. Casablanca is two flights for me as I need to bed down back at Rabat. Either that, or I have to pay transient fees for the aircraft in Casablanca."

"I understand, here is some money for all the troubles. I am sorry about yesterday. That won't happen again." Jerry handed a thick envelope to Buck. It would more than cover his costs.

"Ok. Thanks." Buck looked at Smitty. "Are you the pax?" Smitty nodded. "You ready to go?" Again, Smitty nodded. "OK. Get in."

Smitty entered the plane through the cargo ramp and door. Buck stopped him and said, "Hey, if you guys are going to pay this kind of money, you can ride in the copilot seat if you wish?" Smitty secured his bags in the cargo area then joined Buck in the front cockpit. After a few minutes, the engine was running and they both waved goodbye to Jerry. Jerry waived back and lamented how this would be the last time he saw Smitty alive. Business was business.

Once in the aircraft, Buck handed Smitty a head set and showed him the 'talk' button on the communication cord. They started engines, taxied out, and took off within 20 minutes.

"Really pretty up here, don't you think?" Buck was trying to generate some conversation.

"Yeah. Every shade of brown imaginable." Smitty didn't ignore him outright, but clearly wasn't up for a significant discussion. The two remained silent for a bit.

Buck again spoke. "Hey, I don't know if I ever told you, but my background was flying USAF Special Ops C-130s. Both Gunships and Talons. It was a great gig but unfortunately, I had to give it up."

"OK, I'll bite. Why?" Smitty's response wasn't much, but it was enough.

"I got an Article 15" Buck paused and looked at Smitty's face. There was no reaction. "You know, UCMJ punishment." Smitty remained still. "I was on a mission in Afghanistan. We had intermittent comms with the forces on the ground who we were providing overwatch in our Gunship. All of the sudden, they were engaged with a Taliban force of far superior numbers. I kept hearing them try to communicate, but it was useless. No one on our crew could make out their message. We watched on our EO (Electronic Optics) and IR (InfraRed) systems as they were getting overrun. It all happened so fast, we couldn't get rounds on the ground before the enemy was too close to discern our guys from theirs. I never heard our forces call 'Danger Close,' you know, the call which would have authorized me to fire even though the enemy was potentially too close to discern from friendly forces. Even without the call, I couldn't take it. I opened up with the 25mm and 40mm cannons. For 10 minutes I raged fury onto the Taliban until they retreated. I prayed to God over and over to guide the rounds away from our forces and onto the enemy because the targeting pod just showed a single blur of images in close contact. The rest of the flight home my crew was silent. The tapes would clearly prove I never received the call. I was grounded for the investigation. Luckily, I killed no friendlies, but my career was over. The Air

Force had me dead to rights. I didn't fight it. I accepted my article 15 and would do it again."

Smitty just looked out the window. "Life's a bitch, then you die. Your story sucks." Smitty was actually significantly moved by the story, but he couldn't escape the fact he was on a mercenary mission targeted on a dear friend.

"Yeah, maybe. Just thought I'd share it. Given the kinda guys I'm flying in and out of the mine, a number of these faces look familiar. Like I've sat at chow hall tables with them in places we don't discuss."

Smitty didn't respond. His eyes continued looking out over the horizon. His talking mood was over. Buck looked over at him. Smitty didn't move. But it was clear to Buck that Smitty was somber. And he'd bet a dollar to donuts a small tear had formed in the corner of Smitty's left eye.

The two didn't speak for the remainder of the flight. Buck landed and taxied in. After shutting down, Buck opened the cargo area and helped Smitty fetch his bags.

Smitty took his bags, set them down and reached out his hand. "Hey, thanks for the flight." Surprised, Buck met Smitty's hand and shook it. Smitty continued. "… and about your story. I already knew it. You were flying over Khost, Afghanistan. I was there, on the ground. Thanks for what you did. If it wasn't for you, I wouldn't be alive." Buck froze. He'd never met any of the ground forces from that mission. They stared at each other and soon to both, the handshake seemed inadequate. They hugged. A hard hug. They needed that hug more than they knew. Their eyes filled with tears. And that's ok.

Smitty and Buck separated. Buck reached into the cockpit, grabbed the thick envelope of cash he received from Jerry and handed it to Smitty. "Here. Take this."

Smitty looked at it puzzled. "What is this for?"

"You. You're the only one I've ever met from that day. The bonds of battle are thicker than anything. Sometimes even family. You need this more than I. All I ask is you consider a new start. New decisions. Buddy, this isn't the place for you."

Smitty just stared at Buck. He took the money, hugged him one more time and walked away. After 15 steps, he stopped, turned around and said, "Thanks…. Thanks, man."

As Smitty walked away, a car outside the airport watched him walk across the tarmac. Jackal was in place. Smitty was a marked man.

Chapter Fifty

The Tortoise and the Hare

The only positive aspect to Curt and Allison's bus ride in North Africa was the fall season brought bearable temperatures albeit still quite hot. The trip to the ferry was adventurous and somewhere in the middle of the African desert, the bus broke down with a flat tire. Curt and Allison were hot, sticky, sweaty and stinky, but they were together and safe and that was all that mattered. As the bus lay stranded on the side of the road, Curt watched every car approach, wondering what actions he could take if it was Nissassa goons. He had no weapon; he was pinned on a bus. He was a sitting duck. Tactically, Curt realized he was better off praying to God than trying to devise a tactical plan. Allison laid her head on his shoulder and slept – something Curt had little of and would likely get none in the next few days. His anxiety and hyperawareness were in overload. He was vigilant to the core. Colors, sounds, smells, emotions. It was a great place to be when in battle. It was a nightmare on a bus stuck in the middle of Morocco.

****

Smitty rented a car at the airport. He drove around hotels in Casablanca, questioning their staff. It didn't take long to find where they stayed. After a few hours of questioning cab drivers around that hotel, he again was able to uncover their trip to the Mohammedia bus station. Smitty jumped in his car and followed their trail. The Mohammedia bus station was small and had one employee. Discovering Curt's continued travel was easy. Smitty again jumped in his car and made his way to Al Hoceima. Smitty was quickly closing the distance between himself and Curt.

Eventually, the bus tire was repaired, and the journey continued. Curt's vigilance slightly eased as cars approaching from behind were fewer. They approached the port of Al Hoceima and saw a ferry at the dock, waiting. The two jumped off the bus and ran. After buying their tickets, they processed through immigration control. Curt handed his 'John Holmes' passport to the border official.... And prayed. Buck had done little favor to Curt. The passport was in the name of a 1970s porn star, and the photo was actually from the FBI's wanted poster.

Fifteen seconds felt like an eternity as Curt stood in front of the Customs official. Luckily, that official neither knew of John Holmes, or the wanted photo. He stamped the passport then opened Allison's. Again, they prayed, and again, the official stamped her passport. They were both approved for travel. Jerry's failure to inform Don about Allison's involvement had proved catastrophic, yet again proving the old military adage, *'Bad news does not get better with age.'*

****

Smitty approached the Al Hoceima bus terminal and watched as the ferry pulled away from the port. As soon as he saw that ship, he knew where Curt was. He didn't have to question anyone. Smitty ditched his rental car and walked up to the ferry ticketing office. The next ferry would be at 0730 the following morning. Much of his closure distance would be lost. Smitty bought a ticket, picked up his bags and walked to a nearby hotel. Given there was little to do, he checked in, cleaned up and set out for an early dinner. He'd made great progress on his pursuit. There was time for a nice break.

Minutes behind Smitty, Jackal pulled into Al Hoceima. Jackal's tracking effort was far easier than Smitty's. Jerry had slipped a small beacon into Smitty's gear. Jackal merely watched an app on his iPhone and knew exactly where Smitty was at any given moment. Jackal pulled into the Ferry parking lot off in the distance. He watched as Smitty purchased a ticket and walked to a hotel. Lighting another cigarette, Jackal slowly drove along the Al Hoceima waterfront. He found a nice hotel, parked the car, grabbed a change of clothes and entered. Behind the desk was a small, elderly man.

"Do you have a room for the night?"

"Yes, Sir! We have many. Would you like a suite, a king bed or a single bed?"

"A king bed would be fine. Do you have one that overlooks the water?"

"Of course. Your passport, please?"

Jackal froze. He had not expected to leave tracks, but at this point, there was few alternatives. He reached into his pocket and handed over his passport. It was a fake.

"Thank you.... Mr.... Corbin. Here is your key. Would you like breakfast?"

"No, thank you. One question. Do you know when the next ferry is?"

"Yes, sir. It is tomorrow at 7:30AM. Would you like me to book you a ticket and add it to your room charges?"

"That would be excellent. Thank you." Jackal turned away and proceeded to his room. Once inside, he checked his iPhone. Smitty was stationary in his hotel just 200 meters away.

****

Back on the ferry, Curt and Allison settled in for the trip. Crossing the Mediterranean Sea would take six hours. They had secured a two-person berthing on the port side. They entered the room and Curt closed the door. The room was small, but more than sufficient. Curt double locked the door and stacked their bags against it. The room included a window that tilted to allow in fresh air. Curt's mind calculated the force it would take to break it and jump into the sea if needed. To many, his thoughts would perhaps seem crazy, but Curt's brain was locked into this mode. 'OK,' he thought. *'Primary entry/exit secure and a secondary exit if needed. Good to go.'* His blood pressure slowly reduced along with his pulse. He looked at Allison as she watched him. This Curt wasn't the Curt she knew. She still loved him but could not hide her concern. "Baby, are you ok?"

"Yes. Of course. I'm fine. Why would you ask?"

Allison looked at the hotel door. "Well, I realize we are fugitives, but are we running from Nissassa or Godzilla? You realize, to get dinner tonight, it will take us 10 minutes just to get out of our room. And I pray the ship doesn't catch fire. Oh, and I saw you look at the window. If you think for a second I am jumping, you've lost your freaking mind."

Curt slumped down onto the bed. Allison was right. The ghosts that haunted him for years were back. He'd fought so hard to rid himself of being this person. The truth was, it would always be in him. "Yeah. You're right. I'm sorry."

Allison comforted him, "Curt, you don't have to be sorry. I understand. Come here." She wrapped her arms around him as they both laid down on the bed. His head curled into her chest. Physically, Curt was much stronger than Allison, but in this instant, he felt far safer wrapped in her arms than he would have felt carrying three long guns. The discovery he was facilitating Nissassa's mission, the lack of sleep, and the demons of Post-Traumatic Stress Disorder (PTSD) overwhelmed him. A single tear streamed down Curt's cheek as his head rested on Allison's arm. They both fell asleep. Tomorrow would be another difficult day.

Chapter Fifty-One

Snakes in the Grass

Smitty was finishing up in the bathroom after a long, hot shower. He stepped out of the hotel and paused as he watched the sun lower on the horizon. It was a beautiful evening in Al Hoceima, the sea breeze was cool, and a bit of humidity filled the air. It was heaven compared to Akjoujt. Smitty walked down the street to the waterfront and found a lovely small seafood restaurant. It would be perfect to watch the sunset. The streets were alive with tourists, travelers and locals. It was a nice atmosphere. Smitty sipped a glass of white wine.

Waiting for his food, Smitty pulled out his phone and opened Google maps. The ferry that Curt and Allison were riding had a final destination of Motril, Spain. Again, he thought, *'Curt, you're making this way too easy.'*

Looking around Motril, Spain, Smitty tried to predict Curt's next move. Malaga was the closest large city. It was a seaside locale which would be full of tourists – a good place to hide. The problem was, Smitty was fairly certain Curt's plan was not to hide. Smitty believed Curt wanted to get to the U.S. as fast as possible. Malaga wouldn't be the place for Curt.

Smitty narrowed down his predictions to Seville and Madrid. Both had large airports with daily flights to the U.S. He had considered that Curt might try to find another large city outside of Spain, but quickly dismissed the idea. Once in Spain, Curt was in the European Union (E.U.) Schengen Area. Any information Spain had, other E.U. nations would as well. Border jumping to evade any pursuit would be pointless, time consuming and expensive. Dinner was served and Smitty closed his phone. He'd call Jerry later that evening and relay the day's activities as well as his predictions. After a deep breath and enjoying the aroma of his food, the next few moments he'd spend enjoying life... something Smitty had not done in quite a while.

****

Also in Al Hoceima, Jackal was out on the town. He'd found a local pub, more his style. The TV displayed a local soccer match, a ceiling fan swirled the air and locals filled the joint. Jackal ate a local chicken dish and drank Casablanca beer. He looked at his phone and opened the tracking app. Smitty was stationary along the ocean front. He closed the app. Jackal had no worries. Tonight would be relaxing and well deserved after a long drive to Casablanca and another to Al Hoceima.

Jackal ordered another beer, watched the game and called Jerry. "Good evening, Boss."

"Jackal. Good to hear from you." Jerry stepped out of the Ops Center. This call would remain private. "What's your status?"

"Sir, I have traveled to a small port town east of Casablanca called Al Hoceima. Our friend bought a ferry ticket to Spain but won't depart until tomorrow at 0730. He has secured a room in a hotel. I too secured a room approximately 200 meters away."

"Perfect. Thanks for the update. You're doing great."

"Thanks, Boss. Out."

Jackal drank a sip of beer. It was a good evening to relax.

Jerry went back into the Ops Center. "Tiny, what's the location and status of Smitty's Cell Phone?"

Tiny moved over to one of the tall racks of computers and electronics. He typed in Smitty's number and after a few seconds, a computer screen with a map pinpointed Smitty's phone, all without alerting Smitty to the ping. "Jerry, according to this current hit, it's active east of Casablanca on the coast. Should I call him?"

"No, no. No need," Jerry quickly responded. "I just wanted to see how his progress on Nover. I'll call him in a bit." Jerry had no intention of calling.

****

At the Baku airport, a U.S. Air Force C-130 offloaded the teams under the cover of night. Two bread vans pulled up and were quickly loaded down with gear and personnel. As the bread vans pulled away, an Azerbaijani Customs official approached the aircraft commander. "Good evening, sir."

"Good evening, officer. How can I help you?"

"May I please have your manifest. Also, why are those vans departing?"

"Sir, here is the manifest. Those vans have our maintenance personnel who arrived yesterday to receive the aircraft. They got out here to meet us, then realized they'd forgotten their tools. Sorry about that. They'll be back shortly."

"Ok. But I am supposed to be the first to meet the plane."

"Yes sir. I know. I can call them back now if you wish, but we have a fuel leak on the #4 engine and it's pissing fuel all over your ramp. I'd like to get that fixed as soon as possible."

"There's fuel on the ramp?!!" The Customs Official's primary concern had now shifted to a potential fire at the airport. "No, no. Please, stop the leak! But please, just not again. OK?"

"Sure. Thanks." The lie had worked. The official reviewed the manifest. It only included the aircrew and their gear. The infill was proceeding smoothly.

Jerry received a text. "ARR GYD. AS FRAGGED," Jerry smiled. It translated as *'Arrived GYD as planned.'* GYD is the three-letter identifier for the Baku airport. The plan was progressing as scheduled.

****

Smitty finished his meal and paid the bill. The cool sea breeze was wonderful, and the strand invited him for a stroll. How could he refuse? Smitty walked along and was struck by the wealth disparities in Al Hoceima, Morocco. Multimillion dollar luxury boats were tied to the docks, the tourists were dressed in the latest fashion. But just 50 meters from the sea the apartments and houses were shabby. The busses, the cars, and the bikes were all twenty years old at a minimum. Smitty stood along the strand and pulled out his phone. There was one last thing to do before retiring for the evening and that was to call Jerry. He pulled out his phone......

Smitty stopped as if he'd seen a ghost. He lowered his phone. It couldn't be. He walked towards what he prayed he was not seeing. It was a vehicle, far newer than those surrounding it but covered in dust. He approached and his heart sank. His fears proved true. He'd driven this truck numerous times. It was a Nissassa truck. Smitty knew there were few reasons one would be in Al Hoceima. His wonderful evening had ended. Placing his phone back into his pocket, there would be no call to Jerry.

Chapter Fifty-Two

Hunting a Jackal

Smitty looked into the vehicle. It was clearly from Nissassa. In the back of the truck was a locked gator case, mounted to the bed. Smitty knew that's where Longbow 23 normally kept his weapon. Very strange, as Longbow 23 was now most likely in Azerbaijan with the two teams. Smitty looked around and found the closest hotel and entered. It was Jackal's hotel and the same elderly clerk at the desk.

"Good evening, sir. I'm sorry, we have no more rooms."

"Ah. I understand. I am arriving a bit late. I was supposed to meet some of my American friends here, but we all arrived individually. Do you think any of them may have checked into your hotel?"

"I have a few Americans tonight. Most are couples."

"No, I think this would likely be one or maybe few guys together."

"Hmmmm. I think I had only one single man check in. Hold on." The man turned around and flipped through some paperwork. Pulling out a single piece of paper, he said, "Yes, here he is. A Mister Corbin. Unfortunately, our hotel policy is to protect the privacy of our guests."

Smitty reached in his wallet and pulled out a $100 bill. He handed it to the clerk and said, "I completely understand, but our group has one night in town, and it would be a shame if I could not link up with him soonest."

The clerk took the money. "Well, maybe this once. I understand." He pocked the cash and handed the Xeroxed paper of the passport to Smitty. The name did not ring a bell, but the photo was clear. It was Jackal.

"Nope. Sorry to waste your time. This isn't one of our gang. They are probably in another hotel. Thanks for your effort and have a great night." Smitty's blood boiled. He had interviewed Jackal for the job and knew exactly the skill sets he possessed. The pieces of the puzzle were coming together, and the picture was clear.

"No problem, sir. Can I help you find another hotel?"

"You are too kind. You've done enough. Thank you and good evening."

Smitty exited the hotel and began a close perimeter recon of the hotel. He noted where there was heavy foot traffic, what were the approach avenues to the hotel. Where and how much law enforcement was in place. What, if any closed-circuit cameras were in the area. His mind was fixated. His anger towards Jerry would have to wait. Now was time to employ his professional skills… and few in the business were better than Smitty. Jackal's hotel was towards the end of the strand. Smitty presumed Jackal was also out for dinner and if so, would have walked to the center of town towards the night life. Smitty walked about fifty meters in that direction and found a small service alley between two buildings. Smitty went into the alley. Picking up an old piece of aluminum, Smitty quickly polished it up and placed it on the sidewalk out towards the street. He walked back to the corner of the building and leaned against it. Hunching down, he lowered his head between his shoulders, looking like a vagrant. His eyes however, focused in on the piece of aluminum which provided a decent reflection of approaching passersby. He blended into the environment like city camouflage.

****

Jackal was finishing another beer. He paid his tab and began his walk back to the hotel. It was late and the nightlife in the heart of Al Hoceima was thriving. He departed the bar and began the journey back to his hotel, a path that would lead him past Smitty. Further from the city center, there were few if any on the streets. 100 meters now from Smitty, he approached, unaware. Jackal saw a man, hunch against the wall. It was Smitty, but unrecognizable from the numerous other homeless vagrants along the business walls of the boardwalk. Jackal dismissed him. His mistake would prove costly. Once within reach, Smitty sprung up, grabbed him by the back of the neck, and swung him into the alley. Increasing speed as they turned, Smitty smashed Jackal's skull into the wall. Jackal fell to the ground, knocked out cold. Looking back out into the street for any witnesses, Smitty found none.

    The two would 'walk' down the strand, Jackal slung over Smitty's shoulder. Acting as if the two had just finished a wonderful night of drinking, Smitty added a small stagger to his gate and carried Jackal back to his hotel. Passersby laughed, chuckled and often thought, *'Typical Americans.'*

    Nearing his hotel, Smitty laid Jackal on the ground by the rear service entrance. Quickly, he circled back to the hotel main entrance, casually walked in, wishing the desk clerk a good evening. Past the desk, he navigated through the closed kitchen to the service door. Picking up Jackal, then walking up the stairs, Smitty struggled a bit, wishing he'd tried to stay in a bit better shape, also wishing the hotel had not installed Closed Circuit TV cameras in the elevator.

    Once in the room, Smitty secured Jackal to a chair, tying his legs together. He ripped the pillowcases into long pieces and anchored Jackals forearms to the chair's armrest. Jackal would be going nowhere soon. Once done, Smitty took a minute and caught his breath. In the bathroom, Smitty soaked a washcloth and filled a glass with water. Turning back towards Jackal, he threw the cold water from the glass on his face. Jackal awoke with a raging headache.

    Smitty spoke. "Hello, Jackal. You have one chance at this. What the fuck are you doing here?"

Jackal's mind raced. He'd not planned for such an evening and scrambled for a lie. "I'm back up for the hit on Nover."

"Fucking liar." Smitty's head motioned down to Jackal's right hand. He ordered Jackal, "Look!" Jackal's hand was heavily tied to the armchair, exposing only the four fingers. "Which one do you want broken first?"

"No! No! No! I'm telling the truth!"

Smitty took a deep breath and calmed himself. "OK. Let's presume you're telling the truth. If that were the case, how could I, as the second highest officer at our Nissassa operation not know about this?"

"I don't know, man! Jerry just told me to track Nover in case you failed."

"Great. That's helpful. So, you also followed Nover, correct?"

"Yes!" Clearly, Jackal had not, but he was now committed to the story.

"And you know he was traveling in a rental car alone to Al Hoceima."

"Yes! Yes! We are on the same job!"

"Ok. Good. One question. What color was his car?"

Jackal was screwed. Smitty knew there was no right answer. Curt wasn't traveling alone, and he had traveled to Al Hoceima by bus, not car. Whatever color Jackal guessed was going to be wrong. "I think it was white!"

Smitty shoved the wet washcloth down Jackal's throat, reached down and bent his ring finger back until it touched the back of his forearm. The joints popped and the tendons tore. Jackal screamed in pain. As Smitty let go, the finger lay twisted sideways over the others, clearly out of joint. Jackal was in excruciating pain. After a minute or so, his screaming calmed down. Smitty removed the washcloth.

"Any other colors you wanna guess? You have three more fingers on your trigger hand."

Jackal's only talent was long range rifle shooting. With a trigger hand full of broken fingers, he'd be flipping burgers and slinging fries at McDonalds after a few more wrong guesses. He also knew there were no international military agreements to protect him as there were when he was in the military. No Geneva Convention. No 'Laws of Armed Conflict.' Jackal was playing in the big boy's arena and his life was in the balance.

Jackal had a reckoning. He softly and slowly said, "Jerry ordered me to kill you after you hit Nover."

Smitty wasn't surprised, but pleased he was getting the truth. "Now, start at the beginning. How did you find me?"

"I drove to Casablanca the night before you flew in. Jerry put an app on my phone that tracked you. I think he put some kind of beacon on you. I swear. I didn't want to do it! Please. You gotta let me go!"

"Let you go??!! Are you nuts!" Smitty shoved the washcloth back into Jackals mouth. Jackal began screaming, albeit muffled, in anticipation of the next destroyed finger. Smitty grabbed his gear and dumped it onto the bed. After a quick search, he found the beacon sewn into the webbing of his backpack. It was approximately the size of three stacked quarters.

Smitty reached onto the coffee table. All of Jackals pocket contents rested there. He grabbed Jackals iPhone. "What's your PIN code?"

"8934." The phone opened. A good sign. Jackal was starting to tell the truth. "What the app?"

"It's called 'Stalker.' It's on the second page of apps." As Smitty flipped through the pages, he saw Jackal's phone background. It was a photo of Jackal, a woman and a young child, Jackal's family no doubt. Smitty opened the app, two dots stacked over each other. The phone geolocated itself and the beacon in the same place.

Smitty closed the app and turned the phone towards Jackal, "Is this your family?"

His voice trembled. "Yes. That's my wife, Joy, and my son, Brandon."

Smitty opened Jackal's contacts. "Joy lives at 354 Sycamore St in Rochester, NY?"

Jackal just looked down. This was all far too much. Again trembling... "Yes."

"Are you still married or are you separated?" What Jackal failed to understand was Smitty was looking for any way out of this situation that would save Jackal's life.

"We are married. I took the job because it was easy, fast money."

"OK, let's call her."

"NO!" Jackal's fear now raged.

"Buddy, I'm giving you a last chance to say goodbye to your wife and kid." Smitty dialed Joy's phone. It rang. Smitty put in on Speaker and held it up to Jackal's face.

She answered, "Hey, Babycakes!! Isn't it late there?" Joy's voice was warm and welcoming – happy to get a call from her man.

Jackal tried his best to clear up his speech. "Hey, Babe.... Yeah, uh, I uh, I just wanted to call and say good night." Smitty stared into Jackal's eyes.

"Awww. That's so sweet. Hey, do you know what Brandon did today? He actually stood up on his own while holding the coffee table! It was so amazing. Well, he's not walking yet but I was really proud of him. He keeps saying Da Da Da Da and I am certain he means 'Dad.' He misses you. I miss you." Joy just rambled, and as long as she was talking, Jackal didn't have to speak, which he could barely do. Tears rolled down the sides of his face.

Joy had finished her story. Jackal spoke, "That's... That's great. He's such a big boy. Look... I uh, I gotta go. Give him a hug for me. I... I Love you." Jackal stifled a huge sob.

Joy understood and said her farewells, "I love you too! Good night, Baby! Dream about me!"

Jackal's head down, defeated. He responded, "Always. Good.... Goodbye."

Smitty hung up the phone. He grabbed Jackal's hair, pulled his head back until his mouth was open. In a swift movement, he shoved the beacon down Jackals throat, holding his mouth closed until it was swallowed.

Continuing to hold Jackal by the hair, Smitty turned him until they were eye to eye. "Buddy, I'm fairly certain this line of work is not for you. You have two choices. The first choice is you will be alive and shit that transmitter out in about a day. I will take your phone and the cash Jerry gave you. I will track you until then. I will leave your credit cards, car keys and your passport on the table. Tomorrow when the maid enters, you'll claim to have been tied up by a prostitute but refuse to go to the authorities. You'll drive back to Rabat, book a ticket to New York and go home. Eventually, you will shit the transmitter out. When you do, you'll put it in your pocket. Once in New York and back with Joy, place the transmitter in your house and leave it. At that point, I recommend you move your family and hide. That's choice one. Do you understand?"

Jackal saw a chance at life. "Yes! Yes!"

Smitty continued, "Your second choice is you'll never shit that transmitter out because your body will no longer be functional."

Jackal started crying. "Please! I want to live!!!" It was all too much.

"OK, option one. Great. Just realize, I have your phone, I have your family's number and address. I also have about five contacts in New York and can dispatch them in a day to do whatever I require. Do you understand."

"Yes!! Yes! I get it!"

Smitty repacked all his gear and took Jackal's room key. He'd be sleeping in Jackal's room that night. Before departing the room, Smitty placed a call on his own phone. He looked at Jackal and raised his finger to his mouth making a 'Shhhush' sound. The phone was on speaker and Jackal could hear the ringing. The other party answered.

"Jerry, hey, it's Smitty."

"Smitty! It's late! What's going on?"

Smitty stared into Jackal's eyes as he spoke. "Yeah, sorry about that. I had dinner and lost track of time. Anyway, I tracked Nover to a town called Al Hoceima, Morocco. It looks like he bought a ticket to get on the ferry to Spain, but that's another one of his wild goose chases, much like his plane ticket back to the U.S. I have a hunch he actually continued east into Algeria."

Jerry looked at Tiny. The conversation was on a conference call and Tiny had heard everything. Tiny just shrugged his shoulders in doubt. Jerry spoke, "Algeria? Are you sure?"

Smitty responded, "Not sure, but look. Nover's passport is flagged so getting into Spain via ferry is going to be far more difficult than transiting a small border checkpoint into Algeria."

Jerry had muted the call and was looking at Tiny while Smitty spoke. Tiny agreed and quietly whispered, "What Smitty says is plausible."

Unmuting his phone, Jerry said, "OK, Smitty. Thanks for the update."

Smitty continued, "Hey, any update on our other business?" referring to the Iranian Operation. Normally, Jerry would have shared this immediately.

"Yes, yes. of course. Everything is as fragged. No problems."

Smitty was keeping up the right impressions, "Really glad to hear that. Take care, Jerry."

Jerry responded, "You too, Smitty. Keep me posted."

"Absolutely." They both hung up.

Smitty looked at Jackal. "If you fuck me, your family dies. You get that, right?"

Jackal sensed he would live. He was calming down, albeit with a broken finger that had swollen to the size of a tennis ball. "Yes, Smitty. I'm sorry."

"Yeah. Me too." Smitty left, walked down the street, and entered Jackal's room. It was late, but he couldn't sleep. His adrenaline rushed. He also needed a plan. In effect, Smitty had just served his resignation letter. In the Nissassa world, those were not met receptively. Smitty stared out the window. The ferry for tomorrow AM was on the horizon and would soon arrive. He'd be on it. Slowly, Smitty realized his only hope out of this was Curt, a guy he'd plan to kill just hours before.

****

Jerry drafted a quick text to Don in DC. *'MSN AS FRAGGED. (Mission is as planned) Loose end likely heading to Algeria, could use assist.'* Don copied it and forwarded to Steve. The first half would be well received. The second half would not. Steve would need to engage his sources to cover another embassy and create yet another small loose end to eliminate a larger one. As Steve read the text, he said out loud, "OK... This is the last one." Smitty's decoy had proven successful.

Chapter Fifty-Three

Identification Friend or Foe

It was quite late when the ferry pulled into Motril, Spain. Curt and Allison had gotten little sleep. As the ship docked, the passengers all processed into Spain. There were only a handful of Customs agents, and the lines were quite long.

After an hour, the agents were processing the passports with less scrutiny given the late hour and the overwhelming line. Holding their breath and looking like giddy tourists in love, the two pushed their passports to the agent. "Hello, Spain!" Curt shouted.

The agent was not amused. "Where are you coming from?"

Allison responded with a whopper of a fabricated story. "Our wedding! We got married in the U.S. and our honeymoon started in Casablanca! You know, the movie, right? Anyway, we are now going to travel around Europe! Isn't that wonderful? Have you been to Casablanca!?"

The agent could not care less. It was far more information than he needed or wanted. With the line growing ever more impatient, the agent stamped the passports and waived them through.

Safely in Spain, they went to the bus terminal and bought two tickets to Madrid. Smitty's guess was right. Unfortunately, the next bus was not until 10:00 the next morning. The town of Motril was shut down for the night.

There would be no further travel until the morning. Curt and Allison found a small hotel and went back to sleep.

****

Back in D.C., Steve sat in his office, burning the midnight oil. It was nearly 0100Hrs. As he worked, a figure entered. Steve looked up…. "Mr. President!? It's late! Why are you up?"

The President dismissed his question. "What are you working on, Steve?"

"Just closing loose ends, sir."

"I presume it is our Nissassa project?" The President was correct.

"Sir, everything is on track, but there is a former asset on the run that we are trying to neutralize."

Curious, the President said, "Are you worried?"

Steve replied, "Not really, sir."

The President continued, "Do I have reason to worry?"

"Absolutely not, sir." Steve would protect the President at all costs.

Slightly changing the subject, the President said, "Good. Before the operation takes place, I'd like to go over a few different courses of action on how we react to the Ayatollah's death. Just you and I at this point. Once the news breaks, we will include the press secretary. Steve, this is going to drastically improve the state of global security. It will be one of the most historic events of this century."

"Yes, Mr. President. I agree. I'll work on some courses of action tonight."

The President cut him off, "No, they can wait until tomorrow. The Op isn't for another few days. Go to bed Steve, it's late."

"Yes, Mr. President."

"Good night, Steve." And with that, the President disappeared.

****

The morning sun warmed Al Hoceima like a favorite old blanket. Smitty grabbed his gear and headed to the ferry. Once onboard, he pulled out his phone. Realizing it was a long shot, he sent a text to Curt. *'Curt, Smitty here. I need to see you. I quit Nissassa and am on the ferry behind you. I'll meet you anytime, anyplace. You say when and where. The only easy day was yesterday.'* The last sentence was a common phrase among SEALS, to Smitty, it perhaps was never more fitting than right now. Smitty pulled out Jackal's phone and opened the tracking app. Jackal was still in the hotel room. The cleaning crew would soon find him. Smitty chuckled thinking about it. He was still not certain if Curt would go to Madrid or Seville. Both were viable. Finally, he pulled out a coin and flipped it. The outcome in his mind was Madrid. That would be the next stop. Another good guess.

****

Curt and Allison awoke in Motril, Spain, around 0600Hrs. They showered and exited the hotel. Waiting for their bus, the two strolled down a village street and stopped for breakfast. For the first time, they were together, in a country outside of Northern Africa and enjoying life. Curt's hypervigilance had calmed, and he was able to enjoy the moment. Allison just stared at him as she sipped her coffee.

"Curt…. What are we going to do? We can't keep running forever. Do you have a plan?"

Allison was right, and Curt knew it. "Well, we're sitting on the southern Spanish coast, eating an amazing breakfast in the sun. I'd say we're doing OK." Curt smiled at her. His answer was sarcastic.

"Great. I guess we apply for Spanish residency?"

"OK. I don't know everything, but I do know this. I need to get to the U.S. I need to expose Nissassa, and I'd like to do it before the events in Iran unfold."

"Perfect! I agree. Now..... How?"

"Yeah. I'm working on that. When we get to Madrid, I can't go to the Embassy as I know Nissassa's connections are deep enough to potentially snare us there. I also don't think my 'John Holmes' passport is going to get me into the U.S. As much as Buck may have helped us, I think there are limits to his abilities."

"So, you don't really have an answer."

"No. Not yet. But we have a 7-hour bus ride to Madrid, and I have time to figure it out." It was the best Curt could offer.

As they ate their breakfast, the port town slowly came to life. The next ferry from Al Hoceima would arrive around 1300Hrs, three hours after Curt and Allison departed for Madrid.

The scenery was gorgeous as their bus meandered north across Southern Spain; the colors were vibrant, much more so than the myriad browns of Northern Africa. Curt gazed out the window and rewound the past forty-eight hours in his mind; trying to assess the events from different perspectives. Their ability to keep moving was good. Where they held up were solid locations. Buck's help could have proved disastrous, but in the end, it was a risk he needed to take. Everything made sense except one aspect. How was Allison able to transit customs? Certainly, Jerry had to at least presume she was with him, and given the amount of security and his passport flagging, Jerry had friends in D.C. with serious power. It didn't make sense. Curt had racked his brain and became bored – never a good thing when on the run as a fugitive. He pulled out his phone, still in Airplane mode. He wanted to turn it on. He wanted to see the news. He wanted to hear from friends to include Ms. Wanda. His wants were strong, but he also wanted to avoid capture. Turning on his phone would be catastrophic. Or would it?????

He looked towards the front of the bus. A sign hung over the driver's head, "WLAN Gratis!" *'That's it,'* he thought.

Curt pulled out his phone and turned it on. As it powered up, he immediately put it in airplane mode, disabling the all transmit and receive connections. He opened his VPN app and scanned through until he found Morocco, the last place Nissassa knew his location. *(A VPN or a Virtual Private Network is a program that masks a device's location, generating a fictitious one in another location.)*

Next, Curt disabled his geolocation services on his phone's settings. *'OK,'* he thought. *'Here goes nothing.'* He activated his Wi-Fi, found the bus server and joined, triple checking his VPN was active.

As soon as the link was established, emails flowed in like crazy. His Apple iChat also loaded up... Many from Kamil and Jawad. He couldn't scroll through them fast enough. He waited until all had loaded then disconnected the phone from all transmit and receive functions again. At least at this point, he could see what was going on in the world.

Curt scrolled through his emails. Many were from Ms. Wanda who was worried about him. He read them all. He smiled, knowing someone like her existed in his life and cared. *'Soon, Ms. Wanda. I'll write you soon,'* he thought. Messages from Kamil and Buck all attempted to be coy, but most failed miserably. Jawad was worried, but in true fashion, continued to update Curt on the ongoing events in the hospital. His emails also contained numerous spam messages. He quickly scanned those and disposed of them. Next, Curt reviewed his text messages. Fewer incidents of spam, but still plenty to sift through. Quickly scanning and disposing of most, he found Smitty's message. His eyes lit up.

"Allison... Look!" He showed her the message.

Allison was staring out the window, admiring the countryside. Startled at his alarm, she read the text and said, "Holy Shit. Do you think it's really him?"

Curt was perplexed. "I think it is. But I'm not sure, and I don't know why he's reaching out."

"What are you going to do?" Allison was intrigued but nervous.

"I'm gonna write the number back." Curt pulled out his burner phone and turned it on. He copied the number and typed *'6 Sep 2007, Zabul.'* The phone texting function was 'old school' in that each letter was a selection from the numerical keypad. The process was far slower than his iPhone but also far safer. No need to tempt fate with more WIFI time.

Allison watched him type and just before he sent it, she stopped him saying, "Hey, you misspelled 'Kabul.'"

"Nope. That's right." He sent it.

Smitty's phone buzzed. He looked down at the unknown number and saw the message. He instantly knew it was from Curt. In reply back, he wrote, *'PFC Mykel Miller.'*

Within seconds, Curt's phone buzzed. Curt smiled. "It's him."

Allison was excited, "How do you know?"

Curt's response was somber. "Private First-Class Miller was someone dear to us. He was killed in action in Zabul, Afghanistan on 6 Sep 2007. Both Smitty and I wear a POW/MIA (Prisoner of War / Missing in Action) bracelet on our wrist with his information."

Allison was also convinced it was Smitty, but not at all sure any meeting would be friendly, "OK, great, but is it a trap?"

"I don't know. It may very well be. But if Smitty is no longer with Nissassa and wants to talk, it is about the best chance, if not the only chance we have to get to the U.S." Curt took a chance. He typed in *'Madrid. MTF.'* (More to follow)

Smitty's hands were sweating, and his heart raced. His longshot was paying off. Soon, his phone buzzed again. He read the incoming text in his mind, *'Madrid. MTF.'* Smitty looked up from his phone and out the ferry window. The coastline of Spain was visible. The land, along with Curt's recent text, were ever so welcoming. Opportunities abound.

Smitty wanted to write back, to write more, to explain to Curt everything was different, but he couldn't afford to over play this. He fidgeted and needed something to do. Reaching for Jackal's phone, he turned it on and then opened the tracking app. The beacon was moving along the Moroccan coastline towards Rabat. Not a 100% assurance yet, but a good sign Jackal was following the plan. Smitty said under his breath, 'Good choice, Jackal. Keep it up.'

****

Nearing the border from Azerbaijan into Iran, a 'jingle truck' slowly progressed to the Astra, Iran checkpoint. The trucks in the area got the 'jingle truck' name from the numerous ornaments and accoutrements drivers hung from their windshields and all over their cabs. It was the driver's version of 'flair' and the more one had, the better.

The Astra customs official stopped the truck and asked for papers. Astra is actually a city in both Azerbaijan and Iran, split by the Astarachay River and sharing beautiful beaches along the Caspian Sea. The driver handed his papers to the guard. The guard walked to the back of the truck and opened the cargo area. Large duffle bags along with bags of grain filled the truck. There was nothing to see. Minutes later, the driver was waived through. He would continue down route 16 which paralleled the Azerbaijan / Iranian border.

The scenery was beautiful as the Astarachay river served as the border, continuing into Iran's Baby Yanlu National Forest. With no other vehicles around, the jingle truck slowed. The two teams emerged from the tree line and jumped into the back of the truck.

An hour earlier, the driver had dropped off the teams on the Azerbaijan side of the river. They waded through the

Astarachay river and waited in the forest. Once inside the jingle truck, the teams continued. They were now in Iran.

Chapter Fifty-Four

<u>Guernica</u>

The bus from Motril pulled into a bustling Madrid train station. Curt and Allison took their bags and searched out a hotel. Now low on cash and exchanging it to their last 35 Euros at the bus station, their only option was to use Allison's credit cards. This was far from desired, but truly their only play. Eventually, they found a place near the train station. If Smitty was telling the truth, their need to hide might be easing.

After dropping their bags, Curt and Allison recon'ed the town. He was looking for a place to meet that afforded protection from any unforeseen twist that Smitty might present. The train station was busy, but too busy. City parks would not be busy enough nor offer enough security. He soon found his meeting place: Queen Sofia's National Art Museum or Museo Nacional Centro de Arte Reina Sofía. There would be security and some people but not enough to blend and hide if Smitty wanted to strike and get away. The museum would be blanketed in security cameras. If Smitty had any ill intensions, he'd need days to plan something in such a location.

It was growing late in the afternoon; the museum would close at 1900Hrs. They had fifty minutes; more than enough time to find an ideal meeting spot in the museum. Curt and Allison paid an entrance fee and entered. As they walked around, they located a grand hall in which Picasso's Guernica hung, the museum's most famous piece of art. It was surrounded by video cameras with a guard standing in the vicinity. It was perfect. Curt viewed the entire room through a tactical and operational lens while Allison was consumed by the beautiful art. This was the spot.

Madrid's siesta or mid-day break was over, and the restaurants were opening. It was time for dinner. Curt felt good. He had a plan. They exited the museum and sought out a small Tapas restaurant in the heart of Madrid.

As they were seated, Allison asked, "Aren't you going to send a text to Smitty?"

Curt responded, "Yes, in due time. I have no intention of giving him too much opportunity."

Confused, Allison said, "Too much time? For what? Curt, come on. The museum is closed. Do you honestly think he'd get to Madrid, break into the museum tonight just to build a plan?"

Curt just stared at Allison. Frustrated, he lashed out. "Uhhh. Yes. Look! Not only does Smitty have the internet at his disposal, which will give him floor layouts and schematics of the museum, he also has resources available to him you can't imagine. I honestly don't know if you're being fucking stupid, naive or both!" His heart raced faster. His pupils dilatated. His blood pressure spiked. He became unwavering in his abuse. "Why do you think we have yet to go to an embassy? If we can't go there, that means Nissassa has the U.S. Government on their side, or at least someone in the government who can pull not only strings, but long and thick ropes. One's big enough to hang us with. YOU NEED TO FUCKING THINK!"

His answer was over the top. Allison glared at him. Slowly, she took her napkin off her lap, pushed her chair back, stood up, and walked away from the table. She didn't say a word. Curt had made a scene and the other curious restaurant guests stared in amazement. Curt didn't care. He knew every datapoint he shared was accurate, but in such a mind state, he could not realize it was far too powerful and hurtful. Given the range of emotions and the other things that happened over the past three days, Curt had little ability to control or interpret the strength of his emotions.

Curt looked around at the other restaurant guests. The women scowled at him. The men just slowly shook their head side to side. It wasn't long that he realized he was in the wrong.

Curt got up and chased her. "Allison, I'm sorry. Hey, wait up. Please stop. Really, I'm sorry."

Allison stopped, turned and looked him square in the eye. "If you ever, ever call me stupid or naive again, they will be the last words from your jaw. Do you understand? How DARE you say such things!!! I have done nothing but try to help you through all this and that's how you repay me? I'm a fucking fugitive because of YOU!" She paused and caught her breath. "Curt, I love you. Of all the people to cut me down, your blade swings the sharpest. Don't you understand that?"

Everything she said was right.

Curt grabbed her hand. "Hey. I am sorry." Curt walked Allison to a nearby park bench. She wept and he sat down with her. He couldn't hide it anymore. "I need to confess something to you that I've never told anyone." Allison looked up. "I didn't just become a doctor to heal others. I also became one to heal me. During my time in the military, I was diagnosed with Post Traumatic Stress Disorder or PTSD. I was ashamed and to this day, I still partly am. I figured if I became a doctor, I could prescribe my own medication and continue to hide my illness from the world. Since we've been on the run, I have not had any of my medication. I could feel my PTSD coming on and without my medicine now, it's getting harder and harder to control. I know it may sound like an excuse, and to a degree it is. I did say those things and I am responsible for them. I am also very sorry I said them. I love you."

Allison hugged Curt. It wasn't the reaction he expected. Tears welled up in her eyes. "Curt, Thank you. Thank you so much. Do you have any idea how important it is that you share that? I was beginning to think you were going insane and you weren't the man I fell in love with. It all makes sense now." She knew in her heart with Curt back on meds and in a normal environment, she could have back the man she loved. "How do we get you medication? There has to be a late-night pharmacy."

"Allison, I don't know. I can't write scripts in Spain."

"OK, what is your medication. Let me do this."

Curt hesitated. Then told her. "Xanax, 5mg dosages, daily." With that, Allison jumped off the bench on a mission she felt confident she could achieve. She kissed Curt and said she'd meet him back at the hotel. Allison waked into the heart of Madrid and Curt watched her go. His love for Allison at that moment grew exponentially. He was a very lucky man.

Curt was hungry but had five euros to his name. The only food in Spain he'd find at that time for that price was street vendors. Luckily, Madrid street-vendors were plentiful, and the food was exceptional, albeit far from healthy. Curt stopped on his way to the hotel, downed some chicken and stood in a park. It was 2200hrs. Curt pulled out his burner phone and turned it on. There were no messages from Smitty. Curt typed in *"Guernica – Picasso, 1100hrs."* He ensured the message was sent, turned off the phone and threw it in a nearby trashcan.

****

Smitty was still on a bus towards Madrid. His phone vibrated as the text from Curt arrived. He read it... and read it again. The only piece that made sense was 1100hrs and Picasso. Smitty cut and pasted the message into Google. A quick scan of the Wikipedia page on the artwork exposed the Museum and Google Maps showed it near the train station. *'When did you get an affinity for freakin fancy art?'* Smitty thought to himself.   No matter, Smitty had a meeting venue. This was good news.

Smitty's bus arrived in Madrid. He took his cash, a substantial amount after acquiring Jackals generosity, as well as the money Buck had given him, and converted it to Euros at the train station. He'd pocket roughly 5000 euros. *'More than enough for a hotel tonight,'* he chuckled to himself. Smitty walked with his bags on his back through Madrid. He could have taken a cab, but for the past few days, he'd not worked out. Frankly, he wanted to burn some energy and exercise his legs. Tomorrow would be a big day. He needed to find a way to prove to Curt he was sincere. Before continuing, he pulled out his phone and placed a call.

"Jerry, Smitty here."

"Hey, Smitty. Is the issue dealt with?"

"Not yet, but I know where he is. Tomorrow I will engage."

"OK, but please, this needs to end, where are you?"

"Algiers. He went exactly to where I thought."

"Algeria? Really?"

Smitty could tell by Jerry's voice something was amiss. Jerry didn't simply question things.

"_____ grea …. Becau ------." *'Click.'* Smitty crafted a garbled transmission and disconnected the call. Quickly he turned off his phone so that Jerry could not return the call.

Looking at Jackal's phone, Smitty saw the beacon was somewhere over the Atlantic. 'Good boy, Jackal. Good Boy.' He thought. He was also certain that Nissassa was tracking that beacon and soon his story would start to unravel. It wouldn't be long before Smitty went from being the hunter to the hunted.

****

Back in Akjoujt, Jerry was incensed. The phone calls to Smitty kept routing to voice mail. "Can someone PLEASE tell me what's going on? Where the fuck is Smitty? Where the fuck is Jackal? Why is his tracker in the middle of the Atlantic Ocean?"

Tiny cautiously approached. "Sir, both of them are out of the local cellular CDMA (Code Division Multi-Access) coverage and our eavesdropping software won't work on other national networks. I can't tell you where they are without getting support from U.S. Gov assets. As for the beacon, I don't know why it's in the ocean other than to suggest that either

Smitty, or perhaps more accurately his bag, is on a flight to the U.S."

Jerry was in trouble. There would be no easy way to tell Don that he suspected Smitty had turned. He became sick to his stomach.

****

Thirty minutes before midnight, Allison entered the hotel room clutching a small white paper bag. "Here ya go." She had a solid look of pride on her face.

Curt opened the bag. It was his medication, in Spanish of course. "How did you do this?"

"A journalist never reveals her secrets." She smiled.

Curt got up from the bed, went to the bathroom and took his medication. Given the state of affairs, he decided to take a double dose. Given he'd not had any medicine for days and it was a double dose, he knew for certain he would be sound asleep in under an hour. Allison watched him dose off. It was the first time since Akjoujt she'd seen him sleep so peacefully. As she stared at him, she wondered what was it that had initially induced his PTSD? How traumatic was it? Was it one incident or many? Would he ever share them? Would she want to know? She did know any of these answers; however, the last few days were clearly some that would have triggered anyone's PTSD. She understood. She was extremely grateful Curt shared his secret and she loved him. She knew she would share in this disease and needed to work out how she would help him manage it through their relationship.

Chapter Fifty-Five

Queen Sofia's Museum

The sun rose in Tehran. City workers were preparing the town square for the Prophet's Birthday in a few days. This year would be a wonderful event and many Iranians looked forward to it. Approximately 100 miles away, the jingle truck had stopped, and the two teams split apart. Each team took a small bread truck loaded with gear to their respective locations. The snatch and grab of the lead nuclear scientist would be easy. The plan was to snatch him in the morning after his breakfast when he was on his way to work. The assassination would be far more difficult. Both trucks continued traveling towards their respective objectives.

****

A few hours after sunrise in Tehran, the sun broke Spain's horizon. Allison awoke and made coffee. Curt remained asleep in bed. Eventually, he smelled the coffee and began to awake. "That was an exceptional night's sleep." he said, "I can't thank you enough." She crawled in bed next to him. She was truly happy that he was happy. They kissed. And then kissed more passionately. The morning sun was not the only thing heating up the room. Things progressed…… until Curt gently pushed her away and said, "Hey, what time is it? We gotta get going!"

'Baby, relax, it's 8 AM. We have plenty of time…. Come back here." She pulled him closer and began kissing him again. Curt did not respond.

Finally, Curt gently pushed her away again and said, "Uh…. Houston, we have a problem."

She looked at him confused. "What?"

"I took a double dose of my medication last night after not taking any for about a week. Since you know about my PTSD, you may as well also know that my medication occasionally causes.. well,... uh,…. Let's just say 'my sailor can't sail.'" Curt looked at her to see if this alarm bell sent her running. She made it through learning about his PTSD, maybe this would be the straw that broke the camel's back. To his surprise, it wasn't.

She smiled and took his comment with the seriousness it deserved. "Well, when your sailor is ready to sail, please tell him I have a secret port that he's welcome in anytime." She kissed him again and got up. "Do you want some coffee?"

Curt was stunned. That was it? Could this be real? "You're not upset?"

"Curt, I love you. You're my best friend. You make me laugh, you make me smile, you attract me. This isn't a big deal unless you make it one."

From med school, Curt knew what she just said was exactly what it said in all the literature and was supposedly absolutely true. But he also was certain that it was a bigger deal than the textbooks led on. "Yes, please."

"Yes, please what?"

"I'd like some coffee." Curt smiled.

****

Across town, Smitty was also rustling out of bed. He'd given a significant amount of thought to his plan. It would be far from conventional but that's perhaps what was needed at this point. He truly hoped it would work. Smitty called down to the front desk and asked to extend his room for the following day. The receptionist confirmed his request. "Gracias," Smitty replied and hung up the phone.

At 1030Hrs, Curt and Allison entered the museum. Curt was partially in disguise with a hat and sunglasses. It was the best he could muster on short notice. They split up and Allison walked into the hall displaying the Guernica. Curt scanned the crowds. They were small at this point. He slowly moved towards a school field trip of children, close enough to appear as one of their chaperones.

The hour approached. Allison looked around. Back in Akjoujt, she had seen Smitty on a few occasions, but wasn't certain she'd recognize him. She didn't have to fret for long. Her eyes quickly fixated on a very unique museum visitor. No sunglasses, no disguise, cleanly shaven, with a military haircut. Far from the bearded man she'd seen in Akjoujt. Smitty wore flip flops, Bermuda shorts, a T-shirt from Mc Ps partially hidden from an extremely loud and unbuttoned Hawaiian shirt. If Smitty was trying to be incognito, he was failing miserably.

Smitty walked to the center of the hall displaying Picasso, emptied his pockets onto the floor in front of him and got down on his knees. He raised his hands behind his head as if he was being placed under arrest. Then he began to sing…. Loudly.

"Anchors Aweigh, my boys! Anchors Aweigh!
Farewell to foreign Shores, we sail at break of day-ay-ay-ay;
Through our last night…………."

The local security guards rushed him. Smitty didn't stop singing. Curt was confused and thought, 'What the fuck is he doing?'

Allison had the same reaction as Curt, *'He's freakin lost it!'* She and others in the museum moved away from him. Could this be a distraction? Curt looked around. In actuality, the safest place in the museum right now was near Smitty. Everything else was unprotected. Curt moved towards Smitty and took his glasses off.

By the time Curt was next to his old SEAL buddy, Smitty was pinned down onto the floor by three guards, his head turned to the left. He could see Curt now. Smitty had stopped singing, he looked at Curt and said, "Hey buddy. The only easy day was yesterday." Smitty's smile turned to tears... "I'm sorry, buddy. I'm sorry I got you in this."

Hand cuffs were now going onto Smitty. He didn't resist. He looked at Curt and said, "Curt, take my room key, room 151. The hotel info is on the key card. You're safe there. Please trust me. I'll see you soon." Smitty looked directly at Curt. His eyes were far from dry. "God, it's good to be back on your side. I feel free!!!" The police stood him up. Smitty, happy with his plan, again began to sing the Navy fight song. He sung it all the way out of the museum.

'*Crazy assed mother fucker,*' is all Curt could think. He took the hotel card and rallied with Allison.

Allison was befuddled by what she'd just witnessed. "Can you believe that!? He's certifiable! And we want him on OUR side? Wouldn't we be better off alone?"

Curt smiled, "No. We're good."

"What!? Wait? Seriously?"

Curt explained. "Yes. He's going to jail. If this was a double cross, there's no chance he could coordinate a thing right now. He made himself vulnerable so that we wouldn't be. I believe him. Let's go."

They went to Smitty's hotel. They walked through the lobby and canvased the place. Curt approached the concierge's counter. "Sir, excuse me. Our key card reader seems to be inoperable. Normally it's a problem with the card, but when we put the card in, the light does not illuminate either green or red. I'm certain it's a problem with the reader."

The concierge motioned to a bellhop and rattled off something in Spanish. He then turned and informed Curt the bellhop would accompany them to their room.

"Thank you, sir." Curt handed the man two euros from his pocket – change from their museum entrance fee and literally their last bit of cash.

The bellhop walked up to the hotel room door with them and took the key. Curt and Allison stood back. Uneventfully, the door swung open, and the bellhop was proud he'd fixed the problem. They looked in the room. It was empty. There would be no tip for the bellhop. He departed, disappointed.

Once inside, they saw all of Smitty's gear. The bed was made and on the coffee table was a note.

> *Curt,*
>
> *Thanks for having the balls to come. After how I treated you, I would have understood if you didn't. I broke your trust and am forever sorry.*
>
> *As it turns out, Nissassa placed a hit on me. That 'hit' has been neutralized and I have made it my mission to destroy Nissassa. I believe this is your mission as well. While I realize you likely do not fully trust me, please remember....<u>'The enemy of my enemy is my friend.'</u> Let me help you expose them. It's the only way I am going to get right with the law, with you, and more importantly myself. Again, I am sorry I got you involved. You should know, I did it because you were the best SEAL I'd ever met.*
>
> *If you look in my bag, there's two thousand euros. It's yours, I'd just ask you to consider bailing me out of jail. Also in that bag are six passports, all are active and will get you anywhere you want to go. Just add a photo and laminate. If you don't want my help, I understand. If you do, come get my ass out of jail so we can plan our next move.*
>
> *Smitty*

Curt looked through the bags. Smitty's letter was accurate, the money and passports were all there. Curt grabbed a wad of cash and headed to the police station. "Allison, go down to the lobby bar. Watch who comes in and out. I'll be back soon with Smitty."

"Go to the bar? You don't trust him enough for me to stay here?"

"No. I trust him with my life. But if he quit Nissassa and there was a hit on him, he's a fugitive just like us." They both left the hotel room. Curt kissed Allison goodbye and made his way to the police station. Curt's team was going to become far more powerful today. And that was a good thing.

Curt arrived at the Madrid police station. After a few mis-directions, he found the place where they detained crazy vagrants. Nearing the hold, he could hear Smitty still singing. He chuckled. After about thirty minutes of discussion with the police, he was able to meet with Smitty in jail. Curt waited in a small room. Smitty approached, hand cuffed and had stopped singing.

Smitty smiled, "Hey, buddy. How did you like my hotel room? Nice, eh?"

"Yeah. Nice. It's lacking live entertainment. Know where I could find a singer?"

Smitty chuckled. "Did you read my note? It's all true. Every word."

"I did. I believe you."

"I meant it. I understand if you don't trust me. Take what you need and take down Nissassa."

"Smitty, I need you. And frankly, I think you need me. Now, can you do me a favor?"

"Sure. Name it."

"Stop fucking singing. I have two officers convinced I'm your psych doc and can get you under control. If I do, they'll drop the charges against you and release you into my custody. Can you do that?"

"Sure thing, Skip... or, eh, Doc."

Curt waived to the guard he was done. After another half hour and some paperwork, Smitty and Curt walked out of the detention center, headed to meet Allison at the hotel bar.

As they walked, Smitty relayed everything that had happened, to include Jackal, the beacon, and his last few calls with Jerry. Both agreed the most important thing was to get into the U.S. as soon as possible. Those passports Smitty had were on a shelf life that expired once Jerry no longer believed Smitty.

They entered the hotel lobby and proceeded to the bar. There, Allison was flanked by two Spanish men, fawning over her. She saw Curt approach and said, "Hello honey! Gentlemen, let me introduce my husband and his friend, Curt and Smitty." The two Spaniards slunk away. Curt smiled and kissed Allison. "Husband, eh? Interesting."

Smitty reached out his hand. "I'm not sure we met formally. I'm Mark. Mark Smith but my friends call me Smitty."

"Hi Mark Smitty, I'm Allison. Nice to meet you."

Smitty and Curt ordered drinks. They needed a plan, but everything hinged on a call to Jerry. Smitty turned on his phone, setting his VPN for Algeria. He didn't dare turn on his cellular service, it would be a dead giveaway if Jerry was tracking him. Using FaceTime on his iPhone, a Voice of Internet Protocol (VOIP) system, he called Jerry. "Jerry, hey Smitty here."

"Smitty. Where are you?"

"Still in Algeria, but I'm looking at Nover right now." That part was true, he actually was looking at Curt.

Jerry looked at his intel officer who was working the call. Per the IP address, the call was coming from Algeria. It was legit and he shook his head up and down to Jerry. "Good news. What's the plan?"

"I can't take the shot right now. I have a small problem. Look, the cellular systems here are garbage and I'm jumping on Wi-Fi nonstop. Sorry about the call the other day. Also, my rental was broken into, and my gear was stolen. I'm trying to secure a weapon on the black market."

Jerry attempted to act surprised, but this perhaps helped explain the location mismatch of the beacon and Jerry. "Oh no! Do you need money? I can wire funds to you. Tell me what you need. We just need that problem to go away."

"Yes. I found a guy, but his best price is $5000 USD for an untraceable semiauto handgun with the serial numbers scratched out. Can you wire me the money via Western Union? I'll find a location here in Algeria."

"Yes, I'll do it right now. Keep after it, Smitty. You're doing great. I must go. Goodbye." Jerry's concerns were eased. A part of him was even remorseful about Jackal's task, but that quickly passed. Evil snakes don't remain remorseful for long. Jerry set up the money wire immediately. The funds patiently waited in Western Union's hands ready for Mark Smith to claim it.

Smitty turned towards Curt. "Five Gs. Not bad, eh?"

"Great job, Smitty. OK, what about the passports to get us into the U.S.?"

Smitty responded. "Mine is good. Yours is as hot as a lava ball. What about hers? How did she get into Spain?"

"With her passport. Yesterday."

"Interesting. Jerry knows she's helping you." Smitty tried to process what was going on, and then he figured it out. "That son of a bitch. Jerry hasn't told Don. Ha ha ha! Hold on." Jerry pulled out his phone. He placed another call to D.C. "Don, Smitty here."

"Hey, Smitty. Why are you calling me?"

"Yeah, sorry about that. Jerry is working our Op and told me to call. Can you activate PP1 and PP2?" I need them for the mission I'm on."

"You need both?" Don knew about Smitty's hit mission on Curt, but activating two passports was odd given he was working alone.

"Yeah. The rabbit I'm chasing is jumping fences faster than I can keep up. I'd normally only ask for one, but this way I only bother you once." 'Jumping fences' was Smitty's way of relaying border crossings.

"Ok. Fine. But please, only have Jerry call me unless it's an emergency. Do you understand?"

Smitty smiled. "Yes, I understand."

Don concluded his call with Smitty by saying, "And kill that fucking rabbit."

The line went dead. Smitty hung up the phone. Puzzled, Curt asked, "What is PP1 and PP2?"

"Passport 1 and Passport 2. The first two in the sequence of six I have up in the room. You and I will now enter the U.S. as 'other' people while the rest of the world thinks we are on this side of the Atlantic Ocean. Not bad, eh?"

"Nice work, buddy. Now, let's get those passports and book flights ASAP."

Once at the hotel courtesy computers, Allison began booking flights. Curt looked at Smitty and said, "Smitty, one question. When is the Iran hit?"

Smitty said, "Hold on." He jumped on another computer and googled Iran Prophet's Birthday. He looked at Curt. "Three days." Curt knew that Iran was ahead of D.C. time, which eliminated one day. Travel to the U.S. tomorrow would also eat a day. That meant they really had only one day in D.C. to take down Nissassa. It wouldn't be easy.

The tickets to Washington were all connecting flights. Eventually, Allison found flights direct to New York. She booked them. They'd be in NYC by 1400Hrs. Recovering luggage, exiting the airport and a three-hour train ride to D.C. would place them in the capital no later than 1900Hrs. The three ordered dinner and were certain tonight they were safe. Now, the time must be spent to devise a plan to stop the events in Iran.

Chapter Fifty-Six

Hopping the Pond

Staff scurried around the White House. It was a high paced work environment, but no one complained. The President was ending his meeting with the National Security Council, discussing the ramifications of Russia's continued failure to live up to arms control agreements. It was important stuff, but given the numerous times Russia broke the rules, it was about as pointless as discussing carbon emissions in China. Once it was over, Steve entered with information for the President's next meeting.

"Steve, sit down. Let's talk."

"Yes, Mr. President."

The door was closed, they were alone. "How's our special effort going?"

"Sir, there's been no change from the earlier status. I plan to meet to discuss it soon. I do have the courses of action you requested though." Steve began to hand a piece of paper to the President.

"No, no, no, no. I'd rather that not end up on my desk. Just tell me the options."

"Yes, sir. First COA is to blame a less than friendly E.U. nation for the effort given the discovered sniper rifle will have originated from Austria, a European nation. The second is to blame a neighboring Middle East nation given their continued strife's with Iran. And third is to distance ourselves from the 'blame game' but rather use the effort to unify the region by calling for an emergency regional summit." Steve looked at the President as he chewed over the ideas.

"Good work. Look, the Ayatollah's death will generate significant tensions. Finger pointing, albeit helpful to protect us in the short run could lead to escalated armed conflict that we'd eventually get sucked into. Can you flush out option three a bit more? Think about what nations would be invited to this emergency summit should the Ayatollah suffer a fateful demise."

"Yes, Mr. President. I'll work on it."

"And Steve. No more papers and no more computers. This is a memory only exercise. Do you understand?"

"Yes, Sir. I apologize."

"Good. Now tell my secretary to send in my next appointment as you depart." Steve left and did as instructed. Once back in his office, Steve arranged another meeting with Don. He needed to know what was going on. Don also needed a few Passports activated. The meeting would be symbiotic.

****

Back in Madrid, Allison headed to bed while Curt and Smitty remained at the bar. It was good to catch up and it truly had been way too long. As they talked, they tried to develop a plan that would achieve the objective but not kill either or place either in jail for life. Every idea raised never generated enough of a flash, nor did it protect them from harm. It was difficult. No matter. They were together. Shipmates. And that mattered. Curt took one more drink and a light came on. "Smitty! I have an idea!" Curt explained the idea to Smitty. He was apprehensive.

"Curt, man, I don't know if I can do that."

"Sure you can! I believe in you! I wouldn't want anyone else."

"Uh... OK. Your call." It was clear however, Smitty was still not comfortable.

As Curt thought through the plan, the more he liked it. "Look, I get it. The plan isn't great, but it's good, and it meets our intent. Are you in?" Curt looked Smitty straight in the eyes.

Smitty lifted his beer and drank the remaining half glass. He set it down, wiped his mouth with the back of his forearm and said, "Let's do it."

"Awesome. Thanks. One thing. We don't tell Allison about your part. Agreed."

Smitty agreed, "Absolutely. She already isn't completely sold on me. No chance she'd accept this."

****

Back in D.C., Don answered Steve's text requesting a meeting ASAP. He hand carried PP1 and PP2 information. They met at the usual spot. "Hey, Steve! Good to see you!"

Steve's enthusiasm was not shared. "Yes. What's the status?"

"Both teams are in country and have recon'ed their objectives. Everything they've seen resembles their training event. They are in comms via satellite link every 12 hours. There have been no snags. Overhead shows Tehran being prepared for the festival and speech."

"Good. What about your loose end?"

"Good news there as well. It looks like that will be eliminated tomorrow."

Steve was cautiously relieved. "OK, thanks."

"Steve, wait. To help with the loose end, I could really use these two passports to be activated."

Two passports to eliminate an issue that could destroy the administration. It was a no brainer. "Consider it done in an hour."

"Great. Thanks." Don was relieved the request was so easy.

"Hey, and Don. Remember, you update me. I don't update you. When the President is asking me for information and I don't have it, I look unprofessional. Don't let that happen again." Steve was dead serious.

Don was conciliatory, "Yeah. Got it. Sorry about that. I'll inform you daily from now forward on this op."

"Perfect. Goodbye." They departed ways into the cool D.C. autumn air.

****

As night fell onto DC, the sun would eventually rise in Madrid. The three awoke and packed their bags. After breakfast, Smitty went through the kitchen to the alley. He found a garbage dumpster and disposed of his sidearm intended to kill Curt. There was no way to fly to the US with it. After packing up, they taxied to the airport. Curt and Smitty were memorizing their passport info as Allison watched the trees of Madrid fly by her window.

Once checked in, they all cleared security and proceeded to customs and immigration. Allison went first and passed through with ease. Then Smitty stepped up. He had cut and crafted a passport photo and the job was professional. Still, the official did not let him pass. In a thick Spanish accent, the official said, "Mr. Moore, where are you coming from?"

"Sir, my hotel in Madrid."

"No, what country. You have no entry stamp into the European Union. In fact, you have no stamps at all. How did you get into the European Union?" Behind Smitty, Curt's stomach knotted. He could hear the entire exchange.

"What? Are you serious! I didn't even notice. My friend and I here (pointing at Curt) went to Casablanca, you know, the place with the movie. These are our first passports and our first time travelling out of the U.S. and we had to go see Humphrey Bogart's best performance. Have you seen the movie? You know, *'Of all the gin joints in all...'*"

The customs official cut him off. "Sir, I don't know the movie. Can I see your friend's passport?" Curt stepped forward and handed it to him.

Smitty spoke again. "I'm really sorry they didn't stamp the passports. I didn't know that was a thing? When we took the ferry across into Spain it was late at night, and no one even looked at our passports. Is that a problem? Geesh, I feel awful." Actually, both of their real passports had been stamped in Motril. Those passports, however, were not the ones they presented.

The customs officer didn't respond and called his manager. As Curt was about to vomit, Smitty was relishing his acting role.

The lead customs official came over. "Gentlemen. You can't just travel around countries without getting your stamps! This is unacceptable and we will be filing a complaint with your consulate. If you were going anywhere other than your home nation, we would deny you travel, but since you are going home, you may go, but you are not welcome back in Spain. Do you understand?" And with that, he forcefully stamped both passports and wrote a note on each in Spanish.

They both nodded, apologized again, and thanked the official. They were through.

Compared to their Spanish Customs event, the flight to NYC was uneventful. The aircraft landed on time. Now in the U.S., they all cleared customs without issue and walked through the airport. Suddenly, Smitty stopped and said, "Wait!" He darted left towards an airport Western Union kiosk. Ten minutes later, he returned with a thick vanilla envelope. "Thanks, Jerry," he said with a large smile. Smitty handed the envelope to Curt.

Curt took the envelope. He knew exactly what it was. He looked Smitty in the eyes and said, "Thanks. I'll pay ya back." All three smiled, knowing there was no intent for repayment.

They continued out of the airport and caught a cab to Grand Central Station; trying to make the next Amtrak Acela to D.C. Once on the train, they composed themselves and took a deep breath. It was already a long day. Smitty reached into his bag. He pulled out Jackal's phone and turned it on. Once on the network, he opened up the tracking app. The beacon was in upstate New York. Exactly where it should be. As Smitty was holding the phone, it beeped and buzzed numerous times with voice messages, missed calls and text messages from Jerry. Smitty handed the phone to Curt. They both smiled at each other.

Curt found Jerry's number and placed the call.

Jerry answered incensed, "Jackal! God Damn It! Where the hell have you been?! You need to keep your phone on! This is completely unacceptable and unprofessional!"

Curt took a deep breath. "Hi, Jerry. It's Curt Nover."

The other end of the line went silent.

Curt continued, "Don't worry, Jerry. You don't have to say a thing. I know where you are. I'm coming for you. Goodbye…. and sleep well." Curt hung up the phone, turned it off and handed it back to Smitty.

Jerry sat there, paralyzed. His world was in a tailspin crashing towards earth. He hastily searched for a number and dialed. On the Amtrak, Smitty's phone rang. Again, Smitty handed the phone to Curt. "Hi, Jerry. It's Curt again. Geesh…. You're making this a habit." The line went dead.

Curt smiled. "That's about the best feeling I've had in a long time." They all felt a sense of heartfelt warmth.

****

Jerry's hands trembled. He dialed Don's number.

"Jerry! I was just about to call you! What you got in the way of an update!?"

"Don. We have a big problem."

"Shit… Is it Nover?"

"No. It's Nover AND Smitty." Jerry sullenly relayed the entire story, now including his suspicions of Allison. Don was livid. There was only one option. Nissassa needed to cancel the Iranian Operation, but that call needed to come from Steve.

"Jerry. You fucked up huge. Look, you need to start looking at options on how to mitigate our exposure on this."

"I know. I know." Jerry and Don continually dreamed about expanding Nissassa. That dream had drastically shifted to finding ways to make the company disappear if needed. Their call ended. Don immediately texted Steve. *"Need to meet ASAP. Problem."*

Steve wrote back, *"In STATE dinner now. Tomorrow 0700hrs."* Don saw the message. It was not soon enough, but Steve was the customer and there was little chance of getting him away from a White House State level dinner. There was no way to expedite the meeting. Precious time would be lost.

Chapter Fifty-Seven

<u>Acquisitions</u>

The N.Y. train pulled into D.C.'s Union Station on time. It was late afternoon in Washington and as Curt predicted, they would have roughly one day to thwart Nissassa's plans. They walked into a makeshift electric shop kiosk and purchased three burner phones, one for each of them. They continued out the front of the building. The autumn leaves had fallen and blanketed DC. The sun was shining, but it was far colder than any temperatures any had experienced in a long time. It felt refreshing.

Curt looked at Smitty, gave him a huge hug. Smitty said, "Good luck, buddy."

Curt quickly replied, "You're the one that needs the luck!" They both smiled and hugged again. Allison, still unsure of Smitty, halfheartedly hugged him. They said their goodbyes and Smitty headed off.

"I really hope you're right about him," Allison said, still unsure.

"I am. Look, his task was to eliminate us as soon as possible. I am a horrible distraction from Nissassa's current mission. Keeping me around serves them no purpose. We're good."

Allison knew Curt was right, but still could not shake off her uneasiness. They both watched Smitty walk away.

Smitty took a cab to the Hay-Adams Hotel, secured a room and dropped his gear. There was much work to be done.

Allison and Curt also took a cab. Their destination was the W Hotel, downtown D.C. They checked in and went to the room. Once inside, Curt looked at Allison, "Hey, I wanted to let you know that Smitty and I have a plan. It involves you and we need your help."

Allison wanted to help. "Anything, just tell me."

"Tomorrow evening, you'll loiter on the north side of the White House tourist area. You need to be along the fence line and directly in the center. You'll see me approach. You must not say anything to me, no matter what happens. Do you understand?"

"Yes... but?"

"No buts..... An event will occur. Once that happens, there will be some minor chaos and then soon thereafter followed by significant press presence. At that point, I need your journalist skills to kick in. You will find an outlet and share everything. Tell them you know me, and you know everything about Nissassa. More than enough evidence will be available. Got it?"

"Curt, what is the 'event?' Please tell me you will be OK."

"If everything goes as plan, I will be fine. Just promise me, you will NOT come near me or give any indication you know me until AFTER the event."

"I promise." Curt hugged Allison. All the actors had their parts.

"OK. I gotta make a call." Curt turned on his burner phone, looked up a number in his real phone, typed it in and made the call.

"Hello?"

"Hey, Kamil. How are you?"

"Dr. Nover!!! It's YOU! You OK?"

"Yes, Kamil, I am fine. Thank you for asking. I need one more favor from you if you can help me."

"Yes, Doctor! I do anything for you."

"Great. I appreciate that. I need you to scan and send me my files and those of my predecessor. I will text you an email address. Can you do that?"

"Yes, sir! Right away!" It was nearing midnight in Akjoujt.

"Ha. It's OK, Kamil. You can do it in the morning. But I must tell you, this is critically important."

"You can count on me! I prove it! I made you dead! I can do this too!"

Curt laughed. "Kamil. You are one of the best. Thank you, my friend."

"Yes, Doctor! Goodbye." They hung up. Curt went to the lobby, created a new Gmail account and texted it to Kamil. One task down, many to go. Curt placed another call.

A voice on the other end answered, "Congressman Donegan's Office."

"Yes, this is Curt Nover, a friend of Jack's. Is the Congressman available?"

"No, Mr. Nover, I'm sorry, he's departed for the evening. Is there something I can help you with?"

"Yes, is the Congressman available tomorrow for dinner?"

"Let me check his calendar, hold on………. He currently has a placeholder, but I believe that is for dinner at home, how do you know Congressman Donegan again?"

"We were on SEAL team together."

"Oh, OK. Hold on." She placed Curt on hold. Less than a minute later she returned to the line, "Mr. Nover, the Congressman will take your call."

The line cut away and rang once, then a voice answered, "Nover! What the hell are you doing in D.C? Aren't you curing cancer somewhere in a shit hole third world country?"

Curt chuckled. It was great to hear a friendly voice. "I already finished curing cancer, hadn't you heard? Hey, what are you doing, screening your calls? You aren't that famous yet." They both chuckled and Curt continued, "Jack, I can't talk long. Any chance we can have drinks tomorrow around 8PM at the Top of the Hay? You know the place, it's a restaurant bar on top of the Hay-Adams Hotel."

"Yeah. I know the place well. I can swing that. I have a dinner date with Bonnie and the kids. I'll wrap that up and meet you at the Hay."

"Great. I look forward to it. I have some crazy news that you're gonna wanna hear. Jack, this is really important. I'm grateful to have friends like you. I'll see you then!"

"Count on it. Can't wait to catch up." They both hung up. Step two complete.

****

Smitty rented a car. He needed to get to the heart of Virginia fast. He drove south on the worst highway in all of D.C., I-395, stuck in rush hour traffic with about fifty thousand other D.C. commuters. It was miserable. He'd never make it to his destination in time. As the car sat parked on the Interstate, he pulled out his burner phone and placed a call.

A male voice familiar to Smitty answered, "Federalist Firearms, Tony speaking."

"Yeah... I wanna buy a cannon. Do you have any?"

Tony too recognized the voice immediately. "Smitty? Is that you? You freaking idiot! What's up?!"

"Hey, I'm trying to get down to your shop but am stuck on 395 in D.C. Any chance you can stay open? I need some supplies on short notice and a bit of range time."

"For you buddy, we are never closed. I'll have the shop open and some beers waiting." Tony was excited to see his friend.

"Great. See ya soon." Smitty hung up. He sighed a bit. He promised Curt he'd keep his end of the deal, but second thoughts ran through his head. It was killing him. Finally, he couldn't take it anymore. Without telling Curt, he'd be making a slight deviation from the plan. He placed another call. The phone rang. A voice answered. Smitty sat on I-395 talking. After a few minutes, the support he needed was acquired. He continued onto see Tony, feeling far better about tomorrow's mission.

****

Back in D.C., Curt had acquired another cab and rode it across the Potomac to the Joint Base Henderson Hall. While it was called 'joint,' every military person knew this was a Marine base. The cab dropped him off at the south entrance and he walked up to the Marine guard.

"Hey, Devil Dog." Curt handed over his Veteran ID card. From the guard's uniform, Curt quickly realized the young Marine was a Corporal and a last name of Ramirez.

"Evening, Sir." The guard looked at the ID. While valid, it was not enough to gain access to the installation. "Sir, you need an Active-Duty card or a Retiree Card to enter. This won't work."

Curt knew the guard was right. "Yeah, I know, sorry about that. Look, I'm in a bind. I need to get a uniform tonight. The drycleaner destroyed mine and all I have is my trident badge."

The guard knew that badge. "Sir, are you a SEAL?"

"No, Corporal, Ramirez. I was a SEAL, and I have to go to some uppity event and need a uniform. Can you help me out?"

The Corporal went into the guard shack and returned with a clipboard and piece of paper. "Sir, the only way you can gain access is on a visitor's pass. If you can fill this out, I will vouch for you as my guest."

"I will! I greatly appreciate it." Curt filled out the form and the guard let him in. The Marine Corps Exchange would close soon so he needed to hurry. Curt ran in and immediately up the stairs to the uniform shop. He gathered all the items he needed, shoes, pants, shirt, jacket, trench coat, cover, shoulder boards, medals, ribbons, and a SEAL badge – which he actually did not have, regardless of what he told Corporal Ramirez. He also grabbed a set of Marine E-5 Sergeants rank and headed to the cashier. Curt paid cash thanks to Smitty and Jerry, grabbed his bags and walked back out of the MEX. He walked another 100 meters out towards the gate. As he passed the guard shack, he called out, "Corporal Ramirez?"

Corporal Ramirez stuck he head out of the shack, "Yes sir?"

"Here, I know someday you're gonna need these and I wanted to be the one who gave them to you." Curt reached in his bag, pulled out the E-5 Marine rank and handed them over. Corporal Ramirez took the rank with a sense of gratitude. He felt it an honor to have his next rank given to him by a Navy SEAL. Holding the new rank in his left hand, the Corporal snapped to attention and saluted Curt. Curt returned the salute, again thanked the Corporal and walked away. The majority of Curt's acquisitions were complete. The evening was beautiful. He walked downhill along Southgate Road. While mostly a parking lot, the street butted up against Arlington Cemetery which was partially illuminated by the U.S. Air Force Memorial on the other side of the street. Given the next day's events, it was a walk quite worthy of Curt's time. He slowly walked and gazed in the cemetery on all the veterans who'd given their life in defense of the nation. As he walked, he got the sense each veteran in that cemetery was supporting him.

At the bottom of the hill, Curt flagged a cab outside the Pentagon Row Mall. He headed back to the W Hotel and met up with Allison where he would begin to put together his uniform.

****

It was late in Virginia, Smitty also had all he needed and was driving back to his hotel. Once in D.C., he stopped at the W

Hotel, ran in and used the courtesy phone to call Curt. "Hey, I got what you needed, can you come down? I'm in the lobby."

"On my way." Curt entered the lobby. Smitty was holding a medium sized bag which had substantial weight. He handed it over. "Thanks, Smitty."

"No worries." They bumped fists. Curt could tell Smitty was a bit more upbeat than normal. "By the way, Tony says hi."

"Awesome. How is he?"

"He's great…. And if World War Three ever approaches, his shop is one of the first places I'm going. The guy has everything. Look, I'm parked out in the registration parking. I gotta go. You ready for tomorrow?"

"Yeah. I'm set. I'll dry run tomorrow in the AM."

"Aye. Good luck, Smitty. You got this." As their eyes locked, Curt flashed a quick smile. They fist bumped again. Smitty turned to leave, and Curt picked up the bag, carrying it to his room.

Chapter Fifty-Eight

No Turning Back

Steve walked up to Don just outside the WWII Memorial. Don had been there for a half hour in the cold. "Alright, Don, what's the problem?"

"Hey, we gotta call off the Op. Things have gone south bad." The concern in Don's voice was not lost on Steve.

"OK. Slow down. What's going on?"

"Nover is still a loose end. Not only that, Jerry had a plan to eliminate Smitty, which unfortunately did not materialize and now Smitty is with Nover, together. We don't know where they are, but we do know they pulled funds that Jerry sent for them from a Western Union at JFK just yesterday afternoon. They are clearly in the U.S. Neither have used their phones or credit cards. This is too much. We need to shut this down."

Steve just stared at Don in amazement. "You waited to tell me this until today!? Are you fucking crazy!"

"I didn't wait. I texted we had a problem and you arranged to meet today."

"This is not a problem. This is a dumpster fire! You call me for something this big. Hold on." Steve pulled out his phone. "Cindy, it's Steve, put me through........ I don't care. Put me through....... "Mr. President, I am sorry for the intrusion. I am on my way to your office now. 10 minutes. I am sorry, it cannot wait. Please clear the room as soon as you can."

The President hung up the phone. "Well, there seems to be a family matter that I must attend to gentlemen. Can we wrap this up in the next ten minutes?"

Steve was furious. He looked back at Don, "You keep by your phone. Do you understand?"

"I got it." Don was scared.

Steve ran to the street in front of the WWII memorial and jumped in a black SUV. Once in, the SUV's lights illuminated, and the vehicle tore off towards the White House. Don watched and realized things were even bigger than he imagined.

Once in the vehicle, Steve placed a call. "Hey, I can't talk much, need you to flag those passports we discussed yesterday and also pull any activity on them. Once you have it, call me. Gotta go."

He placed another call to a contact in the Department of Justice, "Hey, it's Steve. Need a favor. I need to create fictitious charges against two individuals. Come by my office in about an hour. Gotta go. Thanks."

Another call as the SUV was entering the White House grounds. "Hey, it's Steve, I need the ADMA in my office in an hour..... I don't care. Thanks." The ADMA was the Associate Director of Military Affairs assigned to the Director of the CIA.

The SUV slowed to a stop in front of the White House door. Steve jumped out and briskly walked in. The next meeting he'd have was not one he relished.

Steve walked into the Oval Office. The President stood behind his desk, his back towards Steve, looking out over the lawn. "I don't suppose it is good news that led you to the decision to shorten my meeting with the Mexican President."

"No, Mr. President. It is not good news. Would you like to sit down?"

"Actually, Steve, I think I will stand for this." The President did not stop looking out the window.

"Sir, the loose end our friend was dealing with has grown out of hand. They are recommending we abort the mission."

The President stood motionless, still looking out the window. His hand gently resting under his chin. After thirty seconds, he said, "Steve.... What do you recommend?"

Steve didn't know. "Sir, I have called for an emergency meeting with the ADMA and also am working with our friends to create some dirt on the loose end. If that all works, we should be able to continue."

The President again didn't move. "You and this Don Harrison fella were West Point Classmates. Is that correct?"

"Yes, Mr. President. And our fathers were also classmates."

"Good…. Good…. And you told me you trusted him. Correct?"

"Yes, sir."

"Good. So, if his little effort in Africa is discovered, how exposed are we?"

"Sir, my only dealing with him is verbal. The funding lines are buried in a Black SOF program code. Even if he were implicated through funding transactions, he will remain silent. I believe that. Also, should he turn, there would be nothing to corroborate the story. We are well insulated."

The President turned to Steve. "The mission continues. You will cancel your meeting with the ADMA, and you'll take no more efforts in support of Don's efforts until I direct differently. Your friend will need to find a way to fight for himself. Should his company be exposed, we distance ourselves and have some friends in the FBI shape their investigation to our liking."

Now was not the time to argue. The President had made his decision. "Yes, sir."

"Steve, I am disappointed."

Steve had never heard those words from the President. They stung. He showed himself out. Steve's loyalty to the President was unwavering. Unfortunately, the reciprocal was not true. The President went to his desk and pressed the intercom button. "Nancy, can you bring me Steve's personnel file? Thanks."

He let go of the button and turned back to the window. *'What a magnificent view,'* he thought.

****

The time now was 0800Hrs. Allison had been awake for hours, unable to sleep due to jet lag. Curt had again taken another two Xanax and was sleeping like a baby. Allison made coffee in the room and looked out the window. 15th Street below was beginning to bustle, runners and cyclists were crisscrossing the White House Oval. *'D.C. is a pretty amazing place'* she thought to herself. Allison went to pour her coffee and saw the bag Smitty had given to Curt sitting on the floor. Out of curiosity, she opened it. On top was a large black vest. Odd, she thought. She started to pick it up and was amazed at the weight. She instantly knew it was body armor. She pulled it out and as she did, she heard a metal thud hit the bottom of the bag. She looked in and saw a black handgun laying at the bottom of the bag. She put everything back, went to the bed and grabbed Curt's arm, "Please get out of bed… now."

Curt woke up a big groggy. "Hey. what? Good morning…"

"Don't you Good morning me. Why is there body armor and a handgun in this room? And don't lie to me. You need to tell me the full plan now. I did NOT agree to this."

Curt sat up, rubbed his eyes and turned to put his feet on the floor. He looked up at Allison. "Any chance I can get a cup of coffee first?"

"Don't get smart with me. You promised you wouldn't get hurt. I am not sure how body armor and a weapon imply you won't get hurt."

"Allison, look…. I can't tell you. I just need you to do your part."

"God Damn it, Curt… I've stood by you. I love you. I know your deepest secrets and fully support you. Someday I need you to trust me. Evidently today isn't that day." Allison began grabbing her things, getting dressed and packing.

"Seriously. Please... not today. Please... not today."

"Are you going to tell me?"

Curt didn't say anything, he tried to take her hand. The truth was, he couldn't tell her. She pulled away.

"Then yes, today." She took her key, her handbag and left, slamming the door behind her. Curt couldn't chase her. If she knew the plan, she'd never support it. There was no way out of this other than to let Allison go and hope she showed up this evening.

Curt got up and drank Allison's coffee. He put on some clothes and went down to the hotel business center. He logged onto his new Gmail account. There were three emails from Kamil. All three were the exact same file. The last email said, 'I send it three times to make shure you get it!'

'Good job, Kamil. Good job,' he thought to himself, 'But it's spelled 'sure.' Curt opened the file and began printing. After five minutes, the printer ran out of paper. Curt went to the front desk and got another ream. It would take another five minutes to complete the printing. Curt took the documents up to his room and placed them in a new brief case he'd bought from the Marine Corps Exchange on Henderson Hall. Another step accomplished.

Curt changed into his work out gear. He went downstairs and out the W. He had not run in D.C. for quite a while and looked forward to it. First, he headed up 15th St. and turned left to run across Pennsylvania Ave. He slowed and walked by the East Wing, White House and West Wing. Tourists were taking pictures, the security was meandering about, protesters were protesting. It was just like any other day.

Curt picked back up the pace and turned left onto 17th St. running south past Constitution Ave. to the WWII Memorial. Again, he slowed down, looking at the fountains, the tourists, and the field of 4,048 golden stars that lay a foundation for the view of President Lincoln at the other end of the reflecting pond. Most who see these stars rarely learned of their meaning. Curt knew. Each star represented 100 American lives lost during the second world war. A catastrophic loss of blood and treasure.

    Curt began running again, circling around the WWII memorial, kissing the palm of his hand and then smacking the World War Two pillar that said "Indiana," his birth state. Curt ran up the length of the reflecting pond, rustling through the wet late-autumn leaves. Nearing the end, he turned left into the Korean War memorial slowing to walk through, paying his respects and seeing the beautiful high glossed black granite stone that read, *'Freedom isn't Free.'*

    Once through, he again ran, going up and down the Lincoln Memorial steps, then north towards the Vietnam Memorial. As he approached, he slowed, again, walking out of respect.

    Curt walked along the walk of black marble containing 58,000 names. He slowed, then stopped in front of plate W10. His hand rose to line 35 and there, he found the name, LCDR EUGENE W NOVER. He rested his hand over it. He paused and looked down, closing his eyes. He whispered to the wall, *'Gonna make you proud today, Dad. The only easy day was yesterday.'* He removed his hand, walked to the end of the memorial and again began to run. Now at an even faster pace. The thought of making his father proud was something that always yearned deep in Curt's heart.

    He crossed Memorial Bridge into Virginia, staring squarely at Arlington Cemetery. He ran along it and around it, circling back towards his hotel crossing back into D.C. on the 14ht St. Bridge. By the end of the run, he was beat. And he also knew what he was doing was right.

    Curt took a shower and a nap, exhausted from his run. His night would be one for the history books.

****

    Over at the Hay Adams, a Ford F-150 truck arrived around 1400Hrs, and a man exited. He threw the keys to the Valet who asked, "Name or Room number please?"

"Put it on Mark Smith," the voice said…. But it clearly wasn't Smitty. The man entered the hotel and picked up the courtesy phone. "Mark Smith's room please." The phone rang. "Smitty, I'm here."

"Perfect, I'll be right down." Smitty's deviation arrived, none too soon.

Chapter Fifty-Nine

The Confrontation - Relived

Curt finished dressing in his uniform and placed his sidearm in his trench coat pocket. He left his room and stepped out of the hotel. He had not seen Allison since the morning. It was an unseasonably cold fall evening in Washington, D.C. Steam rose from the Potomac River and the city street manhole covers. It was a clear night, but the Capitol lights drown out most stars.

Rush hour traffic had calmed, and the city pace eased. Evening meals had started across the city's restaurants and Old Ebbitt Grill on 14th St, NE was standing room only. Curt walked quickly up the street heading to the White House.

As he approached the north side of the White House, he noticed only a few tourists braved the cold. A few protesters were huddled in their makeshift shanties confronting the crisp night air for their worthy cause. As expected, the security forces were in mass for all to see. Curt scanned his environment, calculating his next few moves.

Then, he saw her. Allison made it. A tear ran down her cheek and there was pain in her eyes. She was waiting for him, along the fence line, as promised. She stood dead center in front of the White House North Fence line and as close as one could get given the security, just as he had asked. He said nothing to her. He didn't have to; his face said it all. It said, *'I love you. I'm sorry, but I have to do this. Someday, you will understand.'*

Inside Top of the Hay, Congressman Donegan waited. Curt was 10 minutes late. No big worry. He looked forward to the meeting. The Congressman drank his scotch and enjoyed the only view the Hay offers, overlooking the north lawn of the White House.

Curt stopped 10 yards from Allison. He opened his briefcase. Curt's medical files along with his predecessors flew across the ground. Medical descriptions and photos of injured and dead men flew into the air. Tourists trying to help grabbed the papers. Many were graphic. Most were victims of gunshot wounds or explosive detonations. Pooling blood, visible organs, and sickening deformities from explosions were commonplace in nearly every picture.

The guards took notice and began to approach the Lieutenant. As they came near, he reached in his service overcoat, withdrew a 9mm Beretta semiautomatic handgun and raised it to his right temple. A quick burst of screams arose from the few tourists present. They backed a safe distance away. Capitol police drew their side arms, pointing them squarely on Curt.

The lieutenant spoke... or rather sang, "Anchors Aweigh my boys... Anchors Aweigh," his voice cracked.

"Drop your weapon!" A guard screamed.

Louder he sang, "We sail at the break of Daaaaaaaay." He was oblivious to the guards around him now. The lieutenant had rehearsed this moment in his head numerous times.

"I said drop your weapon, Lieutenant, or we will be forced to shoot."

****

In the Top of the Hay, customers pointed out towards the north lawn. There was a commotion in front of the White House. Congressman Jack Donegan along with others filled the windows. He looked down and saw a Navy uniform and knew. "Shit! It's Nover." He raced out of the restaurant.

****

The Lieutenant heard the security officer now ordering Curt to drop his weapon. He slowly turned and stared directly into the officer's eyes and said…. "Not if I shoot first." Curt's back was against the fence. He faced out towards the Hay Adams Hotel and smiled like a man possessed. He clearly wasn't bluffing. His finger started to squeeze the trigger. Allison screamed along with many other unsuspecting tourists. The guards stood there frozen.

As Curt stood there, he was stunned. Standing 50 yards in the distance was Smitty…. Curt thought, *'This wasn't the plan. Smitty was supposed to be at the Hay Adams! After all this, did Smitty double cross me? He couldn't have!'*

Curt's eyes widened and his facial expression quickly changed to surprise and fear. It was now too late.

CRACK! A shot rang out. Curt fell to the ground. His left hand opened. A U.S. Navy SEAL Trident fell from out; clinking as it hit the ground. His right hand released the sidearm which also fell simultaneously to Curt.

Allison, and many others screamed louder. No!!!!!! No, No, NO!!!!!!

Capital Security radios cracked to life, "SHOTS FIRED!! SHOTS FIRED! WHITE HOUSE NORTH LAWN!" External emergency flood lights powered on around the residence. White House Marine Guards and security details began protocols to seal and barricade. The Capital Police encircled Curt and began asking each other, "Who shot? Who shot? Who shot?" None of them answered. Which meant only one thing to them. The victim was the likely trigger puller.

****

Congressman Jack Donegan pushed his way through the fleeing crowd. "CURT! CURT!" He screamed, praying he was not too late. He'd heard the gunshot and knew things were grim. A Capitol Hill police officer stopped the Congressman, identifying him by his Congressional pin. "Congressman, you should NOT be here!" Trying to shield the HVT (High Value Target).

Jack screamed, "Get the fuck off me! I'm a SEAL! I'm good! I know him!" He threw the officer off him and continued to push his way through until he was behind the encirclement of security guards. Curt laid motionless in the middle of them. Jack's heart sank.

Chapter Sixty

Walking Dead

Curt lay on the ground, his weapon and his trident next to his open hand. A security officer rushed up and kicked his weapon away, then knelt to administer first aid. He rolled Curt's head over. Puzzled, the officer looked over Curt's condition. There was no entry or exit wound. There was no blood. He also quickly realized the Lieutenant was wearing body armor, with a clear indentation in the middle front plate. Curt was alive.

****

Before the presumed fatal shot, unbeknownst to the majority witnessing this calamity, a dark figure slowly stirred on the Hay-Adams Hotel roof top. In his hands, a black rifle barrel protruded in the direction of Curt. A targeting scope centered on Curt's chest. The shadow was the actual shooter.

****

Curt's eyes opened. The Security officer shook him and said, "Lieutenant," he continued, "That was about the dumbest thing you've ever done. Are you acting alone?"
Curt was finally coming to. His chest hurt as if he was kicked by a mule. "No, I'm not alone. As you can see, I didn't take the shot. No further shooting will take place as long as you

do not move me." This put the officer in a bind. They clearly wished to immediately removal of the shooter. However, it was clear Curt was not the shooter.

The Officer transmitted on his radio, "Other actors. Not a Lone Wolf. Repeat NOT a lone wolf."

Allison watched Curt through the Security Police legs. Wait. What? HE MOVED! HE MOVED! HE'S ALIVE! She didn't know how, nor did she care. She knew her part of the plan was coming into gear. She began picking up as many of the photos and records as she could. Off in the distance, news crew vans were stopping on H Street and scrambling to get as close to the action as they could. Guards were trying to corral Allison and the other onlookers. No matter, she and other tourists had more than enough.

Helicopter search lights flooded the area, scanning the trees in Lafayette Square as well as the rooftops of local buildings. All of them, to include the Hay-Adams were void of any irregularities. The dark figure on the Hay Adams had long since retreated.

****

Inside the White House, Security took action. "Mr. President, come with us. There have been shots fired outside the White House." The President got up and followed the security into a safe room. The same was happening with his other family members.

****

Capital Security rolled Curt onto his stomach and handcuffed his hands. He winced in pain as the body armor had stopped the bullet but broke one of his ribs. A small price to pay. Once cuffed, the police sat him against the fence, feeling for other weapons, finding his body armor and punishing him with questions about potential other active shooters. As they did, Congressman Donegan finally pushed through, "Curt! Thank God! You're alive. Now, I'm going to kill you myself! What on God's Green Earth are you trying to prove?" The police immediately recognized Jack as a Congressman and also realized he knew the shooter. It was an easy decision to let him stay.

"Jack, I'm going to say this once. Someone in the U.S. Government has a contracted mercenary hit on the Ayatollah which will take place tomorrow in Tehran during his Prophet's Birthday speech." Jack, along with all the Security guards looked at Curt as if he had three heads.

One of the security guards spoke up, "Buddy, you just came here, dressed in uniform, sang the Navy Fight song, somehow shot yourself and lived... and now we're all supposed to believe this?"

Curt paid no attention to the guard. He stared in Jack's eyes. Jack somehow knew there was some truth to Curt's story. "Jack.... Find Smitty. He has what you need."

"OK. I'll get you out of jail as soon as I can." Jack stood up and walked away, back towards his car at the Hay-Adams. If Curt went to all this trouble, Jack had to at least accept Curt believed his story. Jack was walking while looking down at his cell phone, trying to type a message, as a man bumped into him. Staggering back slightly, Jack quickly said, "Excuse me," and looked up.

"I think you may be looking for me." It was Smitty.

Jack and Smitty hugged. "Buddy, please tell me you have something."

"Sure. I have the team members names currently in Iran, the U.S. Air Force flights that brought them in as well as the ones which will bring them out. I have enough fake passports to choke a horse and all the contact information you need on Nissassa to bring down the operation. What I don't have is safety."

"Brother. I got you." Jack brought Smitty with him to his car and they sped away.

****

The local news media vans had now set up and were broadcasting live from the scene. The first reporter to pause for a commercial was Fox 5 D.C. During the break, Allison walked up to the reporter. "Hi, my name is Allison Donley. I am a journalist. I know the man who was shot, and I have his full story. If you don't want it, I understand, and I'll go to the next outlet." The reporter looked at her as if she'd won the lottery.

"No, No, please. We are back on the air in 30 seconds. Speak to me."

"His name is Curt Nover. He is a doctor and former Navy SEAL. He did this to expose a massive plot which potentially will involve the assassination of a world leader."

The reporter's mouth remained open. The camera man looked at her, "15 seconds."

Allison said. "I have proof," and waived the documents in her hand.

"OK, you're on...." The reporter pulled Allison next to her into the camera shot.

The light came on and the cameraman signaled she was live, "This is Kate Jackson again, back in front of the White House. I am here with Allison.... Allison Donley who claims to know the victim. Allison, what can you tell us?"

"Thanks, Kate... Yes, the victim, Doctor Curt Nover, is a former Navy SEAL and is currently assigned to a Doctors Without Borders mission in Akjoujt, Mauritania. While on that mission, he discovered a U.S. company, Nissassa Incorporated, was secretly training mercenaries to conduct missions for the

U.S. Government. The mercenaries used the local people of Akjoujt as live targets. These photos and medical records prove this."

Kate pulled the mic back, "Yes, Allison. Interesting, but why go to these lengths?"

"Good question, Kate. Unfortunately, as I understand Curt did not know how deep the U.S. Government involvement is. He has traveled from Akjoujt, through Morocco, to Spain to the U.S., the entire time being hunted by a Nissassa Assassin."

As the report flooded D.C., and the rest of America, smart phones and computers googled Nissassa, Inc. It was a real company. A quick scan of the board members revealed little to no mining experience but plenty of military experience. Social Media flooded. The story was out.

Allison continued, "The second reason for all this. Within the next two days, an assassination from Nissassa will be attempted in Tehran." With that, the international embassies on Massachusetts Ave. (Embassy Row) and elsewhere in D.C. sprung to life.

****

Jerry sat in Akjoujt watching the news. There was nothing left to do. He ordered the destruction of all the equipment and full evacuation. He sent a member to get full gas cans with a plan to torch the building. He then called Buck, "Buck, I need you... Now!"

"It's 4AM!" Buck was still in bed in Rabat.

"Buck, it's an emergency."

"OK, double pay." Buck was asleep in his aircraft. It wouldn't be difficult to get there.

"Done. Just hurry!" Jerry put down the phone. He opened the safe and started packing as many bags of cash as possible. He loaded a truck. Others were loading their vehicles as well. Nissassa's gate was wide open. The only positive aspect was the villagers of Akjoujt were asleep. The last thing Nissassa needed was a full out mob riot. By the time they woke and learned the news, Nissassa would be abandoned. The Ops center stunk of gasoline. Jerry lit a match and tossed it and ran. The building was soon engulfed in flames.

Jerry jumped in his truck and began driving to the airport. His rear-view mirror filled with the flames of Nissassa.

****

Back in Rosslyn, Don had driven quickly to the office, entered, and was rapidly shredding every document he could. It was his only option.

Chapter Sixty-One

Trapping Scurrying Rats

Jack drove with Smitty across D.C. towards Memorial Bridge. He placed a call. "Chairman, there's a crisis, I'm on my way to your house now."

"Hey, Jack. I saw the news. Is this Donley person's story legit?" The Chairman of the Joint Chiefs responded.

"Admiral, I believe so, and I have further information. Please have the guards waive us onto Ft Myer without delay."

"OK, Jack. You got it." Admiral Hershey summoned his staff and soon the access to his house would be open on Fort Myer. Jack drove up to the door and parked. They exited the vehicle and received a cursory security pat down from the Army's Military Police. Once inside, Smitty began explaining the entire story. After three minutes, Admiral Hershey stopped him.

"Son, hold on." He turned to his staff. "Get my video camera. I want this recorded." Smitty stared again. It took him approximately a half hour. As he wrapped up, the Chairman's phone rang again. It was the White House. One of his staff answered, copied a message and hung up. He turned to the Chairman, "Admiral, the President is convening of the Security Council. Your helicopter will be here in three minutes." The Admiral nodded.

Admiral Hershey pulled the tape out of the recorder and handed it to his aide. "Take this to the other Chief's Houses as well as the Commandant's House and tell them I direct they view it tonight. Tomorrow, we will have a Tank at 0800Hrs. Also, contact the U.S. Defense Attachés in Mauritania and Morocco. Explain to them the situation and instruct them to work with the Ambassadors and host countries to ensure no

Nissassa personnel enter or exit Mauritania or Morocco. This is on orders of myself. Do you understand?"

"Yes, Admiral." His aide took the tape and proceeded to the Pentagon. In the Watch, he called the Defense Attaches and relayed the message.

The Admiral got up from his chair, "Thanks, Jack. Look me in the eye. Did you know anything about this?"

Jack was a bit surprised by the question. "Squirts, do you think I would have brought Smitty here if I did?" The formal designations dropped. 'Squirts' was the Admiral's callsign from younger days. No one in the military now would dare refer to him in such a manner. A Congressman, however. No issues.

"Fair point. But sometimes you political types execute some wild schemes. And if you call me 'Squirts' in public, I'll kill you myself."

The Admiral began walking. His helicopter could be heard in the distance. He stopped and looked back at Smitty. "What are you waiting for? I'm not going to the White House alone." Smitty jumped up and joined the Chairman onto the bird. They soon lifted off, flew across the Potomac, landing onto the White House lawn. The flight took less than two minutes. It would normally be a 15-minute drive; worse with traffic. *'Funny,'* Smitty thought. *'I'm gonna be in the White House while Nover sits in a D.C. Prison cell. Good times.'*

As the helicopter landed, the Admiral walked in with Smitty behind him. The council members sat at the table. Smitty was seated in a row behind the Admiral. Small chatter existed amongst those at the table, the back row remained silent. The President walked in, "Ladies and Gentlemen, the President of the United States." Everyone stood up.

"Council Members, I apologize for calling a meeting at such an hour but there seems to be an issue. The media has run with a narrative about some crazy mercenary operation funded by the U.S. Government. Frankly, I think it is all a bit crazy, so I welcome your thoughts on how to deal with this."

The crowd remained calculated. Secretary of State Marleen Baker spoke first, "Mr. President, I have no evidence to confirm this activity is true. My Assistant Secretary for African Affairs assures me she knows nothing of this Nissassa." She was being truthful. The State Department activities that supported Nissassa were done at far lower levels and hidden from her.

"Thank you, Madam Secretary. I agree, this all seems to be some sort of malarkey."

Soon thereafter, others began to speak, also relaying their organizations did not have any evidence to support the claims levied by Ms. Donley.

Finally, Admiral Hershey spoke, "Mr. President, before we dismiss this, I'd propose that the current lack of evidence neither validates or invalidates the claims," Admiral Hershey stared at others in the room. They all fell silent.

"Yes, Admiral. Good point. But I think we would all agree without supporting evidence, this story seems a bit far-fetched, don't you agree?"

"Yes, Mr. President, I do agree, if, in fact, there truly was no supporting evidence."

The President stared at the Chairman and noticed a man in the room he had never seen before. "Admiral, do you have knowledge of this operation?"

"Mr. President, I did not until one hour ago. However, I do now have what I believe to be credible evidence that at a minimum merits investigation."

The President paused. "Well, Admiral, may I recommend we convene a smaller group of just us in the oval office and have you share what you know. This is an issue of vital national security, and I don't believe it is for everyone's ears.

"Yes, Mr. President, as you wish, but the evidence I have is currently being shared with the other Service Chiefs, the Commandant of the Marines and the Defense Attaches of Mauritania and Morocco. I apologize if I overstepped here but all of those entities are subordinate to me and I thought given the claim about the Ayatollah, you'd likely wish to move fast, should the information be substantiated, of course."

The President knew at that moment, there was no way to put a lid on Nissassa. He'd need to be just as surprised as the others and play no cards that would even hint to implicating him. Steve stood behind him. Most humans would have been white as a ghost, but not Steve. He acted every bit the part of a surprised observer.

The President finally responded, "Yes, well, since you've shared it across the Pentagon, perhaps it is better to share it across the interagency as well. Please proceed."

The Admiral attempted to recall and articulate everything that Smitty had told him. When he was finished the room was utterly silent.

"Admiral, thank you very much for sharing all of that, but your story is perhaps just that, do you have any evidence? It appears to me you've just regurgitated this young journalist's story."

"Mr. President, I do. The gentleman sitting behind me was a senior employee of Nissassa." Gasps were heard in the room. "He can verify and substantiate the data I've shared. Mr. President, I agree we should be holding a National Security Council meeting, but may I recommend it not be about the existence of a U.S. Government funded mercenary institution but rather on how we stop an assassination against the Ayatollah." There was a fairly substantial pause.

Everyone's head turned to the President. "Yes, Admiral, perhaps you are correct."

****

Back in Morocco, Buck had picked up Jerry and was now flying back towards Rabat with about 200 pounds of cash in unmarked bags. The sun was coming up and the landing was smooth. As Buck turned off the Active Runway, three Moroccan Police Vehicles turned on their lights and stormed towards the aircraft. Buck stopped and shut down his engines. With weapons drawn, the police surrounded the aircraft. Buck and Jerry opened the door and exited with their hands in the air. The aircraft doors were closed by the police and a tug pulled up to tow Buck's aircraft to an impound area.

****

Don sat in his office. It was pointless to run. Soon, the door knock came, and he answered it. After a short Miranda right reading, he was in handcuffs walking out the door.

****

The teams in Iran turned on their satellite telephones at the prescribed time on every 12 hours per the 'check-in' plan. They dialed the number. It would be the final call to confirm they were in place and ready to go. There was no answer. Both teams tried to call a few more times. The phone rang and then disconnected. The team members tried to dial again. Again, the number disconnected. The failed communications were written off to poor satellite coverage. No worries. The sun was coming up and they would soon be executing their respective operations.

Chapter Sixty-Two

<u>Saving Evil</u>

Worlds apart, Smitty and Jerry explained in detail both Iranian team plans to U.S. Authorities. One voluntarily, the other under duress. They also relayed contact information for the teams; however, their phones would likely remain off. There was no further scheduled communications with the teams. At this point, the most realistic and viable plan to stop the teams was share the plan with Iranian authorities and have the team members arrested. Doing so clearly would expose the U.S. to a horrible black eye. There had to be a better solution. The Interagency kept working through options. They needed a better plan, fast.

****

It was now midnight in DC. Allison had sprung Curt from jail. As he walked out of the hold, she ran up to him and hugged him, "I LOVE YOU SO MUCH!"

"Ouch Ow!!! Easy! My chest is killing me." Curt opened his shirt a huge bruise covered his chest.

"What's that from?"

Curt told her, "It's where someone shot me."

She was stunned, "Who shot you!??"

"Yeah. Long story. It was supposed to be Smitty, but it wasn't. So, I am not sure." Curt looked at her with a smile. "Can we go back to the hotel? I really could use some Motrin."

Just as they were walking away, a black SUV with police lights screeched to a halt in front of them. An officer jumped out, "Curt Nover?"

Curt had little desire to speak to press or anyone else for that matter, "Who's asking?"

The gentleman asking the questions didn't care. "Get in."

Curt was in no shape to fight. He kissed Allison goodbye. The back passenger door opened. In the other back seat Congressman Donegan greeted him, "Hey, Nover. How are you doing?"

"Great, Jack. Bars close in an hour. Are we going drinking?"

Jack chuckled, "Yeah. In a couple hours. Get in."

As they drove away, Jack looked at Curt. "Buddy. I wish you would have come clean about all this earlier. It's 10AM in Tehran and the Ayatollah speaks in a few hours. We have no diplomatic relations, no embassy, and no forces other than potentially clandestine, but if so, the CIA isn't speaking, and the President isn't pushing. Frankly, I think the CIA Director is comfortable with an assassination. Our options are not good."

Curt looked at Jack. "Yeah... I understand your point, but tell me how I could have come forward in any other meaningful way that would have garnered this gravitas? I can't think of any. As for what to do.... Sadly, I don't know. I don't even know who we can trust in the U.S. Government. The only reason I risked trusting Smitty was he's our Bro. And the 'Bro network'....." Curt paused and a light came on in his head. *'THAT'S IT! THE BRO NETWORK!'* "Where is the crisis planning cell on this issue? I have an idea."

"Curt, it's at the White House. Why?"

"Jack, we gotta go there. Now."

"Curt, I am not sure I can get you in."

"Jack. Make the call. I have a plan."

Jack called and after a few minutes, his SUV would enter the White House grounds. Jack and Curt were whisked from their vehicle and down to the crisis room. Curt overheard some of the idea's staffers were pitching to stop the assassination. Most bordered on insanity. Communications experts were on conference calls being asked what options existed to turn on a distance wireless satellite phone remotely. The answer clearly was *'it's impossible.'*

Others conjured up ways to get a drone strike into Iranian airspace and target the teams before they executed. These were just two of the plans Curt overheard.

On the walls of the room were Video Conference TV screens with the EUCOM, CENTCOM, and SOCOM Commanders. All the commanders were joined by their senior staff in the video at their conference tables.

Jack looked at Curt. "OK, Nover, you're on." Curt walked up to one of the staff standing around Secretary of State Baker.

"Ma'am, I understand the Secretary is busy, but if I could borrow you for a second, I think I have an idea. May I ask you to listen in on my video chat with SOCOM?" The staffer obliged and they both sat down at the crisis room conference table. It was filled with computer screens, microphones and headsets. They both picked up a headset and mic. Curt looked at the White House Communications staffer in the room and asked to be patched to the SOCOM commander. With a few flips of some switches, they were all connected. "General Etcher? Sir, this is LT, er or, Curt Nover." The message traveled to MacDill Air Force base, the home of SOCOM.

General Etcher pushed his mic. "Nover, go for SOCOM."

"General, you may not remember me, but years ago, we were part of an operation together. I was on a SEAL Team at the time, and we were on a multinational effort in Afghanistan. It was called 'Pinching Daggers' with two other nations."

"Nover, copy. Yes, I remember. Good mission. Something like 20 EKIA (Enemy Killed in Action). What's your point?" The rest of the crisis room was still scurrying, few if any paid attention to Nover.

"Well, sir, the head of that op from the U.K. was Major Tinning, now Colonel Tinning. Ever since that op, I've stayed in contact with him. He's now the British Defense Attaché to Iran."

Every set of eyes in the SOCOM conference room widened. So did the State Department staffer. She raised her hand and shook it violently in the direction of the Secretary Baker. Secretary Baker was on her way over. The seed was planted.

While the plan had merit, it was not without opposition. For quite a while, Secretary of State Baker and White House staff expressed serious reservations about exposing an embarrassing situation to a key ally. In fairness, they had a point. It was an embarrassment. Had another option arose from the crisis planning team, it would have been far easier to eliminate this idea. Unfortunately, there were no other reasonable options, nor was there much time remaining. The White House called the British Prime Minister, and the Secretary of State summonsed the British Ambassador to the U.S. The plan was set into motion.

Chapter Sixty-Three

Tying Loose Ends

In a small village just outside Tehran a residence phone rang. "Hello?" The owner answered in Persian.

The message was relayed in Persian. "Sir, there are strange people around your house. You must call the police immediately."

The owner of the house answered, "Excuse me, who is this?"

"Doctor, I am a friend. I recommend you protect yourself and your family. Call the police now." The line went dead. A local Iranian young man handed the burner phone back to Colonel Tinning.

The Doctor did as he was instructed. He decided not to go to work and to stay home until the police arrived. The Nissassa team surrounding the house would sit and wait. There would be no opportunity to snatch the scientist today. As the grab and go team saw police cars arrive at his residence, the call was made to pull back and abort the mission.

In Tehran, the crowd packed into the square. Security was tightened given the news out of the US, but the defiant Ayatollah was even more determined to speak. Overlooking the square, a roof top door slowly opened. An individual cautiously transitioned through the door with a large bag on his back. He silently closed the door and turned to secure his vantage over the square.

Stunned, the individual stopped in his tracks. There on the roof he saw Colonel Tinning wearing Bermuda shorts, a Hawaiian shirt, and sunglasses while drinking a beer sitting in a plastic lawn chair. "Hey, Mate! You trying to get a good view too?" Longbow 23 was speechless. The Colonel continued, "No worries, mate. Take my chair. But hey, here's the news out of the U.S. Your op is exposed." The Colonel passed over numerous news articles about the previous day. "My name is Colonel Tinning. I'm the UK Defense Attaché and former SAS. Either it's a really good guess that I found you, or someone gave me a little message to tell you to go home. Your call mate, but I hope you bloody get it right. Cheers!" And with that, Colonel Tinning departed.

Longbow sat on the roof for another minute. He read through the articles. Finally, he raised his hand to his earpiece. "Alpha Team, Longbow 23, Abort." And with that, the assassination attempt would be no more.

****

As Colonel Tinning walked out of the building, he picked up his phone and called back to Curt. "Nover. A few pints should cover it, eh?"

"Tins, you rock. Thanks."

"No worries, mate. When you coming to visit?"

"When you get a better posting." They both laughed then said their goodbyes.

By now, numerous staff members had surrounded Curt in the crisis room. The President's staff was also in the room. Nover set down the phone, looked up and said, "It's off." General Etcher in SOCOM threw a thumbs up on the screen. While others in the room applauded, to include the lower-level White House staff. Ironically, they were so elated, they burst in to the Oval Office and shared the good news with the President. It would be received with well faked exuberance.

Back in the crisis room, Admiral Hershey patted Curt on the back. "Good job, son."

Curt stood up to address the Chairman, "Thanks Admiral. Sir, can I have a word. I didn't do this alone and could use a few favors."

The Chairman accepted his offer, "I welcome the discussion. Let's step out in the hall and see what we can do."

****

The next morning on Joint Base Henderson Hall, a mean and grizzly Gunny Sergeant marched into the morning chow hall. He walked up behind Corporal Ramirez and screamed. "RAMIREZ!!!! Stand up!"

Ramirez did as he was instructed. "Yes, Gunny." The room grew quiet.

"Ramirez, why are you out of uniform?" The table of Marines all looked at their battle buddy. His uniform was pressed, he had now stray cables. One looked under the table quickly. His boots were perfect. They saw nothing wrong.

"Gunny?"

"Son! I'm giving you one last chance!"

"Gunny?"

With that, Gunny pulled out a piece of paper and screamed, "Attention to Orders!" The room rapidly stood up. "Effective today, October 19, Corporal Ramirez is promoted to the rank of Sergeant, United States Marine Corps. Signed, Commandant of the Marines, AND Chairman Joint Chiefs of Staff." The entire mess hall erupted in applause. Ramirez smiled and thought, *'Jesus, SEALS really can do anything.'*

****

In Rabat, Buck was undergoing more hours of interrogation than he'd ever hoped for when the door flew open. An Air Force Colonel walked into the room wearing his camo uniform. "Are you the guy who goes by the nickname, Buck?"

"Yeah."

The Colonel handed a piece of paper to the interrogator. After reading it the agent got up and left. The Colonel asked, "You OK?"

Buck responded, "I could use a drink."

Chuckling, the Colonel said, "Come with me." Buck's handcuffs were released. Buck followed the Colonel out to the airport ramp. His plane was sitting there. "My name is Colonel Frasier. I've received a call from the Pentagon. It seems there were a few mistakes made. I've been directed by the Chairman of the Joint Chiefs to remedy them. You're free to go. Your aircraft is over there."

"Thanks, sir. Thank you." Buck shook the Colonel's hand then walked up to the aircraft. As he opened the cockpit door, he noticed an envelope on the aircraft commander's seat. He lifted it up and opened it. Two clunky objects fell out onto his seat as he pulled out the paper. One was a Distinguished Flying Cross Medal and the other was a Bronze Star Medal with Combat Valor. He opened the note. It was handwritten and clearly on fax paper.

> "Buck,
>
> I understand our military may have let you down. Please accept these as well as my gratitude for your bravery and the selfless service you provided on the night over Khost. Both of these will have papers following soon. Major Retired Doug Theissen, our country owes you an apology and a debt of gratitude.
>
> – Signed, Admiral 'Squirts' Hershey
> Chairman, Joint Chiefs of Staff."

Tears welled up in his eyes. He looked around to make sure no one was looking. Only one person was, Colonel Frasier. Buck wiped his eyes, cleared his seat and opened up the rest of the aircraft to perform his preflight check. As he did, he noticed Jerry's bags were still in the cargo hold. Buck jumped out of the aircraft and chased down the Attaché. "Colonel Frasier, Colonel Frasier!"

The attaché turned around, "Yes, Buck?

"There are still bags on the aircraft that are not mine!"

"Buck, those bags aren't mine either. If I understand correctly, the U.S. Government and a gentleman named Nover owe you a debt. I don't know anything about 'bags of money,' but I do know that there are many who are grateful for your actions. Take care, Buck." With that, the Colonel walked away.

Chapter Sixty-Four

We'll Always Have Paris

The weather in Casablanca was perfect. It was November now, a few weeks after Nissassa's fall. In a famous local bar, Rick's Café, Curt, Smitty and Allison sat as tourists, eating, drinking and admiring the memorabilia from the famous movie that shares the city's name. The music was loud, the place was festive and packed.

Smitty looked at Curt, "What a great idea, buddy. I had never been here."

"Me either! And it was perhaps the only place in North Africa I looked forward to visiting."

"Hey, do you think they'll ever find who in the U.S. Government was supporting Nisassa?"

"Smitty, with the way our government works and the ability of our politicians to lie? I doubt it. Jack says there is a Congressional Inquiry, but I don't see Jerry or Don coming forward. They'll take their secrets to the grave. That said, we still did good. I believe that. And you should as well. By the way, was Nissassa someone's name or was it some mythical creature? I never figured it out."

Smitty smiled…. "It was neither. But, if you spell it backwards, you might figure it out."

Curt thought for a minute and then smiled… "Very cute."

Smitty nodded, they clinked beer mugs and took a chug. Allison was in heaven. 'Her' Curt was back, and she was falling farther in love by the day. She put her arm around him. He looked at her, moved in closer and found comfort and warmth in her grasp.

Out at the Casablanca airport, Buck was closing up his aircraft and catching a cab. He'd received a 'surprise' invitation and given work was slow, he'd flown in from Rabat that afternoon. The cab arrived at Rick's Cafe, Buck tipped generously and headed to the door. As he walked in, the place was packed. He stopped at the entrance and looked around. Eventually, he saw Curt, Allison, and Smitty seated in the middle of the restaurant.

Curt quickly spotted Buck at the door. "BUCK!" Curt screamed. The rest of the bar followed quickly and screamed "BUCK!" Everyone laughed and the liveliness continued. The atmosphere was almost as if it were a private party. Buck loved it.

Buck hastily made his way to the table. Curt and Smitty stood. They all hugged. It was a great occasion.

Buck said, "Damn, it's great to see you guys!"

"You too, Buck!" Smitty poured him a beer.

They raised their glasses and Curt toasted, "Cheers, Buck! To saving the free world!"

The bar patrons overheard them, they too raised their glasses, and screamed, "CHEERS!" Again, the entire bar laughed.

They all sat down. Buck got serious for a second, "Curt, how the hell did you pull it off? I watched the news. But did you flinch and miss shooting yourself?"

"Oh, no. I got shot. Right in the chest! The plan was for Smitty to set up a sniper location and shoot me with a low caliber round which wouldn't penetrate body armor."

"No Shit!?" Buck was beside himself.

"Well, that WAS the plan. But the last thing I saw before I got hit was Smitty standing about fifty yards away, so, I still don't know who shot me.

"Yeah, about that. I gotta confess. I didn't take that shot." Smitty's shoulders slumped a bit as he spoke. "Curt, I just didn't have the confidence."

Curt was surprised but understood. "OK…. But who took the shot?" Just as Curt asked the question, a young American lady in her late twenties carrying a baby boy entered the restaurant. Behind her, Jackal walked in, his finger still bandaged. Smitty waived at them and brought them to the table.

Puzzled, Curt watched Smitty waive them in and said, "Who the hell is that?"

"His name is Jackal. He's also an ex-Nissassa employee."

As Jackal made his way to the table, Curt spoke up, "You let a guy with a broken finger take the shot!!!!???"

Jackal, now close to the table, overheard the comment and responded. "Even with a broken finger I coulda put that bullet through a straw at 200 yards." They all laughed. Smitty hugged Jackal, shook Joy's hand and tickled Brandon under his chin. Introductions were made and they all sat down again.

Smitty looked at Curt, "Buddy, did you hear Jackal? That was the kind of confidence I needed to take that shot and I didn't have it. He's a good kid. I kinda feel bad about breaking his finger."

Curt responded, "You broke his finger?"

"Yeah, I thought I told you that.?" Smitty laughed as did others. For Jackal, it was still a bit too soon.

Joy sat down near Allison who lit up seeing Brandon. They started up a conversation like they were old friends.

Curt stood up, raised his beer and faced Jackal, "Well, I guess I ought a thank you for shooting me so perfectly….." They both laughed, clinked their beers together and hugged. Another toast was made, and more drinking was accomplished.

Buck turned to Curt, "Hey Doc, what are you going to do now?"

"I don't know, Buck. You need a co-pilot? I heard you have the means to pay well." They both smiled.

Buck continued, "Uh, No, I meant about Allison."

Curt took a second to reply. "Well, that's a great question…." And with that, Curt's chest swelled a bit. His swagger was switched on as he jumped up on the table and screamed "CAN YOU BELIEVE IT!" In seconds, Rick's Café fell silent…..

Curt, standing on the table, looked down at Allison. Holding a beer in one hand and with his best Humphrey Bogart impression he said, *"Of All the Gin Joints in All the Towns in All the World, She Walks into Mine…..* and I wouldn't have wanted it any other way." He reached out his hand and pulled Allison up from her seated position. A few applauses sprung up across the bar. Next, Curt knelt on the table looking into her in the eyes, "Allison Donley, will you marry me?"

Allison nearly fainted towards Smitty, hoping he may be able to catch her. She however was wrong, as Smitty too almost fainted. The crowd gave a quickly muted roar, awaiting her answer. Tears welled up in her eyes. She tried to say yes, but couldn't breathe… Finally, her head started nodding up and down. It was all the patrons in Rick's Café needed. The place exploded. Curt jumped down, grabbed Allison like a rag doll and swung her off the table. Holding her in his arms, like he'd never let her go.

Finally, the crowd settled, and Buck looked at Curt, "Congrats buddy. I can't believe you. You're freaking as crazy as I am. Why did you come back to Casablanca?"

"Buck, it was a place I always wanted to visit since I saw the movie. More importantly, I wanted to thank you in person. Without you, the world today would be a far more dangerous place."

Buck blushed a bit. "Curt, it's I that should thank you. Those medals mean the world to me, and the money doesn't hurt."

Curt turned towards Buck and couldn't help himself, quoting yet another line from Casablanca, "Buck, *I think this is the beginning of a beautiful friendship*."

They both laughed, clinked their beers yet again and took another drink. Buck spoke, "I still can't believe you're here… and this crowd! Why are they so lively?"

Responding coyly, Curt said, "Buck, there is an open tab. Someone bought the bar. They've been drinking for free for three hours."

Buck was happily surprised. "For free!!?? That's AWESOME! Who's buying the bar?"

Curt smiled at him and said, "Buck, you are my wealthy friend…. You are….. Cheers."

The End.

Too all who struggle with PTSD, please remember, help is never further than a phone call away.

The Veteran's Crisis Help Line: 1-800-273-8255

The National Suicide Prevention Lifeline: 1-800-273-8255

You are not alone

****

Thanks for reading. If you have time, please consider leaving a review on Amazon.

Just scan the QR code with your camera!

Made in the USA
Middletown, DE
08 December 2021